MURDER ON ALCATRAZ

A PEYTON BROOKS' MYSTERY

Volume 4

ML Hamilton

Cover Art by Karri Klawiter

www.artbykarri.com

MURDER ON ALCATRAZ

Peyton's adventures would not be possible without the constant support of my family, particularly Mom and Dad, who always take on the terrifying first drafts. In addition, I want to thank my readers, who allow this dream to continue. I am honored by you.

"Killers can seem smart when you can't figure out who they are."

-- *Governor Pat Brown*

CHAPTER 1

The waters of the bay surged over the bow, casting frothy white spray on the deck. Fog rolled beneath the bridge, obscuring the view of Alcatraz, but occasionally search lights would cleave the fog in two, offering a glimpse of the island. The roar of the motor and the sound of the water slapping against the boat's hull drowned out most other sounds.

Peyton gripped the table in the boat's cabin and bent her knees, trying to roll with the pitching of the small vessel. She could feel a tingle of nausea in the back of her throat, but tried to ignore it. She realized she hated riding on the bay – it was always choppy, always nausea-inducing no matter the weather. Reaching up, she pulled the life vest away from her throat and tried to concentrate on what the park ranger was telling them. A map was spread on the table and he was pointing at various buildings, but it was so hard to hear what he was saying.

Jake sat next to the ranger, his head on his folded arms. If possible, he was feeling worse than she was. Being from landlocked Nebraska, he certainly wasn't used to the violence of riding on the bay. Honestly, it was embarrassing that she didn't fare any better. She'd lived in San Francisco her whole life. This wasn't her first time going to Alcatraz.

"You okay?" said Marco, leaning close to her and speaking into her ear.

She nodded, not trusting herself to talk. She didn't want to vomit all over the park ranger's map.

"Here's the boat dock. It's a short walk to the chapel where the body is," the ranger shouted. "We evacuated the island after the shooting, but we aren't sure where the suspect is. We think he may have mixed in with the tourists as they left."

Peyton and Marco exchanged a look. Just wonderful. Cops didn't like the word *think*. She glanced around. Holmes and Smith sat on a bench at the back of the cabin, both of them holding on tight. Bartlet was nowhere to been seen.

"Where's the kid?" she shouted.

Holmes pointed out the cabin door. She could see the silhouette of someone bending over the side of the boat.

Turning back, she nodded stiffly. She was afraid she might be joining him in a moment.

"Here's how we play it," said Marco. "When we land, SWAT goes in first. They'll secure the buildings. Once we get the all clear, we'll go on scene."

The ranger shook his head. "There's a lot of area to secure." He glanced out the window at the second boat that rode to the left of them. "Are ten SWAT enough?"

"We only need to secure the chapel. We'll grab the body, get off the island, and come back tomorrow when it's light. Then we can do a more thorough search. If our suspect didn't leave with the tourist, he just might be willing to give up after a night out here."

They fell silent as the boat dropped speed. The SWAT boat went in first, cutting in front of them and pulling up to the dock. Peyton left the table and walked to the cabin door, pulling it open. Gripping the rail, she slid past Bartlet and pulled herself to the bow, staring up at the island as it loomed over them.

The SWAT boat bumped against the dock, then someone jumped off, hurrying to secure it. A moment later, dark clothed, heavily armed police officers swarmed onto the dock and raced up the pale concrete roadway toward the top of the island.

Search lights cut across the dock, illuminating the SWAT boat for a moment, and the surge of the waves smacked against the island, driving the boat into the dock. Marco appeared at her side, both of them staring up at the massive rocks which made Alcatraz famous.

Carefully, the captain eased their boat in behind the SWAT vessel and his assistant secured it. The park ranger appeared at Peyton's other side, surveying the island as well.

"John had four months left before he retired," he said.

Peyton gave him a sad smile. "I'm sorry. Were you friends?"

"Yeah, we worked together for seven years." The ranger tipped his hat back on his head. He was in his late thirties with red hair and a blanket of freckles across his nose and cheekbones. Peyton could see a patch of ginger hair sticking out beneath the hat.

Jake staggered up to the rail and gripped it, closing his eyes. "Why the hell couldn't we fly out here in a helicopter?"

"Too many cops and probably too much fog," said Marco. "Besides, there's nothing wrong with boating over."

"Yeah, well, having your stomach bounced into your esophagus is what's wrong. You're lucky I have an iron constitution. You almost saw the pot roast I had for dinner."

"You're just a land lubber, Ryder. Getting out on the bay is good for you. Puts hair on your chest."

Peyton gave him a wry look. Her stomach was finally settling, but she dreaded the return trip and honestly, she didn't want any hair on her chest. She reached up and unbuckled her life-vest, slipping it over her head. Her heavy ponytail bounced against her back as she straightened her flak jacket and checked her gun. Marco pulled off his own vest and tossed it behind him.

Pulling the shoulder radio out of his pocket, he secured it to the flak jacket and selected a channel. Smith and Holmes joined them, removing their own life-vests. Bartlet was still hanging over the side of the boat.

"I think we're it," said Holmes. His blond hair was cut so short, she could see pink scalp in the light from the cabin. "The kid's done for."

Peyton glanced back at him. "Tell him to go inside and lay down. He'll be safe here."

Holmes walked back to him.

"Can I go lay down?" asked Jake.

7

"Nope. You have a job to do."

Jake grumbled something she couldn't hear.

The radio crackled and Marco keyed it to talk. "Come again," he said.

"Building secure."

Peyton reached for her gun, pulling it out. "Stay here," she told the ranger.

He nodded.

Holmes returned to the bow, taking the lead with Smith. They climbed down onto the dock, followed by Marco. Peyton waited for Jake as he retrieved his case, then the two of them descended the ramp onto the dock.

"Stay behind me," she told him.

He nodded.

Taking a flashlight off his belt, Smith turned it on and swept it up the concrete walk. They began climbing in the eerie dark, the sound of the waves crashing against the rocks below them. Besides the search lights, the flashlight and the light from the cabin on the boat, the island was shrouded in darkness. The shadow of trees rose around them as they climbed and off in the distance, Peyton could see the lights from the City, illuminating the fog.

They came to the chapel, or what had once been the chapel, a few minutes later. A SWAT officer waved them to the door and they ran for the interior. Peyton's heart was pounding as they crossed the open courtyard, knowing they might not be able to see, but anyone could be lying in wait from the buildings above them.

Two more SWAT officers stood over the body lying in the middle of the room. Low benches created an obstacle course ending at a small stage with a video screen in the center of it. No one had moved anything, preserving the crime scene.

As they arrived, Peyton lowered her gun. Smith shined the flashlight on the body, starting at the khaki clad legs, rising to the black belt with an empty gun holster, and ending on the bloom of red covering the chest of the ranger.

He lay on his back, his arms flung wide, his eyes still open and staring at nothing. His hat had fallen off his head and lay behind him. The bullet had hit the edge of his badge and dented it into his chest cavity. He was in his early sixties, Caucasian, balding.

"What happened to his gun?" she asked.

Marco shook his head. "That's troubling."

Jake set his case down and reached for his camera. Peyton turned around, trying to survey the scene. Behind them was the door, a reception desk and then the benches. It looked like this was a gathering place for the start of the tours. She tracked a path from the door to where the victim lay.

"The shooter must have been standing in the doorway."

Marco nodded. "The ranger said they were showing a video about the history of the prison, like they do before every tour. It was the last tour of the day."

"How many people were in here?"

"He estimated about thirty."

"Did anyone see the shooter?"

"It was dark and it happened so fast. A couple of people reported the shooter was wearing a Giants' ball cap, pulled low over his face, so they didn't get a good look. Plus it was dark in here because of the video."

"Didn't Defino say someone saw him take a hostage?"

"That's what one person reported."

"How did they get out if he was shooting from the entrance?" She looked at one of the SWAT officers. "Are there other exits to this building?"

"Yep, there and there." The officer pointed to his right and behind the screen.

Peyton started to walk toward the screen. Her boots made a sharp report on the concrete floor. The only other sound was Jake, moving around the body as he took his

9

pictures. She'd just reached the small stage when the sound of a gunshot echoed in the room.

Everyone reacted. Guns snapped into the air and Jake dropped to the ground, covering his head. Peyton exchanged looks with her fellow officers, then Marco's radio crackled.

"Gunfire!" came a frantic voice.

Marco pressed the button on the radio. "Where?"

More crackle.

"What did he say?" demanded Peyton.

Marco shook his head. "Come again! Where's the gunfire?"

"Power house. Power house!"

"Where's that?" Peyton wished she'd paid more attention to the map.

"This way," said Marco, moving to the door with the SWAT on his heels.

"Smith, Holmes, stay with Jake!" she shouted, following him.

Jake looked up at her, the whites of his eyes showing. "Peyton!"

"Stay here!" she ordered, then followed Marco back into the night.

Fog had seeped onto the island, curling around the trees and gliding along the ground. Marco and the SWAT raced up the hill toward the gunfire and Peyton followed. It was so dark, it was hard to distinguish shapes in the shifting shadows. Her fingers tightened on the grip of her gun. Her heart pounded so hard, she could hear the rush of blood in her ears.

Another spatter of gunfire sounded above them. Peyton could see figures slipping through the fog, converging on the buildings rising before them. She had nightmares like this, running through the dark, unsure whether the person beside her was friend or foe. She didn't want to get shot, but she sure as hell didn't want to shoot a fellow officer.

The power house was an oblong building, built right over the edge of the cliffs. They fanned out, covering the walkway that ran along the cliff's edge, and eased along the outer wall of the building. Peyton tried to pinpoint where she'd heard the gun fire, but the crash of the waves on the rocks below them distorted the sound. The search light cut across her face and she tried to duck out of it as it passed over her head.

Marco was to her left and she watched him reach up and silence the radio. She understood why, but the cut off from information made her feel weak. Why the hell did it have to be night?

The SWAT swarmed the building. She could see them slip inside the broken windows, and she wondered if she should follow. There hadn't been any sound of gunfire in the last couple of minutes. Maybe they'd gotten the guy.

Climbing up the walk, she looked over the cliff. Frothy white waves slammed into the rocks, casting spray into the air. She caught motion above her and looked up, but the search light cut across her eyes at the same moment, blinding her.

"Peyton, down!" she heard Marco shout.

She started to lift her gun, but something slammed into the rock next to her. She felt fragments spray her face and she stumbled back, losing her footing on the damp concrete. She landed on her backside as another bullet slammed into the rock again.

"Peyton!"

She blinked, trying to clear her vision, lifting her gun in a defensive posture. She could see the outline of someone standing on the walkway above her.

She saw a flash of light, heard the sharp report of the gun, and braced herself for the impact, but it was the dark figure who suddenly convulsed, its arms flinging out to either side. To her left, Marco opened fire, the percussion of his gun deafening in the still night. The figure was thrown backward by the impact, then his arms flailed and he vanished over the edge of the cliff.

Peyton thought she saw another shadow suddenly break away, racing in the opposite direction, but she wasn't sure because a moment later the entire walkway was covered with SWAT officers.

Marco grabbed her, hauling her to her feet. "Peyton, are you hit?" His grip bit into her arm and she couldn't think straight. *What the hell just happened?*

"Peyton!" He shook her, then his hands were searching over her flak jacket frantically. "Peyton!"

"I'm okay," she gasped. "Marco, I'm okay."

He stopped searching her, then he caught her in a bear hug, holding her so tight she couldn't breathe. She gripped him in return, burying her face against his chest.

"Anyone hit?" came a voice beside her.

"No, we're fine," rumbled Marco's voice beneath her ear.

"Marco, what the hell just happened?"

He eased her back and cupped her face in his hands. "Are you sure you weren't hit?"

Her cheek stung beneath his hands, but all she could do was grip the front of his jacket. "What the hell happened?"

"He shot at you."

She touched her cheek. "My face hurts."

He turned her as the search light passed over them and stepped back so he could look her over. "You've got some cuts on your face, but I don't see any other injuries. Are you sure you're okay?"

"I'm fine. Are you okay?"

He gave a tight nod.

It suddenly hit her that he'd shot someone. He'd killed someone for her. Her eyes filled with tears and she pulled him back against her, hugging him as tight as she could. He held her and stroked his hand through her tangled ponytail as waves surged against the rocks below them.

Peyton hugged the blanket around her, watching the divers pulling the body out of the surf and onto the rocks. SWAT had set up huge search lights to illuminate the area. Thankfully, the body had caught on some flotsam and floated near the cliff wall because it was dangerous getting into the water around Alcatraz, especially at night. The water was freezing cold and the waves pounded so against the island.

Police were combing the island, searching for a second gunman based on what Peyton thought she saw. So far, no one reported finding anything, but it was difficult with so much abandoned area to canvas.

Jake brought her a Styrofoam cup and she took it, taking a sip. The bitter bite of coffee assaulted her tongue, but she didn't care. She was too shocked to do much of anything but stand on the edge of the cliff and watch the divers work.

"Sorry. There wasn't any sugar."

"It's fine."

"You okay?"

She glanced over her shoulder where Captain Defino was debriefing Marco. She knew the captain would want to talk with her next, but she didn't know what to say. Marco had killed someone to protect her. The salty spray stung in the cuts on her cheek.

"He'll be all right, Peyton."

She looked back at Jake and exhaled. "I should have been the one to shoot. He was in my line of sight. He was shooting at me."

Jake looked down. She knew he didn't know what to say.

"Did you find anything on the ranger's body?"

"Nope. Just the usual effects – license, credit cards, keys."

The divers had rolled the shooter's body into a basket. The sound of rotors came across the bay and both Peyton and Jake turned to see a helicopter leaving the City, headed toward Alcatraz, the beam of its lights scanning the water. She watched it for a moment, then heard footsteps coming down the walkway from the water tower. She looked up as Smith came to a stop beside her.

"Did you find anything?"

"SWAT heard an outboard motor on the southwest side of the island. We went over and found marks on the beach, headed toward the water. Probably a Zodiac or something like it. It's too dark to see anything."

"So there was another shooter?"

"Looks like it."

She tried to replay the moments in her mind of just before Marco fired. She had seen a flash, then heard a report. The shooter had thrown out his arms a moment before Marco fired. What the hell was going on?

"I don't get it. So there were two shooters. One stored a Zodiac on the beach. How come the rangers didn't find it?"

"They stick to this side mostly. This is where the tours are conducted. If they go to the other side, it's once a day, maybe. He could have had it hidden in rocks or something."

"We need to get an APB out on the Zodiac. Also alert Marin that he might have landed over there."

"I'll get on it. There's something about this freakin' island that screws with your head. So many strange things happen out here."

"I know, but why? Why set up a raft out here, then wait on the island, shoot a ranger, and…what? What's the reason for this whole thing?"

Smith shook his head. "That's why you're the detective, baby girl." He nodded at her cheek. "You need to get that looked at."

It was getting harder to speak. The helicopter had arrived and banked in over the rocks where the divers had the body. The wind created by the propellers kicked up sand and debris, throwing it into the air. Peyton and Jake turned away, protecting their eyes, while Smith ducked his head, pulling his hat down low.

Placing a hand over her eyes, Peyton squinted at the helicopter as it lowered a cable. The divers connected the basket to the cable, then waved the helicopter off. The big bird lifted into the air, the cage swinging back and forth beneath it, then it banked toward the courtyard in front of the chapel where the first body still lay.

Jake followed it as it passed over their heads, then he looked back at Peyton. "I gotta go, but I'll be right down there if you need me."

Peyton nodded, watching the body swaying in the wind kicked up by the machine. Not one damn thing of this made sense.

Captain Defino walked over to her. Peyton wasn't sure of the time, but she figured about an hour and a half had passed since the shooting. It was surprising how fast cops could mobilize when one of their own came under fire.

In less than half an hour, boats had converged on the island, bringing the sheriff's department and some of Marin's police force. Defino had ridden over on a Coast Guard vessel. The divers were Coast Guard.

"I've arranged for the Coast Guard to take you to the hospital."

Peyton frowned at her. "I'm fine, Captain. I don't need to go to the hospital. I wasn't hit."

"You're shivering, Peyton. I'm afraid you might be in shock."

"I'm fine." She pulled the blanket tighter, trying to force her body to stop shaking.

"I want a doctor to look at those cuts."

"They're nothing."

"You at least need a tetanus shot."

She glanced over her shoulder at Marco. He was talking with a man she didn't recognize. "Who's that?"

"Peyton, don't change the subject."

She looked back at her captain. "I'll go to my doctor tomorrow."

Defino narrowed her eyes and Peyton knew that look.

"Please don't make me go to the hospital, Captain. I need to stay here."

"We've got this under control."

"You don't understand." She realized the violent shuddering wasn't helping her case. Damn it, why couldn't she stop shaking?

"What don't I understand?"

"I should have taken the shot. He was in my line of sight."

"You slipped."

"I shouldn't have. Marco shouldn't have taken the shot."

"Peyton, can you hear yourself? You need to go to the hospital. This is the third time you been in a shoot-out this last year, the second time you've been shot at."

"There was a second suspect. I know it. He got away. He's out there somewhere."

"We'll find him."

"I should have taken the shot, I should have been the one to kill him."

Defino looked beyond Peyton and motioned to someone out of her sight. Peyton started to turn, but Defino pulled her back around. "Look at me."

Peyton stared into Defino's eyes and realized her damn teeth were chattering. "Officer Forman is going to escort you to the boat now. You're going to the hospital." When Peyton started to protest, she shook her head. "That's an order, Inspector Brooks."

Peyton bit her lower lip and nodded.

The officer took her elbow and turned her around. She looked over at Marco as the officer led her toward the boat dock. His eyes met hers and then he gave her a short nod, nothing more. Peyton turned away, focusing on keeping her footing as they wound down toward the boats.

*   *   *

Jake set his case beside the body and removed his camera. Two SWAT officers stood over the body with their assault rifles at the ready. They never once made eye contact with Jake, but surveyed the area with that alert stance of trained gunmen.

Jake ignored them and focused on the body. The rocks and surf had battered the man's face into a shapeless mass of bloated flesh. Three neat holes riddled the center of his body, right over his heart. Marco didn't mess around when he shot. His eyes traveled up and fixated on the collar around the man's neck.

"Shit," he said.

He snapped a number of pictures, then knelt by his case and fished out a pair of latex gloves, pulling them on. He was distracted momentarily as Peyton passed him on the road to the dock. She was being escorted by an officer who had a firm grip on her arm, and she never looked around. He wanted to go after her and see what was going on, but he had a job to do.

The man wore a pair of black slacks. His shoes had been knocked off in the surf, but the black shirt with the white collar was still in place. Jake patted the pockets of his trousers, feeling for a wallet. He found one on the right side in the front, but the salt made the fabric so stiff, he couldn't pull it out.

Reaching for his fabric scissors, he carefully cut the seam on the pants and pulled the pocket away, revealing a battered brown leather wallet. He eased it out and set the scissors on the ground, pulling apart the two halves. A driver's license was visible in the plastic window and he scanned the name. *Patrick Reynolds, 45, brown hair, brown eyes, from Boston, Massachusetts.* He pried open the bill fold and pulled out a bank ATM card, a MasterCard, and an ID card.

"Who is he?" came a voice behind him.

Jake shifted and found Marco standing at his back. His eyes were fixed on what was left of the man's face, or maybe he was staring at the collar. "Adonis, you probably shouldn't be here."

His eyes came to rest on Jake. They were hard and cold. "Just tell me his name, Ryder, damn it."

Captain Defino appeared behind him, crossing the courtyard at a quick walk. Jake really didn't know what the protocol was in this case, but he figured she could handle whatever happened next.

"His name was Patrick Reynolds."

"Patrick Reynolds?" Marco rolled the name around his tongue as if it were bitter.

"Father Patrick Reynolds," Jake finished.

* * *

Peyton rested her head against the pillow on her elevated hospital bed and closed her eyes. The sedative they'd given her made everything feel warped and wobbly. She just wanted to close her eyes for a moment, then she'd demand they release her.

She shifted and the IV tubes pulled in her arm. What an annoyance! She didn't need an IV, and she sure as hell didn't need their damn tranquilizers. At least the shivering had stopped, and at least, they'd given her a private room off the emergency room and hadn't made her remove her clothes. That is after they made sure she hadn't been shot. There were some things being a cop got her.

"There you are, sweetheart," came a familiar voice.

Peyton cracked open an eye and found Abe standing in front of her, his long face distorted by the drugs. "Why the hell are you here?"

"Marco called me." He reached up with his elegant, long fingers and turned her head so he could look at the side of her face. "Did they give you a tetanus shot?"

"I think so, but they have me so hopped up on drugs I don't know what they did to me."

Abe reached for the chart dangling on the end of her bed and read it. "They gave you a sedative. Woowee," he whistled. "A really strong one."

"Yeah, I was a little suspicious when they put it in a dart gun and shot me in the ass, but who am I to argue with doctors?"

Abe laughed. "We need to get you out of here."

"Really? That would be peachy."

Abe went out the door. A few minutes later a nurse came back in and began fussing with Peyton's IV. Abe sank into a chair by her bed.

"Why do you keep getting yourself in this trouble?"

She rolled her head on the pillow and looked at him. Abe always looked like his teeth were too big for his mouth, and in her drugged state, his dreads bounced around like snakes. Good thing she trusted him with her life.

"You're right. Clearly I was looking for trouble, going out to Alcatraz in the middle of the night and running around on the island with guns."

The nurse gave her a startled look, but Peyton ignored her.

"Did you get me checked out?"

"What do you think our good friend is doing here, Peyton? Substituting your IV bag for vodka?"

The nurse looked back at him and frowned.

Peyton couldn't help the smile that tugged at the corners of her mouth. "Why not? All the best movie stars combined sedatives with vodka."

19

He reached out and took her hand. "My heart about stopped when Marco called me at 1:00AM. Now, mind you, that's been a dream of mine for a long time, but…"

She squeezed his hand. "I'm sorry, Abe."

He kissed the back of her fingers. "Unless you're gonna tell me you're quitting, don't give me your mea culpa."

"Mea culpa?"

"Means *I'm sorry.*"

"I know what it means, but that's all I can give you. I'm not quitting."

"I know."

The nurse pressed a piece of gauze over the IV tube where it entered Peyton's arm, then slowly drew the needle out. Peyton watched her, but her thoughts were on her mother. Abe's words brought emotions to the front. Her relationship with her mother was strained because of her job, and now Abe voiced nearly the same thing. Was she being selfish staying in a job everyone hated? And what about Marco? He wouldn't have killed anyone if she'd been doing something else.

The nurse placed surgical tape over the gauze and grabbed Peyton's free hand, placing it over the site. "Apply pressure for a few minutes." She grabbed the clipboard and snapped some papers onto it, then held it and a pen out to Peyton.

Peyton gave her a quizzical look. Did she hold the gauze or did she sign?

Abe reached over and signed on the line for her. The nurse gave him another aggravated look. "I'm her husband," he said with a smile.

Peyton almost burst into laughter, but the nurse didn't crack a grin. For a moment, Peyton was sure she was going to protest, but then she gave up. It was just too late and she didn't really give a damn about who signed out a cop who needed a sedative.

"I'll get a wheel chair." She left the room, carrying the clipboard with her.

Peyton swung her legs over the side of the bed and started to climb down. "I'm not getting in no wheelchair."

"Peyton," said Abe, standing up.

She landed on the floor and her knees buckled. Abe caught her under the arm and hauled her upright.

"This is why you need a wheelchair."

"No, I need you to help me. I'm not kidding, Abe. I'm walking out of here."

He gave a long suffering sigh, but he shifted around where he could slide an arm about her waist. "You are so damn stubborn, woman. Do you know how hard it is being your husband?"

They shuffled their way to the door. Peyton couldn't believe how wobbly she felt. Everything seemed to be tilting. What the hell had they given her? Once they made it to the triage center of the emergency room, a few nurses turned to look at them, but they were too busy to offer more than a passing glance.

In Peyton's drugged state, the walk through the emergency room was surreal. People coughed or moaned or tried to talk over the loud droning of the television set. Lights from the ambulance at the entrance flashed across her eyes. Finally the cool of the San Francisco fog enveloped her and they shambled across the parking lot, dodging cars and other people who were going in the opposite direction.

Abe used his remote to unlock his Mini Cooper and then pulled open the passenger side door, handing Peyton down into the seat.

"I'll drive."

"The hell you will," he scolded, then reached around her and tried to buckle her seatbelt.

She swatted his hands away and did it herself. With a bemused expression, he shut the door and hurried around to the driver's side, folding himself into the tiny vehicle.

"What's say we go dancing?"

Abe chuckled as he started the car. "Not on your life. I'm dumping you off at home and then I'm going to bed. I need my beauty sleep. It's Jake's turn to babysit you."

She rolled her head on the seat and watched him back the Mini out of the parking space. "Actually, I need you to take me to Marco's. I don't want him to be alone tonight."

Abe stopped the car and looked over at her. "Sweetheart, you're going home and getting some sleep. Vinnie's with Marco tonight, so he isn't alone."

"Are you sure? How do you know?"

"He told me. Remember, he called."

"How do you know he wasn't lying so you wouldn't be worried?"

"Because he told me Captain Defino ordered it."

Peyton looked back out the front windshield as Abe put the car in drive. If Captain Defino ordered it, she knew Marco would never violate that. Still she wanted to see him and apologize, beg him to forgive her for what she'd done to him, but Abe was right. If he was with Vinnie, he didn't need her.

CHAPTER 2

The sedative hit Peyton harder than she expected and by the time she pulled herself together, showered, walked Pickles, and drank a half-pot of coffee, it was nearing 11:00AM when she pulled into the precinct parking lot.

Instinctively, she looked around for the Charger, but it wasn't there. That gave her a jolt. She had no delusions about the previous night. She knew exactly what had happened, but not having Marco waiting for her made it all the more real…and terrible.

Her fingers curled around the steering wheel, then she forced herself to release it and thrust open the car door, climbing out. She walked quickly across the parking lot and jogged up the stairs, pulling open the glass door.

Captain Defino and Jake stood around Maria's desk, but they turned as she entered.

Defino squinted at her. "What the hell are you doing here, Brooks?"

Peyton hesitated. "I work here, or else I think I do. They pumped me so full of narcotics last night I'm not sure I'm not still in Wonderland."

"I meant why are you *here*? You should be home."

Peyton let the door close at her back. "I have a case to work on, Captain."

She felt Jake's eyes searching her, but she didn't want to meet his look. Truthfully, she'd been glad he was gone when she got up this morning. "We need to get a list of the people on that last tour."

"Done," said Jake.

"We need to interview them and see if they saw anything."

"We've arranged interviews for this afternoon, Brooks," said Defino.

"Then I guess I just need to fill out my report." She moved toward the half-door.

"Not yet. I need to see you in my office," said Defino, turning her back and walking into the room.

Peyton happened to meet Maria's gaze, but the assistant lowered her head and studied something on her desk. Peyton wished she'd act normal, make some cutting comment about her hair or her clothes, anything but this.

She walked to the half-door and pulled it open, trying to think of some jab, but she realized she didn't have anything. She went to Defino's door and entered.

The captain was already seated and she pointed at the hard melamine chair across from her. "Sit."

Peyton sank into it and adjusted her gun. Was this where Defino took it from her, relieving her of duty? She'd been the one with the clear shot last night, but she hadn't taken it. Twice now she hadn't taken the shot when it was available to her.

Defino just sat and stared at her.

Peyton shifted in the chair and looked at the back of Defino's picture frame. She knew it housed a photo of the captain's husband, Colin.

"Captain, look, I'll do whatever I need to, go to the shooting range, repeat classes, whatever, just don't take me off this case."

Defino frowned. "You think I'm relieving you of duty, Brooks?"

Peyton shrugged.

"You did nothing wrong last night. How many times do I have to tell you that? You didn't have the best shot, Marco did. You were under fire and he told you to get down. You did what you should have done."

"I should have known the shooter was there."

"No one knew he was there. He surprised everyone. It was dark and cops were running all around. There's no way to anticipate how something like that gets out of control."

Peyton rubbed her hands on her thighs. "Well, if that's all, then I really need to get back to the case."

"Not yet."

Peyton looked up at her. She knew Defino hadn't called her in here for nothing. Her thoughts immediately went to Marco and she felt a suffocating worry. Was he all right? She should have called him this morning. She should have gone over to his apartment.

"The shooter was named Patrick Reynolds."

Peyton narrowed her eyes. That wasn't what she'd expected. "Okay?"

"*Father* Patrick Reynolds."

"He was a priest?"

"According to the ID Jake found."

"Where does a priest get a gun?"

"He used the missing gun from the ranger."

That made sense. What didn't make sense was why? "What was he doing on Alcatraz?"

"He was taking a few boys from his parish on a field trip."

"I need to talk to those boys."

"Maria arranged interviews for this afternoon."

"Have we contacted his parish?"

"Not yet."

"I'll do that now." She started to rise.

"Brooks."

Sinking back into the chair, she clasped her hands in her lap.

"I'm sure you know Marco's on administrative leave until Internal Affairs clears him."

Peyton swallowed hard. "I know."

"They contacted me first thing this morning. They wanted to put you on leave as well."

"Me?"

Defino's expression never wavered, never softened. "I fought them. I couldn't lose both of you right now, but they have a mandate."

"Wait." She held up a hand and let it fall. "You said I didn't break protocol out there. Why are they questioning me?"

"As I told you last night, you've been in three gun battles over the last year, twice someone's taken a shot at you. And now, your partner's killed someone."

"He had no choice!" Peyton surprised herself with the violence of her reaction. She'd never spoken to the captain like that before. It suddenly dawned on her what the captain said earlier. The shooter was a priest. Marco killed a priest. "I'm sorry, Captain. I didn't mean…"

"Save it."

Peyton drew a deep breath and released it. "What's the mandate?"

"You're to have sessions every morning with the department psychiatrist until he determines that you are fit to serve. You've been allowed to keep your gun, but only if you complete these sessions. If you miss even one, you will be immediately removed from duty."

"I already had three sessions with the shrink after the Peña case…"

Defino leaned back and a faint smile touched her lips. "You had three sessions with a psychologist who you completely snowed. He was so charmed with you that he allowed you to spend your time telling him ridiculous stories about your dog and Abe."

Peyton's mouth fell open. "You read my file?"

"It was my duty, as difficult as it was."

"That's a violation of my privacy. Aren't counseling sessions confidential?"

"Not when you sign a release. And these sessions won't be either. I will be fully updated on everything you say. I can't give you a gun and turn you loose on the public if I don't know whether you're fit or not, Brooks."

"I'm fit."

"We'll see." Defino tapped a finger on her glass desk. "This man is a trained professional, Brooks, and he won't be conned by your witty repartee. If at any time, he feels you are not fit, he will pull your badge, so I wouldn't play games with him. I would answer him honestly and seriously. Answer his questions and nothing else. No stories, no anecdotes, no silliness. Just answer him with the truth."

"I answered the last guy with the truth."

"Really?" Defino speared her with a look. "Not once did you discuss your father's death or the estrangement with your mother. And I don't remember seeing a thing in there about your failure to establish intimate relationships with men."

Peyton felt her jaw clench.

"I'm serious, Brooks. You take this seriously and you be honest, or I will take your badge myself."

Peyton forced herself to nod.

"You start tomorrow at 8:00."

"I'll be here with bells on."

"I look forward to it. Dismissed."

* * *

Peyton left the captain's office and stopped at Maria's desk. Jake wasn't there and she was just as glad. The previous night he kept looking at her as if he expected her to suddenly shatter into glass shards, as if she'd ever been that delicate.

"Can you let me know when the boys get here?"

Maria nodded.

"I'll be at my desk, trying to find out something about this priest." When Maria still didn't answer, Peyton moved around her desk.

"Brooks?"

Peyton stopped and turned around.

"Have you talked to Marco?" The concern in Maria's voice was real.

"No, I was going to call him right now, see if he's okay."

"Jake said Vinnie was going to be with him today."

"Good. That makes me feel a little better."

Maria started to say something, then stopped. With another nod, she turned away.

Peyton pulled out her phone and thumbed it on. Pressing the icon to dial Marco, she held it to her ear as she walked to her desk. Sinking into the seat, she listened to the ringing, praying he would pick up. If he didn't, she didn't know what she'd do.

"Hey," came his voice. He sounded so normal, she couldn't immediately respond.

"Hey."

"Where are you?"

"I'm at work."

"Why the hell are you there?"

She smiled. *So Marco, so normal.* "I work here. You forget that?"

"No, but I thought you might have. Abe said you were loopy as hell last night."

"When they shoot you full of horse tranquilizers, that's what happens."

"You get a tetanus shot?"

She rubbed her upper arm, feeling the twinge beneath the skin. "Yeah. And they scrubbed the hell out of the cuts as well. I was afraid they were going to rub off all my beautiful brown."

He laughed.

Peyton closed her eyes at the sound. Her throat felt so tight, she forced herself to breathe.

"You gotta stop doing that to me, Brooks," he said in a low voice. "My heart can't take it."

Her fingers tightened on the phone. "I'm so sorry…"

"Don't you dare finish that."

She forced herself to stop. "Is Vinnie with you?"

"Yeah, and my mom."

"Defino said I have to have counseling sessions with the psychiatrist, a real ball-buster apparently."

28

"Good thing you don't have balls then. Honestly, I'm more worried about his manhood, going up against you."

She smiled past the lump in her throat. "You have to have them too."

"I know."

"Hurry up and prove you're all right. Defino needs you back here."

"Defino needs me?"

"Okay, Maria also misses you."

"That all?"

"And Jake."

"Well, hell then, I better hurry. Can't have Jake going around missing my ass."

She blinked back the sudden tears in her eyes. "I'll talk to you soon, okay?"

"Yeah. Hey, Peyton?"

"Yeah?"

"Watch yourself, you hear me. Promise me you'll take it easy when you go out on a call."

"I will. Bye, Marco Baby."

"Later, Brooks."

The line went dead in her hand. She stared at the display, then reached for her computer, powering it on. She did a quick search for Patrick Reynolds. That was too broad, so she narrowed it to Father Patrick Reynolds. That pulled up a few entries, but nothing in San Francisco.

She swiveled in her desk chair and leaned back, looking across at Jake's desk. She couldn't see what he was doing beyond the partition. "Jake?"

He popped up so quickly above the partition she figured he'd been waiting for her to call him. "Yep, Mighty Mouse."

"You get anything out of the shooter's wallet on what parish he belongs to?"

He picked up something on his desk, then came around the partition, strolling over to her. He handed her a piece of paper with copies of Reynolds' driver's license and church ID card. She pulled out her notebook and scribbled the name of the church onto it, then reached for the mouse. She typed in the name of the church and waited for the search engine to load.

Jake sank down in the chair between her and Marco's desk. "You sure you should be here?"

She didn't make eye contact with him. The last time she'd been shot at he nearly quit on them, but Marco had talked him out of it. They had another nine months of friendship between them now. She knew it would be even harder for him now if he had to take pictures of her dead body.

She clicked on the first church that came up on the search list. Scrolling down, she found the contact link and pressed it, then scribbled the number in her notebook.

"Peyton?"

She set the pencil on her desk blotter and turned to look at him. "Look, Jake. I know how scary this all seems to you. People getting shot at – it's insane, but it happens in this business. It's probably not the last time it'll happen to me. And the reality is I may get shot someday."

"This is the very pep talk I've been hoping you'd give me all freakin' day," he said.

"This isn't a pep talk, this is a reality check. I'm just telling you what you already know. I have to be here. This is what I do, who I am. I'm a cop, Jake, and that's a reality you're going to have to square yourself with or choose the alternatives."

"And what are those?"

"Go back to the bank or go back to Nebraska."

He shifted in the chair and leaned closer to her. "You know I can't do either of those things now. I'm in this too deep."

"Then we don't need to discuss it."

He pushed himself to his feet and leaned over her. "I guess not, but you might make a bit more effort by telling me useless platitudes even though we both know they're bullshit. That's what friends do for each other."

She frowned up at him. "They lie to each other?"

"Yes." With that, he walked away.

Peyton thought about what he said for a moment. He had a point. She didn't do the comfort thing very well. It was part of her problem with her mother. She'd never been good at showing other's the soft, vulnerable side to herself.

Pulling out her phone, she typed in the number for the parish and leaned back in her chair as it rang. It rang four times before someone picked up. "St. Matthews' Church?" came a woman's voice.

Peyton realized she hadn't thought this out. Her knowledge of the Catholic Church was limited to what Marco told her. Who did she ask for? What did she say?

"Hello?"

"Yes, this is Inspector Peyton Brooks from the San Francisco Police Department."

"Inspector Brooks, we have been instructed by Father Mark to direct all inquiries from law enforcement to Bishop George Alton at the Diocese. I can give you the number."

"Wait. Father Mark? Who is that?"

"He's our priest."

"Who's Father Reynolds?"

She was silent for a moment.

"Hello?" said Peyton. "Are you there?"

"Yes. Father Mark is our priest. Father Patrick was the vicar."

Vicar? She wasn't sure what that was. "Can I speak with Father Mark? Is he available?"

"All police inquiries have been directed to the Diocese, Inspector Brooks. I can give you the number."

Peyton bit her lower lip. "Can you at least tell me how long Father Patrick was a vicar there?"

"All inquiries have been directed…"

"Yeah, I got it. Give me the number."

31

The woman rattled it off and Peyton wrote it in her notebook. "Have a blessed day, Inspector Brooks," said the woman, and before Peyton could say goodbye, she hung up.

Peyton held the phone out and stared at it. What the hell was that about? She wondered if Father Mark had been called down to the M.E.'s office to identify the body. She sent a quick text to Abe, asking if he got the body, then dialed the number to the Diocese. A man picked up on the first ring. "Our Lady of Redemption, how may I direct your call?"

Peyton decided to be a bit more discreet. "I'd like to talk to Bishop George Alton, please."

"Bishop Alton is very busy this morning. May I tell him who is calling?"

Peyton tapped the edge of the notebook on her desk. "Inspector Peyton Brooks from the San Francisco Police Department."

"Inspector Brooks, I will let him know you called and ask him to return your call. Can you give me the best number to reach you at?"

Peyton told the man her number, repeating it to make sure he got it right.

"I'll have him get back to you as soon as possible. Anything else I can do for you?"

Peyton dropped the notebook on the desk. She recognized a stonewalling when she saw one. "No, just please impress on him how important it is to return my call."

"Of course. Have a good day, Inspector."

"Thanks." Peyton hung up and laid her phone on her desk. A moment later a text from Abe came through. He'd gotten both bodies from Alcatraz to process. She typed another text to him, asking him if anyone had identified the priest's body. He confirmed that a Father Mark Shannon had been in early that morning to give a positive identification. She thanked him and told him she'd call him that night, then she checked the time.

The boys were due in for an interview in about an hour, so she didn't have time to go out to the church. That would have to wait for tomorrow. Clicking on the word processing program, she decided to begin her report.

*   *   *

Peyton poured herself a mug of coffee and reached for the sugar, but she stopped with her hand on the lid. Pushing it away, she picked up the black coffee and took a sip. The bitterness smote her taste-buds, making her shiver. At least the heat drove some of the lethargy away.

Maria stuck her head inside the break-room. "The boys are here. I set them up in the conference room."

Peyton nodded and left the coffee on the counter, following Maria across the squad room to her desk, where she retrieved her notebook. As she headed toward the front of the building, she could hear Defino talking to someone. She slowed as she came around the corner, finding the captain talking to a group of people in the lobby.

She caught sight of Peyton and motioned her forward. "Inspector Brooks, I'd like to introduce you to the parents of the boys." Peyton's gaze passed over the three women and two men. "As I'm sure you remember, the boys were on a field trip with Father Reynolds at the time of the shooting. I was just explaining to their parents how we plan to proceed. The boys are already in the conference room."

Peyton forced a smile and held out her hand to the woman on the far left.

"This is Ms. Barber, Matt Barber's mother."

The woman met her eye directly and gave her a firm shake, then released her. Peyton shifted to the couple next to her.

"Mr. and Mrs. Gafney, parents to Joey Gafney." They each shook her hand, but Mrs. Gafney kept her eyes fixed on the conference room door.

Peyton turned to the last couple.

"And finally, Mr. and Mrs. Pooley, parents of J.C. Pooley. I told them they could be in the room as you questioned the boys, and that I would be in there also."

When Peyton gave her a surprised look, Captain Defino tilted her head, indicating it wasn't open for discussion.

"Great," she said, trying to keep the sarcasm from her voice. "After you?" She held the half-door open as they walked through.

Three teenage boys sat at the table. The parents arranged themselves behind their sons, taking seats Maria had obviously set up earlier for them. Matt Barber was about fifteen, Peyton guessed, with a shaggy mop of brown hair and friendly brown eyes. He had his hands clasped nervously in his lap and he wore a polo shirt buttoned up to the top. Joey Gafney was a year or two older with blond hair that feathered back from his face, showing the line of acne along his cheekbones. He had a t-shirt with a picture of Jesus on it that said, *What would Jesus do?* Finally, J.C. Pooley was a large boy with shoulders like a linebacker and a paunch to match. He wore a Niners' football jersey and a Niners' ball cap over close-cropped brown hair.

Peyton took a seat across from them and reached for her business cards, smiling at them as she passed the cards around. She was aware of Captain Defino leaning against the wall behind her. "I'm Inspector Brooks," she said.

Immediately, J.C. Pooley's father grabbed the card from his son's hand and read it.

Peyton ignored the gesture and reached for her notebook, setting it on the table in front of her. She slid the pen out of the spiral binding on top. "Do you mind if I take some notes while you talk to me?"

The boys all shook their heads *no*.

"Great. Let me start by saying how much I appreciate you coming in and being willing to talk to me. It will help us figure out what happened yesterday. I'm sure you're still shaken up from the experience, so if at any time, you want to take a break, please don't hesitate to let me know."

J.C. gave a grunt, but Matt nodded vigorously.

"Okay, let's get started. I know you all went to Alcatraz on a field trip with Father Reynolds, right?"

"Yeah," said Joey.

"Does that happen often?"

"What do you mean?"

"Do you go on field trips with Father Reynolds often?"

"Do you mean Father Patrick?" asked Matt.

"Right, Father Patrick."

"He just started at St. Matthews," said Joey.

"When?"

"'Bout three months ago."

The other boys nodded.

Peyton jotted a note in her notepad. "Great. Do you know where he came from?"

The boys glanced at each other. Matt turned and looked at his mother. His mother shook her head.

"No," said Matt tentatively. "I don't know."

"Okay. Let's talk about what happened yesterday, all right?" Peyton could sense the shift in atmosphere. Joey's parents moved restlessly in their chairs. "I know it's hard, but I really need to know what you saw and heard."

"Okay," said Joey.

"You were on the last tour of the day, right?"

"Yeah."

"How come you went out so late?"

"Father Patrick said it would be spookier if we went later," offered Joey. Peyton guessed he was the de facto leader of the group.

"Did he just invite the three of you?"

The boys shared a look, but Joey answered. "No, he was trying to start this youth group. It was supposed to be more, but he said only the three of us signed up to go."

"I see. So once you got to the island, you were taken to the chapel to watch a video?"

"Yeah, of the prison."

"I saw benches in that room. Were you standing or seated?"

"We were sitting in the last row. Father Patrick was standing behind us."

"Was it dark in there?"

"Yeah, they turned the lights out so we could see the video."

Peyton leaned forward. "Can you tell me what happened when the shooting started?"

J.C. shifted weight in his chair and Matt looked at his clasped hands. Joey considered his response for a moment. "The video was loud, but all of a sudden I heard a strange pop. People started screaming and we hit the floor."

"Is that what you all heard?"

J.C. nodded, but Matt looked up at Peyton. "I saw the guard or whatever he was fall over backward, then Joey pushed me down."

"Where was Father Patrick?"

"I'm not sure," said Joey. "Everyone was screaming and running for the exits. Someone pushed me in the back and I fell."

Matt dropped his eyes again and stared at his hands.

"Matt?" said Peyton. "Did you see Father Patrick?"

He shrugged. "I'm not sure. Joey's right. It was crazy in there."

"That's okay. What do you think you saw?"

"I thought…" He hesitated and glanced back at his mother. She put her hand on his shoulder for support. "I thought I saw someone in a ball cap grab him around the neck and pull him back toward the door."

"Did you recognize the ball cap?"

"I think it was a Giants cap, but I'm not sure."

"Then what happened?"

36

"Someone fell over me and I couldn't see anything. Next thing I know a guard was pulling me up and pushing me toward the door."

Peyton made a few notes on her pad, then looked over at Joey. "Do you remember anything else?"

"No, I didn't see Father Patrick, I just followed J.C. out of the building."

Peyton shifted toward J.C. "Do you remember anything different than the other two?"

"Nothing. I didn't really hear the shot even. I just heard everyone scream."

Peyton read back through her notes. "Did anyone else know about the field trip?"

"It was posted on the bulletin board for weeks," offered Joey's father. "A lot of people had to see it."

"Why did Father Patrick pick Alcatraz?"

Joey shrugged. "He thought it was fascinating that you could take a trip out there and see it. He said he liked history and stuff."

"How often did the youth group meet?"

"We were just getting started. We met a few times."

"How many people belonged to it?"

"I don't know. Each meeting it seemed like different people showed up. There were about six of us regulars."

"Boys and girls?"

"Yeah."

Matt briefly closed his eyes. Peyton noticed he was clasping his hands tightly in his lap.

"Matt, is there anything else you remember?"

Matt shook his head.

Peyton leaned toward him. "Matt, anything you can tell me would help. Is there something else you want to say?"

Matt looked up at her and his brown eyes were sad. "I heard something, but it was wrong for me to listen."

"On Alcatraz?"

"No, at the church, during one of our meetings."

"Okay, what was it?"

"I shouldn't have been listening."

"Well, sometimes we hear things that we shouldn't, but if it helps us understand what happened on Alcatraz, I think it's okay for you to tell me. I know it was terrifying – what you went through out there, but I'm really trying to make sense of it."

"You get hurt out there?" Joey motioned to Peyton's cheek.

She gingerly touched the cuts. "Yeah, you guys were right, it was spooky out there and by the time I got off the boat, it was incredibly dark."

"I heard Father Patrick's dead. Is he?"

Peyton glanced back at Defino and she nodded that Peyton could continue. "Yes, he's dead."

"Did the guy who took him kill him?" asked Matt.

"That's what I'm trying to figure out. That's why I need your help, Matt. What did you hear at the church?"

Matt rubbed his palm on his jeans. "Father Mark didn't want Father Patrick to start the youth group."

"Why?"

"I don't know. Father Patrick said it was important to him."

"Father Mark knew about the field trip, though, right?"

"He had to know," said Joey. "Dad's right. It was posted on the bulletin board."

"Do you know why only the three of you signed up?"

"No. It was the first field trip, so we just figured the others weren't interested in it."

"Okay. You've done real good, all of you. My direct phone number is on those cards I gave you. If you remember anything else, or think of anything, please call me."

Joey and J.C. nodded.

Matt met Peyton's eye. "I didn't see the guy's face who took Father Patrick. It was too dark."

"I understand."

"Maybe I didn't even see that right. Maybe the guy was trying to get Father Patrick out."

"Maybe."

"But why would he put his arm around his neck?"

"I don't know, but I'll try to find out."

J.C.'s father stood up. "If that's all, I think we should leave."

Peyton nodded. "Don't hesitate to call me though if you think of anything at all, even if you think it's nothing."

The boys nodded and rose. Peyton shook hands with them, then Captain Defino walked them out. Peyton followed her and watched them as they walked across the parking lot.

"Why do you think Father Mark didn't want Father Patrick to start a youth group?" asked Defino.

Peyton sighed. "I can guess, can't you?"

"Yeah." Defino looked over her shoulder at her. "Maybe we need to talk to Father Mark?"

"I'll head out there now."

"Do it tomorrow after your session with the psychiatrist. Right now, I think you should go home and get some rest. You look like hell."

"Thanks, Captain. And here I thought I looked like a super model."

Behind her, Maria made a choking noise.

Defino smiled. "Go home, Brooks, but make sure you're here bright and early tomorrow for your session."

Peyton rolled her eyes. "Why ever would I be late for that? It's gonna be the highlight of my day."

Defino laughed. "Actually, I'm certain it'll be the highlight of his day, poor bastard." With that, she headed toward her office.

CHAPTER 3

Peyton arrived at the precinct precisely at 8:00AM for her session with the psychiatrist. He was waiting for her in the doorway of the conference room. She didn't have time for coffee or to go to her desk.

He held out his hand and grasped hers in a firm, authoritative grip. "Inspector Brooks?"

"Yes. Peyton, actually."

"Peyton, I'm Dr. Ferguson, but if we're going to be on first name terms, you can call me Don." He was middle aged with a thinning crown of blond hair and watery blue eyes. His clean shaven face was long and his chin square. He wore an out-of-date suit with a pale blue shirt and a yellow tie. He was average height, but his hands were large and calloused.

"Excellent."

When his brows lifted, Peyton remembered what Defino had warned her. No stories, no anecdotes, no silliness. Just the bald truth. She hated feeling like everything she said was open for interpretation and study.

"Come in." He motioned into the conference room.

She really wanted some coffee, but she figured that would seem like a crutch to a man like him. She followed him obediently inside. He shut the door behind them, then went around the table, taking a seat. He pointed to the chair at the head of the table and Peyton sank into it. She suppressed the urge to say *no couch*, but it was hard. In fact, this whole thing was going to be hard. How was she going to act normal when the entire set up made her feel like a goldfish in a bowl?

A legal pad sat on the table before him and he picked up a pen. "Do you mind if I take notes while we talk?"

"Do I have a choice?"

He set the pen down again. "We all have choices, Peyton. Certainly there are consequences for those choices, such as this one. I'm certain you'd like to be anywhere else right now, but you have to attend these sessions in order to remain on active duty; however, you could always choose not to attend."

Peyton heard the implied threat. "Take notes," she said. She could pretend like she had a choice, even though she didn't.

"Good. Now, let me explain something to you. My philosophy has always been to ask questions I want an answer to. I don't play around trying to get you to reveal something you are trying to hide. If I want to know, I'll just come out and ask it. Understood?"

"Sure."

"Good. Now, as I understand it, you've been in three shoot-outs over the last year. Twice you've been shot at and one resulted in the near fatal shooting of someone right next to you. This last incident ended with your partner killing a suspect."

He wasn't kidding about getting right to the heart of it. "You have the facts right."

"You must feel like a target."

"I'm a cop. We *are* targets."

"Most cops go their entire careers without getting shot at, Peyton, yet you've had three close calls in the last year."

She forced down the sarcastic quip she was going to make. "You're right."

"That would make anyone wonder if they're in the right career."

"It would. It certainly makes those around me wonder."

"What about you?"

Peyton braced her elbow on the arm of the chair and rested her chin on her hand. "No, I haven't thought about changing careers."

He picked up the pen and jotted something down on the pad. Peyton couldn't read it upside down, besides the fact that it looked like chicken scratch.

"Let's talk about your father."

Peyton's brows rose. "Wow, you weren't kidding. You wanna hop into bed without even buying me dinner."

He glanced up from his pad. "Should I take that to mean you don't want to talk about your father?"

Peyton forced herself to remember Defino's warning. No silliness, no stories, just the truth. "No, I don't want to talk about my dad, but that doesn't mean I won't."

"Do you feel you've gotten over his death?"

Peyton lowered her arm. "No, I haven't gotten over his death. Who gets over something like that? But I don't see how that has anything to do with me being in three shoot-outs this last year."

He made a non-committal shrug. "Perhaps you put yourself in dangerous situations."

"Of course, that must be it. It couldn't be that I'm a cop."

He gave her a half-smile and tapped the pen on his pad. "People often use sarcasm for self-defense."

"Don't read anything into it. I use sarcasm for everything."

"Why did you feel the need to fulfill the last wish of the man who killed your father?"

That took her aback. She blinked at him a few times, then sucked in a full breath and held it. Gradually, she released it. Staring at the table, she tried to come up with a plausible answer, but nothing came to her. "I don't really know." She glanced up. "Except I gave him my word."

"Is that important to you? Your word?"

"When all is said and done, it's all we've got."

"That must have been hard."

Peyton nodded. "I don't think I did it for him. Not for Luis Garza. I did it for his mother. I knew what that loss was like and…I don't know."

"What?"

"I just felt I had to get closure."

"Did you?"

Peyton pulled her upper lip between her teeth. "No, but I guess I understood a little better. That's probably all that I'll ever have, just a better understanding. How one moment changes your life forever."

"Let's talk about your mother."

Peyton fought the smart retort that rose to her lips.

"Your relationship with her is strained, yes?"

Peyton laughed. "You could say that."

"Because of your father's death?"

"That and my job and her current boyfriend."

"She doesn't approve of your job?"

"Why would she? Not after my father."

"You mentioned her boyfriend. It can be hard for children to see their parents move on."

"It's not that…well, not entirely."

"What is it then?"

"He wants to pretend her previous life never happened, including the mixed-race daughter she has."

"Ah, I see. Have you expressed this to her?"

"Why? She'd feel obligated to break it off with him and right now, he fills a need for her. Even if he wasn't in the picture, there's too much between us as it is."

"Is that why you get emotionally involved in the cases you're assigned?"

"Emotionally involved? I don't think I get emotionally involved."

"Really?"

Peyton knew she'd entered a dangerous topic, but she didn't know how to deflect it. "I have never received a complaint about my work ethic."

He lifted a few pages on his tablet and reviewed some notes he'd scribbled there. "Let's see." He shifted a few more pages, then looked up at her. "Currently, you have a murder suspect renting a room in your house. Not only that, but you got him a job."

"Well..."

"You allowed a prostitute to come into your home and take a shower. Later on she betrayed you."

"That was..."

"And in your last case, instead of turning over an open and shut case to the D.A., you stonewalled him and continued working it past all reason, even against the advice of your partner."

Peyton leaned forward. "If I hadn't kept working that last case, we would have sent an innocent man to prison. As for Jake Ryder, he was also innocent."

"And the prostitute?"

Peyton stopped. Flattening her hand on the table, she drew a deep breath. "I was trying to save her."

"Here's what I think. Your father is dead, your mother is estranged, and you have no siblings, so you fill that void with the people around you, making them into your ersatz family."

"Most people would feel that's healthy."

He flipped a few more pages. "Most people wouldn't bring a murder suspect into their house. Not only that, but you have a failed romantic relationship with the assistant district attorney, call the medical examiner your best friend, and then there's your relationship with your partner."

Peyton slumped back in her seat. "What does that mean?"

"Do you deny that you are exceptionally close to your partner?"

"That happens when you trust your life to someone every day for eight years. You can't possibly understand that sort of a bond."

"Relax, Inspector Brooks. My job is counseling cops. I understand that relationship quite well."

"So what are you implying?"

"You were badly shaken yesterday after the shooting. Your captain ordered you to be seen by a medical professional who deemed it necessary to give you a tranquilizer."

"Yeah, someone shot at me, damn near hit me." She pointed to the cuts on her cheek.

"Is that really why you were shaken up, Inspector Brooks?"

"Of course it was."

"And yet the last time you were shot at, you didn't need any medical assistance. In fact, a man was shot right next to you and you continued working the case as if nothing had happened. What changed this time?"

"I don't know."

"I think you do."

"Well, I don't. Maybe it was because it's happened so much lately. Maybe it was the environment."

"I don't believe that's true."

"Well, I don't know then."

"I really think you do, but you're afraid to admit it to yourself."

"What the hell does that mean?"

"Why was this time different?"

"I don't know."

"Yes, you do."

"No, I don't. It just was."

"Why?"

"Because."

"Because why?"

Peyton slammed her hand down on the table. "Because I should have been the one to shoot. It should have been me, not Marco. I should have killed him."

Closing her eyes, she lowered her head.

Doctor Ferguson picked up his pen and wrote something on his pad. She could hear the scratch of the tip across the paper. Forcing herself to breathe in and out, she calmed herself. This had to be a bad thing. There was no way that much writing indicated anything other than disaster.

"I suppose you want my gun now."

"Not at all."

Peyton opened her eyes and looked at him. "What?"

"We're finally getting somewhere."

"And where is that?"

He smiled. His face didn't soften much as a result, but he was a little less intimidating. "Were you and Inspector D'Angelo always close?"

Peyton gave a bark of laughter. The question was so unexpected. "No, he hated me at first."

"Why?"

Peyton allowed herself to lean back in the chair. "I guess I can be a little overbearing at times and he was uptight."

"Overbearing how?"

Peyton smiled in memory. "I told his date one time that I was his wife."

Ferguson gave her an amused look. "You did what?"

Peyton remembered Defino's warning about telling silly stories. "It's nothing."

"I disagree. It lets me get to the heart of this situation, lets me understand the dynamics of your relationship. It bears directly on why you feel you should have taken the shot when everyone else indicates he had the better angle."

"I don't know. It was a long time ago."

"What is this dissembling really about, Inspector Brooks?"

"Captain Defino told me not to waste your time with anecdotes and silly stories."

"I see."

"She told me to answer your questions and nothing more."

"You mean she didn't want you to do to me what you did to the other psychologist you saw?"

46

"Exactly."

"Tell me the story, Inspector Brooks. I'll deal with your captain myself."

Peyton sighed, but she was relieved. This seemed a hell of a lot safer than talking about the shooting. There was absolutely nothing Doctor Ferguson could get out of her first meeting with Marco.

* * *

Peyton opened the door to the precinct and stepped into the lobby. A counter lay in front of her and beyond that was an unmanned desk. The door to the left opened on a conference room and the door to the right was closed. Peyton moved to the counter and leaned over, trying to peer into the rest of the building, but she couldn't see anything beyond a couple of brown partitions.

The outer door opened and a huge man stepped through. He was at least six four, massive shoulders, and had one of the handsomest faces she'd ever seen. He had wide cheekbones, a square chin, and broad forehead. His nose cut a straight slash in the middle of a Patrician face. With his dark black hair pulled back in a ponytail and heavily lashed blue eyes, he was gorgeous.

He eyed her up and down. "Hey."

"Hey," she returned.

Behind her she heard heels on the tiled floor. A young Hispanic woman with an hour-glass figure came around the corner and approached the desk. She spotted Peyton first and her nose crinkled up as if she smelled something bad, then her gaze lifted to the young god behind her. A smile bloomed across her lips, lighting up her eyes.

"Hello. I'm Maria Sanchez." She checked an appointment book on her desk. "And you must be…"

"Peyton Brooks." She held out her hand over the counter.

Maria ignored it and went to the half-door on the left side and pulled it open. "This way."

Peyton pulled her hand back and eased around the counter into the inner sanctum of the precinct, but once on the other side she wasn't sure where to go. She turned back to Maria, but the woman was fixated on the man.

"And you must be Marco D'Angelo." Her eyes tracked him up and down and Peyton thought she thrust her chest out just a bit.

"You've got me," he said in a deep rumble, holding out his hand. He gave her a lazy smile.

She beamed at him and took his hand, sliding her palm along his until her fingers touched his wrist. Peyton wanted to make a gagging motion, but she was afraid it wouldn't look professional.

"I have a meeting with Captain Defino this morning," she suggested.

Maria looked over at her and made the same crinkling motion with her nose. "This way." She pointed to the closed office door and led the way. Knocking at the door, she turned the handle and leaned inside. "Your nine o'clock is here."

"Send them in," came a feminine voice.

Peyton frowned. For some reason she'd expected Captain Defino to be a man.

Maria held the door open. "Go right in."

Peyton went first, stepping into a dark office whose blinds were closed against the sunlight. She glanced back over her shoulder and watched D'Angelo enter. He had to turn sideways to get beyond Maria and she gave him a sultry look as he passed.

Peyton rolled her eyes, then faced forward again. A stocky woman of medium height rose from behind a glass desk and motioned them forward. She had short brown hair and a business pants suit that looked stiff and proper. Across from her sat a middle aged Caucasian man with a barrel chest and enormous hands and next to him was an Asian man who shifted in his seat with quick, sharp movements.

"Officers Brooks and D'Angelo?"

"Brooks, ma'am," said Peyton.

D'Angelo just nodded.

"I guess I should correct myself. Inspectors Brooks and D'Angelo, right?"

"Yes, ma'am."

She motioned to the two men at her desk. "This is Inspector Bill Simons and Inspector Nathan Cho." She gave a slight smile. "These young people are our two latest hotshots. Both graduated at the top of their class."

Simons gave a grunt, but he didn't seem impressed. Cho rose quickly and held out his hand to Peyton.

"Welcome aboard."

"Thank you," she said, watching as he moved to D'Angelo and also shook his hand.

"Thank you, gentlemen," said the captain, motioning to the door. "That will be all. I need to debrief our young detectives now."

Simons lumbered to his feet, forcing Peyton to back up nearly into D'Angelo. She felt tiny between the two massive men. "Good luck," said Simons and followed Cho from the room.

Defino motioned to the vacated chairs. "Have a seat."

Peyton hurried to the one on the right and sank into it. She clasped her hands in her lap and plastered an uncomfortable smile on her face. She was excited about this new opportunity, but she was also nervous. Most detectives rose through the ranks after a long career as street cops. She really wasn't sure she was ready for this advancement, but her previous captain had encouraged her. They were short on detectives and he felt it would be a great opportunity for her. She hadn't actually believed she'd pass the tests, then to test out as one of the highest in her class…it was all happening so fast.

Captain Defino sat down again and picked up a file in front of her. "Give me a minute to review this," she said.

Peyton nodded and watched D'Angelo lever his long legs into the unforgiving melamine chair next to her. He wore a ribbed sweater and it pulled tight across his chest, outlining the muscles in his abdomen. Peyton looked away. She wasn't immune to so much masculine beauty, but this guy was too much. There was no way that much muscle had also graduated top of his class.

While Defino continued to look through the file, Peyton fidgeted. She'd never been very good at waiting. The captain had a crystal stapler sitting on the edge of the desk closest to Peyton. She'd never seen anything like it before. The staples were visible in the carriage and she couldn't help but wonder if you could actually see the sharp edges fold in when you pressed the top down.

Reaching out two fingers, she depressed the stapler. The mechanism moved down, advancing the staple, but as soon as it came in contact with the metal clip in the lower part, the staple disappeared from view. She leaned forward to see where it went, but suddenly realized Defino had stopped turning pages. She looked up to find the captain watching her. Defino reached out, taking the stapler from her and setting it to the side.

Peyton gave her a tight grin and leaned back only to catch the smug smile on D'Angelo's finely sculpted lips. She shot him a glare and folded her hands again.

"Well, everything seems to be in order," said Defino, closing the file and laying her hands on top. "Maria will show you to your desks and as soon as we get a case, I'll hand it over to the two of you."

Peyton lifted her head. "The two of us?"

Defino nodded.

Peyton pointed between her and D'Angelo. "The *two* of us?"

"Right. Is something wrong?"

Peyton shifted forward in her chair. "Do you mean I'm going to be working with…" She pointed her finger at the man sitting next to her. "…him?"

"Yes."

"Him?"

The captain glared at her. "Inspector Brooks, is there a problem?"

"No, I just thought…"

"You thought what?"

"I thought I was going to be working with one of the inspectors who were in here earlier."

"Simons and Cho?"

"Right."

"Simons and Cho have been partners for years. I'm not breaking up a team like that."

"But, Captain?" She held out a hand, indicating D'Angelo.

Defino folded her hands on the file. "What exactly is your problem with Inspector D'Angelo? He graduated with nearly the same scores you did."

Peyton closed her mouth. No use making enemies the first day. "Nothing. I have no problems."

"Good. Then please go out and have Maria get you some desks."

"Thank you, Captain," said D'Angelo, flashing her that lazy smile.

The captain's stern façade vanished and she beamed at him. "You're very welcome, Inspector D'Angelo."

"Marco, please."

"Of course, Marco."

His smile dried as he glanced back at Peyton, then he went to the door and pulled it open. Peyton followed him out.

Marco, please, she mouthed.

Maria simpered with delight when he told her what Defino requested. She led them around the corner of the precinct and to a pair of desks which were arranged nose to nose, the front ends touching each other.

"Take your pick," she said, but she leaned into D'Angelo and pointed to the one on the right. "That one is closest to the break-room and faces the front of the precinct."

"Good call," he said, winking at her.

"Let me know if you need anything," she called over her shoulder as she made her way back to her desk.

D'Angelo walked over to the desk on the right and pulled out the chair.

"What makes you think that's your desk?"

He glanced up at her. "If you want it, just say so."

Peyton clenched her jaw, but she moved to the desk on the left. "I don't really care. I wouldn't want to disrupt your view of Maria's cleavage."

He moved toward her, taking a seat on the edge of the desks where they touched. "What's your problem with me, anyway?"

"I don't have a problem." She rolled the chair back and forth.

"Yes, you do. Look, if this is going to work, we've got to be honest with each other. Is it me or do you hate all men?"

"I like men. I love men." She caught herself and closed her eyes as that maddening smile bloomed across his mouth. Lifting her hand, she let it fall against the top of the chair. "It's just I thought I'd get a seasoned partner, someone like Simons or Cho, not a..."

"Not a what?"

In for a penny, in for a pound, she thought. "Not a GQ underwear model."

He crossed his arms over his chest. "How do you think I feel? They give me a pixie with three inch heels. Where's Peter Pan, sweetheart?"

Peyton gave him a wry smile. "I can still kick your ass."

He rose to his full, impressive height and moved a step closer until he towered over her. "You can't reach my ass, honey."

She glared him down, but he just gave her that slow smile and turned away.

"How 'bout a cup of coffee?" he said over his shoulder as he headed for the break-room.

* * *

Marco lived on the second floor of a walk-up on the edge of the Sunset. She found the building and climbed the narrow staircase to his door. After knocking, she put her hands in her back pockets and rocked on her heels.

She could hear music and muted voices on the other side, so she knew he was home, but no one came to the door. She knocked again, louder this time. Someone fumbled with the chain on the other side and then the door swung inward.

Marco stood in the entrance with only a sheet wrapped around his waist. Peyton's brows rose as she took in the naked planes of his chest, all hard angles and defined muscles, sweeping down to a washboard abdomen.

"What are you doing here?" he growled at her.

"We have a case." Involuntarily, her eyes tracked lower over the sculpted lines of his belly.

"See something you like, Inspector Brooks."

She lifted her gaze to his. Damn, but his face was every bit as gorgeous as the rest of him. "Yeah, unfortunately it doesn't come with a brain."

He gave her that lazy smile of his. "I suppose you won't wait outside."

"Not a chance."

He threw back the door and she stepped in, glancing around. She'd always thought bachelor pads were the stuff of movies, but if so, Marco bought into it with conviction. A broken down couch, a massive recliner, two wine crates and a flat screen TV made up his living room. A galley kitchen with an enormous stainless steel refrigerator and a two burner stove occupied the right half of the room. An open bedroom door with a king size bed lay to the left. She guessed the bathroom had to be through the bedroom.

"Make yourself at home," he said, heading toward the left.

She glanced after him as he disappeared around the door.

"I've gotta go," he told someone.

"Who's here?"

"Don't worry about it. I've just gotta go."

"What the hell do you mean you gotta go?"

Peyton wandered over to the couch and took a seat.

Suddenly a blond woman appeared in the bedroom doorway, glaring out at her. She had a blanket wrapped around her body. "Who the hell are you?"

Peyton flashed her a smile. "His wife," she said mischievously.

"His wife!" She disappeared behind the door again. "She's your wife!"

"My what?"

"She said she's your wife. You told me you weren't married!"

"I'm not married."

The woman gave out a frustrated scream and Peyton heard something hit the door. A moment later, Marco came scrambling out, wearing only an unbuttoned pair of jeans, carrying a sweater and his shoes.

He dumped the sweater and shoes on the recliner and gave Peyton a furious look. "You told her you were my wife?"

Peyton shrugged.

Behind him the woman continued to swear, throwing things around as she searched for her clothes.

"Why did you tell her you were my wife?"

"Come on. Really? That's what you like?" She held a hand toward the bedroom.

He glanced over his shoulder and they both watched as the blond struggled to pull her dress over her head. She was still calling Marco a number of choice names, but her voice was muffled by the fabric.

"What's wrong with her?" He buttoned his jeans.

"She's a giant Barbie doll."

"No, she's not." He sat down in the chair and pulled the sweater over his head, then reached for his boots.

"The hell she isn't. She can't even dress herself."

He tugged the first boot into place. "Maybe I like Barbie dolls."

Peyton pushed herself to her feet and moved close to him. He looked up at her as she leaned down near his face. "Really? And here I thought you might like something with a bit more spice."

His lips parted.

Peyton licked her own lips, then moved away from him and headed toward the door. "Come on, D'Angelo. We got a dead body to investigate."

He tugged the other boot in place and scrambled to follow her, grabbing a jacket and his gun out of the closet by the door. Peyton stepped into the hallway, waiting for him, but he hesitated and glanced back at the bedroom.

"I need to lock up."

Peyton started moving down the hallway. "Forget it. You don't have anything worth stealing."

"What's the case?" He pushed open the door to the stairs.

"Vehicular manslaughter. We've just got to go out there, sign off on it, and the D.A. can decide if he wants to prosecute. Usually he doesn't. Not worth it."

They jogged down the stairs and he followed her into the parking lot. Their brand new precinct-issued Charger was waiting for them near the stairwell and he unlocked the door.

Peyton slipped into the passenger seat as he slid behind the steering wheel.

"How did you get over here?"

"Cab. You weren't answering your damn phone, so I had to come over. Maybe you can try taking it off vibrate once in a while."

His eyes snapped to her face and she knew he'd caught her double entendre. "Look, you and I need to set some boundaries if this is going to work."

"Fine."

He started the engine and put the car in reverse. "Where we going by the way?"

"The Embarcadero."

He cranked the wheel to the right and pulled out of the parking lot. "So first rule, we respect each other's privacy. I won't comment on who you're sleeping with and you don't comment on who I…"

"Bang."

He scowled at her. "Sleep with."

"Fine."

"Two, we don't share our personal lives with each other. We're partners, but we're not going to pretend we're friends. I don't want to hear about your life and you don't want to hear about mine."

"Fine."

"Three, we don't see each other socially outside of work. I have my friends and you have yours."

Peyton rolled her eyes. "Whatever."

"Do you agree?"

"Yeah, fine."

"Four, we avoid each other's homes. I'll keep my phone on in case you need to get a hold of me, but you don't come over any more and I won't go to your place."

"Fine."

"Do you have any rules?"

"Yeah."

He glanced at her as he made the next turn. "What is it?"

"You try to keep your clothes on when we're together."

He exhaled in aggravation.

"Well?"

"You enjoyed the show."

"Yeah, and I enjoy a good juggling act once in a while, but if you see it too much, you realize it's just balls going around in a circle."

He eased the car to a stop at a light and shifted to frown at her. "What?"

"You heard me. So do you agree?"

"Fine," he said. "I'll keep my clothes on when we're together."

"Thank you."

He shook his head in disgust and started driving again.

* * *

Peyton stopped talking. She realized she was getting caught up in the story, remembering those first few days with Marco. God, he'd been so uptight and she'd done everything in her power to goad him.

Ferguson was smiling at her. "You weren't kidding. No wonder he hated you."

Peyton smiled in return. "Yeah. He even asked Captain Defino to move him." Rubbing her hands on her thighs, she met his gaze directly. "What are you really trying to find out?"

"Exactly what I said, Inspector Brooks. I need to know why you feel you should have taken the shot and why it shook you up to the point of needing a tranquilizer."

"I didn't need the damn tranquilizer."

"The doctor in the emergency room clearly felt you did. Are you suggesting you know more than a medical professional?"

Peyton wasn't going to touch that. "So what now?"

"I'll see you back here tomorrow morning at 8:00."

"And Marco?"

"I meet with him for the first time tomorrow at 10:00."

"You won't tell me when he can come back to work, will you?"

"No, but even if I could, I haven't begun to take him apart yet."

"You're going to share everything I say with the captain, aren't you?"

"I'm going to give her a final report. I will tell her whatever I need to tell her to back my report, but don't worry." He leaned closer to her. "I won't tell her you told me any stories."

Peyton let out a dramatic sigh. "Well, that takes away all my worries at once."

He laughed. "Glad I could help. See you tomorrow, Inspector Brooks."

Peyton pushed herself to her feet. "See you tomorrow, Doctor Ferguson." With that, she left the room.

CHAPTER 4

Peyton drove her little green Corolla out to the St. Matthews' Church and pulled into an open parking space. She had a lot to choose from. Beyond the Corolla, there were only three other cars in the lot.

The church was small, built in the mission style so famous up and down the coast of California. The pink adobe bricks showed a dull salmon in the afternoon sunlight as she entered the gate and walked through a small flower garden before the front doors.

White stucco covered the bricks in the vestibule and stained glass windows rose from floor to vaulted ceiling beside the doors. One was of the Virgin Mary in a flowing white robe and the other of John the Baptist.

She searched the vestibule for an office, but found only a small room with a screen and two chairs. She went to the double doors, leading into the church itself. The right door was open and she peered in. The vaulted ceilings rose in a peak overhead and a long aisle ran down the middle of the church, drawing the eye to the altar. Behind the altar was a wooden depiction of the crucifix. The eyes of Jesus bled tears of blood. Pews lined either side of the aisle, row after row leading to the stairs before the altar.

A man knelt in the first pew, the silver of his head bowed over his clasped hands. Peyton didn't want to disrupt his devotion, so she turned back toward the door and came up short. A younger man in black with a priest collar stood behind her. He had very light brown hair and close-set brown eyes that bulged a bit.

"Can I help you?"

Peyton reached for her badge and held it up. "I'm Inspector Brooks from the San Francisco Police Department. I'm looking for Father Mark Shannon."

He smiled, but the smile didn't reach his eyes. "You've found him. How can I help you, Inspector?"

She glanced over her shoulder at the praying man. He also wore black and hadn't moved since she came in. "I was hoping we could talk about Father Reynolds, but..." She indicated the other man with her hand.

Father Mark looked beyond her and then clasped his hands at his waist. "Father Michael is busy with his invocations and won't be bothered by us."

"Isn't there any other place more private we can talk?"

He held out his hands indicating the church. "Where else would you go, Inspector? This is a house of God and He hears all."

Peyton wasn't really worried about God hearing, but who was she to argue? "You were the one who identified Father Reynolds' body at the morgue?"

He nodded. "So unfortunate. I do hope you will be able to get to the bottom of what happened. I worry for the soul of the man who took his life. I understand he was an officer of the law as well."

Peyton didn't answer that. "I interviewed the boys who were with Father Reynolds at the time."

"Yes, I know."

"They mentioned that he hadn't been in your parish for long."

"No, he was transferred here three months ago."

"Transferred? From where?"

"I am not at liberty to divulge this, but I can say that priests are transferred frequently wherever there is greatest need."

"Did you have need here?"

"Of course we did."

"When I called I was told he was the vicar here. Can you tell me what that means?"

"A vicar is an associate priest. I am the head priest of this parish and Father Patrick was my assistant."

"How many vicars are there?"

"Only two. Well, now there is one." He gave her a sad smile. "Father Michael and Father Patrick were assigned under my care."

Peyton glanced over her shoulder at the praying father, but he still didn't move. She shifted weight. "Please forgive me, but I'm a little confused, Father."

"Understandable. The Catholic Church can appear confusing to those not of our faith."

"No, that's not what I mean. Yesterday, when I talked with the boys, they told me Father Reynolds was starting a youth group."

"Yes, that was his ambition."

"But you were opposed to it?"

"Opposed is a strong word."

"What word would you choose?"

"Cautious."

"Cautious? Why?"

"We have many youth opportunities for young people in our parish. Another seemed superfluous."

Peyton narrowed her eyes. "You opposed him..."

He held up a hand in protest at her word.

Peyton corrected herself. "You were cautious because you didn't think there needed to be another youth group? Is that right?"

"Precisely."

"Why did only three boys sign up for the trip to Alcatraz?"

"Many of the parents didn't see the religious reasons for such an excursion."

"Really?"

Father Mark held out his open hands.

"You know what I find strange, Father Mark?"

"You are the detective, Inspector Brooks, not I."

"You don't seem particularly interested in how Father Reynolds was killed."

"He was shot by an officer. That is the only word we were given. I have to assume it was a horrible mistake. He was unfortunately caught up in a crime not of his making and was an innocent bystander."

Peyton resisted the impulse to touch her cheek. She didn't want to give him any information about the case that wasn't already common knowledge. "I need to know why Father Reynolds was transferred here, Father Mark."

"I'm afraid I can't give you that information, Inspector Brooks, any more than you can tell me what really happened on the island. We each have our limitations, now don't we?"

"If I go to the Diocese, will I get the same answer?"

"I do not speak for the Diocese, Inspector Brooks, but I would assume you'd get the same response."

Peyton looked down in frustration.

"Excuse me," came a voice behind her.

She turned and glanced up. Father Michael was passing by in the aisle. His face was lined and his eyes were a pale, watery blue. He met her gaze and gave her a pointed look, then he eased past. "Father Mark," he said, inclining his head.

"Father Michael."

"I'll just continue my work on the roses, by your leave."

"Certainly."

Peyton watched him walk toward the double doors. When he reached them, he paused and glanced back, catching her eye again. Peyton looked away, not wishing to draw Father Mark's attention.

"Did Father Reynolds have any family I should notify of his death?"

"His parents died years ago and he had no siblings. The church was his family."

"No aunts, uncles? Grandparents?"

"None that I know of."

"If you tell me where he came from, I could search for them."

Father Mark gave her that same soul-weary smile. "You know I can't do that, Inspector Brooks."

Fighting a wave of frustration, she reached into her pocket for a business card and passed it to him. "If you decide you can tell me anything else, I'd appreciate a call."

"The same could be said for you. I would like to know why a priest in my parish was gunned down by one of your officers, Inspector Brooks. It might help me give solace to the boys who were involved."

Peyton nodded and moved around him, headed for the door. Crossing the vestibule, she stepped outside, relishing the feel of the sun on her face. Father Michael was trimming the rose bushes on the edge of the garden, closest to the parking lot.

Peyton went down onto the walk and moved toward the gate. "Good afternoon, Father Michael," she said.

"Good afternoon to you, child," he answered.

She walked toward the Corolla.

"Inspector, you might spend a few moments looking for your keys," came Father Michael's voice behind her.

Peyton paused by the door of the little green car. Look for her keys?

Suddenly she understood and she patted her pockets as if she couldn't find them.

"If you meet me at St. Mary's Cathedral tomorrow at noon, I have information to share."

Peyton went still, not sure she'd heard him correctly. "St. Mary's? On Gough?"

"Yes. I go there once a week to pray."

She could hear the snick of his pruning shears. "I'll be there."

He didn't respond, but the sound of his shears grew louder.

Peyton located her keys and pulled them out, unlocking the Corolla and slipping into the seat. Once she had the door closed, she looked over at Father Michael, but he was busy struggling with a particularly thick branch and never looked up.

Feeling bewildered, Peyton drove away. She needed to think through everything and the only one she knew who could help her figure it out was Marco. Time to pay him a visit, family or no family.

* * *

Jake entered the precinct and pushed open the half-door. Maria looked up from her desk. "Where you been all day?"

He held up the camera bag across his shoulder. "Abe wanted me to take pre-autopsy pictures of the priest before he started cutting on him."

Maria made a face. "You got a letter. The mailroom brought it to me. It has no return address on it, just your name and our P.O. Box number. I put it on your desk."

"That's strange. Why would I get mail?"

"I couldn't tell you, but here's an idea. You could open it."

Jake gave her a tight grin. "I wonder why I never thought of that. What did I ever do before I met you?"

"Got yourself arrested for murder."

Jake bit his lip to stop from commenting. They were never going to give that one up no matter how long ago it had been. As he strode back to his desk, he marked that Peyton's desk was empty. By the time he'd gotten home the previous night, she was already in bed, and he hadn't seen her this morning. He was worried about her, but he knew she wouldn't appreciate his concern.

He set the camera on the desk, studying the envelope. It was a standard business size envelope with no return address as Maria had said. His name and the precinct P.O. Box were typed across the front. Leaning closer, Jake felt pretty sure the letters were from an actual typewriter. Running his fingers across his name, he could feel the indention where the keys had pressed into the paper, the edges slightly bleeding into the grain.

Pulling out his chair, he retrieved his evidence case from beneath his desk and opened it. Picking up a pair of tweezers, he used them to turn the letter over so he could see the back. There was nothing written on the back either.

He reached for a pair of scissors and used it to cut open the flap, then he picked up the tweezers again and lifted the bottom of the envelope, shaking the contents onto his desk. A white card fell out and written in bold red font across the front were the words *Clean-up Crew*.

Jake stared at it, transfixed, his heart picking up speed. Using the tweezers, he flipped the card over. On the back, written in someone's round looping stroke was a message. Jake leaned closer, sorting out the words. *Ranger collateral damage*.

He sat down hard in his chair, feeling a cold sweat break out on his body. It had been three months since the last time he'd found a card. The man had been Allen Brill, living in a flop house on Isadora Duncan Lane. He'd been hung from a ceiling fan and the card had been resting in his bound hands. The first murder was a bum at a BART station, shot in the back of the head, execution style. He and Abe had discovered his name, Wayne Kimbro. Both men had served time for child molestation. Now this.

Grabbing two separate evidence bags, he carefully placed the card and the envelope in them and sealed them shut. Maybe Forensics would be able to get DNA or a fingerprint from either of them, although he doubted it. They'd found nothing on the other two cards Jake had recovered. Staring at the card, he folded his hand over his chin. It bothered him that the killer now knew his name. How?

They'd kept the connection between the other two killings secret. No one had known about the cards. Staring at the words on the back of the latest card, Jake knew it had to do with the priest killed on Alcatraz. The death of the ranger had been accidental. So all along, the real target had been the priest.

He reached for his mouse and pulled up the sex offender registration, typing in *Patrick Reynolds*. The search engine wheel spun around for a moment, then turned up nothing. He typed in *Reynolds* only and pressed enter again. Nothing. He broadened the search to the national level, but still he found nothing.

Rubbing a hand over his eyes, he realized he wished Peyton were here. Why was he targeted for this message? How did the killer know he was the one who processed the other two bodies? It never occurred to him before that someone might know he was involved. He didn't like feeling as if he were a mouse to the serial killer's cat.

Picking up the evidence bags, he hurried to the front of the precinct. Maria shifted away from her computer as he stepped up to her desk.

"I need to talk to the captain."

Maria frowned at him. "You're all pale. What's wrong?"

"Please, Maria. I need to talk to the captain now."

Captain Defino's door opened and she stepped into the entrance. "What's wrong, Jake?"

He held up the bags. "Simons and Cho's serial killer made contact."

"What?" Defino came forward and took the bags. She shifted them so she could read both of them, then she looked up at Jake. "Holy shit," she said.

Jake blinked at her. Well, that wasn't really the comforting reassurance he was hoping for.

* * *

As Peyton knocked on Marco's apartment door, she thought back to the story she'd told the psychiatrist that morning. When she thought about it, she couldn't believe she'd actually spoiled his date that way, but he made her so aggravated at first. She just hadn't been sure how to deal with him. How much the two of them had changed over the ensuing years.

Her smile faded as the memory of Alcatraz came back to her. So much had changed. He'd taken his first life all because she hadn't pulled the trigger when she should have. How was she ever going to make this right for either of them again?

The door opened and Vinnie's friendly face met her. "Hey there, sweetheart, come on in."

She stepped through the door and into Vinnie's warm embrace. Hugging him back, she took a moment to compose herself. Marco's apartment hadn't changed much over the years, but she'd made him get rid of the wine crates and replace them with a real coffee table. He'd upgraded to a larger flat screen television, but the broken down couch was now a sleek modern set with low arms in a dark microfiber. She'd even talked him into getting a bistro set for his galley kitchen, so she didn't have to eat on her lap on the rare occasions she had dinner at his place.

But his recliner hadn't changed and he was lounging in it as she stepped into the room. Immediately he rose to his feet and came toward her. Even in stocking feet, he towered over her five four frame.

"You did get a tetanus shot, right?" he scolded.

"Good to see you too, partner." She placed her hands in her back pockets and rocked on her boot heels.

"Answer me."

"Yes, I already told you that."

Mona, his mother, came out of the kitchen, wiping her hands on a dishcloth. She caught Peyton in an embrace much the way Vinnie had, then she held her off and cupped her cheeks in both hands. "Look what they did to your face."

Peyton gripped her elbows and smiled at her, but her gaze lifted to Marco again. He looked surprisingly normal. His hair was loose, just touching the line of muscle on his shoulders, and he had a bit of stubble on his chin, but other than that, he looked just as he always did – powerful and confident, unbending.

Mona hooked Peyton around the waist, turning her toward the kitchen. "Have you eaten?"

Peyton thought for a moment and couldn't remember the last time. She'd missed lunch going out to the church, and last night she'd grabbed a peanut butter sandwich before she'd fallen into bed. This morning she hadn't even had time for coffee.

"No, not yet."

"I'm making manicotti. Come, sit down." She pulled out a bistro chair and handed Peyton into it.

Marco came over and took the other chair, while Vinnie dropped onto the couch, propping his feet on the coffee table. The Giants game was on the television, but he reached over and turned off the sound.

"How's Antonio, Vinnie?" Peyton asked, anything to avoid the way Marco stared at her.

"He's finishing the last of his physical therapy next week. He should be cleared by the doctor for normal routine by then."

Three months ago, Vinnie's teenage son had been in an auto accident that left him with a severely damaged leg and a paralyzed best friend. They'd found the guy who hit the boys, but it didn't begin to fix their devastating losses. Now she'd only brought more grief to a family who'd experienced enough for one year.

"Did you have your session with the psychologist?"

Peyton met Marco's gaze. "Psychiatrist. Dr. Ferguson. He's a definite ball buster. His first question was about my father."

Marco sighed and leaned back in his chair.

Mona set a plate in front of Peyton, heaped with manicotti in a marinara sauce. Next to it, she placed a basket of garlic bread and a glass of red wine. "Can't eat Italian without wine," she said, patting Peyton's shoulder.

Peyton smiled at her and accepted the fork she held out. For the first time all day, she felt a twinge of hunger. Mona waited until she took her first bite, then she went back to the stove.

"This is amazing, Mona," said Peyton around a mouthful.

Mona waved her off.

"What else did he ask?"

"About my mother and why I feel the need to get personally involved in my cases."

"Did you find an answer to that?"

Peyton picked up her wine glass, giving him an arch look over the rim.

"No, then," he said.

Taking a sip, she lowered it. "He said I've built an ersatz family with my friends to fill the void of an empty relationship with my mother."

"Smart man."

"Just wait 'til he's playing around in your head tomorrow, D'Angelo."

He gave her his patented Marco smile. Peyton ducked her head and went back to eating. Mama D'Angelo knew her way around a kitchen to be sure.

"Are you going to tell me about the case or not?"

Peyton stopped with her fork halfway to her mouth. Behind her, Mona went still. Glancing up, she saw Vinnie looking over at them. She wished it was just her and Marco, but there was no way either of the D'Angelos was going to leave this alone now.

Setting the fork on her plate, she picked up her napkin and wiped her mouth. Resisting the impulse to grab her wine, she twisted the napkin around her index finger. "Marco, I…"

"Tell me what you found out today. I know you researched the priest."

Peyton nodded. "He was a vicar at St. Matthews' Church. He'd only been there a few months, but he'd started a youth group. He'd taken three boys from that group to Alcatraz on a field trip."

"What do you mean he'd only been at the church for a few months?"

"He's a transfer."

"From where?"

"I don't know. I talked with Father Mark Shannon, who's the head priest of that parish, and he said he couldn't tell me where he transferred from or why. Earlier when I called on the phone, I was told all inquiries were to be made at the Diocese with Bishop Alton."

Vinnie looked away as if he were considering what she said.

"Have you talked with Bishop Alton?"

"I was going to do that tomorrow."

"He won't tell you anything," said Vinnie. "The Catholic Church is very closed-mouth about these things, especially now with all of the scandals surrounding the cover-ups."

"That's the feeling I got too." She set the napkin by her plate. "When I was leaving the church, though, I ran into a second vicar, Father Michael. He was praying in the church when I talked with Father Mark, so I know he heard our conversation. As he left the church to tend some roses, he made deliberate eye contact with me."

"And?"

"And when I went to my car, he told me to pretend like I was trying to find my keys. Then he said he'd meet me at St. Mary's on Gough tomorrow at noon. He said he had information to give me."

Marco frowned. "You're not going there alone."

"It's a church, Marco."

"I know, but you're still not going there alone."

"And who is going with me?" she said, although she already knew.

"I'll meet you there at noon."

"You're on leave, plus you have a session with Dr. Ferguson tomorrow."

"At 10:00. I'll be done before noon."

Peyton shook her head. "You can't violate Defino's orders, Marco."

"I can go to a church, Peyton. I'm a Catholic. She can't tell me what I do with my spare time."

Peyton couldn't help the smile that lit her face. Having him there would go a long way toward making things normal again. "Okay. I'll see you there at noon." She looked back at Mona. "Thank you for the food. It was delicious."

"Are you running off, dear?"

"I need to get home and let Pickles out. He's probably starving."

"Of course. Get some rest, all right?"

"I will. Thank you again, Mona."

"Anytime, dear."

Peyton rose to her feet. "You okay?"

Marco looked up at her as she stood. "I'm fine, Brooks."

Peyton nodded. "I'll see you tomorrow, then."

He gave her an inclination of his head, but as she moved past him, he reached out and caught her wrist. Startled she looked down into his face.

"I'm okay, Peyton," he said.

She bent down and kissed his cheek, lingering there a moment. There was so much she wanted to say to him, so many things she wanted to beg him to forgive, but his family was there and so it went unsaid. "See you tomorrow," she answered, fighting back a rush of tears.

"Tomorrow," he said and released her.

Vinnie stood up and walked her to the door. "I'll walk you to your car," he said.

Marco turned at that, but Vinnie ushered her out the door before he could come after them. Peyton followed him as he went to the stairs and pushed the door open, then side by side, they descended toward the parking lot.

"How is he really, Vinnie?"

"He's Marco, all bluster and bite."

Peyton didn't know how to answer that. She didn't think Marco's brother would appreciate her apology.

"Look, Peyton, I actually want to talk to you about something."

They reached the bottom of the stairs and Vinnie pushed open the outer door. They walked across the parking lot to where her Corolla waited before he continued. Peyton pulled out her keys and turned to face him.

She wasn't sure if he expected her to open the conversation. If so, he was going to be disappointed. Facing Marco was hard enough, answering to his family was harder.

"Have you considered finding a different career?"

Peyton blinked. That hadn't been what she expected him to say. "Different career?"

"You've almost been shot twice. Don't you think that might be a warning?"

"I understand your concern, but this is my career, Vinnie. This is what I do."

Vinnie looked down at the asphalt. "I don't want to hear from my brother that you've been killed, Peyton. You're like family to us."

"I appreciate that, but…"

He glanced up and speared her with his blue eyes, so like Marco's. "And not to be calloused, but more than that, if you quit, he will."

Peyton took a step back and bumped into her car. "What?"

"If you quit, we can talk him into quitting as well."

"What makes you think that?"

"Because…"

"Vinnie!"

Marco's voice carried across the parking lot. Vinnie closed his eyes and bit his bottom lip. Peyton glanced between the two brothers, but before she could respond, her phone vibrated in her pocket. Automatically, she reached for it and pulled it out. A text message appeared on the screen from Maria.

She thumbed it on and read it. *Come back to the precinct. Important.* Peyton curled her fingers around the phone. "I've gotta go," she said, reaching for the door handle.

Vinnie nodded. "Think about it, okay?"

Peyton slipped into the driver's seat. "I will." She looked back at Marco, but he hadn't left the doorway. "Talk to you soon." She pulled the door closed and started the ignition, leaving Vinnie standing where he was.

* * *

When Peyton arrived at the precinct, Maria didn't speak, just pointed at Defino's door. Peyton pushed open the half-door and crossed to the captain's office, turning the knob and stepping through. Simons, Cho and Jake occupied the space before her desk. Defino stood at the window, looking out. It was one of the few times Peyton remembered her blinds being up.

"Captain?"

Defino turned at her entrance. "Brooks, did you go to St. Matthews' Church today?"

"Yeah." She gave Simons and Cho a bewildered look. "What's going on?"

"What did you find out?"

"Not much. Father Shannon wouldn't tell me why Father Reynolds was transferred there or from where. I thought I'd go to the Diocese tomorrow, but a second priest, Father Michael, asked me to meet him tomorrow at St. Mary's at noon."

Defino squinted at her. "What?"

Peyton shrugged. "He said he had information for me."

Simons and Cho exchanged a look.

"Sounds fishy to me," growled Simons.

Peyton gazed pointedly at Jake. "What's going on?"

"Jake received a letter today," said Defino.

"Okay?"

"It contained a business card."

Peyton felt her stomach drop. She could imagine where this was going. "From?"

"We don't know."

"It said *Clean-up Crew*, just like the others," offered Jake.

"And on the back it said the ranger was collateral damage," finished Defino.

Peyton considered that. "Which means the priest was the real target?"

"Apparently."

"Wait. This doesn't make sense. It was the priest who shot at me."

"So that one of you would kill him. Suicide by cop," said Cho.

Peyton shook her head. "That doesn't make sense. This *Clean-up Crew* character killed his other two victims himself. Why change his M.O. now?"

"Actually it fits. He's had a different method of death for each of them," said Jake. "Kimbro was shot execution style. Brill hung."

"And Reynolds shot by a cop," finished Cho.

Peyton rubbed her eyes. This was too much to take in. "I don't get it. The other two were convicted sex offenders. Have we searched for Reynolds on the data base yet?"

"I did, but I didn't find anything," said Jake.

"Did you search only California? Maybe you need to look nationally."

"I did that too. Still nothing."

"I can get my head around why he picked Kimbro and Brill. He found them on the data base, but why Reynolds?"

"That's what we need to find out," said Defino.

"Maybe I'll learn something at my meeting tomorrow."

"You're not going to that meeting, Brooks," said the captain.

"Why not?"

"This case belongs to Simons and Cho. I'm officially taking you off it."

"What?" Peyton pushed forward between the men. "You can't do that, Captain. We haven't made a definitive connection between Reynolds and the others."

"The card left with Jake does just that. Look, I don't like where this is going. He knows too much about us already. He's manipulating us at every turn. He knows about Jake, he had inside information about Reynolds that we don't even have. You could be walking into a trap tomorrow, Brooks, and I can't chance it."

"He's a serial killer, Captain. He's going to stay to pattern. We've just got to unravel the pattern. I can't miss that meeting tomorrow."

"She's right," said Simons. "That meeting is the only chance we have to establish the pattern, Captain, and this priest isn't going to talk to us. He expects to meet Brooks tomorrow. It has to be her."

"We'll also be there, Captain. We'll get established in there before the meeting time, so she isn't there alone," suggested Cho.

Peyton knew she should tell them she wouldn't be alone, but she was sure Defino would never let her do it if she thought Marco might be there, unarmed. She'd just have to call Marco and make sure he didn't come.

"Captain, don't take me off this case. We gotta throw everything we've got at it. If the media hears we've got a serial killer, it's only going to complicate things."

Defino was clearly torn. She turned back to the window and stared out at the failing light. Peyton met Jake's eyes. She couldn't read the emotions there – probably a mixture of fear and excitement both. Oh, lord, she had so much to answer for – first Marco and now Jake. She should have just left him alone, counting his money and living paycheck to paycheck working at the bank. The thought of a serial killer marking him made her feel sick inside.

Defino spoke with her back to them. "Simons and Cho will run point on this. Brooks, you do whatever they say."

"I will, Captain," she promised.

Defino turned and pointed a finger at her. "I'm not kidding you, Brooks. You play this one by the book. No funny business, no silliness. If they tell you to back off, you back the hell off at once. Got me!"

"Yes, Captain. I got you."

"And keep a weather eye out, all of you. I hate feeling like we're being played."

Peyton released her held breath with a nod.

CHAPTER 5

Marco took a seat at the table in the conference room.

"Let me get you some coffee, baby," said Maria.

He smiled up at her. "I'm good, but thank you."

She gave him a worried look. "He should be here any minute."

"It's all right." He glanced toward the door. "Is Brooks around?"

Maria's face showed her disappointment. "She's meeting with Cho and Simons right now. You want me to tell her you asked for her?"

"No, I'll talk to her soon."

Maria patted his shoulder and left.

Marco took out his phone and read Peyton's message again. *Meeting off. Don't come to church.* He didn't know what the hell that meant and she wouldn't answer when he called her. Why was the meeting off?

"Sorry to keep you waiting," came a voice behind him.

Marco put the phone away and glanced up. A man with thinning blond hair and blue eyes walked into the room and pulled the door shut behind him. He held a legal pad in one hand and a cup of coffee in the other. He went around the table and set both down, then held out a large hand.

"Dr. Donald Ferguson," he said.

Marco took his hand, noticing that the doctor's grip was firm. "Marco D'Angelo."

"Yes, nice to finally meet you, Inspector D'Angelo." He took a seat and picked up his coffee, taking a sip. "Would you like a cup?"

"I'm good."

Throughout the introductions, the doctor's gaze measured him. Then he looked down and flipped through a few pages of notes, reaching for a pen in the breast pocket of his dated brown suit. "I met with your partner again this morning."

Marco didn't respond. He didn't think it required one.

Dr. Ferguson looked up at him. "She's quite something."

"That's one way of putting it."

"Your captain told her not to tell me any stories, but so far, she's regaled me with quite an array of anecdotes."

Marco nodded. He could just imagine.

Dr. Ferguson studied him a moment more, then set down his pen and clasped his hands over his legal pad. "Let me start by telling you the same thing I told her. I believe in being direct, Inspector D'Angelo. If I want to know something, I'll come out and ask it. I don't mince around."

"Fine."

"So let's start with the elephant in the room – the shooting. I've counseled many cops in your situation and let me just tell you that they experience a myriad of emotions after something like that. Feelings range from sadness to guilt to anger. Pretty much anything is normal."

Marco nodded.

"You must feel quite conflicted."

"I'm fine."

The doctor frowned. "Fine?"

"Yeah, I'm fine."

Picking up his pen, he acted as if he wanted to write something down, then he stopped. "I find that difficult to believe, Inspector D'Angelo."

"Well, it's the truth."

"There has to be more to it than that. The man you shot was a priest."

"He also shot at my partner."

"And that's all?"

Marco held out his hands. "Look, I don't go much deeper than that. You want complexity, talk to my partner, but with me, pretty much what you see is what you get."

The doctor stared at him a bit more, then he looked through his papers again. "I see you have three older brothers."

"Right."

"Both parents are alive."

"Yep."

"And quite a number of nieces and nephews."

"All true."

He glanced up. "You have a fairly strong network of people supporting you, don't you?"

"Yes."

"Each of your brothers is married and has children."

"That's right."

"But you don't?"

"No."

"Doesn't that present a problem?"

"How so?"

"Is there any pressure on you to get married?"

"No."

"Why not?"

"I don't believe cops should marry."

"Why?"

"It isn't fair to the spouse."

"And no children either?"

"That's right. I don't want children."

"Because it isn't fair to them?"

"Exactly. This career is all consuming and the risks are too great. Best not to bring anyone else into it."

"So you prefer random sexual encounters with unknown women?"

Marco could guess how that would sound, but he didn't really care. It had no bearing on if he was fit to hold a gun or not. "Yes, then no one gets hurt."

"Let's go back to the shooting."

Marco didn't answer.

"You say you have no feelings over the priest's death."

"I didn't say that."

The doctor lifted his chin in interest. "Okay, what did you say?"

"I simply said he shot at my partner. That didn't leave me with any other choice. I had to return fire."

Ferguson steepled his hands. "You are a practicing Catholic, right?"

"I'm not sure what you mean by that. I don't go to church every week or anything. I'm more of a holiday Catholic."

Ferguson smiled. "But you do consider yourself a Catholic, yes?"

"Yes."

"Doesn't that cause conflict since you shot a priest?"

"No more so than anyone else. He shot..."

"...at your partner. I know." The doctor gave a wry shake to his head. "I mostly counsel police officers, Inspector, and I've always been fascinated by the partner relationship. I mean we choose our friends, but we don't choose our family and most of the time we don't choose our partners. I've seen partners who have hated each other, fought like mad, but in a life or death situation, I've seen those same partners sacrifice themselves for the other one without a second thought. It is a bond forged like no other."

"That's right."

"But does it really go beyond everything, including our ties to our spiritual well-being?"

Marco sighed. "Look, I don't know what you want to read into it. I shot a man, he died. He was a priest. The only thing I focus on, the only thing I knew then and I know now, is he fired a gun at my partner and I did what I had to do to protect her."

Ferguson shuffled a few papers, glancing at them. "She told me the story of how she ruined your date during your first case by telling the young woman she was your wife."

Marco smiled. "Yeah, she did that."

"She says you hated her, asked to have a new partner."

"I did both. She was not at all what I envisioned for myself. I wanted someone professional and detached, but I got her."

"You said she was complex. I'm just beginning to see that. Weren't you furious that she ruined your relationship with that woman?"

"I was pretty pissed, but it's hard to stay mad at her. I was sure we couldn't work together, but she proved me wrong. Did she tell you she doesn't like dead bodies?"

"No." Marco could hear the amusement in his voice.

"Homicide detective who doesn't like dead bodies." He shook his head in bemusement. "Our first case was a vehicular manslaughter, and when we got out there, she just kept looking at the sky. She wouldn't look down."

Ferguson smiled.

"I was already pissed at her, but that just seemed like too much."

"How did you work through it?"

"I don't know. She gets to you and then she's so damn smart. If *you* aren't careful, she'll have you wrapped around her finger too."

"I can already see that. So if she wouldn't look at the body, how did you work the case?"

Marco laughed, remembering that case. He'd been so sure that there was no way he and Peyton would ever work, but now he couldn't envision this job without her.

*   *   *

Marco pulled the Charger up to the police blockade and turned off the ignition, setting the brake. Two patrol cars had the Embarcadero blocked off and a uniform was directing traffic through a narrow section on the far side. It had to be getting close to midnight. Fog snaked in from the bay, curling around the warehouses and seeping onto the street.

He reached for the door handle and pushed it open. Half-an-hour ago, he'd been enjoying a night at home…well, he'd been enjoying Amber, but he pushed that thought aside. No use dwelling on what would never be now.

He'd been so damn excited to get this opportunity. He hated being a street cop, he hated the constricting uniform and the strict grooming policy – no beard, no hair longer than your shirt collar. And he hated the boredom. So much boredom. For great spans of time, nothing happened and then it was mostly picking up drunks.

He climbed out and surveyed the scene. He could see the body in the middle of the street and straddling the median was a late model Buick Century. A woman was sitting on the curb, weeping into her hands, while another uniform stood guard over her. While he took everything in, the passenger door opened and *she* got out.

All of five feet tall with a ponytail of curling black spirals, she exuded an energy that grated at his composure. She wasn't classically pretty, no Amber to be sure, but there was something exotic about her mixed blood and her dark eyes that drew men's attention. Then again, there was her mouth.

He didn't believe in hitting women, his mother would kill him if he ever even thought about it, but this one deserved a good smack on the ass.

Yep, he'd been so excited to be a detective, until they'd paired him with her.

"What you waiting for, Handsome? News cameras to capture that pretty face?"

He clenched his jaw. Yep, a good old fashioned slap on the ass.

He followed her over to the patrol cars. She flashed her badge at the uniform and stepped between the barricades. Marco trailed after her as she and the uniform surveyed the scene.

"Woman over there says the man just jumped out at her, waving his arms in the air and screaming at her. She couldn't stop and ran him over."

"Is he homeless?" she asked.

The uniform gave her an arch look. "No, he's dead."

Marco smiled and looked at the man's name plate. Officer Smith. He liked him. He was stocky, but it was mostly muscle, middle aged, but he had a thick head of hair and an enormous mustache. Marco never understood why a beard didn't meet the grooming policy, but a mustache did.

Brooks turned to face the officer, putting her hands in her back pockets. "That's real cute." Her eyes also dropped to his name plate. "Officer Smith, but what I was asking is does he look like he's a homeless man? Maybe he was schizophrenic and he walked into traffic not knowing what he was doing. If you wanna bust my chops, by all means, go for it, but make sure you understand the question first?"

Smith glanced back at Marco and they shared a commiserate look, then he faced her again. "He didn't appear to be homeless, but why don't you take a look, Inspector?" He drew out the title deliberately.

She hesitated. Marco leaned forward so he could see her face. She was chewing on her bottom lip.

He needed to store that information away. He might have just found her tell. "What are you waiting for? News cameras to capture that dulcet voice of yours?" he mocked.

She glared at him as he walked over to the body. Smith followed him, but she didn't. Hunkering over the man, Marco could clearly see tire treads going up his back. His leg was bent at an unnatural angle and half of his head was caved in. If they turned him over, he was sure they'd find all sorts of horrific road rash. Shifting to view where the car was, he tried to visually measure the distance between the two.

"It looks like she knocked him down, then dragged him for a spell before crashing the car onto the median."

"That's what I thought," said Smith.

"We getting a crime scene photographer out here?"

"Yeah, Chuck Wilson from the precinct. We woke him up."

Marco nodded, then looked over his shoulder at Brooks. She was pacing in front of the patrol car.

Smith also looked at her. "That one's got a mouth."

"Yep, and apparently not a lot to back it up. You gonna come do your job, Brooks?" he shouted at her.

She finally came over to him, striding quickly, her boot heels tapping on the roadway. She looked everywhere but at the body. Marco exchanged a look with Smith. "The body's down here, Brooks."

She glanced at him, then away. "I see it." She curled her arms around her middle.

He half-smiled and pointed at the man's head. "See how his skull's caved in?"

"Yeah." She kept her head elevated.

"And look at his leg? You ever see a knee facing the wrong way before? Must be just jelly and bone fragment in there?"

She closed her eyes and swallowed hard. Smith gave a snort of laughter and levered himself to his feet against Marco's shoulder.

"And look at the tire tread, going right up the back of him. She must have dragged him under the car for a spell before driving right over the top of him."

Brooks' eyes snapped to his face. "Tire treads?"

"Yeah, perfect imprint. You could probably tell the tire just by looking at it." He emphasized *looking*.

She glanced at the body, gave a little shudder, and looked over at the car on the median. "They go up his back?"

"Yep, right up his spine. Probably turned that to jelly as well."

She swung back to him, pinning him with that dark gaze. "Up his spine?"

"Yeah, look." He pointed.

She faced him directly. "Didn't Smith say the man jumped in front of her and waved his arms, screaming?"

Marco's face grew serious. "That's what he said."

"Well, if I'm jumping out in front of a car…" She made the motion with her body, using the closest patrol car as a model. Marco rose to his feet and moved near her. "Then the car's going to strike me here." She angled her hands into her thighs. "And the wheels are going to go…" She swept her hands up the front of her body.

Marco sighed. "Not over the back of you."

They both turned and looked at the woman. She was still sobbing into her hands.

"She hit him deliberately," said Peyton.

Marco reached for his handcuffs. "And according to the academy, we call that murder."

* * *

Smith brought the suspect into interrogation, placing a tissue box at her elbow and stepping back. She grabbed a handful and covered her face with it, continuing to sob. Peyton and Marco watched her from the other side of the one-way mirror.

Captain Defino entered the observation room and stood next to Marco, studying her as well. "Okay, who's going to question her?"

"I will," said Marco, preempting his partner.

Peyton gave him a dark look, but didn't dispute him.

"You're on," said Defino.

Marco walked to the door, but paused a moment to gather his thoughts. Women usually responded well to him, so he just had to strike the right balance here. He should be sympathetic, but also assertive. She'd killed a man in cold blood, after all.

Opening the door, he stepped inside. She didn't look up at him, but continued to sob into the tissue. He nodded for Smith to leave, then took a seat diagonal to her. Smith handed him a paper listing her name and address as he passed by.

Marco glanced at it, then placed it on the table. "Ms. Warren, right? Lily Warren?"

She gave a nod, her face covered.

Marco drummed his fingers on the table. This was going to be a lot harder if she wouldn't look at him. "Ms. Warren, I'm Inspector Marco D'Angelo."

No response.

"Ms. Warren, I'd like to talk about the accident."

Her sobs grew louder.

"Ms. Warren, did you know the man you struck with your car?"

Her shoulders began shaking violently.

Marco grimaced. God, he hated crying women. And she wouldn't look at him. How the hell was he supposed to get anything out of her?

He drummed his fingers on the table again, hoping she'd get control over herself, but if anything, she seemed to be crying harder.

"Ms. Warren, we got the man's name. It's Adam Collins. Do you know this man?"

She folded over on herself, pressing her forehead to the table.

Marco shot a glance back at the mirror, knowing that his partner was enjoying this. Frustration warred with annoyance inside of him. "Ms. Warren, I want to help you, but it's very difficult with the crying. Could you try to stop? Please."

The volume increased, and the entire table shuddered.

Damn it all, his first interrogation and this was what he had to deal with, really? How the hell was he going to make it as an investigator if he couldn't even get this done?

"Ms. Warren, please. I want to hear your story."

She reached for another tissue and added it to the pile, but she didn't lift her head.

"Dear God, woman, shut up!"

The moment the words left his mouth, he closed his eyes. He could just see the smug smile on Peyton's face.

Sobs became wails.

Pushing himself to his feet, he headed toward the door. Smith was the only one to give him a sympathetic look as he stepped into the observation room.

"You're up," said Defino to Peyton, motioning out the door.

She couldn't resist giving him a smug smile as she passed him and headed into the interrogation room. Marco took her spot next to Defino and they watched her take the seat he'd vacated a moment before. She just sat there, studying the paper Smith had given Marco and saying nothing.

Marco didn't want to broach the topic that was bothering him most, but he didn't know when he'd get another chance. It had to be now or never. "Captain, this isn't going to work."

She looked over at him. "What isn't going to work?"

"This partnership. It's just not going to work."

"How so?"

"We're both too green for this."

Defino glared at him and he resisted the impulse to squirm. "Why don't you tell me what the real problem is?"

Marco looked down. "She's the problem. She's a handful."

"A handful?"

"She's got a mouth on her and she's opinionated and..."

"You got a problem with women, D'Angelo?"

Marco's eyes snapped to Defino's face. Behind them, he heard Smith clear his throat. "No, ma'am, I don't have a problem with women. I've never had a problem with women."

"I don't mean in your bed, hot shot. I mean working with them, collaborating with them."

"No, ma'am. I have never had a problem working with women." He was distracted as Peyton leaned forward in her chair.

Defino waved him to silence.

"You know what works better?" said Peyton conversationally. "You need to get mascara that isn't waterproof, so it runs down your face. There's something about a woman looking all messy that brings out the protectiveness inside of men."

The woman's shoulders stopped shaking and the sobbing died down. She looked up at Peyton, her eyes damp, but not nearly as red and swollen as they should be for all the crying she'd been doing. "What?"

"I don't know what it is. The bastards see a woman crying and they get all flustered, like they don't have brains or something. It's about the only way we can get them to do a damn thing."

"Tell me about it."

"You know, it's all about playing the game, finding the way to control them without them realizing it. Crying, playing helpless."

Lily nodded, sitting back in her chair. "Let them think they control you."

Brooks laughed. "I got a guy to change my tire the other day just by telling him I didn't know how to use the wrenchy thingy. He thought it was cute. The poor bastard was wearing a suit and all."

A faint smile touched Lily's lips. "Jackass."

Peyton pulled her chair closer. "So what was it with this guy?" She looked at the paper. "Adam Collins. Was he a boyfriend?"

She nodded. "Three years."

"He hit you?"

Lily looked away, lifting the wad of tissue to press against the corner of her eye. "Legs, ass. I haven't worn a dress in months."

"He hit you there so it wouldn't show?"

Lily nodded. "He got this braided hemp from a street fair in the Haight-Ashbury. Said he was going to use it to tie up the dog or something. Bastard beat me with it nearly every day." She met Peyton's gaze. "I wanted to strangle him with it."

"But you weren't strong enough?"

"No."

"How'd you get him on the Embarcadero?"

She shifted in the chair and shook back her hair. "He liked going to the bars down there. He'd drink until closing, then tell me to pick him up. He got picked up for drunk driving once and didn't want it to happen again."

"Bet that also kept you on a tight leash."

"Damn straight."

"So he went out tonight? What time did he call you?"

Lily gave a laugh and pressed the tissue to her nose. "One. Early for him."

"How'd you get him walking down the Embarcadero?"

"I pulled up in front of the bar, but I kept the doors locked. He came out and tried to get in, but when he couldn't, he got pissed. Started banging on the window."

"Weren't you afraid he'd break in?"

She drew a deep breath and released it. "I guess I didn't care. This has been going on for three years. I figured one of us was going to kill the other."

"Then what happened?"

"Some guys outside the bar yelled at him to knock it off." She shook her head with a wry smile. "Typical coward. He wouldn't mess with them."

"Of course not."

"He starts walking away, swearing at me, threatening to kill me when we get home."

Peyton leaned back. "So you ran him down?"

"I don't think I planned to do it, but when he started calling me such filthy things, I lost it." Her eyes fixed on the paper. "I wanted him dead."

Peyton reached over and clasped her hand. "I'm going to get a pad of paper, Lily. Will you write it all down for me?"

"Yeah." She squeezed Peyton's hand in return. "I'm going to prison, aren't I?"

"That's up to a jury, but a lawyer should be able to argue acute duress and get you a reduced sentence."

Lily let her head fall back. "I don't really care. All that matters is I'm free."

Smith moved to get Peyton the pad of paper she wanted and Defino glanced over at Marco. Marco met her look.

"So, you want me to get you a new partner?"

Marco's attention focused on the tiny woman with the black, curling hair. "No. Don't get me a new partner."

*　*　*

Marco fell silent, realizing he'd divulged more than he intended. Talking about Peyton was easy, he guessed. She was such an integral part of his life now.

Dr. Ferguson wrote some notes on his legal pad, but Marco didn't even try to make out what he said. It didn't matter. He likely wouldn't understand the psycho-babble anyway. He splayed his hand on the table.

"So, do I get my gun back?"

The doctor looked up through his lashes, his hand stilling on the paper. "No, Inspector D'Angelo, you don't get your gun back. We've just begun."

Marco resisted the impulse to show his frustration. He didn't have time for this bull shit. He needed to get back to work. Peyton was going to that church in an hour and she'd told him to stay away. He didn't like her going on the streets alone, he needed to be back where he belonged, in the loop again.

"Why not?"

Ferguson looked up. "Why not?"

"Why can't I have my gun? Go back to work? I'll keep meeting with you like she's doing, but I need to have my job back."

Ferguson folded his hands. His smug way of controlling Marco's life nettled him. He didn't like anyone having this much control. "If I were asked if I think you are well enough to carry a gun, what do you think I'd say?"

"What?" Marco frowned. What the hell did that mean? How the hell should he know what went on in a psychiatrist's head? Nothing good, he was sure. Then it hit him. "You want remorse, don't you? You want me to bang my head against the wall and rail at God that I killed someone."

"I want honesty."

Marco drew a deep breath and held it. Gradually he breathed out. "I can put on an act for you if you want."

"And I'd know it was an act."

"I gave you honesty. I told you why I don't feel anything. It was my job and I did it."

"You killed a man, Inspector. You killed a priest. Your supposed lack of emotion about it would have me concerned that you're a sociopath, if I didn't think it was all an act."

"An act?" Marco couldn't believe what he was saying. How the hell did this bastard think he knew more about him than he did himself? He *didn't* feel anything. He wasn't lying. When the priest pointed a gun at Peyton, he was left with no other choice. There wasn't a moral issue here, there wasn't an emotional one. Someone pointed a gun at his partner and he'd reacted. That the man wound up dead was secondary to everything else. The only important thing was that Peyton wasn't.

He met Ferguson's gaze. "What do you want from me?"

"I want to see you here tomorrow at 10:00. We'll pick up from there."

Marco fought to maintain his composure. "Fine. I'll be here at 10:00."

"Good. It was nice to finally meet you, Inspector D'Angelo."

Marco clenched his jaw, but he forced himself to nod. The bastard wasn't getting anything else out of him. He just wasn't going to bend that far. Without making eye contact, he pushed himself to his feet and went to the door.

CHAPTER 6

Marco walked out to Maria's desk. "Where's Brooks?" He glanced at the clock over the conference room door. 11:10? He couldn't believe he'd been in with the psychiatrist for so long.

Maria smiled up at him. "She left with Cho and Simons a few minutes ago."

"Where?"

She gave him a sad look. "I can't tell you that, baby."

They both stopped talking as the conference room door opened and Ferguson stepped out, carrying his legal pad and coffee cup. He gave them an inclination of his head as he walked toward Defino's door and knocked. Defino called for him to enter and he slipped inside.

Marco stared after him.

"He creeps me out," said Maria.

Marco looked back at her. "You and me both." He gave Maria his lazy smile. "Come on, Maria, tell me where they went."

"You know I would do almost anything for you, baby, but I can't. You need to go home and get some rest. If you need anything else, I'd be happy to do it, though."

He rose to his full height. "Is Jake here?"

"Yeah, he was at his desk last I saw."

Marco gave her a wink and walked toward the back. He ignored the two empty desks where he and Peyton started most of their days because that only increased his frustration. Jake was messing with pictures on his computer, but as Marco came around the partition, he minimized the window.

"Were those of the priest?" he asked, nodding at the screen.

"What?"

"Ryder?"

Jake leaned back in his chair. "What are you doing here, Adonis? I thought you had a session with the shrink."

"I did. We're done." He grabbed a loose chair and turned it around backward, straddling it and folding his arms across the top. "Why is my partner dodging my calls?"

"Ask her. She hasn't said more than five words to me for the last two days."

That gave Marco pause. "Is she all right?"

Jake lifted a hand and let it fall against his thigh. "Hell if I know. She's been quiet and you know how strange that is for Peyton."

"What's going on with the case? Is she going to that meeting with the priest at St. Mary's?"

Jake looked away. "You're on leave, Adonis. I don't think I'm supposed to be telling you anything."

"Okay, then just nod if I hit on something."

Jake reached for his mouse and clicked on the internet, bringing up a search window. "I'm working, D'Angelo."

"Maria told me she was meeting with Cho and Simons earlier today. Defino's obviously worried about this meeting with the priest, so she didn't want her to go alone, but why Cho and Simons? Usually she sends Smith or Holmes with her on something like this."

Jake refused to look at him.

Marco narrowed his eyes. "Cho and Simons are involved because the priest is connected somehow to that case they're working."

Jake blinked rapidly a few times.

"The *Clean-up Crew* case, right?"

Blinking continued.

"Did you find a card on the priest's body?"

Jake clicked the mouse, his eyes scanning the screen.

"No card on the body, but the case is still connected." Marco folded a hand over his mouth as he thought. "If the card wasn't on the body, it had to be at the scene?"

"Just stop, D'Angelo, please. I'm not going to tell you a damn thing until Defino says I can."

"On the ranger's body then?" Marco dismissed that. "No, the ranger wouldn't be connected to the priest at St. Mary's." Tilting his head, he studied Jake's profile. "Something happened last night after Brooks came to my apartment because she was all set to have me go with her to St. Mary's, but this morning I get a text telling me to stay away."

Jake's eyes tracked to his face involuntarily.

"You made the connection to Simons and Cho after she left my place, didn't you?"

Blinking ensued.

Marco gave a grim smile. "The card was delivered here last night, wasn't it?"

Jake shifted his chair and stared at the screen, but Marco saw his tell anyway.

He pushed himself to his feet and turned the chair back around.

"Where are you going?"

"Home, just like everyone wants," he lied.

"No, you're not. You're going to St. Mary's, but I didn't tell you a damn thing, D'Angelo."

"Yes you did, but I'll keep that close to my vest in case we ever play poker again."

"If you go out there, I'll go to Defino."

Marco leaned on the desk, bringing himself close to Jake. "No, you won't."

"And why won't I?"

"Because you don't want her going to that meeting without me watching her back any more than I do."

Jake turned back to the screen. "Freakin' assed cops," he muttered as Marco walked away.

*　*　*

95

St. Mary's Cathedral was a massive white stone building with red bricks leading to the remodeled entrance. The enormous saddle roof of the building had recently earned it a spot on the list of top San Francisco architectural structures, but some less charitable people felt it resembled a massive washing machine agitator. The interior of the cavernous Cathedral was lined on either side by wooden pews leading to a set of stairs, which rose to the altar. Behind the altar was a massive cross made of stain-glassed windows, allowing the summer sunlight to filter through.

Peyton entered the Cathedral, feeling small and insignificant to its massive size and importance. It demanded silence and reverence just by the sheer magnitude of it, her footsteps echoing on the hardwood floor. To her right sat the organ, a collection of pipes raised above the floor on a platform that resembled a concrete octagon. She crossed around the baptism font and moved toward the sanctuary. A few other people occupied the pews, sitting in pairs or singularly, but she didn't see the grey headed priest.

Cho had told her to take a seat in back by the door, so she could get out quickly if something went wrong. She had a hard time believing anyone would try anything in a church, especially the old man she'd met at St. Matthews, but she didn't want to take any chances.

She walked to the second pew from the back and slid into it. A folded down kneeler lay before her and above it was a bracket where the hymnal was stored. Bracing her hands on either side of her, she glanced around again, trying not to appear obvious.

Simons entered and moved up the far left aisle, taking a seat about ten rows before her. She resisted the urge to look behind her, but she suspected Cho was on her right. Across the aisle from her about four rows up was an older Hispanic woman, counting her rosary and genuflecting. Peyton could hear the low cadence of her voice as she went through the ritual. A young couple was sitting at the front of the church, looking around. Peyton wondered if they were checking it out with an eye toward a future wedding, and directly behind them was a man in a flannel shirt who appeared to be sleeping. Still no Father Michael.

Peyton shifted, lifting her leg to rest her foot on the kneeler, but she thought better about it and set her foot on the floor again. She was aware of someone taking a seat behind her, but she resisted the impulse to turn around.

"Relax, Brooks, you aren't going to burst into flames just for sitting here."

She closed her eyes briefly at his familiar voice, feeling a surge of relief that he'd come. "I told you to stay home."

"You send me a text and then refuse to answer my calls. What did you expect me to do?"

"Cho and Simons will see you."

"And what if they do? I told you before – Defino can't tell me I'm not allowed in a Catholic Church."

"That's not why you're here," she hissed.

He leaned forward until he was right behind her ear. She could feel the warmth of his breath on her scratches. "No, but when were you going to tell me this case is connected to the serial killer?"

"When you are reinstated."

He started to say something more, but stopped and sat back. Peyton realized she was tense as a man dressed in black took a seat beside her, close enough for her to touch. If he wanted to do anything to her, Cho and Simons were too far away to prevent it. As always, she felt relieved that Marco was behind her.

"Excuse me," said the man, reaching for the kneeler and lowering it.

Peyton moved her feet out of the way and glanced at him as he levered himself to his knees, clasping his hands on the back of the pew before him. A rosary lay across the backs of his hands. He muttered something under his breath and then crossed himself, his head bent toward his hands, his eyes closed. She was certain his white hair and lined face were familiar, but she'd only seen him briefly the day before.

He finished his prayer, then reached back and braced himself on the pew. Peyton automatically caught his elbow, helping him into the seat beside her. Once he was settled with a grunt, he patted her hand fondly.

"Thank you, dear. These old knees don't bend as they once did."

Peyton released him and gave a tense smile. "Father Michael?"

"Yes, dear." He leaned back and looked up at the ceiling. A cross had been inlaid in the white stone with mosaic glass. It crossed over the entire expanse of the Cathedral. "Lovely, isn't it?"

Peyton looked up with him and nodded. "It's stunning."

He folded the rosary in his clasped hands and laid them in his lap. There was a serenity about him that Peyton envied. She'd never learned the art of stillness, but she realized Marco had it as well.

"I'm glad you were able to meet me here," he said. His voice was pitched low, so only she could hear and she realized it could be mistaken for prayer, except that she could hear him clearly. She wondered if Marco could.

She wasn't sure how to proceed. She could see Simons in front of her, his back ramrod straight, aware of everything around him. She didn't want to scare the priest off, but she really didn't have time for idle conversation. Not with a serial killer on the loose.

"Did you know Father Reynolds well, Father Michael?"

He fingered a rosary bead with his thumb. "Do you know I entered the seminary at 18?"

Okay, then. Clearly they weren't going to get right to the point. "No, I didn't."

"I've been a priest for 60 years." He shot a glance at her. "I'll be you aren't even half that old yet, are you?"

"No."

"60 years is a long time to dedicate to anything, even one's faith, isn't it?"

"Yes, it is."

He drew a deep breath and then released it, his thumb rubbing back and forth across the beads. Occasionally Peyton caught a glimpse of the crucifix resting against his palms. "The Catholic Church has done much good, fed many who were hungry, gave shelter and comfort to those who were lost."

Peyton lifted her eyes to the stained-glass cross behind the altar. "I'm certain it has."

"But like all things touched by man, it has its flaws."

Peyton rubbed her hands on the thighs of her jeans. She wasn't sure how to answer that.

"That is the true human condition," he continued. "We always strive to overcome temptation, evil, but it's everywhere we look, in everything we do. Most especially we have to face it in ourselves. By giving us free will, our Divine Creator has made an imperfect creation."

Peyton looked at his worn profile.

He briefly met her gaze and gave her a grim smile. "That surprises you because you think I am criticizing our Lord and His Purpose, but I'm not. You see, that is the reason for our struggle, the reason for everything we do, the very reason for our existence. You, yourself, my dear, are a part of it. You strive always to chase back the chaos, battle the evil in an imperfect vessel. Don't you now?"

"You have a point."

He nodded. "Oh, we are creatures of weakness, so torn between the lofty calling of our souls and the base needs of our bodies. And none of us are immune to that weakness." He leaned close to her and touched her shoulder with his. "I myself have a great fondness for the grape, if you know what I mean."

Peyton smiled. "I do."

He gave a low chuckle. "The Catholic Church has done much good, but it has also suffered much evil."

Peyton felt a chill go up her spine.

"Sometimes we are so filled with our own hubris that we fail to face what we know to be evil in ourselves. We fail to protect those who have need of our protection. We fail to help those who need help even from themselves."

"Was Father Reynolds one of these?"

Father Michael's fingers rubbed and rubbed the beads. "He was."

"Where did he come from, Father Michael?"

"Boston. He was moved here three months ago."

"Why?"

Father Michael met her gaze and in his eyes, she saw his torment.

"He committed evil acts with children, didn't he?" she said.

Father Michael gave her a nod, then looked away.

"Did Father Mark know?"

"I'm certain he did."

"Is this why he opposed the youth group?"

"I believe so."

"Did he tell you that?"

"No, he did not. The Church is very circumspect about such accusations."

"Do you believe they were just accusations, Father Michael?"

His grip on the beads tightened and his eyes darted back and forth across the pew.

"Father Michael?"

"I know they were not."

Peyton wasn't sure how to answer. She didn't want to grill him like a criminal, but she had to know how he found out about Father Reynolds if the church didn't disclose it. If she knew how he found out the truth, they might be able to determine how the serial killer did as well.

"I have been a priest for 60 years, Inspector. I have given my life and my soul to the Church, and I have never regretted that decision."

"I understand."

He patted her knee as if she were a young child. "Perhaps you do, but I think you may be too young to understand a life of such dedication and faith. What I tell you now, I tell you so that some good may still come of Father Reynolds' unfortunate life, and so the officer who shot him may find some peace."

Peyton felt a catch in her heart at that, especially with Marco sitting right behind them.

"What I tell you I tell you because it can no longer hurt anyone, but you must understand how difficult this is for me."

Peyton studied his profile. "How do you know the accusations against Father Reynolds weren't just accusations, Father Michael? How do you know what he did in Boston?"

He shifted on the pew and met her gaze. "I know…" He let out a quivering breath and his large knuckled hands constricted around the rosary. "I know and that has to be enough for you."

* * *

Peyton leaned against Cho and Simons' Crown Victoria. Marco stood to her right and Simons before her. Cho sat on the hood of the car, his hands folded on his knees. None of them had spoken since Peyton told them what Father Michael said.

Finally Simons stirred, wrapping his arms around his massive barrel-chest. "I still don't understand how the killer knew about the priest and I especially don't understand how he knew he was going to Alcatraz."

"You don't think that priest could be our serial killer?" asked Cho.

Marco and Peyton shook their heads.

"He wouldn't have had the mobility or the strength to get to the other side of the island or drive the Zodiac over the waves in the bay," said Marco.

"Maybe our killer is a parishioner of the church," said Peyton.

"Would the church have a parishioner list?" asked Simons.

Marco shrugged. "It would, but that doesn't mean anything. Do you have any idea how many Catholic churches there are in the City? Most Catholics have a local parish church, but that doesn't stop them from going to whichever one is closest, and they don't necessarily get on the church rolls. That way they can avoid the tithe."

"The field trip was posted on a community board. The killer might have seen it there," said Cho.

"But how did he know Reynolds had been transferred here from out of state?"

"He must have inside information on the church. That's the only way," said Simons.

Peyton's phone buzzed. She pulled it out and thumbed it on. A text message from Abe blinked across the display. Cho and Simons were still discussing the case, but she felt Marco's gaze zero in on her.

She glanced up at him. "It's just Abe."

He didn't seem convinced. "About what?"

"Wondering when we're gonna have a night out again, go dancing or something."

Marco looked down and she knew he didn't believe her. She hated lying to him. She hated it more than anything else, but she was in so difficult a position with him right now.

"We should head back to the precinct and debrief the captain," she said, pushing away from the car. "I'll call you later," she told Marco.

He didn't answer.

Simons put a heavy hand on his shoulder. "Hang in there, bud," he said. "I remember when they put me on leave for shooting that tweaker in the Haight Ashbury, I thought I'd go stir crazy."

"Yeah." He looked up and speared Peyton with his eyes. "It's a bitch."

Peyton grabbed the door on the car and pulled it open.

"Later, D'Angelo," said Cho, hopping off the hood as Simons climbed behind the steering wheel.

Peyton sank into the backseat and closed the door as the engine roared to life and Cho threw himself into the passenger's seat. Marco stepped back from the car, placing his hands in his pockets. She glanced up at him as Simons pulled away from the curb and steered the car into traffic.

The ride back to the precinct was done in silence, and once there, Peyton climbed out and thanked Simons, then asked them to debrief the captain for her. They agreed and she walked across the parking lot to her car.

Abe's message hadn't been about a night out. He wanted her to come to the M.E.'s office because he had information about the case that he wanted to share with her. She drove her Corolla over to his office and parked in back.

Each time she came, it got a little easier moving from the car to the back door, but without Marco beside her, she felt a rush of bile in her throat. Pulling out her card, she swiped it across the pad and then pulled open the outer door.

A guard waited at the podium and handed her a clipboard to sign in. He was the same guard that usually manned the post during the weekday, but he never tried to make conversation with her. She didn't make much effort herself.

Walking down the hall, she came to Abe's lab and glanced through the glass in the door. A body lay on the table, covered in a white drape and Abe wasn't anywhere to be seen. She was reluctant to go into the lab unless he was there, especially with a body on the table.

"Hey, sweetie, you finally decided to come down?"

She turned with relief to see him walking down the hallway with his long stride. His dread locks bounced on his shoulders with each step and he wore a white lab coat. The lab coat was his only allowance toward professionalism because he had multi-colored beads on the end of his dreads and he wore a shirt that looked like it might have been wallpaper in a previous life. She could see a flash of purple slacks beneath the lab coat and he had green snakeskin cowboy boots on his feet.

"Nice shoes."

He stopped and turned his ankle out, showing them off. "Best faux anaconda money can buy."

She felt some of the tension ease from her as he gave her a toothy smile.

"You putting anything on those cuts?"

"Why is everyone so worried about my face?"

He took a dramatic step back, pressing one elegant, long fingered hand against his chest. "Oh my, the little cat is showing her claws."

"I'm sorry. It's been a bitch of a day."

"Or two, I'm guessing."

"Yeah, or two."

Abe pushed the button on his lab and the automatic doors opened. "Come in."

Peyton hesitated on the threshold. "You got a dead body in there, Abe."

His brows lifted. "I'm a coroner, sweetie. What do you think I do all day? Crochet?"

"That wouldn't surprise me."

"Well, actually I do. I made the most delightful little beanie." He came back and put an arm around her shoulders, guiding her into the lab. "It's green and pink. You would love it."

She had to smile. Abe made it impossible not to.

He brought her to the bench that ran along the back wall and pulled out a stool. "Sit down."

She perched on it, trying to avoid looking at the white draped form a few feet away. "Is that the priest?" she said, glancing at the beakers he had arranged on shelves above her head.

"Yep. I thought I might show you something, but we'll work our way up to that." He went to the body and retrieved a plastic bag on a lower shelf of the table. He brought it over to Peyton, hooking another stool with his foot and dragging it over. He sat down next to her, blocking her view of the body.

It was cold in the room, so Peyton clasped her hands together and pressed them between her knees. "What's that?"

He opened the bag and took out a smaller one. Shaking the contents into the bottom, he laid it on the counter before her. Three bullets tented the plastic along the seam of the bag. "Recognize these?"

".40 caliber." She felt a prickle of sweat at her temples.

He reached into the larger bag again and pulled out another smaller bag, holding it up before her. "Recognize this?"

Peyton reached for it. "That's a 9mm. Where did you get this?"

"I pulled one out of the ranger's chest."

"Is this it?"

"No."

Peyton set the bag on the counter. "What do you mean no?"

"I sent the 9mm I found in the ranger on to ballistics." Abe fingered one of the .40 calibers. "They'll have to confirm this, but we both know these came out of Marco's Glock."

Peyton couldn't meet his eye.

"He's a clean shot, Peyton. The priest probably didn't feel a thing – took him through the heart."

She swallowed and closed her eyes briefly.

"I did the autopsy on the ranger next and found the 9mm, but this one…" He touched the single bullet in the bag. "I found this by accident."

"What do you mean?" She finally met his gaze.

"Even though I had Marco's bullets, I wanted to be thorough. The priest's body was so bloated and battered by the rocks and waves, I probably wouldn't have found it, except I always take an x-ray of the entire body as the last thing I do." He picked up the bag. "This little baby was swimming around in what was left of our priest's brain."

"He was shot by the same gun as the ranger?"

"Not officially confirmed, but yeah, I think it's safe to say that."

Peyton tried to remember that night. She had seen a flash of light just before Marco opened fire or she thought she had. She grabbed Abe's wrist, pulling down the bag. "Which one killed him?"

"What?"

"I thought I saw a flash of light just before Marco fired. Could he have been dead already?"

Abe's face grew grim. "Peyton, it's impossible to know that. Two of Marco's bullets were lodged in his heart."

She swallowed hard and nodded. "What did you want to show me on the body?"

Abe shook his head. "I don't think it matters, but I'm pretty sure I found the entrance wound."

"Where?"

"Behind his right ear. Clean shot."

Peyton stared at the 9mm. She was sure she'd seen a flash just before Marco fired, but who would believe her? Everything had happened so fast that night, and no one knew what was going on until it was already over. Either way, bullets from Marco's gun had been inside the priest's body. There was no disputing that.

* * *

Marco was sitting on her stairs when she got home that night. She slowed as she came up the walk and frowned at him. "Why aren't you inside?"

"Jake has the Giants' game on and he can't let a single call go by without commenting on it. It was either wait out here or strangle him."

She smiled. "Come on up. I'll order Thai. That should shut Jake up for a while."

"No, not tonight. I'm not good company right now."

Peyton felt a twist in her gut. "Did Vinnie go home?"

"Yeah, but my mom's still there." He had his hands clasped before him, his forearms resting on his knees. "I'm all right, Brooks. I just don't want to make small talk right now."

"Okay."

He lifted his eyes and pierced her. "What's going on with us right now?"

"What do you mean?"

"You duck my calls and you aren't telling me things."

She leaned against the railing. "I'm not ducking your calls, but I'm in a tough spot here, Marco. Internal Affairs wanted to put me on leave, but Defino fought them. If I step out of line, they're gonna pull my gun too."

He studied her intently and she resisted the urge to squirm. He knew she was only telling half the truth.

Finally, she couldn't take it and looked down at the stairs, bracing her foot on the last one. She didn't want to keep things from him. They'd shared everything for eight years now, but she didn't even understand what she was feeling. Guilt and grief and worry warred inside of her. She hated that he'd killed someone for her, but at the same time, she was humbled by his sacrifice. And then there was the shame that she hadn't taken the shot herself. It was hard being around him right now, but she hated not having him there. He was her stability, her center, her equilibrium.

"Look, just tell the psychiatrist whatever he wants to hear, so you can get back to work. Everything feels off kilter right now and I've never had to deal with this before."

"You wanna tell me what he wants to hear because I can't figure it out."

"I wish I knew. I feel like I'm just one wrong word away from being committed." She forced herself to look at him. "Please understand. My hands are tied. With this serial killer, Defino can't afford to lose both of us. I need to play it by the book with them, so I don't get my badge yanked."

He didn't answer, just stared, and Peyton knew he didn't buy a damn thing she said. She felt a gulf growing between them and it scared her deeply, but she didn't know how to stop it from happening.

Pushing himself to his feet, he came down the stairs until he towered over her. She looked up at him, wishing she knew what to say, anything to stop this distance from continuing. "You better watch yourself, Brooks," he said. "I won't be there if you need me."

A chill shivered over her and she wrapped her arms around her stomach. She expect him to pull her in for a quick hug, or a kiss on the top of her head as he always did, but he just brushed past her and stepped onto the walkway. Peyton stood where she was, fighting tears as the Charger roared to life behind her. Whipping around, she started to go after him, but he pulled away from the curb and never once looked back.

CHAPTER 7

Peyton sat in her usual spot at the conference room table. Dr. Ferguson tapped his pen against his legal pad and gave her a speculative look. Peyton would have given anything to be anywhere else right now. She hadn't been sleeping well, and these 8:00AM meetings were beginning to prey on her.

"So, here we are at our third session."

"Really? And it only feels like five."

He fought a smile. "Does that mean you aren't enjoying our talks?"

Peyton gave him a disbelieving look. "I was fine until you made my head your playground. Now everything I do feels off."

"What do you mean?"

"I mean I can't talk to my partner without it being strained."

"And this bothers you?"

"Of course it bothers me. He's my partner. We've shared everything with each other for eight years, but now I can't even tell him what's going on." She leaned forward on the table. "You've got to let him come back to work."

"That isn't your concern, Inspector Brooks. That's my decision to make." He flipped a few pages on his pad. "Right now, I would suggest you be more concerned with yourself than him."

Peyton slumped back in her chair, feeling lost and defeated. "Why can't you understand? We're partners, we do this job together. Keeping him away isn't good for either of us." She drummed her fingers on the table. "You said you understood cops, you understood the bond between two partners. You've got to know this isn't normal. We work in tandem, we're a team. We complement each other. And with the case we've got right now…"

"The serial killer?"

Peyton hesitated. She wasn't aware Defino had told him this much. She knew the captain wanted to keep this information from the media. It was bound to set off panic in a city like San Francisco. "Anyway, with this case, the captain needs all of us working it."

He scribbled something on the pad. "As I said, Inspector Brooks, you should be more concerned about yourself right now."

"What does that mean? Are you going to pull my gun?"

He glanced up at her, surprised by her directness.

"You're not the only one who shoots straight, Dr. Ferguson."

"Then answer me this. Are you sleeping well at night?"

"If I say no, what happens?"

"If you say yes, I'll know you're lying."

Peyton sighed. She hated playing cat and mouse with him. "What do you want me to say? If you let Marco come back, things will work themselves out on their own."

"You mean you'll suppress everything that you're feeling and pretend everything is normal again."

"Isn't that what everyone does? Isn't that how most people face each day?"

"Most people don't have to deal with what the two of you have faced lately, so no, suppressing what you're feeling isn't normal, and let me tell you, Inspector Brooks, in my experience, cops who have been through what you have do not last long unless they confront what they're feeling."

Peyton looked away. There was no way to win this with him.

"When you say things are strained between you and your partner, what do you mean?"

"It's always been so easy between us, but right now, I feel like we're both measuring out every word."

He steepled his hands and pressed them against his square chin. "That's not completely true. It hasn't always been easy between you, now has it? You told me yourself that he hated you at first, asked for a different partner."

"That was at first. It didn't take us long to work it out, then we became friends."

"That's not the way he tells it. Seems to me it took longer than you remember."

Actually, Peyton remembered very well. Marco was determined to keep her at a distance no matter what she did, even when Abe came into the picture, and that was saying something because it was hard to thwart Abe when he was determined.

*   *   *

Peyton and Marco entered the M.E. building for the first time. They'd been called down by the Medical Examiner assigned to their first case, an Abraham Jefferson. The guard at the podium outside the door told them his lab was in the basement.

Jogging down the stairs, Peyton felt a flutter of anxiety in her stomach. She wasn't sure what she was about to see. During the academy, they'd taken a class on autopsies and forensics, but she hadn't watched the video when they'd showed it, staring instead at her notes.

As they turned into the hallway, Marco moved in front of her. He didn't seem to have any trepidation at all. "Here it is," he said, pointing to a nameplate attached to the door.

"Do we knock?"

He gave her a dark look and pressed the button for the automatic doors. They swung open, revealing a sterile lab with a metal table in the center of the room. A body lay flayed open on the table, and Peyton quickly looked down, only to have her gaze fix on the drain in the floor. Oh, lord, that wasn't good.

"Well, well, well," came a deep voice.

A man moved in front of the door, drawing Peyton's attention. He was tall, nearly as tall as Marco, with long limbs and a slender build. He had a pleasant face, colored a brown darker than her own, with a wild mane of black dread locks. As he smiled, he revealed a mouth that overflowed with teeth and eyes that laughed.

He fixated first on Marco and gave him a lazy, thorough perusal. "Slap me and call me Daisy, you are about the prettiest cop I have ever seen. Tell us your name, gorgeous."

Marco took a step back, his face twisting into a frown.

Peyton immediately felt her anxiety decrease and she pushed in front of Marco, holding out her hand. "I'm Inspector Peyton Brooks and this is my partner, Marco D'Angelo."

His dark eyes passed over her and he smiled again. "Aren't you adorable?" He took her hand, then to her surprise, he spun her around. "Good thing the department suspended the height requirement, isn't it, cutie?"

She smiled. "We're looking for Abraham Jefferson."

"You found him."

Peyton blinked in surprise. This man was not at all what she expected from the staid Medical Examiner's office. "Come again?"

He placed a long fingered, elegant hand in the center of his chest. "I am Abraham Jefferson, but my friends…" He gave Marco his lazy look once more. "And lovers, call me Abe."

Peyton glanced up at Marco, but he seemed completely bewildered. "Nice to meet you, Abe."

"Same here, sweetie. Peyton, huh?"

"Yep."

"Does your partner speak, Peyton?"

"Only when necessary. It's one of our rules."

"Rules?"

"We have rules."

Abe's brows rose. "I see." He turned around and walked back toward the body, his lab coat swinging around him. "I don't believe in rules."

Peyton guessed as much just looking at him. He wore a paisley print silk shirt beneath the lab coat and a pair of pinstriped black pants, ending in a pair of pointed dress shoes.

"So I called you down here 'cause I thought you might want to know a little about your vic from the other night."

Peyton stayed where she was. She didn't think she needed to get any closer to the body on the table to hear what he had to say.

Marco gave her a shake of his head as he walked over and stood on the other side of the table from Abe. "What did you find?"

Abe gave him a dreamy look. "A voice as mellifluous as angels singing."

Peyton could see Marco's back stiffen. "The dead body talked to you?"

Abe barked out a laugh. "No, handsome, I meant your voice." He glanced back at Peyton. "You coming, sweetie?"

Before she could answer, Marco shot a scowl at her. "She's afraid of dead bodies."

That did it. She stormed up to the table, forcing herself to look down. The corpse had a grey cast to his skin and a suture line ran from the middle of his throat all the way to his groin and extended out to either side. She fought down the rush of bile and looked instead at the cool metal of the table. The two men would never know the difference.

Abe brought his head down into her line of sight. "Gonna be hard being a homicide detective, isn't it?"

"You mean with Prince Charming as my partner."

Abe smiled. "I like you."

She held his gaze. She liked him too.

He offered Marco a sultry look. "And I like looking at you."

Marco's jaw clenched so hard she could see a muscle bulge in his cheek. "What did you find?"

Abe moved down the table and lifted the vic's hands. "Notice the knuckles?"

Peyton forced herself to look. They were grey and stiff, but she also noticed they were abnormally large.

"He liked punching things, our friend here. The bones in his fingers have calluses, areas where extra calcium has been deposited to repair fractures." He moved up to the vic's head. "He also had signs of brain trauma."

"From the car?"

"No, I found a blood clot on a CT scan. He was a ticking time bomb."

"He used to beat his girlfriend. Could that be why?"

"Certainly a possibility. I thought it might be helpful for her case. Maybe the D.A. won't want to prosecute?"

"Thank you," said Peyton.

"Glad to help."

Peyton took a step away from the table. "It was nice meeting you. Hopefully, we'll be working together again."

"Oh, I'm certain of it. I get most of the homicides from the precinct." He leaned closer to her. "Love the drama."

She laughed. "See you later then." Turning, she headed for the door, Marco on her heels.

"Goodbye, gorgeous. I can't wait to see *you* again," Abe called after them.

Marco faltered, but then his long stride took him past Peyton and out the door. Peyton shot a smile over her shoulder at the M.E. and he waved good naturedly after her. She jogged to catch up to her partner as the door closed behind her.

Marco grabbed the rail and pulled himself up the stairs, but after a few, he stopped and turned around.

Pointing down the stairs, he glared at Peyton. "He should be reported for sexual harassment."

Peyton came to a panting halt. "What? He just flirted with you a bit."

"It was unprofessional."

"Oh please." Then she gave him a crafty look. "What's your problem, D'Angelo? Are you homophobic?"

His eyes widened in astonishment. "No."

"No?"

"No, I'm not homophobic. Why can't any of you take this job seriously?"

"We do take it seriously, but you take it to the point of ridiculousness. You're gonna burn out before you're thirty the way you're going. Why can't you lighten up just a little?"

He loomed over her and Peyton took a step back, hitting the rail behind her. "Lighten up? That was a dead body back there and he's making quips about my looks? Are you kidding me?"

"No, that would be against the rules."

His mouth opened, but nothing came out.

"Look, you're upset because another man called you handsome. I get that you have a problem with your looks."

"I should report him."

"Because he said you were gorgeous? I've said the same thing, but you haven't reported me. Do you really want to come across looking like a bigot?"

"Bigot? Because I want a little respect?"

Peyton gave him a wry look. "You gotta earn that respect, D'Angelo, and right now, all anyone sees is an uptight cop who can't take a joke."

"I can take a joke. I don't think he was joking."

He did have a point. "What do you want me to say? I'm not going to tell you to report him. He's clearly good at what he does. So he flirted with you a bit. Let it go. In fact, why can't you enjoy the attention?"

"You don't get it, do you? This is a job, Brooks, a job. We protect the public, we stand between them and the bad guys. It's a sacred duty."

Peyton burst into laughter. She couldn't help it.

"What the hell!" He walked up a few stairs, then came back down, clearly agitated.

"I'm sorry, but when you start spouting off like a freakin' action hero, it's really damn funny."

"You are impossible!"

"I'm sorry." She leaned against the wall. She couldn't stop laughing and his anger only made it funnier.

He stopped pacing, putting his hands on his hips. "I have another rule."

Her laughter dried to a smile. "Of course you do."

"You back me up when I think something is wrong. You don't mock me."

"What are you saying? You want me to report him?"

He sighed and slapped a hand against his thigh. "No, I'm not gonna report him, but I am going to ask that he not handle any of our cases."

"I'm not backing you up on that, D'Angelo."

"Why the hell not?"

"Because it's just stupid. He's a good M.E. Do you really want to get a reputation for being a hard-ass this early in your career? Do you want Defino to think you aren't a team player? Look, you're right about one thing. We all have to work together. This is like a puzzle and we each have our roles. I'm learning to put up with your uptight ass, you could learn to overlook a few things yourself, okay?"

He stared at her in bewilderment. Clearly, he didn't think he was being difficult at all. Clearly, he thought he was the only one who was having to make allowances, but something must have registered because he straightened and drew a deep breath.

"Okay. Point taken."

She raised her eyebrows in surprise.

He shrugged. "Besides that, I guess he does have good taste."

Peyton laughed and pushed him in the stomach, starting up the stairs. "Don't worry, D'Angelo. He just hasn't gotten to know your personality yet."

*   *   *

Marco dropped a folder on her desk. "Sign it."

She picked it up and opened the flap. He'd typed up the report for their vehicular manslaughter case. "Wait. I thought we'd write it together."

"It's done. Just sign it."

"Do I get to read it?"

"Whatever." He went back to his desk and threw himself into his seat.

She picked up a pen and placed it against her lower lip as she read. "What's *pre-mediated* mean?"

"What?"

"Here, you say the attack wasn't *pre-mediated.*"

"Premeditated."

Peyton pursed her lips, then made a notation on the paper.

"Are you correcting it?"

"Yeah."

"Why?"

Peyton looked over the file at him. "I'm guessing Lily Warren probably wouldn't want the D.A. getting confused about what happened."

"How would he be confused?"

She tapped the pen against the paper. "So is *vehuncular* a scientific term then?"

"What?"

"It says *vehuncular manslaughter.*"

He jumped to his feet and grabbed the report from her, reading it himself. "It's a typo. Just sign the damn report."

Peyton's brows rose.

"Is there a problem?" came Defino's voice behind them.

Marco visibly composed himself. "No, Captain. We're just discussing our report on the last case."

"I see." She moved beyond them, headed toward the break-room. "We certainly want to make sure we represent the department at our finest now, don't we, Inspectors?"

"Yes, Captain," Marco answered, turning and watching her walk into the break-room. He shifted and looked down at Peyton. A lazy smile tilted the corners of his mouth and his blue eyes sparkled. "Fine, why don't you write it then?"

"What? No, I'll edit it and then you can fix it."

"Obviously that would be a waste of effort. Since you are far superior at this, I think you should write all of our reports."

Peyton glared at him. "I'm not your damn secretary, D'Angelo. Just learn to spell."

His smile grew wider. "That really hurts, Brooks."

"What?"

"The way you make fun of my disability."

"Disability?"

"Yes, didn't you know?"

"Know what?"

"I'm dyslexic. I can't spell."

Peyton narrowed her eyes on him. "Bull shit."

He winked at her. "Really?" Then he leaned on the desk, bringing himself closer to her. "Just how do you want to play this, sweetheart? Do you want to call me a liar in front of the captain this early in your career? Do you want Defino to think you're not a team player?"

She clenched her teeth, but Defino came out of the break-room, carrying a cup of coffee, so she gave him a sweet smile instead. "Touché."

He rose to his full height, then turned away. "Want a cup of coffee, partner?" he called over his shoulder.

Peyton didn't answer, but turned to her computer, clicking on the word processing program. Then she began typing the report with angry strokes. Bastard had her and she knew it. He returned and took his seat again, whistling happily as he clicked on his computer screen. *Probably looking at naked women*, she thought as she typed.

*　*　*

Peyton came back from the restroom and slowed to a stop. Her father was sitting in a chair next to Marco's desk and the two of them were laughing. She couldn't remember ever hearing Marco laugh before.

She approached slowly and her father looked up, his face beaming into a smile as he spotted her. "There she is." He held out his arm and she stepped into it, bending down to kiss his cheek. "How are you, sweetness?"

"I'm good. What are you doing here, Daddy?" He was wearing civilian clothes, a collared shirt and jeans.

He hooked his arm around her waist. "I came to take you to lunch. You got an hour to spare your father?"

She smiled at him, wrapping her arms around his shoulders. "Always. How about Japanese?"

He made a face. "You know I don't like Japanese." He leaned toward Marco and dropped his voice. "What's with the raw fish anyway?"

Marco smiled. "I don't know, sir."

Peyton stared at him in bewilderment.

"Let's do Mexican. I've been dying for a taco for weeks now, but your mother won't let me have any."

"Okay. Mexican it is. There's a great place around the corner."

"Excellent." He looked at Marco. "Want to join us?"

"Daddy, we don't do social things here. We're strictly professionals."

Ben looked confused, but Marco gave her a cunning smile. "I'd be honored, sir."

She frowned at him. She didn't want him going to lunch with them. She wanted time with her father by herself.

"Great." Ben pushed himself to his feet. "Lead the way then."

The San Francisco fog was creeping into the City as they walked down to the Mexican restaurant on the corner. It was busy this time of day, but the hostess found them a quiet booth in the back. The high walls of the booth were painted purple and large terra cotta suns decorated the backs.

Peyton slid into the booth after her father and Marco sat down across from them. The hostess placed a bowl of salsa and a basket of chips in the middle of the table. "What can I get you to drink?"

Ben glanced at his daughter, then he smiled up at the hostess. "A Margarita with salt on the rim. Your mama won't let me have one of those either."

Peyton smiled. "Water, please."

"Same," said Marco.

Ben took a chip and broke it, placing a piece in his mouth. "How long you been on the force, young man?"

"About a year, sir."

"You and my daughter are about the youngest detectives I've seen."

"Yes, sir. How long have you been on the force?"

He nudged Peyton with his shoulder. "Going on twenty-three years. Peyton's mom wants me to retire in a few years, but I don't know what I'd do with myself."

"I understand."

Peyton gave Marco an arch look. Where was all this charm coming from? "You're off today, Daddy?"

"Yep. Got another two days, then it's back to the beat."

"Why didn't Mama come with you?"

"She's getting her hair done." Ben shook his head. "Women and their hair." He ran a hand over his thinning closely cropped black crew-cut. "Just shampoo and go for me."

120

Marco smiled. His own hair was pulled back in a ponytail, resting on the collar of his shirt.

Peyton tried to hide her disappointment. Her mother never wanted to talk about her job. In fact, she'd tried to discourage Peyton from taking the test to become a detective. Peyton couldn't understand it. Police work had been in the family for generations.

The hostess brought back their drinks and set Ben's Margarita in front of him. His eyes lit up and he licked his lips. As the woman walked away, he held the drink up as if he were going to make a toast.

"To the force. May your careers be as rewarding as mine has been."

Marco picked up his water glass and touched it to her father's, then he tilted it against hers, giving her a pointed look.

Peyton sneered at him and touched his glass.

Her father took a long sip, then smacked his lips. "Damn that's good."

Peyton laughed and wrapped her arms around his, placing her chin on his shoulder. "I'm glad you came, Daddy. I've been missing you."

He kissed her forehead. "You need to come home for dinner more often. Your mama would like that."

"Would she?"

He gave her a frown. "You know she would. She's just worried about you. That's all. So am I, but now that I've met your partner, I feel a whole lot better." He took in the breadth of Marco's shoulders. "What do you bench press, young man?"

"310 or so, sir."

"Good. Keep it up. You don't want to go to seed." He patted his own stomach.

Marco smiled.

Peyton rolled her eyes. "Really, Daddy, that's what impresses you."

"It helps, sweetness, but more than that, it helps knowing there's someone who's got your back. That's important. If you take nothing away from this lunch, take this. Someday it's gonna come down to the basics, the most fundamental moment of any cop's life, and when you hit that moment, all you can hope is the man at your back is willing to lay down everything for you when you need him."

Peyton and Marco locked eyes.

"That's what I want, baby girl, I want to know that when you need him, your partner is gonna be there for you."

*   *   *

Peyton fell silent. *When you need him, your partner is gonna be there for you.* Oh, God, how much she missed her father, his words of wisdom, his unwavering support. She realized Marco had taken that place for her. When all else failed, he was there, always at her back, always supporting her.

"Sounds like a remarkable man, your father," came Dr. Ferguson's voice.

Peyton blinked and remembered where she was. She could only nod. All these years and the grief could come back so strong, so powerful, choking her.

"Almost prophetic."

Peyton met his gaze. "Maybe."

"He obviously saw something in Marco, something he liked."

"Yeah." She smiled in memory. "Talking to him was the first time I saw Marco the man, not the cop."

"So what bothers you most about the shooting?"

"What?"

"What is it that keeps you up at night?"

She thought for a moment, but she was still too conflicted to make sense of it. "I wish I knew."

"Could the strain with your partner be caused by you yourself?"

"I thought that's what you were supposed to tell me."

"I don't tell you things, Inspector Brooks, you discover them."

"Well, this isn't helping me discover a damn thing."

"I disagree. I think you're facing a lot of stuff you didn't want to face."

"I wish you'd tell me what that is."

"If I did, I wouldn't be a very good psychiatrist, now would I?"

Peyton looked away.

"I'll see you tomorrow, Inspector Brooks, bright and early. Try to get some rest tonight, all right?"

Peyton pushed herself to her feet. "Yeah, thanks for the advice." What the hell! How much was the department paying for him to tell her what she already knew? Get some sleep and then everything will be just hunky dory. Damn idiot!

CHAPTER 8

Peyton dragged her white board into the conference room after Marco had his session with Dr. Ferguson. Marco left the precinct without saying more than a short hello to all of them. Peyton watched him cross the parking lot, feeling her heart in her throat, but it did no good. She couldn't fix anything right now.

Marco was pissed that she wasn't sharing the case with him, but just that morning, Defino had made it clear he wasn't to be in the loop. She was furious that he'd shown up at the church, so furious that she'd threatened to take Peyton's badge herself. Peyton couldn't risk it. She needed to be on this case.

Cho and Simons entered the conference room a few minutes later, followed by Jake and Defino. Defino positioned herself next to the white board, refusing to take a seat, but Jake sat at the head of the table, pulling out his computer tablet and thumbing it on. Cho and Simons took seats on either side of him.

"Okay, Brooks," said Defino. "Let's start listing each of the murders."

Peyton wrote the three men's names across the top. *Kimbro. Brill. Reynolds.* Beneath them she wrote their occupations: bum; parolee; priest. Under that she wrote method of death: execution style gunshot; hanging; death by cop. In parentheses, she wrote *gunshot* for Reynolds as well. Under Kimbro, she wrote *card in back pocket.* Brill, *card in bound hands.* Reynolds, *card delivered to precinct.* Stepping back, she surveyed the board. The others did as well.

Defino rubbed her forehead as if she had a headache. "What else do we know?"

"Serial killers usually operate with a pattern. So far the only pattern is the *Clean-up Crew* card," said Peyton.

"And the fact that they were all child molesters," offered Jake.

Peyton held out her hand to him in agreement, then added it to the board.

"Suspected," said Cho. "We still don't have proof for Reynolds."

"Right," said Defino.

"The method of death could also be a pattern," said Simons.

"How?"

"Each one was different. That lack of a pattern is almost a pattern."

"You're right," agreed Peyton.

"How does he pick them?" asked Defino.

"We believe he got the first two names from the Megan's Law Directory."

"But not Reynolds."

"No." Peyton covered her mouth with her hand.

They fell silent and studied the board for a moment.

"Unless," said Jake, and he began typing on his tablet. "Unless, the church also has an on-line bulletin board where they list activities."

Peyton looked over at him as he searched. He clicked on something, then shifted the tablet so Cho could see.

"I'll be damned. Well done, Preacher."

Defino walked around the table and looked over his shoulder. "It's right there for anyone to access," She shook her head in amazement. "That's the entire diocese, Jake. Isn't there one for that single parish church?"

"Not that I can find. They don't even section it out by parish. It's just everything jumbled together."

Peyton set the dry-erase pen down. "He used the same database to find his first two victims, then changed it for the third. If he holds to pattern…"

Simons leaned his bulk forward. "…the next victim will be on the church event board as well."

Peyton touched her finger to her nose.

Defino straightened and looked at both of them. "How the hell will we figure it out in time? There are hundreds of events listed on here. Everything from softball games to birthday parties to baby showers."

Jake's eyes were moving rapidly back and forth. "We have to find those events that are listed by men, then we have to search each man's name on the Megan's Law directory. If we find a match, we've found our guy."

"That won't work. Reynolds wasn't on the Megan's Law directory," reminded Cho.

"It still might work. We can start with a general search and see if something comes up. If we'd looked for Reynolds in any search engine, it likely would have mentioned his transfer here," reasoned Peyton.

Simons closed his eyes briefly. "This is going to take weeks."

"What's the time between murders?" asked Defino.

Cho narrowed his eyes. "Kimbro was about three months ago, Brill two weeks later."

Peyton shook her head. "The timing isn't part of the pattern, the opportunity is."

"That makes it even worse."

Defino strode quickly to the door and leaned out. "Maria, get me four laptops in here stat."

Peyton could hear Maria's heels as she hurried away from her desk.

Defino looked back at them. "Call whoever you need to call, people, 'cause we may be here all night."

* * *

Jake looked up as Peyton set a coffee mug by his elbow. "Thank you. What about Pickles?"

Peyton took a seat beside him, cradling her own mug. "I called Abe. He's gonna take him over to his place for the night."

"Marco wouldn't go over?"

"I can't get a hold of him."

Jake heard the worry in her voice. "He's probably with his brother or parents, Mighty Mouse."

"Yeah."

"He's frustrated because he can't get back to work. That's all it is."

"He accused me of ducking his calls. I feel like he's paying me back."

"Adonis wouldn't do that with you and you know it."

Peyton shook her head. "This whole thing is such a mess, Jake. I just don't know how to make it better. Every time I talk to that psychiatrist, I feel like I'm going to say the wrong thing and get my badge pulled. Defino is riding me about telling Marco anything and Marco is pissed that I won't." She held a hand over his tablet. "And this case...the chance of us figuring out who the next victim is...well, it's slim and none."

"We'll get him."

"How? Serial killers avoid getting caught for years."

"But they do get caught. Eventually he's gonna mess up and we'll get more evidence against him."

"We've got four bodies already. How high is this count going to go?"

Jake shifted in his chair and leaned closer to her. "Where is this coming from? Don't talk like this, Peyton. You are the cop who kept working my case after everyone else had closed it. You're the cop who faced her father's killer to stop a gang war. And you're the one who wouldn't give up on a troubled rock star when everything else pointed to his guilt."

She met his gaze and tears glimmered in her eyes. "Marco was with me for all of those."

"And he'll be back again soon."

"Will he? And if he is, will it ever be the same?"

"Why not? Why wouldn't it be the same?"

A tear escaped and rolled down her cheek. She swiped it away violently. "Because he killed someone for me."

Jake started to respond, but Defino entered the conference area. "Anything?"

Peyton turned her head away.

Defino sensed the charged atmosphere and hesitated.

Jake reached for a piece of paper he'd printed out. "I started making a list, so we don't duplicate our efforts. If we check off an event, I think we should put it on here, so we don't keep researching the same ones."

"Good idea." Defino's gaze shifted to Peyton. "Where are Cho and Simons?"

"They took a break, but they'll be back," answered Jake.

"Okay. Let's debrief in five minutes. We'll list everything on your chart and review what we've researched." She came around the table and put a hand on Peyton's shoulder. "Brooks, why don't you get some fresh air to clear the cobwebs?"

Peyton nodded and rose to her feet. Jake followed her with his eyes as she left the room. He thought Defino might go after her, but she didn't.

"What's going on?"

Jake didn't want to betray Peyton's confidence, but he also didn't want Defino becoming more concerned than she already was. It would devastate Peyton to be taken out of action right now.

"She's just tired, Captain. There's been a lot going on lately and she's worried we won't figure out the serial killer's next victim in time."

"Nice try, Ryder."

"What?"

"I get you're trying to protect her, but I'm responsible for everyone here. I have to put the strongest, most capable cops on the street, so if she told you something that speaks to her state of mind, I order you to disclose it."

Jake knew Defino could be a ball-buster when she needed, but he'd never had her direct her authority at him before. His mind scrambled trying to think of what to say without giving too much away.

"Ryder." The warning in her tone was implicit.

"I told you the truth, Captain. She doesn't think we'll find the victim in time."

"Fine, but this has to do with Marco, doesn't it?"

"Yeah, she wants him back at work. They're a team, Captain, one of the best teams you've got and she's not used to working without him."

Defino eyed him with her squinting stare. He knew she sensed there was more. "Understand this, Ryder. If she goes out in the field and she isn't one hundred percent, she could be killed. We deal in life and death and a cop who isn't focused, who isn't well, doesn't stand a chance."

Jake swallowed hard. He wanted to break her stare, but he knew he couldn't. She was right, but he was more afraid what inaction would do to someone like Peyton. If Marco was suffering for it, Peyton would be worse. It would give her too much time to obsess over what happened.

And then there was reality. They were facing down a serial killer who had no problem continuing his rampage. Jake wasn't much concerned with the three child molesters, he figured it was a sort of justice, but he'd killed an innocent man in the ranger and called it *collateral damage*. He'd taken a life and it was just collateral damage. Such a monster had to be stopped.

"Here's the thing, Captain. You've got a serial killer running around this City with ample opportunity and hundreds of targets to pick from. We're chasing shadows in the night with this guy and you know it. Maybe Peyton isn't one hundred percent, but can you really risk taking her off this case right now?"

Defino straightened. "You're a man of many surprises, Mr. Ryder, you know that?"

"I'll take that as a compliment, Captain."

She gave him a faint smile. "You do that."

Cho and Simons came back into the room, Simons carrying a pizza. "Can't think when my stomach is eating itself," he grumbled.

Jake smiled at him and pushed his tablet aside to grab a slice.

* * *

Marco pushed the food around the plate, creating designs in the marinara sauce.

"Don't you want seconds?" asked his mother.

He blinked up at her, remembering where he was. His parents' familiar kitchen surrounded him with its homey smells of garlic and oregano. Terra cotta plates hung on the wall behind him and an antique china cabinet sat to his right, bursting with brightly colored plates that his mother claimed came directly from Italy. Marco never disputed it to her face, but he and Franco had once inspected the etching on the bottom and unless Taiwan was a province in Italy, he figured she was pulling someone's leg.

"No, thank you, Mama," he said.

"Did you see Bernardo's new mini-van?" asked his father. He was sopping up the sauce with a piece of garlic bread, his head bent low over his plate.

"Eat like a human," scolded Mona, slapping his arm.

He made a kissing motion with his lips, but went right on eating the way he was.

"Are you sure you don't want seconds? I have some left-over risotto. You like the risotto. You know, with the chicken."

"No, Mama, I don't want any risotto. I don't eat meat, remember?"

She picked up the bread basket and held it out to him. "Have more bread? There's no meat in that."

He took a piece to please her, but set it on his plate. He could feel her worried eyes on him, searching him. He tried to remember what his father had asked him. Something about Bernardo. *Right, mini-van.*

"Bernardo got a new mini-van, huh?"

His father nodded, moving the mouthful of food into his cheek so he could talk. "One of those tricked out numbers with the video player in back for the kids."

"Nice."

"What about dessert? I have ice cream. I can put some chocolate syrup on it."

Marco shook his head. "I don't want dessert, Mama."

"What's wrong with you? You never pass up seconds or dessert. You love ice cream and chocolate."

He did when he was ten...well, that wasn't completely true. Working with Peyton, he ate more sweets than he probably should.

"I'm just not hungry tonight."

His mother reared away. She measured all well-being by a person's appetite.

"I got a burger earlier," he quickly amended.

"Burger?"

"Veggie burger."

His father gave a grunt of disgust. "That's not a burger."

Marco smiled at him.

His mother settled her napkin by her plate, folding her hands on the table. "Tomorrow is Saturday, Marco."

He glanced over at her, stilling the aimless motions he was making with his fork. "Yeah?"

She looked him directly in the eye. "I want you to come to confession with me."

His father stopped eating.

Marco settled his fork on the plate and leaned back in his chair. "What?"

"You need to go to confession with me. You need to give this burden to the Lord."

"What burden?"

She dropped her eyes. "The priest. You need to confess what happened."

"Why?"

"Why? Because you must ask for forgiveness. You must ask for absolution."

"I did nothing wrong. He shot at my partner and I stopped him. That's all."

"You killed a priest, Marco."

"Because he would have killed my partner." He leaned forward on the table. "Are you saying you'd rather I didn't fire on him? That I let him shoot Peyton?"

She gave him a wounded look. "Of course not. I love Peyton. I know you did what you had to do to protect her, but…"

"But what?"

"But he was a priest, Marco," said his father.

"Who was also a child molester. Are you going to defend that, Papa?"

"No, I can't defend that."

Marco gave a short nod of his head, but his mother was still watching him with a pained expression.

"You aren't eating. You're angry all of the time," she said.

"Because they won't let me go back to work."

"I don't think that's what it is. I think the priest's death is weighing on your heart and confession will ease your mind and soul."

"No!" Marco slammed his hand on the table, making his mother jump. "I don't regret what I did. I killed him because I had no other choice and you know what, I would do it again…" He drew his lips back against his teeth. "…and I will if it comes down to it."

Her face grew stern. "You can lie to me and your father. You can lie to that psychiatrist, but you cannot lie to God. He sees into your heart and He knows what is in there." She closed her eyes and pressed a hand against her heart. "I fear for you, my son, I hurt inside watching you.

Until you go to confession and absolve yourself of this, you will be haunted."

Marco pulled in a deep breath and held it, trying to force his jaw to unclench, but it was no use. Pressing his hands flat against the table, he levered himself to his feet. "Thank you for dinner, Mama."

She opened her eyes and looked up at him. The hurt in her expression made him feel sick inside, but he didn't know how to give her what she wanted. He wasn't going to confession. He had nothing to confess.

"Talk to you later, Papa."

"Come over on Sunday and watch the baseball game with me."

Marco inclined his head in agreement, then he eased out from behind the table and headed toward the living room. His jacket lay over his father's recliner and he pulled it on, reaching for the phone he'd left in its pocket.

A number of calls from Peyton showed on the display, but he shoved the phone back into the jacket pocket, ignoring it. Now would be an especially bad time to talk to her. After their last conversation on her stairs, he was sure his present mood would do permanent damage to their friendship.

His mother trailed him and he turned, forcing a smile. She held out her arms and he moved into them, ducking his head to kiss her cheek. "I'll see you Sunday."

She kissed him back, cupping her hands on his cheeks. "I love you, Marco. No matter what, I love you."

"I know, Mama." He stepped out of her hold. "Good night."

She walked him to the door and watched him jog down the stairs to the street. As he climbed behind the steering wheel of the Charger, he was sure she was watching him out of the front windows, but he didn't look up.

He started the car and pulled into the street. He didn't want to go home and Vinnie would be busy with his family now. Instead, he drove out to the wharf and walked into the *Fiddler's Green*, an Irish pub right off Beach Street. A guitarist was playing in the corner and the bar was crowded. He found a stool at the wooden bar and took a seat.

The bartender came over. "What'll it be?"

"Just a cola. Whatever you've got on tap."

With a nod, he walked away again.

Marco shifted and looked out at the people crowded at tables or standing in clusters talking. A television was positioned in a corner by the door, showing a soccer game. Marco couldn't make out who the teams were.

When the bartender settled the cola in front of him, he reached for his wallet and gave him a ten. The man went away to make change while Marco took a sip. As he lowered the drink, his eyes caught on three women at the other end of the bar. Two were brunette, but one was blond. They were smiling at him, but when he caught their eye, they giggled and whispered amongst themselves.

The bartender gave him back his change. "You've got admirers," he said.

Marco nodded and took the bills, leaving two on the bar.

Grabbing the tip, the bartender moved away again.

The brunettes were urging the blond to approach him. He studied her. She was tall and shapely in a red minidress, her straight hair pulled back on the left side with a comb. She lifted her drink and placed the straw against her lower lip, giving him a sultry look with her heavily lashed eyes. She wasn't his usual type. He usually liked women a little less California girl, but what the hell. She was clearly interested.

Marco motioned the bartender over. "What's she drinking?"

"Long Island."

Marco gave him another ten. "Send another one over to her and keep the change."

The bartender held up the bill in a salute and went to make the drink.

When he delivered it to the blond, she and her friends giggled and whispered over it, but she didn't acknowledge him in any other way. Suddenly Marco realized he didn't care. He wasn't in the mood to put out the effort to charm her. It was pointless. Crossing his arms on the bar, he shifted on his stool so he could see the television. He watched the two teams, one in green and one in red, race back and forth across the field, the ball bouncing from one end to the other. No matter how many times he watched it, he would never understand soccer. Who wanted to go around chasing a ball with their feet?

"Thank you," came a feminine voice behind him.

He looked over his shoulder to see the blond standing at his elbow. Looking at her this close, he realized she wasn't as young as he was beginning to think. Still, she was pretty and she had a smoking hot figure.

Shifting around, he held out his hand. "I'm Marco."

She took it, giving him a charming blush. "Lisa."

"Lisa, nice name. You from around here?"

"Yeah, I have an apartment out in the Sunset and I work at a law firm on Market. Paralegal."

He nodded. "Excellent."

"What do you do?"

He thought about that one for a moment. "Good question. Right now, I'm talking to a beautiful woman."

She giggled and ducked her head, taking a sip of her drink. "I meant for a living."

He stood up and offered her his seat.

Her eyes widened at his height, but she sat down, setting her drink on the bar. Shooting a look at her friends, she made an "o" out of her mouth. Marco glanced at them and noticed they were fanning their hands before their faces.

"So, what do you do?" she asked again.

He gave her his lazy smile. "Let's say I'm exploring my options."

Her eyes tracked over him as she sipped at her drink. "I see."

135

He leaned on the bar, bringing himself closer to her. "What exactly do you see?"

Slowly she licked her lips. "Why don't you tell me?"

*   *   *

Peyton pushed the laptop away and reached over, picking up Jake's list and studying it. They'd gone through over a hundred events and nothing added up. Everything that seemed likely resulted in a dead end. There was no way they were ever going to find the next victim in time.

Cho rolled his neck and gave a huge yawn. "What time is it?"

Peyton glanced at her phone. "1:00AM."

Defino closed the cover on her laptop. "Okay, what have we got? Is there anything at all that flags a warning?"

"Not so far."

"I got a baseball coach with a record," said Simons.

They looked over at him in interest.

"But when I pulled it up, it was a DUI from five years ago."

Peyton rested her head against the back of her chair.

"Okay. Let's call it for tonight. We'll get back at it tomorrow at noon."

"Noon? That's letting a lot of time go by, Captain," said Peyton.

"You have your session with Dr. Ferguson at 8:00, then Marco's in here at 10:00. In the meantime, Simons and Cho, go out to St. Matthews and see if Father Mark will tell you who might have a criminal record in his parish."

"He's not gonna tell us that, Captain," said Cho.

"Tell him why we need to know. If he wants to save a member of his parish, he might be willing to lift the cone of silence."

"It's worth a shot," said Simons, pushing himself to his feet. "Brooks, it's your turn to get us lunch. I want a chicken parm from Lucca's."

"Fine."

"I want the smoked salmon," said Cho.

"Got it."

As they walked out of the room, Peyton glanced at the captain. "What do you want, Captain?"

"Salami on rye."

Peyton rose to her feet and patted Jake's shoulder. "Let's go. Leave the Daisy here and we'll come in together tomorrow."

"Sounds good. I'll bet the Daisy won't start anyway. She doesn't like having her beauty sleep interrupted."

Peyton followed him out to the lobby.

"Brooks?" came Defino's voice behind her.

Peyton turned around.

"Don't be late for your session tomorrow."

She didn't need the reminder. "I won't be."

"Good."

Turning away, Peyton followed Jake into the parking lot. As they walked to her car, she pulled her phone out and pressed the contact for Marco's number. Placing it against her ear, she listened to the ring as she unlocked the doors and slid into the driver's seat.

Marco's voice mail came on, but she didn't leave a message. She'd left three already.

"No answer?" asked Jake as he slid into his seat.

Peyton set the phone down in the cup holder and shook her head. "No, I'm starting to get worried."

"He's probably asleep, Mighty Mouse. It is 1:00AM."

She sighed. "You're right."

"Peyton, I know he's fine. Adonis wouldn't do anything stupid and you know it. He's too…"

"Too what?"

"Uptight."

Peyton gave him a reassuring nod, but he didn't know Marco the way she did. Marco was capable of plenty of stupid as she'd seen many times in the past.

* * *

The heavy bass of a blues track broke the stillness of the room, repeating itself over and over again. Marco blinked open his eyes and stared around in confusion. The soft pink of the walls, the unfamiliar pillow beneath his head disoriented him at first.

The blues piece continued playing to his right.

"Oh, God, what the hell is that?" came a feminine voice next to him.

He rolled his head on the pillow and then closed his eyes. The blond from the previous night lay next to him on her stomach, her hair a tangled mess, covering her face. He pulled back the covers and rolled into a sitting position, reaching for the jacket he'd thrown over the chair next to the bed.

Digging into the pocket, he pulled out his phone and pressed the display, holding it to his ear. "Yeah?" His voice came out rough.

"Where the hell are you?"

Vinnie.

"What time is it?"

"7:00AM. Peyton's been trying to get you all night, but you wouldn't answer. Mom said you left their house pissed off last night."

"I'm fine." Bracing the phone between his shoulder and ear, he reached for his clothes and began pulling them on.

"Where are you?"

"I had a date."

"You had a date? With who?"

"Lisa."

"Who the hell is Lisa?"

"Don't worry about it." He rose to his feet and hiked his jeans around his waist, glancing over his shoulder at the blond. She'd rolled to her back, pulling up the covers and combing the hair out of her face. Her mascara was smeared under her eyes. He reached for his shirt.

"Are you going to call Peyton?"

"Yeah, I'll call her."

"Fine. I'll call Mom and let her know you're all right."

"Thanks."

"Why don't you come by my office later and I'll take you to lunch?"

Marco hesitated, one arm through his shirt. He understood the concern of his family, but they were starting to smother him just a bit. "I've got plans."

"With Lisa?"

"Sure." That worked.

"Okay. What about dinner tonight? Rosa wants you to come by."

"Not tonight. Look, Vinnie, I'm fine, okay? Stop hovering."

"Yeah, you're fine. Okay, look, I'll call later and we can talk some more."

"Great." He tried to keep the sarcasm out of his voice, but it was hard.

"Bye, little brother."

"Bye."

He pulled his shirt on and began buttoning it as he pushed Peyton's number. The phone only rang twice before she picked up. "Hey," came her voice.

He sat down on the edge of the bed and reached for his boots. "Hey. Sorry I missed your call. Is everything all right?"

"Yeah, I was just getting worried. I'm sorry I bothered Vinnie, but I didn't know what else to do."

"It's okay. I got into it with my mom last night and just didn't feel like talking to anyone." He pulled one boot on, stamping his foot to get it in place.

"About what?"

He gave a grim laugh. "It's a long story. I'll tell you later. Don't you have your session with Dr. Ferguson soon?"

"Yeah, can't hardly wait."

"I know what you mean."

"What about dinner tonight with Abe and Jake? You free?"

Surprisingly, he realized he missed that madness. "Yeah, just tell me where."

"I'll text you later, okay?"

"Okay." They both fell silent. He glanced over at the blond. She was watching him closely. "Hey, Peyton?"

"Yeah?"

"I'm really sorry I missed your call last night."

"I know. I'm just glad you're all right. I was getting worried, D'Angelo."

"I know. Talk to you soon, okay?"

"Yeah, bye."

He hung up and slipped the phone into his pocket as he reached for his other boot.

"Who's Peyton?"

"What?"

"Who is Peyton? The woman on the phone?"

He rose to his feet and grabbed his coat. Giving her a wicked smile, he said, "My wife."

Her eyes widened, but he didn't wait for her to respond, backing to the door and pulling it open.

CHAPTER 9

"So, our last session was less than productive, wouldn't you say?" asked Dr. Ferguson.

Marco scratched his forearm. "Why do you say that?"

"I asked you questions and you gave me one word responses. We really didn't get to the heart of anything."

"Is that why you won't give me back my badge?"

"How can I clear you for duty, when you won't communicate with me?"

"What do you want to know?"

"How are you?"

Marco placed his arms on the table. "Here's what I don't understand. If I tell you I'm fine, you say I'm lying to you, or worse in your estimation, I'm lying to myself. That's grounds for denying me my gun. If I say I'm terrible, you report to Defino that I'm unstable and that will be grounds for denying me my gun. You said you were direct. Tell me what it is you want to hear and I'll let you know if I can give it to you."

Dr. Ferguson smiled. "Psychiatry is not an exact science, Inspector, no science is. As you can imagine, the human animal is unpredictable. I can't tell you what I'm waiting to hear until you say it."

Marco held up a hand and let it fall. "Where does that leave me?"

"Yesterday, you mentioned that your mother and brother had returned to their respective homes. What did you do last night?"

"I went to dinner at my parents."

"And?"

"And what? My mother made spaghetti and garlic bread, I ate and I left."

"Your mother is a devout Catholic, isn't she?"

"Yes."

"How is she handling this situation?"

"She's worried about me as any mother would be, but she's always been supportive of my job."

"Who isn't supportive of it?"

"What?"

"By specifying that your mother is supportive, it's implying that someone isn't supportive. I was wondering who that was. Your father?"

"No, he's never said a word one way or the other. In fact, last night he agreed with me when…" Marco stopped and looked away.

"When what?"

He straightened. "My mother asked me to go to confession with her today."

"I see. Did this cause friction between you?"

"Friction, no, but I didn't see the need. I did my job and that's all there is to it. I don't regret it and I'd do it again if the situation arose."

"Do you know the purpose of confession?"

"To absolve us of our sins."

"In a Catholic vision, yes, but in a psychiatric view, it's a bit different." Dr. Ferguson set down his pen. "Confession allows humans to find a way to admit our guilt and find a release from it. If you think about the things people confess, they range from disrespecting one's parents to carnal temptations to heinous crimes. Beyond the release of guilt lies the hope that by confessing our failings, we will find the strength to resist the temptation to sin again."

Marco frowned. "Are you saying she hopes that if I confess to killing the priest, I won't be tempted to do it again?"

"No, I think she believes that the weight of his death is pressing on you to the point of suffocation and you need to give the burden to someone else. I think she believes that it will be the only way for you to find peace."

Then what was this shit about temptation and sin?

"Who doesn't support your job choice?"

Marco was still thinking about his mother, so he had to think over their previous conversation. "My brother, Vinnie. He wants me to quit."

"Did he tell you this?"

"Yeah, but he also talked to Peyton about it."

"Did that make you mad?"

"Of course it did. He blamed Peyton for me continuing on in this career."

"Did Peyton tell you this?"

"No, Vinnie told me."

"Is she the reason you're continuing in this career?"

"What?"

"Is Vinnie right?"

Marco picked at a string on his shirt sleeve. "I was a cop before we were partners."

"But that was eight years ago. What about now?"

"No, she's not the reason." He looked up and met Ferguson's gaze. "In fact, if anything, she was the reason I almost quit."

*   *   *

The divers hauled the body out of the bay.

Half of his clothing was torn away, showing a bloated, grey corpse. It was impossible to tell age or ethnicity. Just deciding he'd been male was difficult enough.

Smith and a few uniforms stood over the body as Peyton and Marco approached. Marco noted that Peyton hung back behind him, her eyes fixed on a spot somewhere out in the bay, watching the fog roll in from the ocean.

"Got any ID?" asked Marco, staring down at the grotesquely distorted features. Hours in a saltwater bath did strange and terrible things to the human flesh. Parts of his cheeks were flaking away.

Smith held out a pair of latex gloves, which Marco pulled on, then he gave him a sopping wet wallet. Marco opened the wallet and thumbed out the man's driver's license. *Joseph Beltran.*

"Jumper?" he asked, looking up at the bridge in the distance.

"Only if he stabbed himself first." Smith bent over and pulled the body onto its side. It made an unpleasant squelching sound. In the dead center of his back was a gaping wound, showing backbone and a spongy grey mass.

Marco bent closer, squinting. "Is that lung?"

Smith started to answer, but his eyes lifted beyond Marco's shoulder. Marco heard boot heels on the concrete, then the sound of retching. He met Smith's look and slowly shook his head. "Honestly, why me?"

Smith gave him a sympathetic smile and let the body settle onto its back again. "She's just green."

"She's certainly green now."

Smith chuckled. "Give her time."

Marco straightened with a weary sigh. "I'm trying, man, I really am." He veered back to the Charger and grabbed a bottle of water out of the cup holder, then he remembered Peyton had stuffed some spare napkins in the glove compartment. He'd thought it was stupid at first, but now he could see a use for them. Gathering the napkins, he walked over to her.

She was bent over a garbage can along the bay walk, her hands curled into fists. The violent spasms seemed to be over for now. He handed her the water bottle and the napkins. She mumbled a thank you and swished the water in her mouth, spitting it into the garbage can.

Staggering over to a bench, she sank down on it and pressed the napkins to her mouth. Marco gave her an annoyed look, but he walked over to her, taking a seat on the end, bracing his forearms on his thighs.

"Can I ask you an obvious question?"

She looked at him from the corner of her eyes. "What?"

Her voice came out rough and he motioned to the water bottle. "Drink some of it."

She lowered the napkin and took a sip.

"Why the hell did you pick homicide?"

"To work with all the hot men."

Marco fought a smile. She surprised him sometimes. "Yeah, nothing hotter than a bloated corpse."

She gave him an arch look.

"You wanna tell me the truth?"

"What truth? So I get a little nauseated looking at dead bodies…"

"Baby, you get more than a little nauseated." He tilted his head toward the garbage can.

She fussed with the cap on the bottle. "My dad's a cop."

He nodded.

"When it came time to go to college, I just couldn't see studying anything else." She shot a look at him. "I tried being a beat cop for a year, but I hated the uniform. Homicide just seemed the most interesting." Shifting on the bench, she folded her leg under her. "Is this why you asked Defino for another partner? You don't think I can handle it?"

He blinked at her. He didn't know what to say. He hadn't expected Defino to tell her. And the truth was she had more experience than he did.

"Well?"

Well, she asked for it. He was honest if he was anything, and there was no point in dancing around the issues between them. If this was going to work, and he wasn't certain it would, she needed to hear it straight.

"Actually, it's your mouth."

"My mouth?"

He nodded. "You got a mouth on you, sweetheart."

"Maybe if you weren't so condescending toward me by calling me *sweetheart* and *baby* all the time, I wouldn't have to bust your chops so much."

145

Fair enough. He did do that, and most of the time he didn't even realize he was doing it. "Okay. Let's say I don't call you condescending names and you don't talk to me like I'm stupid."

She sighed. "Is this one of your *boundaries* you like to set?"

"Yeah, let's say it is."

"Fine. I won't talk to you like you're stupid."

"Good. That doesn't solve the problem of you puking every time you see a dead body, though."

"This is the first time that's happened." She gave a shiver of distaste. "I'd have been fine if you didn't talk about seeing his lungs."

He nodded without conviction.

"And it wouldn't hurt you to smile once in a while."

"Yeah it would. That would be too personal," he said, pushing himself to his feet. "Look, Brooks, I'll watch your back, I'll cover you in a shoot-out, and I'll even take a bullet for you. Just don't expect me to be your best friend."

The look she gave him said he was daft. "Clearly a smile means we're joined at the hip."

"You just said you weren't going to do that anymore."

She stood up and threw the napkins in the garbage. "Come on, D'Angelo. I said a smile, I didn't give you a damn friendship bracelet."

"I just want to make sure you know we're just work partners."

"Well, I guess the matching sweatshirts are out," she said, moving back toward the body.

He stopped and held out his hands in frustration. Someone really needed to teach this hellcat some respect.

*　*　*

Marco returned to his desk carrying a soft drink. It was close to 5:00PM, but he wanted to do a little more

146

research on their bridge diver, Joseph Beltran. Had anyone filed a missing person's report? Did he have a past record?

He slowed when he caught sight of Abe waiting by their desks. He wore a pair of black slacks that flared at the bottom, a bright green silk shirt tucked into the waistband of his trousers, and a thin black tie.

"What are you doing here?"

Abe whirled to face him, placing a hand over his heart.

Marco grimaced. Did the man have to be so damn theatrical?

"Hello, Angel. I thought you'd gone for the night. If I had known I'd get the pleasure of seeing you, I would have dressed for the occasion."

Marco gave him a speculative look. Dressed for the occasion? "Clearly you're dressed for something."

"We're going out."

Marco almost choked on his soda. "We're?"

"Peyton and I." He motioned to her empty desk, then he turned, his dreads swinging with the motion, and gave Marco a sultry look. "Although, I would be delighted to take you out anytime, gorgeous."

"I'll pass." He pulled out his chair and sat down, reaching for the mouse.

"Ready," came Peyton's voice.

"Aren't you just a hot little number!" said Abe.

Marco glanced up. Peyton's hair was loose, he'd never seen it like that, and it spiraled in curls down to her shoulders. She wore a black skirt, red pumps, and a silk tank-top in pale pink that showed off her toned arms. He couldn't believe the transformation. In her everyday get up, she was cute and all, but now…he blinked and blindly reached for his soda. What the hell!

Abe took her hand and twirled her around. "Girl, you are going to get all the straight men hot and bothered tonight."

147

Marco forced himself to look back at the computer monitor. "The fog's in. You're gonna freeze in that get-up, and where are you gonna put your gun?" The minute the words left his mouth, he realized he sounded like an old man.

She grabbed her leather jacket off the back of her chair. "I'm not taking my gun into a nightclub."

Involuntarily, his gaze trailed over her. "You might need it, dressed like that."

She sucked in an aggravated breath, but Abe shifted back toward him. "Why don't you come with us? Then you can protect her virtue with all that hot, hostile testosterone."

Marco started to answer, but Peyton put her hand on Abe's arm. "You're crossing a boundary, Abe. We're not best friends, we're just work partners."

Marco threw himself back in his chair. Damn her, she'd promised to stop the mocking. "What is wrong with being professional?"

"Nothing at all, D'licious," said Abe, "but this is after work and there's nothing wrong with having a little fun either."

"I have fun. I just don't like to mix work with that fun."

They both looked at him as if he were an idiot.

"What? Why can't you keep your home life separate from your work life? I've never understood why people have to make friends out of people they work with. It's stupid."

Abe came to the spot where their two desks met. "You spend most of your time with the people at work. It might be nice to like them, wouldn't it? And for you, a man who has to rely on those *work people* for his life, you might try to be a little more accommodating. Now, I like a man who's all butch and stuff, but come on, Angel, you keep growling at people and they may not want to help you out if you need it."

He pointed a long finger, pressing it to Marco's desk. "Case in point. If you keep building walls between us, I might just decide not to tell you that your jumper was stabbed with a military grade knife."

Marco frowned. "What? How do you know that?"

"Size of wound, striations on the bone where he nicked a rib, and what's more…" Abe leaned even closer. "The killer must have had military training."

"How do you know?"

"The angle of the strike. He knew what he was doing because that blade passed between two ribs and clean into the heart."

Marco looked over at Peyton.

"Maybe the victim was also in the military?"

Marco nodded.

"I can stay and we can run it."

"No, go. I'll check his background, but the rest can wait until tomorrow."

"Okay." She slipped her leather jacket on and Abe straightened, offering her his arm.

"Later, Angel'D," he said as he led Peyton toward the front.

"Later." Marco watched them go, then looked back at the computer. What the hell was happening to him? Friday night and he was the one sitting here working instead of going out. Bull shit. He could get some friends together and…

He slumped back in his chair. He didn't have any friends. His friends from high school had all gone away to college, while he'd stayed here. And he had a strict policy about making friends at work. He used to go out with his brothers, but they were all married and having kids now. No late nights for them.

His eyes drifted toward the front of the building. No way was he going to follow Peyton and that crazy M.E. He couldn't let her know that they'd gotten to him. If he gave even this much ground to her, he'd be wearing her matching sweatshirts by Christmas.

* * *

Marco unlocked the Charger and pulled open the door. "He was a Marine, a tour of duty in Afghanistan. Last year he was honorably discharged with a Purple Heart and was diagnosed with PTSD."

"Shit," said Peyton, sliding into the passenger seat.

"His mother lives close around here." Marco started the Charger and put it in reverse. "She hasn't been notified yet."

Peyton didn't respond as they pulled out of the precinct parking lot and onto the street.

"So, did you have a good time last night?" he asked conversationally.

She glanced over at him. "Yes."

"Yes? That's all?"

"Any more would be crossing the boundary, now wouldn't it?"

He fought the wave of annoyance every conversation with her created. He didn't want to go back to Defino and ask for another partner again, but she was making it hard.

They pulled in the parking lot of a small apartment complex and exited the car. The complex had two stories and the doors were on the outside. In fact, it looked like an old motel that had been converted into apartments circa 1970.

"Which one?"

Marco glanced at the note he'd taken. "203. Up there."

They walked to the stairs and began climbing.

"How do you want to do this?" he asked.

She paused. "I hadn't given it much thought. Wow, this is going to be hard."

"Yeah."

With a shake of her head, she continued climbing. Marco was bewildered. What the hell did she think she was going to do? Just go in and tell the mother her son was dead? Shouldn't they have discussed it before they got to the door?

A window box beside the door was overflowing with red geraniums. Marco stared at them, feeling his heart begin to pound. How the hell did you deliver this sort of information? He could imagine his own mother receiving this news and it made him feel sick inside.

Peyton drew a deep breath, then knocked. Marco reached out to touch her elbow, hoping she'd tell him what she planned, but the door opened and a middle aged woman looked out. Her hair was cut short and she wore glasses. She had on a waitress uniform from one of the cheesy 50s diners near Market.

The minute she saw them, her eyes went wide.

"Mrs. Beltran?" asked Peyton.

She nodded, lifting a hand to her throat.

"Mrs. Beltran, I'm Inspector Brooks of the San Francisco Police Department…"

"He's dead, isn't he?"

Peyton blinked. "What?"

"My son. He's dead."

Marco wanted to bolt. He couldn't stand the look in the woman's eyes, the devastation and dawning comprehension.

"I'm sorry, ma'am," said Peyton.

The woman made a strange noise, half between a sob and a gasp, then her knees crumpled. Peyton moved first, catching her, then Marco stepped forward, getting an arm around her waist and lifting her to her feet again. They staggered over to the first chair they found, a battered recliner, and got her into the seat.

Peyton sat down in front of her on a stool and took her hands.

"How?" Tears glimmered in the woman's eyes.

Peyton glanced around, then pointed to a box of tissue on a rickety wooden end table. Marco retrieved it and held it out to her. Peyton placed it on the woman's knee, but she didn't take one.

"How did my son die?"

"He was stabbed."

"Stabbed?"

"Yes."

The woman made a strange gasping noise. Marco didn't know what to do. Peyton looked around, then left the stool and located the kitchen to their right. Marco watched after her as she grabbed a glass off the dish-rack and filled it with water, carrying it back to the woman.

"Take a sip." She closed the woman's hands around the glass and helped her lift it to her lips.

Tears raced down the woman's face as she lowered the glass and Peyton handed her a tissue, taking a seat on the stool again.

"Your son was in the military, Mrs. Beltran?"

"Yes, Marines."

"How long?"

"Eight years." She motioned to a sofa table against the wall. A picture of two young men in Marine uniforms smiled back at the camera.

Marco picked it up, studying it, then he handed it to Peyton. She gave the woman a sad smile. "He was very handsome."

Mrs. Beltran nodded. "Looks just like his father." Her hands shook and she closed her eyes. "I knew this day would come. I knew someday someone would show up at the door and tell me this, but there's no way to prepare yourself for it."

"No, there isn't."

"I thought it would be someone from the military. He served in Afghanistan."

"When did he get out?"

"About a year ago. They diagnosed him with PTSD. He got caught in a road side bomb, messed up his head." The tears flowed faster. "He wasn't the same when he came back."

Peyton looked at the picture again. "Who's the other young man?"

She gave a wounded smile. "His best friend, Richie, Richie Sundmore. They were friends since high school. Did everything together, even enlisting."

"Where's Richie now?"

"He's still in the military. I think he was headed for Iraq last I heard."

Peyton handed the picture back to Marco and he replaced it on the sofa table. "You said he wasn't the same when he came back."

"No, he would hardly leave the house and he'd get spooked over the littlest things. Car backfire. Slamming door. 4th of July was hell."

Peyton nodded. "Was he able to work?"

"No, but lately…" She balled the tissue up in her hands. "Lately he was better."

"Any reason?"

"He met a girl." Mrs. Beltran smiled through her tears. "He was so in love with her and she seemed so good for him."

"What's her name?"

"Stacey?"

"Stacey what?"

Her smile grew grim. "I can't remember." She pressed a hand to her forehead. "I can't remember what her last name was."

Peyton took her hand. "It's okay. We can figure it out."

Mrs. Beltran nodded distractedly.

"Is there someone I can call? Your husband?"

"My husband died ten years ago, Inspector."

"Anyone else?"

She shook her head, then paused. "My sister. She lives in San Bruno. She might be home."

"Can I have her number?"

"It's in the kitchen. Just press speed dial and number one. It'll ring her directly."

"Okay." Peyton rose and went into the kitchen.

Marco looked after her. He didn't want to be left alone with this woman. He didn't know what to say. Peyton had struck just the right tone with her, honest, but sympathetic.

"Do I have to identify the body?" She made that strange gasping noise again.

Marco thought of the bloated and battered body they'd recovered and hated the thought of this woman being subjected to that. "He had ID on him, so I don't think it'll be necessary."

She stared blankly in front of her, as if she saw something he couldn't. "Do you think he was murdered?"

Marco wasn't sure how to answer that.

She looked up at him, her eyes meeting his, and her grief was so stark and raw that he almost bolted again.

"It looks that way," he forced himself to answer.

Peyton came back into the room. "She's on her way over."

"Thank you, Inspector." Curling her hands on the arms of the chair, she levered herself upright. "I think I need to lie down."

Peyton caught her arm and steadied her.

"I'm sure you have things to do."

"We'll wait for your sister to arrive." She put her arm around the woman's waist and helped her walk toward the bedroom.

Marco stared at the recliner, uncertain what to do. It didn't bother him to look at dead bodies, but this...this was a nightmare. He didn't think he could ever do this again.

When Peyton came back out, he studied her. "How did you know what to say?"

"What?" She gave him a bewildered look.

"How did you know what to tell her?"

"I don't know. They went over it in the Academy."

"Yeah, but this was so much worse. So...real."

Peyton nodded. "I know." She glanced over her shoulder toward the bedroom. "Look, we have at least a half hour before the sister gets here. I'm gonna call the D.A. and see if we can get a warrant for Beltran's phone records. We need to find out who this Stacey is."

"Good thinking."

"I noticed another door back there when I took her to her room."

"You think it's his?"

"It's worth a look around, isn't it?"

"Yeah, I'll do that."

"Keep an ear out for her. She fell apart when she got to her room, but she didn't want me to stay. I don't think she wanted me to hear her crying. If it gets real quiet, though, we better check on her."

"Got it."

As she pulled out her phone to call the D.A., he walked through the tiny kitchen and into a hallway beyond. He could hear crying coming from the door at the far end, so he knew that was the mother's room. The bathroom door was open, so he tried the only other door directly across from the kitchen.

It opened onto a bedroom not much bigger than a closet with a twin bed. The covers were so tightly made up, it could only have been done by a trained military professional. An American flag draped down the wall over the bed and a dresser was shoved up beneath the only window. Marco walked over to it and opened the blinds.

Pale sunlight filtered into the room and he shivered. Just a couple of days ago, Joseph Beltran woke up here and began his day, not knowing it would be one of his last. He'd survived a tour in Afghanistan to end like this, a body floating in the bay.

A small desk sat on the wall opposite the window and Marco walked over to it. A black box lay in the center of the desk on a loose pile of papers. Marco carefully lifted the lid. A heart shaped medal with George Washington's profile lay nestled in a bed of purple silk. With just the tips of his fingers, Marco traced the edge of the medal, running the pad of his thumb across the purple ribbon.

Tilting his head, he noticed the medal lay on top of a newspaper article. Closing the lid, he carefully shifted it to the side and picked up the article. The headline read *Marines Receive Joyful Homecoming.* A group of Marines stood together in what appeared to be the San Francisco Airport. Marco quickly scanned the article. It had been written less than a month before, but Mrs. Beltran said Joseph came home nearly a year ago.

The article talked of the families that had come out to greet their returning heroes, the joyful reunions, the hugging and sobbing. A few of the Marines were quoted, sharing their happiness to finally be home. One even mentioned that this was the first time he'd held his baby son.

The article continued on another page, which had been carefully cut out of the newspaper and stapled to the back. As he lifted up the first page, he saw a second picture of a smiling Marine, his arm around his pretty, young wife.

Marco's eyes widened. The Marine was Richie, the same man in the photo Mrs. Beltran had on her sofa table. Scanning the caption below it, Marco caught his breath.

Backing to the door, he hurried into the hallway. "Brooks?"

She appeared in the entrance to the kitchen. "The D.A.'s working on the warrant. We should have it by this afternoon."

Marco held out the article. "I don't think we'll need it. Look at this."

Peyton frowned at him, but she crossed the room and took the paper from his hand. "What is it?"

"Look at the second page."

She lifted it and studied the picture.

"Read the caption."

Her mouth fell open and her eyes snapped to his face. "This is Gunnery Sergeant Richard Sundmore and…"

"And his wife, Stacey."

*　*　*

Marco fell silent.

"Wait." Ferguson leaned forward. "What happened?"

Marco gave him his slow smile. "I think our time is up, Dr. Ferguson."

He bit his bottom lip and looked down at his notes. "Very clever, Inspector D'Angelo. Seems you've taken a page out of your partner's book, dazzle me with stories to keep me happy."

"Did it work?"

"Do I get the rest?"

"Peyton can finish it for you."

Ferguson chuckled. "I think you're extracting a bit of revenge against me, Inspector."

"No, she just tells a better story."

"I don't know about that." He made some notes on his pad, then folded his hands on top. "You learned to respect her there, didn't you?"

Marco nodded. "I know everyone has a problem with how involved she gets in our cases, even I get pissed at her, but if I ever have to have someone on my team, she'd be my first choice. She's what every cop should be."

"And yet, that involvement almost got her shot during your gang case."

Marco held out his hands. "We carry guns, Dr. Ferguson. The one thing they impart on you in the Academy is that there will come a time when you have to draw it, which means there will come a time when we will be on the receiving end of gunfire. And more than that, every cop knows that at some point in his career he may have to not only draw that gun, but fire it. If you carry a gun, odds are you will kill someone at some point."

Ferguson studied him, then he picked up his pen and wrote some more. Marco dared to hope he might have found the "right" thing to say, that maybe he would be reinstated, but when the doctor looked up again, his expression was exactly the same.

"I'll see you tomorrow, Inspector D'Angelo," he said.

"You do know tomorrow is Sunday, right?"

"You do know detectives don't work traditional hours, right? Besides, you have plenty of time to yourself as it is."

Marco forced a tight smile. "Tomorrow it is then."

CHAPTER 10

Peyton placed protective glasses over her eyes and covered her ears with the bulky ear protectors the firing range gave her. She drew her gun out of its shoulder holster, bracing it with her free hand. The target lay directly before her and she took a deep breath before depressing the trigger. Firing off a number of rounds, she waited a moment, then pressed the button next to her to advance the target forward, so she could check the accuracy of her shots. Four out of the six shots were dead on, the other two near enough to stop someone cold. She pressed the button and the target rolled back to its spot as she drew on it again. She emptied the rest of her clip into it, then drew the target back to her for another inspection.

Pulling out the clip, she loaded another 15 rounds into it, then ran through the process once more. After reloading a second time, she holstered her gun, pulled off the ear protection, and removed the glasses.

As she turned to go, she came face to face with Holmes, one of her least favorite uniforms. Raising his brows over his blue eyes, he gave her a smug look. "Practicing?"

Her fingers tightened on the ear protectors. "Yeah, you?"

"I come here once a week."

"Where's Bartlet?" Peyton figured a cop as green as Bartlet could use firing range practice whenever he could get it.

"Back at the precinct. He's a natural shot."

Peyton gave a non-committal nod. "Good for him."

Holmes pursed his lips and rocked back and forth. "You heard from D'Angelo?"

"Yeah."

"How's he holding up?"

"You know Marco, never gonna give anything away."

"Yeah. Tough Italian."

"Yeah."

He gave her a serious look. "And you?"

Peyton frowned in surprise. When the hell had Holmes ever given a damn about her? "Frustrated."

"About?"

"The case, Marco's suspension…"

"The shooting." He nodded at the firing range behind her.

Peyton blew out air. "Yeah." No use pretending it was different. "I keep going over and over it in my mind and I arrive back at the same conclusion. I should have been the one to fire on the priest."

"You know, I usually take any opportunity to get on you about something…"

"Really? You? I hadn't noticed."

He gave her a smile. "Anyway, we were all out there that night and it was freaky. In my fifteen years on the force, I've never been that sure I was going to be shot."

Peyton nodded.

"Here's the point, and if you ever tell anyone I said this, I'll flat out deny it." He pointed a finger in her face. "Whatever happened out there, you did exactly what you had to do. None of us got shot and that's pretty freakin' amazing. So, stop beating yourself up over this. If you really need something to worry about, I'm happy to supply it, but this isn't it."

Peyton was surprisingly touched by his comment. "Thanks, Drew. I appreciate it."

He gave a careless shrug. "I can let this one slide. You're bound to do something soon that will give me fuel for more ribbing."

"Of course. You're a real gem, ain't ya?"

He patted her shoulder as he moved past her. "Just treatin' you like one of the guys, Brooks."

Peyton had to smile.

* * *

At noon, they gathered in the conference room. Peyton arrived a few moments later, bringing lunch from Lucca's. She passed the sandwiches around and Defino sprang for sodas. Jake accepted his pastrami on a sour dough roll and pulled it open as he thumbed on his tablet.

He pulled the paper log out of his evidence case and slid it into the center of the table, then entered the church bulletin board address on the tablet, while he took a bite of his sandwich. A shock of pepper struck him first, then garlic exploded in his mouth. He looked up at the others in surprise.

Bill Simons had taken a huge bite and nodded around his mouthful. "Good, innit?" he mumbled.

"Like freakin' heaven," said Jake in awe.

Peyton smiled over at him. "How long you been in San Francisco, Jake?"

"Since college."

"And you haven't had Lucca's before?"

"Never got the opportunity."

"A Lucca's virgin," quipped Simons.

They all laughed and continued eating. Jake scanned over the list of events and found ten brand new ones. He started clicking on them to eliminate any that weren't run by men. That brought it down to six.

"Marco sure loves a Lucca's sandwich," remarked Simons to Peyton.

"Yeah, he does."

"Wait," said Jake, glancing up, "I thought he was vegetarian."

"They serve vegetarian, Jake."

Jake eyed his pastrami. "Seems like a waste to me."

"Enough chit chat," scolded Defino, "Let's get to work."

Silence descended in the room as they searched the bulletin board and researched events, adding new items to the chart when they eliminated something. Hours came and went. Cho went out and replaced their sodas with coffee and still they searched. At one point, Peyton left to call Marco and Abe to reschedule dinner to later that night. Another hour passed, then Peyton reached out and picked up the list, scanning it.

"Nothing's fitting, Captain. What are we going to do?"

Jake scrolled up to glance over the earlier entries. One caught his eye – a camping trip for this very weekend, but the destination was Huddart County Park in Woodside. "Hand me the list, Peyton."

She passed it over to him and he searched it for the camping trip. It wasn't on there.

Defino looked over at him. "What you got?"

"There's a camping trip to Huddart Park in Woodside for this weekend."

"I saw that," said Cho, "but it's not in San Francisco."

Peyton glanced over at him, then back to Jake. "Who's running it, Jake?"

Jake tapped on the entry. "Lewis Booker."

"I'm on Megan's List right now," said Simons. "Spell the name for me."

Jake did.

After a moment, Simons shook his head. "Nothing."

Peyton was clicking on her own keys. "Hold on."

Jake watched her as she typed into the keyboard.

"I've got a divorce decree and a custody order."

"Open it," said Defino.

Peyton clicked on the link and they waited while the computer pulled up the information. Her eyes shifted as she scanned the page. Cho got to his feet and moved to her side, leaning over her so he could see the window as well.

They both sucked in air and Cho turned to Defino. "His wife has temporary custody of the kids."

"Why?"

"He's under investigation for child molestation, Captain."

Defino was up and moving. "Let's get out to that park. What the hell time is it?"

"5:00PM," answered Peyton, glancing at her computer screen.

"Shit. We've got less than two hours to sunset and Woodside is a good 45 minutes away."

The three inspectors went into motion.

"Cho, take Smith, Holmes and Bartlet. Brooks, get on the phone to the ranger station at the park and alert them. I'll call the sheriff's department in San Mateo County and get clearance. Simons, get flak jackets and…"

"Bring the car around."

"Good." She paused and looked at Jake. "Nice job, Mr. Ryder."

Jake gave her a grim smile. "Thank you, Captain."

Peyton paused on her way out the door. "Call Marco and Abe and tell them dinner is postponed. I'll call later."

He nodded, then caught her arm to stop her. "Be careful, Peyton, okay?"

"I will. Oh, and Pickles really needs a walk."

Jake gave her an aggravated look. "I'm serious."

"I know." She patted his hand. "I'll be careful." Then she was gone.

*　*　*

Peyton tried to reach the ranger station at Huddart Park repeatedly as they drove toward Woodside, but there was no answer. Then she put a call into the local police force in Woodside and asked them to go to the park, since they could arrive there faster.

It was nearly 6:00PM by the time they reached the entrance to Huddart Park. Coastal redwoods rose around them and the filtered light was dim beneath the weight of the trees. Peyton undid her seatbelt as Simons pulled up to the ranger's booth and showed his badge. A tall, thin ranger stepped out to meet them, followed by a female sheriff's officer in uniform. Glancing over her shoulder, she could see the patrol car with Smith and the others pull up behind them.

"Have you located Lewis Booker?" demanded Smith.

"A group checked in yesterday afternoon, saying they belonged to St. Matthews' Church," said the sheriff's officer. "We went out to the campsite, but someone there told us they'd gone hiking hours ago. We haven't been able to locate him."

Peyton gripped the headrest behind Simons.

"We have a ranger waiting in the campsite for them to return," offered the ranger.

"We need to find Booker stat," said Simons. "How many officers can you get out here to start searching?"

"It'll be dark in about two hours," said the ranger.

"Yeah, so we better haul ass."

"What about a cell phone?" asked Peyton.

"Did the person at the camp know if he had a cell phone on him?"

The sheriff's officer shook her head. "Everyone in the group stored their cell phones in a locked box back at the campsite. The idea was to commune with nature, no distractions, get close to God."

"Shit," said Simons, hitting the steering wheel.

Peyton opened the back door and climbed out. "Take us to the campsite and call everyone you can get to meet us there. We've got to fan out and search every trail."

The ranger pointed to a jeep parked behind the station and the three of them ran over to it.

"Deputy Janice Miles," said the sheriff's officer.

"Peyton Brooks."

Miles opened the passenger side door and motioned Peyton inside. She slid into the seat and looked over at the ranger, searching for a name tag. A small silver one rested on the left pocket on his shirt, Thomas Aiello.

"How big is Huddart Park?"

He started the engine and threw the car in reverse, turning it deftly up the road heading deeper into the park. "Over 12,000 acres."

Peyton felt her stomach drop. How the hell were they going to cover that much ground before it got dark?

Picking up the radio beneath the console, the ranger called for all available park personnel to meet at Toyon Campground 2. The drive to the campground took a good ten minutes. Peyton stared at the digital clock on the dashboard and fidgeted. They were rapidly losing daylight

As they pulled into the area, a group of people had gathered around another ranger. Peyton threw the car door open and climbed out. Simons and Cho were right behind them, followed by Smith and the other two uniforms.

"Do we have maps of the trail?" she asked, heading over to the group.

Ranger Aiello grabbed a handful out of the back of the jeep and carried them to the picnic table in the middle of the campground. The second ranger came over and Peyton showed him her badge.

He motioned to the people gathered around. "Some of St. Matthew's party is returning now. They were told to meet back here by 6:00PM, before it gets too dark."

"Has anyone seen Lewis Booker?"

The ranger shook his head.

Peyton turned to Aiello and waved him forward. "Give everyone a map. Pair up and select a trail. Deputy Miles, write down which teams take which trail and stay here to coordinate the search as people return. Make sure to question the rest of the St. Matthew's group and see if anyone remembers where Booker went."

"Got it."

Peyton took a map from Aiello and handed it to Simons and Cho. Then she passed one to Holmes and Bartlet. A third went to Aiello and the other ranger. "Anyone else coming?"

"A couple more. But it'll take a while for them to get here," said Aiello.

"We can't wait." She nodded at Miles. "You send them as soon as they get here."

"Done."

"Smith, you're with me." She grabbed a map and held it out for Miles to mark a course. While she waited, she watched the others depart, her eyes catching Simons and Cho as they moved toward the start of their trail.

Miles handed her the map and Peyton laid it on the picnic table so she and Smith could orient themselves. "Here's the campground." She placed her finger on the spot, then looked up. "That must be the trail."

Smith nodded and led the way. The campers parted, allowing them to pass, but they were murmuring, confused by what was happening. Peyton didn't have time to interview them, so she pushed through without answering any questions.

They took to the trail, a well-worn path leading into the forest. Redwood trees rose up on either side of them and the amount of light immediately dropped.

"Do you have a flash light?"

Smith pulled one off his belt and held it out to her. She folded the map and shoved it in the back pocket of her jeans, then turned on the flashlight to make sure it worked, clicking it off again. Smith's radio crackled and Holmes' voice came through, indicating they'd found the start of their trail and were beginning down into a canyon.

Sounds from the campsite quickly faded away to be replaced by an occasional rustling in the underbrush. Soon the trail began to climb and Peyton pulled at the neck of her flak jacket, wishing they didn't have to wear the bulky garment. Woodside in summer was a great deal warmer than the City.

As the light faded, she tried not to get herself spooked. They were staying on a clear trail and only had to turn around to find their way back to the campground. Still, it felt a little too like Alcatraz for her. Sure, the terrain was vastly different, but the circumstance was eerily familiar. Since the start of this case, they'd been behind the 8 ball, unable to get a jump on their opponent, uncertain of his next move.

And it made her miss Marco all the more. She liked Frank Smith very much, but he wasn't Marco.

A rock twisted under her foot and she stumbled.

Smith glanced over his shoulder at her. "You okay, baby girl?"

"Yeah. Just trying not to imagine the sorts of things running around out here."

He gave a tight laugh. "Like what?"

"Werewolves. Zombies."

"I think Zombies like cities better, more brains to find."

"Are you saying people are smarter in cities?"

"Hell no. I'm saying there's more of them."

She laughed. "But werewolves, yes?"

"Werewolves, aliens."

"Space aliens?"

"Yeah, don't they always come down in a forest or something and suck people up?"

"I think that's wheat fields, isn't it?"

"Corn. It's corn. That shit always freaks me out when I see it growing."

Peyton laughed again. He was making her feel less afraid. "You're right. Corn is freaky shit."

He turned and smiled at her in the fading light.

Just as he turned back around, they heard a woman's scream.

It cut through the still forest like a siren and they both froze.

"Where the hell did it come from?"

Smith shook his head.

Peyton realized she had her hand on her gun.

Then the woman screamed again.

Her heart kicked into her ribs, but she could finally pinpoint the sound. "Over there." She pointed to her left.

"Leave the trail?"

Peyton drew her gun and nodded.

Again came the scream – a high, terrified shriek that sent birds rocketing into the air and lifted the hairs on the back of her neck. She took off running toward the sound, dodging trees and fallen branches, brambles and bushes, with Smith right behind her.

They tore through the underbrush and landed abruptly in a wide part of another trail where a bench had been placed to look at the trees. A body was huddled at the base of the bench and Cho was bending over it. Behind him stood Simons, bent at the waist, fighting desperately for his breath.

The woman stood to the side, hunched over, covering her face with her hands, sobbing brokenly. Smith went to her as Peyton walked across the clearing to Cho, her chest rising in a rapid pant, her gun gripped in her hand.

Cho also held his gun, but his left hand was feeling at the man's jaw for a pulse. Peyton looked over his shoulder, then gave an involuntary gasp and backed up. The man's throat had been slit from ear to ear, a bib of blood staining the front of his shirt.

She turned away, closing her eyes and fighting for composure.

"God damn it!" growled Simons, straightening and walking in a crazed circle.

Peyton couldn't look at the body. "Is it Booker?"

"Shouldn't I wait for a CSI?" asked Cho.

"We have to know, Nathan. If it isn't him, we've got to keep looking." She couldn't believe how reasonable her voice sounded when she felt panic edging up inside of her.

Holmes and Bartlet burst through the trees, followed a moment later by Aiello and the second ranger. Bartlet's face blanched at seeing the body and he turned away, going to the head of the trail.

"Holmes, get on the radio and get every unit out here to scour this park. Maybe the killer is still here."

"On it."

Peyton forced herself to look over at Cho as he pulled the man's wallet out of his back pocket. As soon as he opened it, he bowed his head. Peyton knew what he found.

"Is it Booker?"

"Yes."

"We need to find the card." She didn't want to give any more away with all these people standing around.

Cho held up the wallet. In a credit card slot next to the plastic window for the driver's license was a familiar white business card with red lettering. Peyton flicked on the flashlight again and shined it on the card.

Clean-up Crew.

∗   ∗   ∗

Jake paced by Maria's desk.

"Sit down. You're making me nervous."

Jake turned to say something to her, but stopped as he saw Bill Simons loom outside the precinct door. The big man pulled it open and stomped inside, followed by Cho, Smith, Holmes and Bartlet. Peyton came last and wouldn't make eye contact with him as she stepped beyond the half door.

Defino came out of her office, her arms crossed as if she were cold. "Everyone okay?"

Simons nodded, but his expression looked anything except okay.

Peyton leaned against the counter before Maria's desk, staring at the toe of her boot. Jake wanted to say something comforting, but he felt like an outsider.

"Where's the body?"

"On its way to the M.E.'s office," answered Cho.

"Here?"

Simons and Cho nodded. "Brooks got them to turn jurisdiction over to us."

"Good. What's happening at Huddart?"

Cho leaned on the counter next to Peyton. "The sheriff's department shut the park down, sent everyone home after they checked their IDs. It was too dark to search any further, but they're going back out tomorrow, see if they can find anything. Their CSIs will go over the crime scene."

"Did we interview the woman who found the body?"

"Brooks did," said Simons.

"How did she find him?"

Simons looked over at Peyton, but she didn't seem inclined to answer, so he continued. "The group had gone into the forest in pairs. They were instructed to find a place to mediate on God's glory. The woman, Joyce Evans, was paired with the youth leader, Lewis Booker. They walked to the bench on the trail and split up with a plan to meet at the bench by 5:30PM, so they could walk back to camp together."

"How far away from the bench did she go?"

Simons shrugged.

"A ways," answered Cho. "She continued up the trail and then went off into the trees. She found a tree that was hollowed out by fire and sat down inside it."

"She lost track of time," finished Simons. "She got back to the bench almost at 6:00. He was already dead."

"She didn't hear anything, see anything?"

Both Simons and Cho shook their heads.

Defino gave a shiver and hugged herself tighter. "Brooks, you okay?"

She looked up and met Defino's gaze. "We screwed up."

"How?"

"We had it figured out. We had the pattern down, we even knew the victim."

"I know, but we just didn't get there in time. We got close, next time we'll get him. He's bound to slip up. And you don't know, he may have slipped up here. Tomorrow the CSIs will canvass the scene and they might find something."

Peyton shook her head. "This was our opportunity."

"There will be another."

"No, we had the pattern, but he'll change it now after these last two kills. There will be another pattern and someone will die before we figure it out. There will *be* another body."

Jake looked down. The silence in the room felt like thunder.

Defino crossed around Maria's desk and reached for Peyton's hand, folding it in both of her own. "That may happen, but it hasn't yet. I have faith that we will stop him and I need you to have it as well."

Peyton met her eyes, then she forced herself to nod, tightening her grip on Defino's hands. Defino gave her a faint smile and released her.

"Go home, everyone. We will get back at it tomorrow."

They all dispersed, moving into the precinct to get their possessions. After they were gone, only Jake and Peyton were left in the lobby. "Come on, I'll drive," he said, taking his keys out of his pocket.

She nodded woodenly and walked to the half-door. He held it open for her and they moved from the lobby into the parking lot. He pulled out his phone and sent a quick text to Abe as he'd promised.

Peyton frowned at him. "What's that?"

"We're still meeting Abe and Marco for drinks."

Peyton shook her head. "I want to go home, Jake. Besides, Pickles needs to go out."

"I went home and fed him, walked him and set him down with a bone."

"Then you came back?"

"Yeah."

"Why?"

Jake unlocked the Daisy. "I needed to know what was going on."

Peyton gave him a faint smile. "Thanks."

He shrugged and slid into the driver's seat, reaching over to unlock her door. She sank into the seat and rested her head back on the headrest, then she shifted back and forth.

"This is the most uncomfortable seat I've ever sat in."

"Hey, it's paid for."

She gave a half-laugh. It was the first laugh he'd heard in a while.

"Come on, Peyton. Let's grab a drink, then we'll go home."

"Fine. One drink."

Jake turned the key on the Daisy and she coughed to life. "Well, to be honest, we're meeting Abe, so who knows how many drinks or what ungodly concoction they'll be?"

* * *

Marco and Abe had a booth in the bar when they got there. Peyton slid into the seat next to Abe and looked at the drink he held. Poured into a martini glass, it was pink and bubbly with raspberries floating on the bottom.

"Do I dare ask what that is?"

Abe beamed a smile at her and held it out. "It's a Flirtini. Try it."

"A what?"

"A Flirtini. Vodka, champagne and a splash of cranberry juice for the beautiful pink color."

Both Marco and Jake stared at him with their mouths open.

"Try it."

Peyton shook her head and pushed it away. "I'll pass."

A pretty blond waitress appeared beside her. "What can I get you?"

Jake tore his eyes away from Abe's drink. "A beer. Whatever's on tap."

"Great. And you?"

"A shot of Jack Daniels," Peyton answered.

Marco's attention shifted to her and he lifted his beer, taking a sip. "You okay?"

She gave him a shrug and watched Abe drink. "Do you really like the taste of these crazy drinks you order?"

"Of course. This one is particularly fun. You get the punch of vodka..." He leaned closer to Jake and Marco. "...and the tickle of champagne."

Marco shook his head with a half-smile, but Jake reared back.

The waitress arrived and set the drinks in front of them. Peyton pulled out her wallet, but Abe stopped her with a hand on her arm. "I have a tab going," he said.

Peyton reached for the shot as the waitress moved away. She downed it in one swallow and gave a shiver as it blazed into her empty stomach. The three men watched her, then Abe tapped Jake's forearm.

"You know how to play that?" He pointed at a pool table in the back corner.

"Pool?"

Abe nodded as he took another sip.

"Yeah."

"Show me how to play."

"You want to play pool?"

"That's what I said, isn't it?"

"Why?"

Abe batted his lashes. "Men seem to love it, so it's a way to meet men."

"Not your kind of men." Jake lifted his beer, but Marco hit him with his elbow.

"Show him how to play."

Jake gave them both a bewildered look. "Why?"

Peyton spun the empty shot glass around with her finger. "So Marco and I can talk, Einstein."

Jake's chin lifted in comprehension, then he pushed himself out of the booth.

Abe gave Peyton a wry shake of his head as he slid out to follow him. "Straight men, lord help us."

When they were out of earshot, Peyton turned to Marco. "How did your session with Dr. Ferguson go?"

"I told him about our case with the Marine who was stabbed in the back."

"You told him stories?"

"Yep, took a page out of your book."

The waitress returned. "Do you want anything else?"

"Another shot," answered Peyton.

She turned to Marco with a brilliant smile. "What about you?"

Marco held up a hand. "I'm good."

As she walked away, she glanced over her shoulder at him.

"She thinks you're hot," said Peyton.

"Stop evading the elephant in the room. What's going on with the case?"

Peyton spun the glass again. "Defino said she'd pull my badge if I told you anything."

"Defino isn't going to pull your badge. She had to put me on leave because of the shooting, but she can't afford to lose you too right now."

Peyton figured he was right, but she knew Defino was worried about her stability and she didn't help it tonight with her outburst. "I don't feel like talking about it."

"So your answer is to down shots?"

"It's worked for us before."

"When did you eat last?"

"I had Lucca's today."

"When?"

"Lunch."

"It's almost 10:00PM, Peyton."

Her first name, spoken by him, brought tears welling into her eyes and she ducked her head. "I hate when you call me Peyton."

"You hate when I call you your name?"

She fought back the tears. "You only call me that when you're angry with me or there's something wrong."

He thought about it for a moment, then lifted his beer. "I think you're exhausted and hungry."

The waitress returned and set the shot down in front of her.

Marco picked up the menus. "Can you bring us a sample platter too, please?"

"You got it," she said with another dazzling smile.

Peyton tossed back the shot. It didn't burn as bad this time.

"Tell me what happened."

As the whiskey warmed her belly, Peyton realized she didn't care if Defino suspended her. She hated keeping secrets from Marco. "Jake figured out the identity and location of the next victim."

"Jake?"

"Yeah."

"The Jake Ryder who couldn't catch a clue just now?"

"Yeah."

"Okay, go on."

"We identified the victim as Lewis Booker. He recently went through a divorce and lost custody of his children."

"Child molestation?"

"Suspected. It was still going through the courts." She curled the shot glass in her fist. "He was a Youth Leader for St. Matthew's and taking a group on a campout at Huddart Park in Woodside."

Marco pulled at the label on his bottle, but he was focused on her.

"We got out there. We had the local sheriff's department, half of our precinct, and every ranger within miles. We scoured that park trying to find him."

Marco stopped pulling the label. "You were too late?"

Peyton banged the shot glass on the table. "We had him, Marco. We knew who the victim was and where, but he still got to him before us."

Marco released his held breath.

The waitress came back with the sample platter and set it in the middle of the table with four small plates. "Want another shot?"

Peyton nodded.

"No, she'll have a beer. Same thing I'm drinking."

Peyton glared at him, but she didn't correct him.

"I'll be right back." Sensing the tension, the waitress backed away.

"You're not my mother, D'Angelo."

"And I'm not your babysitter. I'm not carrying your ass into your apartment tonight."

Peyton let it go, looking over at Abe and Jake playing pool. Abe wasn't taking it very seriously and the pool cue was waving dangerously close to some patrons talking at a table near them.

Marco dished up a plate of food and pushed it over to her. "Eat something."

"I don't think I can. My stomach's in knots."

"Then you won't be drinking any more either."

She picked up a fried zucchini and bit off the end.

"Look, this is why every cop fears getting a serial killer. You're always operating two steps behind him."

Peyton pressed a finger to the table. "But we had him. We figured out the pattern." She held up her hand. "Then we lost him. Five people are already dead and there will be another."

"You don't know that."

"I do. We had the pattern, but he changes it after two killings. Where do we begin to look now?"

"Who got this last body?"

"It should go to Abe."

"Okay, each killing was done in a different way. How'd he do this one?"

"Slit his throat."

"Then let's take this apart logically. In order to slit someone's throat, you have to get them from behind and you have to subdue them. Quickest way is an arm across the upper body."

"Right." Peyton took another bite, watching him.

"What's the first instinct if someone grabs you there?"

"You grab their arm."

"And you dig in, trying to dislodge them, right?"

"Right."

"Epithelials under the finger nails."

"What if he wore a long sleeved shirt?"

"Your other hand is going to go on the hand and try to pull it away."

"Gloves."

Marco braced his head on his hand. "Okay, so you figured out he used internet sites for all four murders."

"Right."

"Where would he go next? Where do most child molesters meet their victims?"

"Chat rooms."

"Chat rooms. And what chat rooms would children frequent?"

Peyton thought for a moment. What did children do on-line? She had so little experience with them. She was sure if she ever had a child, she would forbid him or her from ever logging onto the computer.

Marco's blue eyes glimmered in the light from the candle.

"Video games."

He gave her a short nod. Leaning forward, he dropped his voice. "I'll bet Stan Neumann knows the most popular ones. He can set up a dummy account on any number of sites, pretend he's trolling for his next victim. Anyone who responds in San Francisco has got to be suspect, right?"

Peyton felt a glimmer of hope rise inside of her. "You're brilliant," she said, then she stood up and leaned across the table, kissing his cheek.

"Your beer," said the waitress, plunking it down rather heavily, then she turned and walked away without looking back.

Peyton and Marco exchanged a look, then they broke into laughter.

CHAPTER 11

"So, I understand it was rough last night," commented Dr. Ferguson, looking up from his notes.

Peyton stopped fussing with a loose curl. "What?"

"Captain Defino told me it didn't go well."

"What exactly did she tell you? Did she tell you about the case?"

"In as much as it pertains to your emotional state."

"What does that mean exactly?"

"I know you lost a man you thought you'd be able to save. She expressed to me that it rattled all of you."

Rattled was a good word. "You do realize that this has to be kept strictly secret, that none of this can leak out of this room?"

"Inspector Brooks, do you have any idea how many years I've worked with cops? Do you think I don't know the importance of discretion?"

"I would hope so. If the media got a hold of this case, there would be panic."

He studied her. "How long do you think you can keep it from them? A family member, another precinct, even a witness is bound to slip up at some point."

"We need to keep a lid on it for as long as we can."

"Understood." He slid his fingers along the cylinder of his pen. "Captain Defino seemed particularly concerned that you blamed the victim's death not on the killer, but you and your partners. Do you still feel that way?"

Peyton shifted in the seat. "This was our chance to catch him and we messed up. We should have found him in time."

"You do understand that the killer does not operate under the same ethical restraints as the police? You have certain protocols to follow, but he has none."

"I understand we have five bodies and there will likely be a sixth before we figure out the pattern again." She braced her forehead with her hand. "Look, Dr. Ferguson, I know you're trying to help, but right now I can't get my head around the fact that we had a chance to save someone and we failed. Still, I'm here and I'm working, so just this once can we not dismantle this situation?"

He studied her a moment longer. Lowering his head, he made a note and Peyton resisted the impulse to sigh in frustration. When he looked up, his expression was intense. "When I met with your partner yesterday, he told me about a case you had with a Marine."

"Joseph Beltran."

"That's right. He said you'd tell me how it ended."

Peyton fought a smile. Marco had hooked him good. "Where did he stop?"

"He'd just found the newspaper article with the picture of Joseph's best friend, Richie, and his wife, Stacey, the girl Joseph's mother said was his girlfriend."

Admiration rose inside of Peyton. Marco was playing him like a fiddle and bringing her into the game. "So, we called Dispatch to get an address for the Sundmores' house and we drove over there. On the way, I called for backup..."

* * *

Marco parked a few doors down from the Sundmore house. The houses on this block almost squatted over the street, so it was impossible not to see anyone arriving. A patrol car pulled up directly across the street from the house and Peyton recognized Smith in the driver's seat.

Leaning over the seat, Marco pulled out two flak jackets from the back and passed her one. "Put this on."

Peyton began to struggle out of her shoulder holster. "I hate wearing a flak jacket."

"You a fan of being shot?" he grumbled as he pulled off his own gun.

"No."

"Then what? It doesn't match your outfit."

Peyton shifted in the seat to glare at him. "No, it restricts my movements."

He paused and looked over at her.

"Why do you have to be hostile every step of the way? Was my comment about flak jackets too personal or something?"

"Okay, I'm sorry."

The apology wasn't enough anymore. "You said you'd have my back, but you have so little respect for me, I have to wonder."

"I keep my word, Brooks. You can trust me."

She threw open the car door. "Can I, because you're making me think I can't." Then she got out, tugging on the uncomfortable jacket.

He climbed out after her. "Look, Brooks…"

"Stuff it. I don't want to hear it. This has gone on too long now. If you want me to trust you, you better start proving it." She bent back in the car and grabbed her gun. "Bring the radio. We might need to communicate with our backup." Then she started walking toward the house.

Smith met her on the sidewalk.

"Why don't you wait by your patrol car?" she said, surveying the front of the house. A driveway on the right led to a single car garage. In front of them was a porch with a couple of metal chairs lined up to the left of the front door. A single window rose behind the chairs, covered with a curtain. As Peyton watched, the curtain moved. "Someone's clearly home."

Smith nodded, catching the motion as well. "Don't take any chances."

"I won't."

Marco jogged up to them. He had the radio microphone hooked to the shoulder of his flak jacket. She didn't even bother to look at him as she started toward the front door. He was on her heels and when they climbed onto the porch, he pressed the button for the doorbell.

Peyton leaned close to the door to listen for voices, but all was silent. Straightening, she caught motion to her left at the curtain again. Marco reached out for the bell again, but Peyton caught his hand. The curtain had pulled back to reveal a man with a crew-cut, holding a gun pointed at a woman's head. She recognized both of them from the photo in the newspaper.

"D'Angelo."

He looked over, then he hooked a hand in the back of her flak jacket, pulling her away. Pressing the button on the radio, he leaned into his shoulder, dropping his voice. "Smith, get SWAT out here ASAP. Also a hostage negotiator."

Peyton shook off his hold. "We don't have time for that."

"The hell we don't."

Peyton reached for the badge at her belt, holding her other hand out and away from her body. "Richie Sundmore? I am Inspector Peyton Brooks from the San Francisco Police Department. I'd like to talk to you." She held up the badge and took a step closer. The woman's eyes widened in terror, but Richie's face remained fixed.

"What do you want?"

"We'd like to talk to you about Joseph Beltran."

"I ain't got nothing to say." His voice was muffled behind the glass.

"Tell you what. Why don't you release your wife and then we can talk, just you and me?"

"Brooks," hissed Marco.

She waved him off.

"I said I ain't got nothing to say."

"I saw the newspaper article about your return. You were in Iraq?"

He gave her a bewildered look. "What?"

"You were stationed in Iraq, right?"

His grip on his wife tightened and she whimpered. "Yeah."

"How many tours did you serve there?"

"One. One was enough."

"I can only imagine what that must have been like."

"You can't imagine it at all."

"You're right. Nothing here compares with that." She carefully replaced her badge. "It must be hard coming home."

He glanced at his wife, then his eyes snapped back up as Marco shifted weight. Peyton stayed stock still. "Yeah, it's hard."

"I read a lot of articles about guys coming home and they all say slowing everything down is hard. They say that when you're over there, you're so wound, ready to react at the slightest sign of trouble, and then you get here, and you're still in that elevated flight or fight stage."

He nodded, his attention focusing on Peyton. "Yeah. Like everything's a threat."

"That's what I hear. In Iraq, you're fighting for your life, but when you get home, everyone wants you to be the same person you were when you left."

He nodded again.

"And I'll bet you want things to be the way they were too, right?"

He briefly closed his eyes. "Yeah, that's right."

"But nothing's the same, is it?"

"No." He stared at his wife.

Peyton could hear sirens coming in the distance. She didn't have much time to end this before SWAT arrived and she didn't want Richie to die. "Richie?"

His gaze shifted to her.

"You don't want to do this. This isn't what a Marine does. You survived Iraq, you can survive this."

"You don't know what you're saying."

"Brooks," Marco warned.

She had to take a chance. She was running out of time. SWAT would not wait.

"Richie, let her go. A Marine would be strong enough to let her go."

"She's a whore!" His voice came clearly through the glass.

"No, she's just as confused as you are. Everything changed when you went to Iraq for her too. She was left here alone and she didn't know if you would make it back alive or not. I know it isn't fair or right, but this isn't the answer."

"What is?"

"That's something we can work out, but you have to let her go."

"She cheated on me! With Joe, with *Joe*."

"I know, but this doesn't solve it. In fact, it dishonors your service. You deserve better than this." He was clearly torn and the sirens were getting closer. "Richie, there isn't much time. SWAT is on the way and you know what that means. You know they aren't going to talk their way through this. Don't let them make the decision for you. You make it. You be the Marine that I know you are. Let her go, please. Let her go."

His eyes scanned the street, then suddenly he pushed her. She hit the window and scrambled for the front door. Marco grabbed Peyton's flak jacket and yanked her behind him as he leveled his gun on the window.

"Drop the gun, Sundmore!" he shouted.

The door opened and Stacey appeared, tears streaking down her face. Peyton grabbed her and together they ran down the stairs as patrol cars and SWAT vehicles filled the street. Whipping around, Peyton looked back at Marco.

Sundmore had his hands raised, the gun dangling from his index finger. Marco eased to the door, then he dashed inside. Peyton started to go after him, but Smith caught her arm and held her back as SWAT fanned out, covering the house.

A moment later, Smith's radio crackled.

"Suspect subdued," came Marco's voice.

"Well done, everyone," said Captain Defino. "Well done. Go home and get some rest."

Smith patted Marco on the shoulder as he walked away from the front of the precinct. Passing Peyton, he gave her a wink. She smiled back at him. Finally, she'd earned someone's respect.

"So, what are you doing tonight, Marco baby?" asked Maria.

He was leaning against the front counter before her desk, his arms crossed. His eyes lifted to Peyton, but she turned away, not waiting to hear what he said. She walked back to her own desk and pulled her jacket off the back of her chair, sliding her arms into it.

She heard his boot heels on the tiles as he walked toward her, but she didn't bother to acknowledge him. He took a seat on the open space where their desks butted up against each other. "I'll drive you home."

"Don't bother. I'll get a ride with a uniform or take the bus."

"You can take the Charger and drop me off at home."

She met his eye. "No thank you."

"Come on, Brooks. Stop busting my chops."

"Fine. Take me home then."

He rose to his full height and swept his arm out, indicating she should go first. She suppressed the sharp retort that came to mind and walked in front of him to the lobby. Maria gave Peyton a snide look as they walked past, but Peyton ignored her.

"Later, Marco baby," she called.

"Later, Maria," he called back, giving her one of his smiles.

Peyton pushed open the outer door and crossed the parking lot to the Charger, waiting while he unlocked it. She sank into the passenger seat and stared out of the window. He got in next to her and started the big engine.

They didn't talk as he pulled out of the precinct parking lot and turned onto the street. The sun was setting behind the buildings and people hustled back and forth across the sidewalk, headed home. After a few moments, Peyton realized he wasn't headed out toward the avenues, but rather down toward the wharf.

"I live on 19th," she said without looking at him.

"I know where you live, I pick you up every morning."

"Well, this isn't the way."

"We're going to get a beer."

She shifted and looked at him. "What did you just say?"

"We just solved a case, probably saved two lives, and I think we deserve a beer."

"Hold on a minute, D'Angelo, what about the boundaries, the rules?"

"We'll add this as a rule. After a successful case, we'll get a beer." He stopped the car at a stop light and glanced over at her.

"I have plans tonight."

"With who?"

"Abe. We're going dancing again."

The light turned, but he didn't move.

"Green means go," she said, nodding at the light.

He started the Charger moving again. After a few moments, he exhaled and his fingers tightened on the steering wheel. "Call him and tell him to meet us."

"What?"

"Tell him to meet us at the bar. We're going to *The Fiddler's Green*."

"*The Fiddler's Green*? Isn't that that Irish Pub on Russian Hill?"

"Yeah, you ever been there?"

"No, I'm not exactly Irish." She motioned to her dark skin and curly hair.

He laughed. "You don't have to be Irish to go there. I'm not Irish either."

"Oh, they're gonna love Abe."

He laughed once more.

She pulled out her phone and sent Abe a text, then leaned back, completely bewildered. She'd given up on her partner. She was sure he was never going to come around, then he goes and does this. She wasn't sure how to take it.

The Fiddler's Green was crowded when they got there. A lot of people had the same idea – a quick drink before going home. As they weaved through the people standing around, she marked all of the woman who followed Marco with their eyes. He did make an impression, so tall and broad, his shoulders cutting a path through the people.

He found a booth in a back corner, away from the crowds. It was near the bathroom and almost behind the bar. He immediately took the seat with the best vantage point, the cop's seat, where he could look out. She slid in next to him, close enough to hear, but far enough away to maintain her distance. She wasn't ready to forgive him just yet.

Her phone vibrated in her pocket, so she pulled it out. *A drink with an Angel, hell yes!* was Abe's response. She smiled, then tucked the phone away.

"What'd he say?"

"He's coming." Peyton didn't think it was a good idea to relay Abe's message.

A waiter appeared. "What'll it be?"

"I'll have a beer. Domestic," said Marco. He lifted his brows at Peyton.

"I'll have the same."

"Any appetizers?"

Peyton picked up the menu. "How about a plate of potato skins?"

"Sour cream."

"Yeah."

187

With a nod, he left.

Peyton reached for the candle in the center of the table and tilted it, watching the wax run up the sides of the round jar. She felt Marco's eyes on her, but she wasn't ready to acknowledge him yet.

"You're good at talking to people."

She shrugged, trying to make a pattern with the wax.

"They calm down when you start talking. I'm not good like that."

"Because you growl."

He held up a hand and let it fall. "I guess."

She tilted her head and looked at him. The candle light flickered in the hollows of his cheeks. "Dead bodies don't bother you at all?"

"No. I mean I don't love them, but..."

She laughed, returning to the wax. "Why did you pick homicide?"

"It seemed interesting. You know, figuring out puzzles."

"I guess so. Finding that article was a stroke of genius."

"Not so much."

But she could hear the pleasure in his voice. So he wasn't immune to praise.

He drummed his fingers on the table. "I wasn't sure about us at first. You know, as partners."

"I know. You still aren't."

"It's not that. It's just..." He stopped as the waiter returned with the two beers and the potato skins. He arranged everything on the table and turned to go.

Peyton set the candle down and reached for one of the small plates, dishing up a potato skin and pouring sour cream over the top of it. Marco reached for his beer, taking a sip.

Peyton bit into the crisp appetizers. The smoky flavor of the bacon was complemented by the smooth bite of cheddar and the tang of the sour cream. "Oh, that's good," she said, closing her eyes in pleasure.

He gave her a faint smile, twirling his beer around.

"Try it," she said, pointing at the plate.

"I don't eat meat."

She paused with the skin halfway to her mouth. "Come again?"

"I don't eat meat."

She eyed him up and down, the way his ribbed sweater stretched taut across his upper body, his biceps straining the sleeves. "You're kidding me, right?"

"Wrong. I haven't eaten meat in years."

"Why?"

"Health, and I like animals."

She set the potato skin down. "Why didn't you say something? We could have gotten something else."

"Don't worry about it."

She reached for her beer and took a swallow. "Wow, that shocks me."

"Why?"

"I just didn't expect it."

"Maybe there's a lot you didn't expect about me."

"Maybe. What were you saying before?"

"I don't remember."

"I said you weren't sure about me as your partner."

He met her gaze as he took another sip of his beer. "You're just not like anyone I've met before."

"How?"

"You challenge everything I say, everything I do. Most women…"

"Most women?"

He dropped his eyes.

Peyton looked out at the bar. Even now, a number of women were looking toward them, well, him, trying to catch his attention. "Oh, I get it. Most women act like Maria around you."

He gave a slight nod.

She grabbed her beer and took a swig. "Get over yourself, D'Angelo. You aren't that gorgeous."

He looked up in surprise. Then they both smiled.

"Well, there you are?" came a loud voice. "Why are you hiding all that pretty back here?"

Peyton glanced up to see Abe standing there, holding a pale gold drink with a blue flame rising off the top of it. He slid into the seat next to Peyton, setting the drink down. Peyton's eyes widened, staring at it.

"What the hell is that?" asked Marco.

Abe placed his elbow on the table and rested his chin on his hand. "It's called Burning Love, D'Angel. You wanna try it?"

"It's D'Angelo," Marco corrected. "No, I don't want to try it."

"What a shame!" He nudged Peyton with his shoulder. "Burning Love is soooo much fun."

Peyton laughed.

"Sounds like an STD," quipped Marco.

Peyton and Abe stared at him in shock. She'd never heard him utter anything remotely close to a joke before.

"Meow," said Abe, then he winked at him. Turning to Peyton, he said, "Come on, cutie. You'll try it."

Peyton shook her head vigorously. "I avoid anything that flames." Then she realized what she said and gasped.

Abe and Marco both laughed at her. She ducked her head, reaching for her beer, and realized she was actually having fun. It was hard to stay serious when Abe was around. And for the first time, Marco wasn't being hostile.

"So, I thought this wasn't allowed according to the by-laws or whatever you two came up with."

"Boundaries," she corrected.

"Whatever." He leaned forward and blew on the flames. Peyton was worried he'd set his dreads on fire. "Anyway, doesn't this cross the line?"

She glanced over at Marco. He shrugged, his eyes fixed on Abe as he tried to take a sip of his drink.

"Sometimes lines need to be moved," he said, shifting his gaze to Peyton.

She smiled at him and nodded.

* * *

Peyton stopped talking. She didn't feel like revealing any more. These sessions walked a tightrope between therapy and voyeurism. Dr. Ferguson hadn't written anything in a good half hour, caught up in the story. She just couldn't figure out how any of this was helping her. He didn't offer advice, he didn't tell her how to get over the anger she felt or the panic that gripped her when she thought of the serial killer running loose. And it didn't restore Marco to her.

"We still have time," he prompted.

"Can I be honest with you?"

"Of course."

"I don't see the point of these sessions. All they do is bring up old memories that have nothing to do with the case we're currently working."

"Everything has bearing, Inspector Brooks. You're frustrated that I've removed your partner and I'm trying to understand the complex bond the two of you have formed. As I told you before, it fascinates me to work with cops. The partner bond is so deep, so complicated, and no two are the same."

"So, what? We're lab rats for you?"

"Not at all, but I'd be remiss if I didn't say that what I learn here with you two will also color my work with other partner units. We see these kinds of bonds in life or death situations all the time. Between cops, between soldiers on the battle field, between firefighters – these are not people who would usually choose to be bonded to each other, but thrust into these situations and the connection is made."

She leaned forward. "How does that help us right now? How does that make me any less angry or Marco fit to return to work?"

"Whether you know it or not, you are learning about yourself through our sessions, Inspector Brooks. You're examining your life with detachment, something you would never do unless it was forced upon you."

Peyton felt that this was a lot of arrogant bull shit. She wasn't learning a damn thing about herself or Marco, except she hated working this case without him. The most difficult case of their career and this psychiatrist was keeping him on the sideline.

"How many more sessions, Dr. Ferguson?"

"I can't tell you that."

"Why not?"

"Why are you angry?"

"Because my partner is on leave."

"That's not why you're angry."

"Then why don't you tell me why?"

"I'm not here to give you answers. You're here to figure them out yourself." He scratched at his chin. "Although, I would ask you to examine what you're feeling a bit closer."

"Meaning what?"

"Are you sure it's anger you feel?"

Peyton felt her shoulders tightened. Oh, she was feeling angry, all right. "Yeah, I think I know anger."

"Directed at whom?"

He was as good a target as any, but she realized she wasn't really angry at him. "At no one. At the situation."

"That's why I know you aren't feeling anger. We can be mad at people, but we can't be mad at situations. When you know what you're feeling, what you're really feeling, then we can stop the sessions."

He waited, sitting on the other side of the table with his yellow tablet and his blue pen, staring at her as if she would suddenly have an epiphany. She stared back at him. Maybe she was wrong, maybe she was angry at him after all.

After a moment, he leaned back, stretching. "See you tomorrow, Inspector Brooks," he said.

CHAPTER 12

Stan Neumann pushed his glasses back on his nose, making his eyes loom larger as he shifted from laptop to desktop, clicking and typing in a manic sort of way. Watching him fascinated Peyton because he reminded her a little of herself, always in motion, never still.

Across the room, Cho was messing with his phone, typing something into it, his focus completely centered on the small device. Big Bill Simons did some awkward stretching thing in the open space behind the table, but Peyton tried to avoid looking at him. Seeing such a big man contort himself couldn't look anything less than obscene.

Jake sat on the table behind Stan, watching him with a look of pained concentration on his face. Peyton observed that whenever he could perch himself on a table or shelf he did so, letting his feet dangle like a little kid.

Hiding a smile, she wondered what Dr. Ferguson would make with all of them.

She couldn't help but wonder what Marco was doing at the moment. Had he been here, he would have positioned himself at Stan's shoulder, prodding him to stay focused with a stern, "Stan!" interjected for emphasis.

Finally Stan leaned back and wiped a hand across his mouth. "Done," he said, still staring at the screen. "I've got a profile set up in as many top games as I can."

Cho looked up from his phone. "Meaning what?"

"I'm posing as a teenager, thirteen. From here I can insert random comments into the chat windows on every game where we've set up a profile. I can lay a trail that a predator might follow and we'll see if we get a bite."

"How certain are you that we will get a bite?" asked Simons, coming to the table.

Stan shrugged. "We'll probably get a bite, but it doesn't mean it'll be in San Francisco, and it doesn't mean our serial predator will be watching."

"This is pissing in the wind," grumbled Simons.

"It's all we've got, Bill," said Peyton.

"I also put in a call to ICAC."

Cho frowned, lowering his phone. "ICAC?"

"The Internet Crimes Against Children Task Force. They'll also help us monitor known sites beyond the gaming community. They said they'd contact us if they get anything in our area."

"Good thinking, Stan," said Peyton.

He gazed up at her with wide eyes and a faint smile.

"Now what do we do?" asked Simons.

"We wait."

Simons rolled his head on his shoulders.

Cho bounced to his feet. "We need to go out and talk with Booker's widow anyway, Bill."

"Yeah, we'd better get on it." He moved toward the door.

"Call us if you get anything, Brooks," said Cho as he followed him.

She nodded, then sat down next to Stan. "How wide does this ICAC cover?"

"They represent eleven counties all over the Bay Area. They cover a lot more area than I can and they can do it 24/7."

"So when do you start chatting or whatever with our system?"

"Already have. I programmed a number of canned responses just to get things going. When you troll these games, you'd be surprised at how similar the comments and conversations are."

"How will you know if we get something?"

"I have it programmed to alert me if certain phrases are used. ICAC gave me the most common ones used by child predators."

"That's amazing, Stan."

He blushed and looked at his keyboard. "Cool of you to say that, Peyton."

"I'm serious. I'm really impressed."

He glanced at her, then rubbed his thumb across the space bar. "Thanks."

Peyton caught Jake making a face behind Stan's back. She glared at him, but her glares no longer seemed to have any impact. Sharing a house for the last nine months had obviously taken the fear out of him.

"So, I heard you're not seeing the D.A. anymore, eh, Peyton?" commented Stan.

"No, we broke it off a while ago."

"Sorry."

"Don't be. I'm not sure lawyers and cops mix well."

He seemed to remember Jake was still there, casting a glance toward his right shoulder. "Remember when we went out to dinner."

"I do. It was fun."

"Yeah, it was."

Except the part where a guy in the bar made a comment about her ass and Stan stepped up to defend her. He would have been physically hurt, if Peyton hadn't flashed her badge. She'd been worried that would demoralize poor Stan, but it hadn't. In fact, he suggested she might want to pull her gun the next time. They hadn't had a second date.

"I guess it's too soon, I mean after the D.A."

Jake made a choking sound.

Peyton ignored him, focusing on Stan. "I decided to take a break for a while, Stan."

"Yeah, I get that. I just went through a break-up too."

"You did?"

"Yeah, you'd probably have liked her. I met her at a convention in Sacramento."

"What kind of convention?"

Stan looked back at the computer. "Graphic novel convention."

"Graphic novel?"

"Comic books," said Jake behind them.

"I know what graphic novels are, Jake," she said.

195

"Really?"

"Yes."

"Do you read them?" asked Stan.

"Sure I do. All the time."

"Which ones?" said Jake with a wicked smile.

"What?"

"Which ones do you read?"

"Well, not so much now, but in the past…" Stan looked at her with such devotion, she hated to disappoint him. "I read them in high school."

"Which ones?"

Peyton shot Jake a glare, but Stan was waiting for an answer. "Archie and…Scooby."

Jake looked like the cat who ate the canary, but Stan gave her a reassuring nod. "Those aren't bad, but my favorite is Batman."

"Oh, yeah, Batman is good."

Maria stuck her head inside the conference room. "Brooks?"

Peyton shifted toward the door, grateful for the reprieve.

"Defino wants you in her office, stat."

"Excuse me," she told Stan sweetly, then she stood up and walked toward the door, punching Jake in the shoulder as she went.

*   *   *

Marco climbed the stairs to his parents' house. It was almost 1:00PM and the game started at 2:00. After his session with Dr. Ferguson, he'd had just enough time to grab a six-pack before heading over. He was actually looking forward to a quiet day with his father – watch the game, drink a few beers, and then have dinner in front of the television. That way he could avoid another conversation about church with his mother.

Just as he lifted his hand to knock, the door swung open and Emilio ran into him. Marco blinked in surprise, catching the boy with his free hand.

"Sorry, Uncle Marco," he said, then he raced down the stairs.

Behind him came his brother Sergio, skidding on the hardwood as he stopped at the door. "Later, Uncle Marco."

"Later."

"Later!" called a little voice as six year old Michel squeezed past, hot on his cousins' heels.

"Slow down, you monsters!" shouted Serena in his ear, leaning out the door. She had her two month old baby in her arms, but he didn't even flinch when his mother shouted. Marco figured the poor thing had gotten used to it in utero. "Hey, baby," she said, reaching up to kiss his cheek. "Come in."

Marco almost bolted back down the stairs. If Serena was here, it meant the whole clan had converged on his parents' house for Sunday dinner. He really wasn't ready for that yet. "I…"

"Marco," shouted Vinnie, coming forward. "The boys run you over?" He took the six-pack from his hand.

His mother came out of the kitchen, carrying a tray of stuffed mushrooms. "There you are. Your father was wondering when you'd get here." She stopped in front of him and held out the tray. "No meat."

He took one and allowed Vinnie to pull him into the room. Rosa hurried across to him and threw her arms around his shoulders, standing on her tiptoes. "How are you, sweetheart?" she whispered in his ear.

He hugged her in return and nodded. When she stepped back, Sofia was there, pulling him down to kiss his cheek. He looked around for his father. Leo occupied his recliner in front of the television. Tonio had been given the seat next to him, so he could prop his leg on the stool. Marco's two brothers, Bernardo and Franco, took up the entire couch, each lounging in a different corner.

197

They acknowledged him with a lift of their hands and a nod. Marco nodded back and placed his hand on his father's shoulder. Leo looked up and covered it briefly with his own. "Grab a chair from the kitchen, Marco. Pre-game's about to start."

Marco hunkered down beside his father's chair so only he could hear him. "I thought it was just going to be the two of us today, Dad."

Leo forced his eyes away from the TV set. "I know, but your mother wanted to make it into one of her Sunday dinners. You know how she is."

Marco forced a smile. "Yeah." Rising to his feet, he clasped his nephew's hand. "How's the leg?"

"Better. I just have the brace now and I can start putting weight on it."

"Good." He moved past him and headed to the kitchen, popping the mushroom in his mouth. He had to turn sideways to avoid Vinnie as he came through the entrance, headed toward the TV with two open beers. He stopped and deposited one in Marco's hand. "I was coming to bring you this."

Marco took it. "Thanks." He let Vinnie slide past him, then he stepped into the kitchen, pausing by his mother to kiss her cheek. She patted him with a distracted hand covered in flour. "Can I make you a sandwich?"

"No, I'll wait for dinner."

His nieces, Cristina and Pia, were folding ravioli at the table. He kissed each of them on the cheeks and picked up a piece of spinach, sticking it in his mouth. They giggled and went back to folding. Carrying his beer, he walked to the back door and opened it, stepping down the stairs and into the yard.

Typical of San Francisco, his parents' yard was small, shaped in a perfect square and paved in terra cotta paving stones. His father had made raised beds along the perimeter and they were choked with grape vines. At one time he'd had plans to make his own wine. That had lasted all of a summer, but the vines had grown into a hoary, gnarled tangle that created a privacy screen from the neighbors. Right now they were lush and green with leaves, a few bunches of grapes visible here and there.

His mother had a bistro set arranged in the middle of the patio, but he took a seat on the stairs instead, lifting the bottle to his lips and drinking. The sun shone down overhead and the warmth seeped into his shoulders. Behind him he could hear the sound of the television and the murmur of voices in conversation, and beyond the walls of the yard, he could hear kids playing and cars rolling past.

The door opened at his back and his brother, Franco, stepped out, holding his own beer. He walked down the steps and took a seat next to him. Marco was a little disappointed. He wanted a moment of quiet to himself. Besides that, he and Franco were closest in age, so they had spent their childhood fighting over everything. They'd never been anywhere near as close as he and Vinnie were.

"So who sent you out here? Vinnie to talk me into quitting my job, Mama to get me to go to confession, or Dad to make me watch the game."

Franco gave a laugh. "No one. I thought a moment of peace sounded pretty good."

"I guess you don't get much of that with three kids, eh?"

"Naw. I can't remember the last time I went to the bathroom without someone pounding on the door."

Marco smiled.

"Vinnie said you had a new girl, that you might bring her over today. Lisa?"

Marco studied the label on his beer. "Yeah, Vinnie didn't get that right."

"Ah, I see. You know Vinnie. He's got everyone's life figured out for them."

"Well, he might have something. He hasn't done bad for himself."

"Did he really tell you to quit being a cop?"

Marco took a sip. "Worse, he told Peyton to quit, so I would."

"He did what?"

"Yeah. I get why he did it, but bringing Peyton into it wasn't okay."

"No, you're right. How's she doing?"

"I don't know. I can't really get her to talk to me. It's been strained between us since the shooting. I think she feels responsible or guilty."

"Why?"

He looked out at the grape vines. He and Franco had climbed behind those vines as kids, making forts and hiding things they didn't want their older brothers to find. That had been the worst thing they'd had to overcome, two older brothers who tormented them. "She feels like she should have taken the shot."

"Should she have?"

"No."

Franco's brows rose. "No?"

Marco scuffed his boot against a rough spot on the stairs. "Do you go to church regularly?"

"What's regularly?"

"Confession on Saturday, mass on Sunday."

"I go to mass when Sofia tells me to."

Marco chuckled. "Devout, aren't you?"

Franco shrugged. "When you only get two days off a week, it makes devotion hard sometimes." He finished off his beer. "Mom asked you to go to confession?"

"She wants me to be forgiven for killing the priest."

"Whew!" Franco leaned back on the stairs, bracing himself with his elbows. "That's a load of guilt to carry around."

"Which?"

"Mom."

"Yeah."

"What do you think? Would it help?"

Marco choked down the immediate defensive response that rose inside of him. He didn't want to ruin this moment with his brother. "Why do you say that? Help what?"

"You. I'm not gonna lie to you, little brother, everyone's worried about you. I didn't know Mom asked you to go to confession, but I've heard all the talk, the concern. Why do you think we're all here today?"

"Not for Mom's raviolis?"

"Well, yeah, for Mom's raviolis, but mostly for you, so you know we're behind you."

"I'm not going to confession, not for that. I did my job and that's all it was. Everyone wants me to be bothered by it. It upsets people that I'm not, but I'm not going to lie to myself or God about guilt I just don't have."

Franco leaned forward and draped an arm across his shoulders. "You sure about that?"

"Yes."

"Then tell me why you're sitting out here on the stairs when there's a game on inside."

Marco looked down into the beer bottle and swirled the liquid around.

Franco tightened his grip, then released him, patting him on the knee as he pushed himself to his feet. Turning around, he climbed back up the stairs and pulled the door open, disappearing inside.

Marco lifted the beer to his lips and took a swallow, but he didn't leave his spot.

* * *

"So, you and Stan, huh?" said Maria, circling around her desk and taking a seat.

"Me and Stan what?"

Maria made kissing noises.

Peyton gave her a practiced smile. "Now, sweety, you know you're the only one for me. You don't have anything to worry about. I would never leave you."

Maria ran her hands over her ample curves. "You wish you could get something like me."

Peyton paused, fighting an amused smile. Maria's lips tightened against her teeth in frustration. She always played into Peyton's hand. "But I would never settle for someone like you," she added.

Peyton leaned on her desk. "So you did a little experimenting, did you? In high school?"

"What? No."

Peyton gave her a wink. "It's okay. I don't kiss and tell." She moved to Defino's door and knocked.

She could hear the captain's voice behind the paneling, but she didn't think it was directed at her. Pushing open the door, she stuck her head inside. "Captain?"

Defino was standing behind her desk with her phone pressed to her ear. She motioned Peyton inside. Peyton shut the door at her back and sank into the melamine chairs before Defino's desk.

"Yes, I understand, but this case is very sensitive. No, I'm not trying to suppress anything, I just don't want to set up a panic situation…no, I understand, but…okay, yes, sir, I'll get back to you first thing in the morning." Defino lowered the phone and drew a deep breath, holding it. Her short brown hair was mussed.

"Was that the Mayor?" questioned Peyton.

"How'd you guess?"

"You get a tick in your cheek whenever you talk to him."

Defino shook her head and leaned on the desk. "A reporter for the Examiner has gotten wind of something and when she couldn't get through to our Media Relations Unit or the Chief of Police, she contacted him."

Peyton lowered her head. This is what she was afraid might happen.

"He misdirected her, but he feels the public needs to be warned."

Peyton's eyes snapped to Defino's face. "Warned? They're going to panic."

"That's what I told him, but it didn't do me any good. We need to sit down and write out our own press release, get out in front of this, so we control the story, not the other way around."

"Captain, this is the very thing a serial killer wants. They want publicity. If we go public with this, we may inadvertently move up the timing for the next target."

Defino's brows rose. "Inadvertently?"

"Abe gave me a word of the day calendar for Christmas."

"Good gift." She sank into her chair. "Do you really think that will make a difference, Brooks? He killed someone when you were right on top of him. This guy is beyond bold."

"I think I don't want to take a chance. Can't we try to convince the Mayor? And to be honest, he owes us one, Captain."

"I don't think he views it that way. We've cost him two big contributors in Claire Harper and Jedediah O'Shannahan."

"Yes, but we haven't divulged his connection to them in the media. I can't promise I won't slip up if I have to give an interview."

Defino squinted at her. "That's blackmail, Brooks."

"Not at all, Captain. You know me. I talk off the cuff and who knows what I might say?"

"All right. I'll try to dissuade him tomorrow, but if not, we still better be prepared."

Peyton replayed the captain's words in her mind. "You said this reporter got wind of something?"

"Right."

"What do you mean?"

"She knew about the priest's death and that a cop was on leave."

"What if she figures out who that cop is?"

Defino slumped back in her chair. "You better alert D'Angelo before *he* talks off the cuff."

Peyton reached for her phone.

* * *

Marco sipped at his cola and watched the people in the mirror over the bar. He wasn't sure why he kept coming to *The Fiddler's Green*, but it was the only bar he knew that didn't feel desperate and seedy, and he didn't want to go back to his empty apartment just yet. Dinner at his parents' house had been harder than he thought.

He loved his loud, boisterous family, but tonight it had felt suffocating. Everyone was acting just a little off. If his mother had mentioned how beautiful mass was that morning another time, he felt like he might explode. Then Vinnie had been almost manic, trying to lighten the mood by dragging everyone into a conversation about the benefits of organic spinach. Even Marco's father, who could usually be called upon to stay solid and centered, had made Bernardo tell everyone about his new mini-van at least five different times. No one gave a damn how the seats folded into the floor. He'd left before dessert, something he knew would send his mother into fits.

"Let me guess. Black Russian?" came a feminine voice at his shoulder.

He shifted and eyed the woman. She was tall, at least five seven, with long legs and a shapely, but slender figure. She was African American, beautiful face, straight black hair that feathered back and cascaded over her shoulders. Her eyes were large, darkly lashed, and a light brown.

"No, I'm Italian."

She laughed. "I meant your drink."

"I know. Just plain cola."

"Can I buy you another one?"

He patted the stool beside him. "Sure."

She sat down and motioned the bartender over. "I'll have a glass of Riesling, and a plain cola for the gentleman."

The bartender was the same one working the night he picked up Lisa. He gave Marco a smirk as he wandered away.

"I'm Genevieve," she said, holding out her hand.

Marco accepted it. "Marco."

"You come here often?"

"Ooh, bad pick up line."

She blushed a little and giggled. "That's not what I meant."

"If you say so."

"I meant, have you been in the City long?"

"I'm serving a life sentence."

She smiled.

"You?"

"I came up from L.A. about three months ago. Moved half a state away without knowing anyone."

"How do you like it?"

"I love it. It's very different from L.A."

"Lot more fog."

"And a lot more charm."

The bartender settled the drinks in front of them, then he moved down the bar again.

She took a sip of her wine and eyed him over the top of the glass. "You look like you belong in L.A."

"Another bad pick-up line."

"No, you just have that movie star look about you."

He made a face and she laughed.

"Okay. I heard it myself that time. So save me from embarrassment. What is it you do, Marco?"

He started to answer, but his phone vibrated in his jacket pocket. He pulled it out, looking at the screen. Peyton's number flashed back at him. "Hold that thought," he said, pressing the contact button. "Hey." He swiveled away from her. "What's up?"

"Hey. There's a reporter from the Examiner snooping around our case. We think she may have figured out who you are."

Suddenly, everything snapped into place. "I think I may have met her."

Peyton didn't immediately answer, then she dropped her voice. "Be careful what you tell her. We don't want to give anything away."

"Got it."

"Be careful, Marco. Don't trust anyone right now."

"I got it. You do the same."

"You know I will. Night, Marco baby."

"Night, Brooks." He shifted back to face Genevieve. She gave him a speculative look.

He shot a glance around the bar. "You know what."

"What?"

"Why don't we get out of here, go back to my place." She straightened. "What?"

"Go someplace private." If he was wrong, he might have just messed up a fun evening for himself, but he didn't think he was. Women usually didn't act so forward, even with him.

She gave a tense laugh. "Slow down, cowboy. We just met. I don't even know your last name or what you do for a living."

"Well, Genevieve, I find that hard to believe. I think we both know what I do. Why don't you tell me what it is you do?"

Her expression shifted immediately. Where she had been seductive and sultry, she now grew serious. "Who tipped you off?"

"Doesn't matter."

She shrugged. "I'm a free-lance reporter for the Examiner."

"Free-lance?"

"I wasn't lying when I told you I moved up from L.A. My name really is Genevieve, Genevieve Lake. I'm trying to land a job at the newspaper, but you can imagine how hard those are to get."

"Well, you're targeting the wrong person, sweetheart."

"I don't think I am. Look, I've done my research. I hadn't been here more than a week when I read a few paragraphs about a bum being shot in a BART station. Shortly after that, I read about a suspicious hanging in a flop house. With a little digging, I found out both men had been arrested for child molestation. Then there was the priest."

"I think we're done, Genevieve."

"Look, I want to be honest with you. I'll tell you everything I found out, if you'll just listen to me."

Marco figured he wanted to know how she'd followed him here. "Go on."

"I found a few paragraphs on an on-line news source about the priest. There was one line in the article, saying the homicide detective who shot him had been put on leave. No name, just that." She pushed her wine away. "So I went to the precinct and waited across the street."

"You staked out the precinct?"

"You know the coffee shop across the street? I ran into one of the uniforms there and casually mentioned the case."

"Who did you talk to?"

"I'm not giving up my source. I don't want to get him in trouble. Besides, he didn't want to tell me anything anyway, but he slipped and said your name...well, your first name."

Bartlet. Damn kid, of course he'd screw up around a beautiful woman.

"Anyway, I noticed you came in one day about 10:00AM. You're kinda easy to remember." She gave him her sultry smile once more.

Marco made an impatient motion with his hand.

She grew serious again. "You left around noon. You did that for the next two days."

"You sat in a coffee shop for three days straight?"

"Free-lance, remember?"

"Right."

"Today I took a chance, being Sunday and all. Sure enough, you showed up at 10:00, left at noon. You had to be the cop on leave, so I followed you."

"You followed me?"

"I had no choice. I had to make contact somehow."

"You followed me to my parents' house?"

She shrugged.

Marco forced himself to calm. "What did you do? Sit in your car all the time I was there?"

"Free-lance." She placed her arm on the bar, leaning closer to him. "I need this story. It's the only way I'm gonna have a chance at a real job."

"As I said, you got the wrong cop, sweetheart. So you followed me here from my parents' house?"

She nodded, her expression troubled.

"And just how far did you think you'd take it?"

"What do you mean?"

He motioned between them. "This. How far would you have let it go?"

"I wasn't going to sleep with you, if that's what you think." She gave him another once-over. "At least, not until we'd dated for a couple of months."

His eyes never wavered. "Why me? Why not work the kid some more? Or one of the other detectives?"

"What kid?"

"I know who you talked to, Genevieve."

She sighed. "Don't report him. It wasn't his fault."

"I'm sure it wasn't, but I'm not a twenty-two year old kid. Why did you think I'd be a good mark?"

"I saw your teeny tiny partner. She looks like a regular kick-ass bitch. I wasn't going up to her." Marco fought a smile at her description of Peyton. "Or the big guy, you know, like a linebacker. I figured he'd chew me out something good. And the Asian guy, he scares me. I'd be afraid he'd pull his gun on me."

"So you thought you'd seduce me?"

"Actually, I was hoping you'd be drunk."

"Well, I'm not."

"Not seduced or not drunk?"

"Not either, and I'm not giving you your story, so you might as well go on home, Genevieve."

She looked momentarily disappointed, then she glanced up at him. "Give me your phone."

"What?"

"Give me your phone, so I can put my number in there. If you change your mind, you can call me. All I need is one good story. We'll control how much information to give out and I promise to be discreet. Please, Marco, it's going to get out anyway. Let it be me. Help me get my career going."

"I'm not giving you my phone and I'm not giving you any information."

She gave him a frustrated sigh, then she glanced around, leaning over the bar to grab a pen. She scribbled her number on a cocktail napkin and passed it to him. "If you change your mind…"

He crumpled up the napkin and placed it in his cola. The brown liquid soaked into the napkin, blurring her number. "Goodbye, Genevieve. I don't talk to reporters, too sneaky. Go stake out someone else's family reunion or something."

She studied him a moment, disappointment in her expression. "The Examiner also has my number if you change your mind."

"I won't."

"Then what about dinner?"

"Dinner?"

"Yeah, you can buy it. We'll call it a date."

Marco pushed himself off the stool. "No, we won't."

Without a backward glance, he walked toward the door, leaving Genevieve sitting on her stool, watching after him.

CHAPTER 13

Marco looked up as Dr. Ferguson entered the room. He took his usual spot at the table, setting down the yellow legal pad. He wore another outdated, rumpled jacket in a blue that should never have been made into a suit. Marco had to wonder if being a psychiatrist for cops paid well, or if he was living off noodles in a cup. He sure dressed like he shopped at thrift stores.

"Just got out of a meeting with your captain."

Marco felt his stomach drop. About him or Brooks?

Ferguson caught the anxious look on his face. "She was warning me about the Examiner reporter."

"Free-lance."

"What?"

"She's a free-lance reporter, so I'm not sure that qualifies as a reporter."

"You met her?"

"Yeah, last night."

"How'd she find you?"

"She followed me from my parents' house."

"Back to your apartment?"

"No, to the…" Marco stopped himself and dropped his eyes.

"To the what, Inspector D'Angelo?"

"The bar."

Dr. Ferguson lifted his papers and glanced through them, pulling a pen out of the inner pocket on his jacket. "How much alcohol have you been consuming lately?"

"It's not like that. I just drank cola."

Okay, that was probably worse.

"I see."

Marco was beginning to hate that psychiatric platitude. *I see.*

"How many random sexual encounters have you had this past week?"

"What? No…"

The doctor's brows rose, his pen poised over the legal pad.

Marco exhaled. "One."

"One? The reporter?"

"No." Although to be fair, that hadn't been far from his mind. "Peyton tipped me off."

"So if Peyton hadn't warned you, you would have taken her home?"

Marco wasn't sure how to answer that. Either way he jumped, he was going to be in trouble. *No*, and he'd be accused of lying. *Yes*, and he'd be crossing another line.

Dr. Ferguson shifted the pen until he gripped it with both hands. "You do know there are other addictions besides alcohol and drugs, right? Food, gambling…sex?"

"It's not an addiction."

"Then what is it?"

His mind spun frantically. How the hell did he answer that? "Whatever it is, it doesn't make me unfit to hold a gun or work."

"It does if you are engaging in self-destructive behavior because of the shooting."

"Look. I already told you. I don't believe cops should have relationships. They aren't fair to the other party, but that doesn't mean I'm a monk, Dr. Ferguson. It doesn't hurt anyone and I'm careful."

"I think it does."

"Who does it hurt?"

"You. You deny yourself a truly meaningful relationship because of some ill-conceived code you've created, one that no one else in your family or your circle of friends maintains, and you've tricked yourself into believing these random encounters are not only acceptable, but beneficial."

Marco didn't answer. What could he say? This idiot didn't understand him or what he felt and he wasn't going to convince him otherwise. It was all well and good to armchair quarterback from across the room, but that didn't mean he was right.

"Should I take your silence to mean this discussion is finished?"

"Obviously, you'll take it to mean whatever you want. You have all the cards on your end of the table, and I'm playing with an empty hand."

"I don't want you to feel that way."

"Well, Dr. Ferguson, that is the one thing you don't control in my life."

He stared at his pad, making aimless swirls with the tip of his pen. "Why don't we go back to storytelling?"

Marco frowned. What did he get out of the stupid stories he and Peyton told? Were they revealing more than he thought they were? It made him shift uncomfortably. The power imbalance in the room hadn't really bothered him before, but right now it felt suffocating. Was he telling this doctor about himself without actually saying anything?

"I don't feel like telling stories right now."

"Why not?"

"Because I feel like everything I say is being measured and catalogued. I feel like a lab rat and you're poking me with needles to see how I react."

Dr. Ferguson studied him for a moment, then he set down the pen. "That is exactly what I'm doing, Inspector D'Angelo."

Marco narrowed his eyes. "Come again?"

"I have been tasked with deciding if you are healthy enough to put back on the street, whether it is safe for me to put a gun in your hand and turn you loose on the public. I take that job very seriously and the only way I can do that is to poke you with needles and see what makes you bleed." He folded his hands on his legal pad. "So far, you have stone walled me whenever I approach a sensitive topic."

"Like what?"

"Your religion, your inability to form monogamous relationships, your attempt to convince me you do not have any remorse. I took a second approach and I got you to tell me stories where I get a glimpse of the man hiding behind the detective's mask. You say I'm holding the cards, but we can play this your way. You choose which method we use from now on."

Marco could feel his jaw clench.

"I'm going to reveal something to you, Inspector D'Angelo. When we first met, you told me..." He lifted a page on the pad and read from it. "You said, 'I don't go much deeper than that.' My experience with you is quite a bit different than what you said. You go a lot deeper, but for some reason, you don't like anyone to know just how deep."

Marco's eyes lifted and pinned him. "Fine. You want a story, I'll tell you a story. Our third case after the Marine was a Unabomber copycat. Killed an old homeless woman in the Tenderloin."

* * *

Dumpsters lined the alley on either side, backing up to the rear doors of businesses with faded paint and few placards to indicate their identity. Dusk was approaching, the sun fading behind the high rises, sucking the fog into the lingering warmth hiding in the narrow spaces between the concrete walls.

The body lay dead center in the alley, legs twisted, hands curled around the piece of metal sticking out of her throat. Her eyes were open, staring up at the gusting fog, flash marks around her lips, her eyebrows partially burnt away, the tip of her nose blackened. Blood flowed down over her throat and chest, pooling beneath her. She wore layers of clothes, men's shoes, heavy socks that bunched around her ankle.

Peyton made a choking noise and turned away. Marco glanced over his shoulder at her, then faced Smith.

"Next time put a cover over the body, will ya?"

Smith nodded. "Yeah, good idea."

A number of uniforms canvassed the alley, and a few witnesses stood on the sidewalk, watching the proceedings. Marco noted a number of cops were taking statements.

"Is Chuck Wilson on his way to take pictures?" he asked Smith.

"Far as I know."

Hunkering down at the victim's side, Marco studied the metal bar. Leaning closer, he tilted his head to see it from the side. "Is that a screwdriver?"

"Looks like it."

Marco grimaced. "Took her in the jugular, eh?"

Smith made an unpleasant face and nodded. "Probably bled out."

Marco looked around. The dumpster directly in front of the body had a twisted and burnt lid. "Bomb?"

"Got a call into the bomb squad, but that's my guess."

Peyton shifted toward them, but didn't look at the body. "See the crate there." She pointed to a vegetable crate lying on its side a few feet away. "She was probably standing on that to look inside the dumpsters. When she lifted the lid, it triggered the bomb."

Marco looked down at the body. "So, was the screwdriver an unfortunate accident, or did he plan to kill someone?"

"Either way, someone died, so now we've got a homicide," answered Smith.

*   *   *

"Pretty crude device, but effective."

Marco glanced at Peyton. She was watching the body being loaded into the van, headed for the morgue. He turned back to the bomb squad sergeant, Pete Nelson. "What was in it?"

"Probably ammonium nitrate and aluminum with some sort of detonator. It was hooked to the dumpster lid, so when someone opened it…" He made an exploding motion with his hands. "Designed mostly for a lot of sound, but there was enough force to propel shrapnel." He looked back at the dumpster. "We need to get it back to the lab before I can give you anything more."

Peyton focused on him. "Are you saying it wouldn't have been fatal if there hadn't been a projectile in there?"

"Some second degree burns, burst ear drums, concussion, yeah, but there probably wasn't enough fire power to kill someone by itself."

"Where would someone get ammonium nitrate?" asked Marco.

"There are a lot of chemical companies around here, pharmaceutical companies, universities, nurseries, illegal sources."

"Do you think you'll be able to get any fingerprints or DNA off the bomb?" questioned Peyton.

"We'll do our best. I'll let you know the moment I find out anything."

"Thank you." Marco held out his hand and Nelson took it, then he shook Peyton's hand and walked back to the dumpster.

Peyton's attention had drifted back to the Medical Examiner's van.

"Come on. I'll buy you a burger. It's been a long time since lunch." He motioned toward the street.

"I don't think I can eat anything."

"Give it a few minutes and you'll be okay again."

They walked to the Charger and climbed inside.

"Who the hell would do something like that?" she asked, staring out at the City.

"Unfortunately, a lot of people. That's the problem. So many sick people are wandering around, preying on others." He started the car and pulled into traffic. "You've got to let it go or it'll give you an ulcer."

"Hard to let it go. She wasn't doing anything, barely surviving as it was."

"I know."

They drove in silence. Marco took her to a little 50's throw-back diner with call boxes and waitresses that served burgers right at the car. He turned off the Charger and pointed at the menu on the box beside the driver's side window. Peyton leaned forward and studied it.

"I'll just have the original cheese burger."

He nodded and started to press the call button.

"And a chocolate milkshake."

He gave her a frown. What was she? Ten?

"Chocolate milkshake?"

She nodded.

He turned back to the box and pressed the button. A badly distorted voice blared out of the speaker. He placed her order, then got himself a vegetarian burger.

"What did you order?" she asked, staring at him in bewilderment.

"Veggie burger."

"Veggie burger? I still can't get over that you're a vegetarian."

"Why does that surprise you so much?"

"I don't know. You just seem like a carnivore."

"How?"

"You know – the whole alpha male thing."

He lifted an eyebrow. "Alpha male?"

"Oh come on, you know what I mean. You growl at everyone, trying to keep them off. Sometimes you might as well beat on your chest."

He gave a bewildered laugh.

"How long have you been a vegetarian?"

"Years."

"Wow."

"It's really not that weird."

"I guess." She leaned back in her seat. "Tell me again why you don't eat meat?"

He shrugged. "I like animals, so it seemed a good idea to stop eating them. And it's healthier. Easier to maintain your weight." He faced her. "You feeling better?"

"Not much. I keep thinking about how senseless her death was and worrying that we won't figure out who did it."

"We'll figure it out, but the why of it always baffles me. Why hurt someone else? What's the reason?"

She shook her head. "I just try to remember what my father has always said. More people *don't* hurt others than do. You have to focus on that and tell yourself the rest are aberrations."

"Smart man, your father."

"Yeah, he is."

"When we went to lunch, I got the impression that you and your mother had a difficult relationship."

"She's not thrilled with the idea of her only child being a cop."

"I get that."

"Your family approve of it?"

He gave a non-committal shake of his head. "I'm the youngest of four boys. All three of my brothers went to college and got advanced degrees. I'm the only one who didn't. I think they felt they failed me in some way, but school really wasn't for me. I mean I did all right. I just didn't love it, you know?"

"I know."

They were silent for a moment, then he glanced over at her.

"Look, I know I've been hard on you."

She gave him a disbelieving look. "Have you? I didn't notice. I just thought it was like junior high when you pull the hair of the girl you like."

He gave a chuckle. "Well, that wouldn't surprise me. You didn't notice I'm a vegetarian, now did you?"

"Touché."

"Anyway, I'm trying to apologize here."

She folded her hands primly in her lap. "By all means, continue."

"It's just you weren't at all what I expected as a partner. I mean, you're all of four and a half feet tall…"

"I'm five four."

"Exactly."

She punched him in the shoulder.

He gave her a smirk as he rubbed it. "And you aren't exactly sugar and spice."

"This is what you call an apology, D'Angelo?"

"I'm getting there. Then there's your issue with dead bodies."

"I'm working on it."

"You're getting a reputation, Brooks."

"Really?"

He nodded. "They're calling you Inspector Repeat because, well…" He made a motion with his hand and she stopped him.

"I get it. Nice of you to defend me."

"Is that what you want me to do? Defend you?"

"No, I'd have to castrate you then."

"Exactly."

"I'm still not getting the apology part of this."

"You're opinionated and mouthy and generally, a pain in the ass. You have questionable taste in beverages…"

"Beverages? What?"

"Milkshake, Brooks?" He waved that away. "And you couldn't keep a boundary to save your life. Your friends are certifiable and ultimately, you're a girl."

The look she leveled on him would have made a lesser man shiver.

"But you're also damn intelligent, observant, and scary good with people. You care…about everyone, and I have no doubt in my mind that if I ever need you, you'll be there."

Her smile lit up her whole face and she pressed a hand in the center of her chest. "You may have taken me on a journey around the world there, but when we finally reached the destination, it was worth it."

He smiled back at her, shaking his head. "You also make me laugh."

"Abe is right. You are so much prettier when you smile."

He closed his eyes and released his breath in a weary sigh.

*   *   *

Marco looked up to see the Medical Examiner, Abe, striding toward them from the front of the precinct. He was carrying a box and a broad smile stretched across his face. Clearing his throat to get Peyton's attention, Marco nodded with his chin toward the M.E.

Peyton swiveled around, then she bounced to her feet, clearly delighted to see him.

"Hey, little soul sista," he said, setting the box in the space between their desks.

"Hey, Abe, whatcha got?"

"Presents." He tilted his head and gave Marco a cool look. "How are you, beautiful?"

"I was better thirty seconds ago."

Abe laughed. "All bark and no bite. Although I don't mind a bite or two." He gave Marco a wink.

Marco fought a smile, looking down at his computer screen. Clearly, his open hostility wasn't having the desired effect and this man was so outrageous, it was hard to keep up the pretense of disliking him.

"Look what I brought you, D'licious." He held up a blob of chocolate on a stick.

Marco frowned. "What is it?"

"My heart."

"Uh, Abe, that isn't a heart," said Peyton skeptically. "It's shaped like a tear drop."

"Sure it is." He turned to her and pointed with one of his long, elegant fingers. "Here are the two ventricles and this is the aorta."

Peyton's face fell. "You mean a *heart* heart. Oh that's nasty."

"Why? It's just chocolate, Peyton…well, and brandy." He turned back to Marco. "I think that's why it didn't hold together as well as I wanted. I used too much brandy." Extending it, he gave Marco a wicked smile. "Unless you'd like another body part."

Marco took it. "This is good. Heart is good."

Peyton peered over his shoulder into the box. "What other parts you got?"

"Brooks!"

She smiled mischievously.

Abe reached in and picked up another blob. "You wanna try some liver?"

She made a face and took a step back, sinking into her chair. "I'll pass. Isn't the liver just a big filter?"

"Pretty much." He looked around and then walked over to grab a chair, dragging it back to their desks. "I'm not only here to distribute chocolate. I got your homeless woman yesterday. The bomb blast?"

Marco set down his heart. "She bled out around the screwdriver, right?"

"Not completely. The blast was stronger than the bomb squad thought. She had significant frontal lobe trauma, bleeding and swelling. Even if the screwdriver didn't get her, she probably would have died from a head injury. The screwdriver just sped things along, mercy almost."

Peyton's expression grew grim.

Marco tried to offer her a reassuring smile, but his phone rang. "D'Angelo," he said.

"Inspector, this is Sergeant Nelson with the Bomb Squad."

"Yes, Sergeant."

"We took apart the device and it was exactly as I told you. Ammonium nitrate, aluminum with a crude detonator, batteries and electrical wire."

"Any fingerprints?"

"Not a thing."

"Any other identifying marks?"

"I'm afraid not. I wish I had more to give you."

"Thank you, Sergeant. I appreciate it."

"I'll send our report over to you tomorrow."

"Thanks." The call disconnected.

Marco gave Peyton a shrug. "They didn't find anything more than what they told us yesterday."

"Damn it." She chewed her lip in frustration, then she looked into Abe's box. "What are those? Kidneys?"

He reached inside and handed them over.

She bit off the left one. "Next time bring the brandy bottle as well."

*   *   *

"You're going to leave it at a cliff hanger again, aren't you?" said Dr. Ferguson. "Am I supposed to find out the ending from your partner?"

Marco leaned forward on the table. "Why don't you cut my partner loose? She doesn't need these meetings. She's fine."

"That's for me to decide, Inspector D'Angelo."

"This case is hard enough on her. She doesn't need the stress of being constantly afraid that you're going to pull her gun. I'm the one who shot someone, not her. Let her go."

"It's funny how much time the two of you spend campaigning for the other one. Did she tell you meeting with me was causing her stress?"

"She didn't have to. I know her well enough to know that these meetings worry her. You're never going to find a more dedicated cop or one who takes her job as seriously.

There's nothing for you or the department to worry about where she's concerned."

"I'll make that judgment myself. This time here is between you and me, Inspector D'Angelo, and I have to wonder if this concern over your partner isn't just another way to deflect attention from the issues we were discussing before."

"I'm not deflecting anything. I've answered every question as honestly as I know how."

"I disagree. When I wanted to talk about the random encounters you have with women, you shut down at once. This is obviously an issue that you feel defensive about and want to avoid addressing."

"I'm defensive because you accused me of it being an addiction. Sort of hard not to get defensive."

"What concerns me is you think this satisfies the need you have for intimacy."

"I said it satisfies a need, but I never pretended it was about intimacy."

"Humans are social creatures. We have a need for deep, social relationships. Sex shouldn't be confused for intimacy, for meeting that need that we have to connect with others."

"I understand that."

"Do you? Are you aware that statistics prove that married men live longer than unmarried men, and divorced men die much sooner than any other group?"

"That's painting the brush strokes a bit wide."

"How?"

"Are you telling me you'll let me come back to work if I get married, Dr. Ferguson?"

"Of course not."

"Then what are you suggesting?"

"You need to be open to a relationship with a woman that involves more than sex. You need to have a connection that is more than physical. You've got to stop picking up strange women in bars and pretending that it meets the need you have for a deep, meaningful relationship with someone."

"Why is it you think I don't have a deep, meaningful relationship with anyone?"

The doctor didn't immediately answer.

"Here's what I think, Dr. Ferguson. We all have our preconceived notions and yours doesn't square with who I am. You want me to gnash my teeth and pull out my hair over killing a priest. When I don't, you want to assign a label to me. Sociopath or psychopath or whatever. Then you want me to tell you how empty and alone I am because I deliberately choose not to pursue marriage. Again another label – fear of intimacy, sexual addiction." He stood up and leaned on the table. "Maybe you're right. Maybe you've got me all figured out. Maybe I am just a label, or maybe I'm not. Maybe the labels are what's wrong. But either way, none of it prevents me from carrying a gun and I think you know that."

Dr. Ferguson reached for his pen, but he didn't break eye contact with Marco.

Marco gave him a lazy smile. "You're just dying to scribble on your pad, so I'll let you get to it." He glanced down at the thin script. "Of course, you'll want to remind me that you'll see me tomorrow morning, so don't let me stop you."

The doctor's jaw tightened, but he gave no other indication of annoyance. "I will see you tomorrow, Inspector D'Angelo, precisely at 10:00."

Marco inclined his head, then turned on a heel and left.

CHAPTER 14

Marco walked out of the conference room and stumbled to a halt. The entire front parking lot of the precinct was filled with people, cameras, and microphones. A number of uniforms were holding them off, keeping them from storming inside the building.

Defino and Maria stood at the counter, watching the mayhem, but they both turned as he appeared. Maria gave him a smile, but Defino scowled at him.

"You talk to that reporter from the Examiner?" she demanded.

Marco started to walk over to her, but Jake suddenly appeared. "They've got the back covered too. They're waiting on the street." He glanced up at Marco. "Hey, Adonis, so you caused this?"

"What?"

"Did you talk to that reporter from the Examiner?" demanded Defino again.

"Free-lance."

"What?"

"She's not exactly a reporter yet."

Everyone stared at him. Behind him he heard the conference room door open and Dr. Ferguson poked his head out. Jake shied away from him and went to stand with Maria and Captain Defino, leaning against Maria's desk.

"D'Angelo, my office now! Maria, get Brooks in here too."

Maria gave him a sympathetic look and went to phone.

"Captain Defino, if I may..." began Ferguson.

"Doctor, your hour is up. I have bigger problems to solve right now." She dismissed him. "Maria, get Cho and Simons in here too. D'Angelo, give Ryder your keys to the Charger, so he can park it up the street and get you out of here when I'm done." She pointed at Jake. "Ryder, wade through that scrum of reporters, do not say a word to any of them and I do mean not one word. Get the Charger and park it up the street, then get back here. When you've done that, tell Holmes and Bartlet they're escorting D'Angelo out of here." A moment later she disappeared into her office.

Marco glanced over his shoulder at the doctor. Ferguson hadn't moved and his mouth was hanging open. Marco didn't think he'd ever been given orders before.

As he walked toward Jake, he reached into his pocket for the Charger's keys.

"Don't you hate getting called into the principal's office?" Jake's smirk was goading. He leaned closer to Marco and lowered his voice. "I sure hope you didn't go under cover with that reporter."

Marco pulled out the keys, glaring at him.

"Get it. Go *under cover* or maybe it should be *covers*."

Maria had the phone to her ear, but she giggled.

"Keep it up, Ryder."

Jake took the keys, jangling them. "This is a red letter day. I get to drive the Charger. I get to run my hands all over her steering wheel and put her in drive."

Marco moved closer until he loomed over him. "If you put one scratch on her, I will do such terrible things to you, Ryder, such terrible things."

Jake dramatically glanced over at the doctor, jerking his head toward him.

Marco smiled chillingly. "Such terrible, terrible things. And don't forget, I know where you live."

Dr. Ferguson took a step forward as if he wanted to say something, but Marco shifted and walked into Defino's office.

*   *   *

Peyton entered Defino's office and stopped dead when she saw Marco sitting in the chair before the desk. "Oh no, you didn't sleep with her, did you?"

226

Marco's expression was incredulous. "Nice to see you too, partner."

Standing at the blind-covered window, Defino glared at her over her shoulder. "Where are Cho and Simons?"

"They're going over all the chat logs Stan has to see if we got a bite. Stan's also contacting ICAC to see if they have anything."

Defino wandered to her desk and sank into her chair. Laying her hands flat on the glass, she focused on Marco. "I'm only going to ask this once. Did you sleep with the reporter?"

"No."

"No? Are you sure?"

Marco gave her a bewildered look. "I think that's something I would remember."

"But you met up with her?"

"She came up to me in a bar."

Defino exhaled and slumped back in her chair. "So you talked to her? How much did you have to drink when you met her?"

"Nothing. I was drinking cola. I didn't tell her anything, Captain. Brooks warned me in time."

"What does that mean? In time?"

"Before anything happened."

"How did she find you?" asked Peyton, moving further into the room.

"She's been staking out the precinct from across the street. The coffee shop. She noticed that I come at 10:00 and leave at noon. She figured I was the cop who shot the priest and was put on leave."

"How long has she been doing this?" demanded Defino.

"Days. Like I said, she's free-lance, so she's been scanning the papers, looking for anything she can get her hands on to break a story. She thinks it'll get her a permanent job as a reporter."

Defino dug the heels of her hands into her eyes.

In the lobby, Peyton could hear the clump of Simons' boots. "Holy shit!" he exclaimed.

She circled around Marco and went to stand by the window. Simons and Cho appeared in the entrance and pushed their way into the little office. Cho took the seat next to Marco, reaching over to shake his hand.

"How ya doing, man?"

Marco shook his hand in return. "I'm fine."

Simons clamped a huge hand on his shoulder for a moment, then released him.

"As you can see, we've got a problem," said Defino.

"Did Stan get any bites on his chat room conversations?"

Simons shook his head.

"Close the door, Bill. We need to decide how we're going to handle this reporter mess," said Defino.

Simons went to the door and started to close it, but Devan poked his head inside.

"Got a moment, Captain," he said.

Peyton moved back closer to Defino. It was getting crowded in here with so many male bodies and she still didn't feel comfortable being in the same room with her ex-boyfriend. Devan acknowledged her with a nod as he stepped into the room. Simons closed the door at his back.

"It's not a good time right now," said Defino.

"My boss got a call from the Mayor this morning."

"Shit," said Defino. "What'd he want?"

"The Mayor's worried that this is getting out of control, so I was asked to come down and give you any advice I could."

"What does he want me to do? Go out there and tell them we have a serial killer?"

"Actually, he does."

"What!"

Peyton realized her mouth was hanging open. She closed it and shot a disbelieving look at Marco.

"They know about the priest and the youth group leader in Woodside. One of the reporters even made a connection to the two previous deaths, the bum and the hanging. And apparently now, D'Angelo has been identified as the cop on leave."

Marco looked down at his hands.

"The mayor wants you to go out there and calm things down, tell them we have a suspect."

"He wants me to lie?" snapped Defino.

"Reassure."

"Me? He wants me to go in front of those cameras?"

"You could send an official spokesperson in your capacity. Someone who can reassure without giving too much away. I can go with that person and coach them through it."

Everyone turned and looked at Peyton. Peyton backed up into the blinds, making them rattle. "Me?"

"You'd be perfect," said Devan, giving her a smile.

Defino nodded. "Not a bad idea."

"No. No, I'm not going in front of those cameras."

"Come on, Brooks, they'll love you. You're cute as a button," said Cho with a smirk.

"Downright adorable," added Simons.

Peyton turned to Defino. "Captain, this isn't fair…"

"What isn't fair is that my precinct is once again a media circus, Brooks. What else do you propose?"

She looked to Marco for help.

Marco shifted in the chair. "The reporter I met was afraid of her. She said she looked like a regular kick-ass bitch."

Peyton held out her hand to Marco, then she frowned and stared at him. *A regular kick-ass bitch?* Hold on. Bitch?

"You talked with a reporter?" demanded Devan.

"No, I met her. I didn't talk to her."

"How did she figure out who you were? You had to talk with her. You must have slipped up."

"I didn't slip up."

"How can that be? Your parking lot is crawling with media, D'Angelo. You must have said something you shouldn't."

"It wasn't me, so back the hell off, Adams!"

Everyone went quiet.

Defino leaned forward in her chair. "Who was it?"

Marco looked away.

"D'Angelo, if one of my cops leaked information, I need to know who it was."

"Captain, this Genevieve Lake is really pretty and she's not opposed to using that to get what she wants. She's hungry and ambitious and desperate for a real job."

"Who talked with her?"

"I can't tell you that."

"You can and will."

Marco folded his hands in his lap. "With all due respect, Captain, I'm already suspended. What more can you do to me?"

Peyton felt panic edge up inside of her as Defino and Marco stared at each other. "I'll do it. I'll give a statement to the reporters," she squeaked out.

Defino broke eye contact with Marco and glanced at her.

"Captain, it doesn't matter who let it slip. Someone did, but it was only a matter of time before that happened anyway. We were going to have to address this eventually. Maybe this is a good thing. Maybe we can flush the killer out if the public knows. And maybe it will scare convicted child molesters, make them lie low."

Defino placed her hand over her mouth in thought.

Peyton tried to wait as patiently as she could, but the tension in the room was like a physical force, pressing down on her. She shifted weight, she stared at the toe of her *kickass* boots, she tried to remember when she'd ever noticed a reporter hanging out across the street.

Turning, she parted the slats on the blinds and peered out. She could just see the edge of the coffee shop. Did she ever run into someone there? She couldn't remember the last time she bought coffee at that shop. It was too expensive, so she usually drank the swill they made in the break-room. In fact, whenever she'd had coffee over there, she never got it herself. One of the uniforms usually made a run…

Her thoughts coalesced. *Bartlet.*

She gasped, but didn't turn around. She knew she'd give it away if she did. Reaching for the plastic turner on the blinds, she started to twist them open without thinking about it.

"Don't you dare, Brooks," came Defino's voice.

Peyton glanced over her shoulder at her. Defino was glaring at her hand. Deliberately releasing it, Peyton wrapped her arms around her middle so she wouldn't be tempted again. "Well, Captain?"

"D'Angelo, you are going home and staying there. Do you hear me?"

"Yes, Captain."

"Simons and Cho, walk him out, follow him home, then report back here once he's inside. Make sure there are no reporters hanging about his apartment."

"On it," said Simons, moving to the door and pulling it open.

"Brooks, park yourself in a chair. You and Devan are helping me write a press release, then you're going out to deliver it."

Marco glanced up at her as he pushed himself to his feet. She wanted to talk to him, she wanted to find out what was going on with him, but now wasn't the time. He gave her a brief nod as he turned toward the door. Cho immediately stepped up behind him, following him out of the room.

* * *

Simons and Cho walked Marco right to the door of his apartment. Marco gave them both a tight smile. "Thanks. I can take it from here."

"You heard the captain, D'Angelo. We got to see you to the other side," said Cho with a commiserate smile.

Marco pulled out his keys and fitted one to the lock, turning. He pushed open the door and blinked in surprise. His mother was scrubbing his coffee table, a spray bottle of cleaner in one hand and a dust rag in the other. She looked up as he stepped inside.

"Looks like you've got a break-in," said Cho in amusement.

"Mom?"

"Hello, gentlemen." She pushed at her hair.

"Ma'am," said Simons, ducking his head.

"Mrs. D'Angelo," answered Cho.

"Come in. I can have lunch ready in about five minutes."

Simons stepped into the room, sniffing. Marco gave him a disbelieving look, although he had to admit that whatever she was cooking smelled delicious.

"We can't stay, ma'am," said Cho, but he was mainly talking to his partner. "We were ordered back to the precinct after we saw your son home."

"Oh, that's a shame. What if I made you up a plate to take with you?"

That drew Cho over the threshold. "That would be awesome, ma'am."

"Just awesome," repeated Simons.

She beamed a happy smile and hurried into the galley kitchen. Marco scowled at them and held out his hands. Simons shrugged, but Cho stepped around him, further into the apartment.

"It smells wonderful, ma'am. What is it?"

"My parmesan chicken. My own special recipe. It's one of Marco's favorite dishes."

"I'm vegetarian, Mom," said Marco with a sigh.

She stopped, holding the spatula over the dish. "Oh, lord, I keep forgetting that." She set the spatula down and Simons' face fell. Reaching back, she grabbed the roll of tinfoil and tore off a large piece. "You gentlemen just take the whole thing with you. You can return the pan to Marco when you see him next." She grabbed two potholders and used them to lift the pan, transferring it to Cho. "Take these too, so you don't burn your hands."

"This is so sweet of you, Mrs. D'Angelo," he said, giving her a goofy grin.

She waved him off, but she was clearly pleased.

"Thank you, ma'am," said Simons. The smile he gave her made him look like he had indigestion. Marco shot him a disbelieving look, he couldn't remember when he saw Simons smile like that, but Simons just shrugged his massive shoulders.

Cho turned, carrying his pan, and they both moved toward the door. A moment later, they were gone, leaving Marco alone with his mother. He wandered to the bistro table and took a seat.

"Why are you cleaning my apartment?"

"It needed cleaning."

"Chicken parmesan, really?"

"Okay, so I also have eggplant parmesan." She went to the oven and pulled out a second pan, placing it on the burners. "Of course I didn't forget you were vegetarian. I might not understand it, but I didn't forget it." She grabbed a plate off the shelf above the sink and reached back for the spatula.

"Then why did you make it?"

"I thought you might have your new girl, Lisa, over for dinner or something. Isn't that her name? I think that's what Vinnie told me." She dished up the food and pulled open a drawer, getting out a fork. She carried both to him and set it down on the table. "What do you want to drink? I bought milk."

He arched one brow at her.

233

She rolled her eyes. "Not even milk? Fine." She threw up a hand and went back to the sink, grabbing a glass and pulling open the refrigerator. She took out the water pitcher and filled the glass, then snatched a napkin out of a holder she'd placed beside the sink, carrying both to him at the table. "Maybe she'll like the eggplant parmesan too."

"Mom, sit down."

She settled herself into the other bistro chair. "What? Is it too tough? I was worried about this eggplant. It seemed like it had been on the shelf a little too long."

He cut a piece and placed it in his mouth. It almost melted against his tongue. "It's delicious as always."

"Good. There's plenty for dinner. Add a salad and a bottle of wine, and she'll be impressed. There's nothing that a woman likes more than a man who can cook. It is Lisa, isn't it?"

He swallowed. "Mom, there's no Lisa."

Her expression fell.

He reached over and took her hand. "I'm sorry. I just said that to get Vinnie off my back."

"Get him off your back for what?"

"He was keeping tabs…" He faltered when he saw the tears pooling in her eyes. "What is this all about? The cleaning, the cooking, the prying?"

She reached out and pressed the napkin flat. "I just want to make sure you're okay. Is that wrong of me after what's happened?"

"No, but I'm fine. You don't have to hover."

"How are you fine? You're lying to your brother, you're making up imaginary girls. Other cops have to escort you home." She held a hand toward the door.

He ignored the part about Vinnie. He was certain his mother would find as much fault with him about the real Lisa as Dr. Ferguson had. "Simons and Cho came home with me to make sure there weren't reporters around my apartment."

"Reporters?"

"They found out about the case and they're poking around for information."

"What information? What do they know?"

"They know a lot. They know about the killings and they know I was the one who shot the priest."

She covered her mouth with her hand. "They know that? Will they come here?"

"That's why Cho and Simons came. To make sure my apartment was clear."

She shook her head, her eyes swimming with unshed tears. "I want you to come home with your father and me. I don't want you staying here by yourself."

"What?"

"It's too dangerous. If they know about the priest, someone might do something, try something."

"Who would try something? What are you talking about?"

She grabbed his hand. "Please go to confession with me, Marco. Please. You must ask for forgiveness, for help. You can't shoulder this burden alone."

He pulled away from her and abruptly stood up. She clutched her hand against her chest. He caught the motion out of the corner of his eyes, and realized she was clutching her hands around a crucifix. His immediate fury bled away.

Coming to her, he knelt before her and drew her hands away, covering them with his own. "Mama, you're going to make yourself sick over this. I know you want to help me, but this isn't helping. I don't need you cooking and cleaning for me, and I don't need you agonizing over my soul. I'm a grown man now."

She cupped his cheek in her hand. "You can't possibly understand, Marco. It doesn't matter how old you are or how old you'll ever be. I'm your mother and I ache inside when you're hurt. Nothing anyone could ever do to me is worse than what someone could do to my children. I need to be here right now. I need to cook and clean and worry for your soul." She leaned close to him. "You keep

235

saying that you're all right. You can shout it from the top of the world if you want, but when I look in your eyes, I see torment and it makes me hurt inside." She shifted her hand to his chin and cupped it. "You can pretend for those police officers, you can lie to your brother, and you can even snow that psychiatrist, but you can't lie to me."

He exhaled heavily. What the hell! Why did everyone think they knew him better than he knew himself?

"Come on. Eat your lunch and let me finish my dusting. Then I promise I'll leave you alone."

He gave a short nod and rose to his feet, his eyes fixed on her cross. He had no illusions about the rest of his day. Mona D'Angelo never gave up on anything. He was going to have to fend off at least one more demand for confession before the night was through.

Going to the television, he reached for the remote. As he pressed the button to turn it on, he couldn't deny it was nice to handle something that wasn't covered in a fine layer of grit. He pushed the channel for the local news and replaced the remote. A shot of the precinct flashed across the screen and a male reporter with very white teeth made a comment about a news conference.

His mother stopped moving beside him. "Isn't that your precinct?"

"Yeah."

"What happened?"

"Peyton's going to hold a press conference about the serial killer."

"Peyton?"

Marco and Mona exchanged a look.

He nodded. "I just hope she keeps her lunch down," he said.

*   *   *

"So, Bartlet was the one who released the information," said Defino.

Peyton opened her mouth to respond, then thought better of it. Of course she would have figured it out the same way Peyton had.

"I could have D'Angelo's badge for insubordination." She pointed at Peyton. "You might just tell him that."

"He was trying to protect the kid, Captain."

Defino's look softened. "I know."

Devan sank into the seat next to her. "You'll still need to have a talk with Bartlet, Captain. You can't have this sort of stuff getting out."

"I'll handle it," she said, pulling her laptop in front of her. "Let's get this press release written."

They worked on the press release for half-an-hour. Midway through Defino sent Smith out to announce that the precinct would make a statement in about fifteen minutes. Peyton rehearsed the release, pacing about Defino's office, until she had it almost memorized. Then Devan spent another five minutes throwing questions at her and forcing her to respond.

Finally, Defino rose to her feet. "You're ready."

Peyton gave her a terrified look. "Captain…" Her heart was pounding beneath her ribs.

Defino came around the desk and placed her hands on Peyton's shoulders, gripping her hard. "Stay on script. And whatever you do, Brooks, don't make some snarky comment if you get flustered." She held a finger up in her face. "And no stories."

Peyton let out a tense laugh.

Defino smiled at her. "You can do this. I have faith in you."

Peyton wished she had more faith in herself, but Defino's praise went a long way to restoring a level of calm. Devan moved behind her and opened the office door. Peyton followed him out into the lobby, but stumbled to a halt when she saw the crowd waiting there.

Maria and Jake were sitting on the edge of her desk, Smith had just come in from the front, Holmes and Bartlet were standing at the half-door, and Dr. Ferguson was leaning against the door frame of the conference room. She searched each of their faces, but the one she wanted to see the most, the one that would give her strength wasn't there. His absence made her stomach knot. She tried to imagine what he would say.

He'd give her a smirk and a quick hug, then tell her, *Man up, Brooks.*

As she followed Devan toward the front, Maria tsked. "Wish you'd let me do something with that hair."

Peyton fought a smile.

Jake gave her a thumb's up. "Try not to cuss."

She punched him in the shoulder.

Holmes shook his head. "Cuss? Try not to throw up."

"It's hard when the last thing I see before going out there is your face."

He chuckled and held the door for her.

"Good luck, Brooks," said Bartlet.

Smith touched her hand. "You'll do fine, baby girl."

She gave him a smile and squeezed his fingers in return. "Thank you."

Devan placed his hand on the door and looked back at her. "Stay on script. Don't let them rattle you." He pushed open the door, then waited for her to go through. Someone had dragged out a podium and set it up at the top of the stairs, Smith she figured, and microphones covered the surface. Peyton faltered.

Devan put a hand in the small of her back, exerting a bit of pressure. "If they ask you something you can't answer, it's best to say nothing. Ignore it."

With the pressure of his familiar touch, she made it to the podium. Cameras snapped around her, but the flash was muted by the brilliant summer day. All of the faces blurred and her heart pounded so hard, she was surprised the microphones didn't pick it up.

"Look at the tops of their heads. Look at their parts. It makes it easier than looking them in the eye."

She did as he instructed. Leaning into the microphones, she said, "Good afternoon. I'm Inspector…" Feedback from the microphones pierced everyone's ear. Devan tugged her back a step.

"Just speak normally."

Speak normally? Cute. The podium came to mid-chest and when she rested her hands on it, she had to lift herself on her toes to make sure her mouth was anywhere near the microphones. She felt like a little kid, trying to sneak cookies off the kitchen counter.

"Good afternoon," she repeated. "I'm Inspector Peyton Brooks of the San Francisco Police Department." She tried to enunciate the words, but she couldn't hear anything in the rush of blood inside her ears. "I've been authorized to answer a few questions you have about a case we are currently working on. Please understand that this is an on-going case and therefore, whatever information I give you will be limited to protect the sanctity of our investigation."

There. Statement delivered.

"Good job," muttered Devan.

Hands shot up. Peyton felt panic skitter over her. He'd mentioned something about questions, but how did she pick who to call on?

The decision was taken away from her.

"Is it true you're investigating a serial killer?"

Peyton searched for the voice and found a man with a long face holding his hand in the air. "We have a number of deaths we're investigating that we believe are related."

"Is it a serial killer?"

Peyton forced herself to remember what both Devan and Defino had told her. Give them a non-answer. "This is an on-going investigation and we are covering all possibilities."

"Is it true that there was a killing on Alcatraz?" said someone else.

"We are investigating two deaths on the island, yes."

"One of them was a priest, right?"

"I cannot confirm that at this time."

"Do you have any suspects?"

"We are investigating all leads and have collected a large amount of evidence."

"Isn't it true that one of the police officers shot a suspect?"

Peyton drew a quivering breath, her hands tightening on the podium. "There was an officer related shooting, yes."

"Where is that officer?"

"By protocol, he has been put on leave pending an investigation. That is standard police procedure whenever there is an officer related shooting."

"Did the killer stab someone while the police were trying to find him?"

Where the hell were they getting all this information? She shot a look at Devan. He gave a nod toward the microphone and pressed a hand against her back again. "Officers were in route to a call when there was an attack. Unfortunately, the victim died."

A woman pushed to the front of the crowd. She was tall, African American, and very pretty. "Is it true that all of the victims are convicted sex offenders? Child molesters?"

Peyton focused on her. This must be Free-lance. "Can I have your name please?"

She looked at the reporters on either side of her, but she faced Peyton again. "Genevieve Lake with the San Francisco Examiner."

"Ms. Lake, this is an on-going investigation and I cannot divulge that information."

"The first two men can be found on the Megan's Law database. The last murder victim had a custody agreement filed with the county, which granted full custody to the mother due to an on-going child molestation case. All public record, Inspector Brooks. I don't think it hurts your investigation to confirm what we can all find out on our own."

Peyton narrowed her eyes on her. If she thought she was a bitch before, who was Peyton to disappoint her? "I think it would be reckless to make assumptions on a case that is currently under investigation. Furthermore, reporting such unconfirmed information would not only be harmful, but unprofessional and amateurish."

Her façade cracked a bit and she glanced at the reporters on either side.

Peyton ignored her, looking out over the rest of the reporters. "Thank you for coming. As soon as we have more information, we will update you." Backing up, she and Devan started to turn away. More questions were shouted at them, but they ignored it.

Genevieve Lake wasn't finished. She took a few steps forward, coming up against a uniform positioned to keep reporters from the precinct. "People are calling him the Janitor, Inspector Brooks. Have you heard that?"

Peyton faltered and looked back over her shoulder. What the hell!

"They're saying he's an avenger, righting the wrongs of the justice system. He only preys on child molesters, monsters, men who deserve to die."

Peyton stared at her, feeling panic well inside. This was bad. This was exactly what they wanted to avoid. Reckless bitch! What was she trying to do?

"Peyton?" said Devan, a note of worry in his voice.

Peyton knew she had to do something, she had to stop this now.

"If the police aren't capable of stopping him from killing under their noses, maybe it's because you know he's right."

Peyton forced herself to walk back to the podium. She gripped the edges hard, the wood biting into her fingers. "Anyone who takes the law into his own hands is not an avenger. Do not confuse reality and fantasy, Ms. Lake. Our justice system was created to keep order and when we deviate from that, when we take the law into our own hands, not only are we criminals, vigilantes, but we invite chaos and anarchy into our lives. Anyone who commits murder is a murderer, plain and simple, and we will stop him!"

With that, she turned her back and walked away.

CHAPTER 15

Dr. Ferguson glanced up when Peyton entered the conference room the following day. She placed her mug on the table and sat down. Nervous energy had kept her up long after she knew she should be asleep. Stan Neumann wasn't getting any hits on his gaming profiles and the clock was ticking. The serial killer wasn't going to wait much longer before he struck, especially now that half the City had painted him as some avenging superhero.

Watching the news conference on the television should have made her feel better. She'd actually handled herself better than she expected, but the *Janitor* comment had taken off and spread across the country within hours. This was just the sort of publicity that serial killers loved. And this one was already bold. What would stroking his ego do? Peyton feared the body count was destined to go up.

"I was impressed with the way you dealt with the press conference yesterday, Inspector Brooks. You struck the exact tone and handled yourself admirably."

Peyton picked up her mug and took a sip. Lately she'd been trying to curb her sweet tooth, but this morning, frankly, she hadn't cared. It took four tablespoons before she could stomach the precinct's tar.

"I know it was a situation you weren't prepared for, but I think you can feel proud of your performance."

She gave him a polite smile and settled the mug on the table again.

He steepled his hands. "Was it difficult to coordinate the press conference with your ex-boyfriend, or whatever young people call them these days?"

"Difficult?"

"Stir up memories, feelings."

"No." And it hadn't. For the first time, she and Devan had been able to work together without it becoming a screaming match. Maybe they were making progress.

"Are you taking another page from your partner's book?"

"Come again?"

"One word answers, silence. That's usually his forte, Inspector Brooks."

At the mention of Marco, Peyton exhaled. "No, I'm not playing any games with you, Dr. Ferguson. I'm just tired of this whole thing."

"The counseling sessions?"

"The counseling sessions, the worry, the stress. By now, you must know whether you're going to pull my badge or not, and you also know when or if you're going to let Marco come back to work. Nothing I say beyond this is going to change anything."

"I disagree. There are a great many things that could change the situation from what it is. Your silence might be one of them."

"I'm not in the mood for threats this morning, Dr. Ferguson."

"I wasn't threatening, Inspector Brooks, I just want us to understand one another. I have very specific goals for our sessions, and silence isn't one of them."

"I have goals too, Dr. Ferguson. One is to get my partner back to work, and here's the truth – Marco *is* my partner and keeping us apart is a mistake. We work better when we're together. We complement and protect each other."

"I think you did fine on your own yesterday."

Peyton gave an aggravated snort of laughter. "Because I imagined him being here and I imagined what he would tell me. When I came out of Defino's office and looked at all of you, the only person I wanted to see, the only person that mattered at that moment was Marco. For eight years, I have known that when I need him he is there." She placed her index finger on the table for emphasis. "When I needed him on Alcatraz, he took the shot. He shouldn't be on leave. He should be receiving a medal."

"At some point, you may have to do this job without him. If he gets promoted or he decides to quit, what will you do then?"

"I don't know. That isn't something I have to face right now. Right now, he's my partner and that's all that matters."

"I think this points to a bigger issue, Inspector Brooks. Your self-esteem, your very self-worth is tied to a co-dependent relationship with your partner. It isn't healthy. We all need to be able to stand on our own feet. While we need a supportive network around us, we need to be secure in our own abilities. You aren't."

Peyton curled her fingers around the mug. Honestly, she'd gone past caring what he said. All the textbook learning and college lectures only went so far. People were more complicated than whatever could be put down into words, but unfortunately, Dr. Ferguson didn't understand that. He was a man trying to force three-dimensional people into his two-dimensional science.

She might as well change the subject. "So, did Marco leave you with a cliffhanger yesterday?"

"You know he did."

"Which one?"

"The story of the bombing. The one that killed the homeless woman."

The one where Marco saved her life for the first time.

"Where did he leave off?"

"No one could get any identifying information from the body or the bomb. You'd run up against a dead end."

Peyton took another sip of coffee. Marco was ingenious. Not only was the story exciting, but it made him look like all kinds of hero when you got to the end, especially if Peyton was the one telling the ending.

*   *   *

The glass doors swished open with an audible hiss as Peyton and Marco entered the large, commercial nursery. Aisles of gardening equipment, pots, clippers, hanging doodads, crowded the interior. Bags of potting soil actually leaked out into the middle of the aisles, forcing people to step over them.

She wasn't sure what good this little excursion was going to do them, but Defino seemed to think it was worth a shot. And to be fair, they had nothing else to go on. A call to Homeland Security had gotten lukewarm results. They said someone would come out to help them with the case, but it didn't seem to be high on their list of worries at the moment.

She looked down the bank of cash registers. Only two were manned, both by teenagers who sullenly scanned the customers' purchases and slapped them into plastic bags. Peyton nodded toward the end. A return counter occupied the far corner of the store and a man in his mid-twenties was staring at something on a computer screen. Since he was the only worker in the store without a smattering of acne on his face, Peyton figured he might be the manager.

They headed in his direction. He glanced up as they got close. His mousey brown hair was combed back from a wide forehead and he had dirt splatters on the orange apron he wore.

"How can I help you?"

Peyton removed her badge and held it out. "Are you the manager?"

His eyes widened upon seeing the badge and he vigorously shook his head. "I'll get him. Look it was just an office party. We didn't even know they were underaged."

Peyton and Marco exchanged a look. Shit. Underaged for what?

"You expect me to believe that," she said, leaning into the counter.

"It was just beer. That's all. Just a few beers and I didn't let them drive."

Peyton released her held breath. Behind her, Marco relaxed. "Actually, we're here about something else." When the clerk's shoulders dropped, Peyton pointed her finger at him. "But don't let it happen again."

He nodded vigorously.

"Can you get the manager, please?"

He picked up the phone and punched in four numbers. He gave the two of them a wary look as he waited for someone to pick up. "Ted, two cops are here, say they want to talk to you." Peyton could hear a voice speaking on the other side. "No, not about that." He covered the mouth piece. "He wants to know what you're here for."

"We want to ask him about some of his products."

The clerk repeated Peyton's request. Listening, his expression changed to one of frustration. "Fine. Yeah, fine." Slamming the phone back on the cradle, he gave Peyton a bored look. "He says he's busy doing inventory, that I can answer your questions. If not, you can leave your card and he'll get back to you as soon as he can."

Marco shrugged.

It wasn't as if this was going to net them anything, Peyton knew, but it annoyed her that the manager didn't feel they merited his attention. "Fine. We're trying to track down materials that might be used to make a bomb."

"A bomb?" He gave her a skeptical look. "This is a home improvement store."

"I understand that, but you also sell chemicals here."

"For home improvement. You know, cleaning and stuff."

Peyton didn't love his attitude. "Do you sell ammonium nitrate?"

"Yeah, it's called fertilizer. Makes your grass green."

Peyton cocked her head at him. "Does every nursery sell it?"

"Yeah, it's sold all over the bay area. Nurseries, home improvement stores, grocery stores."

"Does anyone buy it in large quantities?"

He gave her a disbelieving look. "Yeah, they're called landscapers. Gardeners. Farmers."

Peyton pressed up against the counter. "I could do with a lot less attitude. Let me school you on something, buddy...COPS ARREST PEOPLE!"

He took a step back.

Marco hooked the tail of her jacket and pulled her away, stepping between her and the clerk.

"Did she just threaten me?"

Marco gave a careless shrug. "She might have." His expression grew hard. "But me, I don't threaten."

The clerk's eyes widened until white showed around the iris.

"Now, here's what you're going to do. You're going to have your manager get me a list of everyone who bought ammonium nitrate in the last month and he's going to do it now."

"The last month? Everyone?"

"That's right. Everyone." Marco gave him a cold smile. "I think it's a good time to get your manager, don't you?"

The clerk scrambled away without a word.

Peyton's phone vibrated. She dug it out of her jacket and lifted it to her ear. "Brooks?"

"Brooks," came Maria's voice. "We just got a call from a professor at Berkeley. He wants to meet with you about a student, said he asked some strange questions during a lecture."

"You got a phone number?"

"I got an address. I'll send it by text."

"Great. Talk to you later, beautiful."

Maria made a gagging sound and hung up.

Peyton put her phone in her pocket as she walked over to Marco. "You think the rabbit will get the manager to come out?"

"I think he better 'cause I go back there next."

"Well, we don't need him. We got a call from a professor at Berkeley, who wants to talk to us about a student. Maria's sending the address."

"Let's go."

They headed toward the doors, which swished open as they approached. As they crossed the parking lot, Peyton pointed back over her shoulder. "That was fun back there."

"It was," said Marco, giving her a smile. "We should do it again sometime."

"We should."

"But next time I say we make him wet himself."

Peyton hit his shoulder with the back of her hand. "I like it."

They both burst into laughter.

*   *   *

In order to reach the University of California, visitors have to drive through the city of Berkeley. Berkeley is built on a series of hills and the streets all branch off the main thoroughfare, University Avenue. Below the city glimmers the San Francisco Bay and above it stretches the Pacific Coast Range, covered in redwoods and oak and eucalyptus trees, dotted occasionally by multi-million dollar homes.

Marco drove the Charger up University toward the campus. Peyton watched the colorful people meandering up and down the street, homeless people intermingled with college students and young couples with children.

"You ever come here when you were a teenager?" Marco asked, glancing over at her.

"My father would have killed me. I had a very tight leash as a kid."

"Cop's daughter and all, eh?"

"You got it."

"He do background checks on your boyfriends."

Peyton glanced over at him. "What boyfriends?"

Marco chuckled.

"You come to Berkeley as a kid?"

"Yep. My brothers used to take me to concerts at the Greek."

"Did your parents know?"

"Yeah, Bernardo went to Cal."

"Ah, that must have been hard on you – living up to your brother."

Marco shrugged. "Vinnie went to Stanford."

Peyton winced.

"Tell me about it."

"Don't you have a third brother?"

"Yeah, Franco."

"Where'd he go?"

Marco pulled into the circle at the start of the campus. "He's a disappointment. San Francisco State. Master's degree in Civil Engineering."

Peyton smiled. "You and me must be hopeless then."

"I think it's you and I, but what do I know?" He nodded at the unmanned information booth. "Wanna grab us a map?"

She jumped out and grabbed one from the plastic holder. Climbing back into the car, she held it so the two of them could view it. "Here it is," she said, pointing at the square on the paper. Looking around, she searched for a parking space. "Think we'll get a ticket if we park there?" She motioned to an open spot at the end of the circular drive.

"I think Defino will take care of it for us. Feel like a hike?"

"Sure."

Marco parked the Charger where Peyton indicated and they climbed out. Using the map to guide them, they began the trek up the steep hills of the campus. Peyton looked around at the interesting buildings and abundance of redwood trees. In some areas, it looked as if the forest had just come into the campus and taken over, and no two buildings looked the same.

"It sure is pretty."

Marco nodded.

They found the physical science building and went inside. The professor's office was on the second floor. There was no reception desk, so she and Marco walked down the hall until they came to the number Maria had texted to them.

Peyton glanced up and down the dimly lit hall, then knocked on the door. A moment later, it opened and a short, stout man poked his head out. He had a grey beard, a bushy mustache and thinning hair.

"Yes?" he asked, blinking at them from behind large oval glasses.

Peyton reached for her badge. "I'm Inspector Brooks and this is Inspector D'Angelo."

He gave them a skeptical look, then stared at her badge. "You hardly look older than my students," he said, pulling open the door and motioning them inside. "Come in."

The office was cramped with bookshelves that overflowed with manuscripts and hardbound books. Three chairs occupied the space, along with the professor's desk chair, but they were piled high with papers and folders. The professor scooped up an armful and turned a circle, trying to find a spot to put it down.

"Please have a seat. I notified campus police as well and they said they'd send someone over." He deposited the pile on a shelf and reached for another.

Marco motioned her into the vacated spot, while he waited for the professor to dispose of his second load. Dumping it on top of the first pile, the professor placed his hands on his hips and gave them a cool look as Marco took the chair and sat down.

"Why don't you sit, Professor?" said Peyton. "I didn't get your name."

"Professor Karl, Albert Karl. I didn't get your name either or I mean, I didn't process it."

"Brooks." She pointed at herself. "D'Angelo."

"Inspectors? Really? What are you, barely twenty-one?"

Peyton decided to deflect that question. "Our receptionist told us that you were concerned about a student."

"Yes, Will Taber. He's a student in my Chem. 1A class. I read an article about the unfortunate woman killed by a homemade bomb and it made me even more worried."

"Tell us what happened, Professor."

"It might not be anything. A lot of people have curiosity."

"Curiosity about what?"

"Making bombs. Every semester I have a student ask me what I would use to make a bomb. I usually dismiss it, it happens so frequently, but Will Taber was different. He didn't just want to know how to make it. He wanted to know how you detonate it from a distance."

"Did you talk to him after class?"

The professor gave her a confused look. "Class?"

Peyton glanced helplessly at Marco.

Lecture, he mouthed.

"Lecture."

"Do you know how many students I have in a Chem. 1A lecture, Inspector Brooks?"

Peyton sighed. No, she didn't know how many students he had. Why should she know that? Was that something all college students knew? "Enlighten me."

He gave her a look over the top of his glasses as if to say there was no hope of enlightening her. "150 on a slow day."

"And yet you knew who this Will Taber was?" There. That should school him.

Marco gave her a brief encouraging nod, but the professor considered her as if she were an experiment.

"He asked so many questions about bombs, I asked the GSIs who he was. One of them remembered him from lab. He asked a lot of strange questions there too."

"Hold on." Peyton held up a hand to stop him. "GSIs?"

"Graduate Student Instructors." He exhaled heavily.

Of course. Peyton bit her lip to stop the snarky comment that desperately wanted to come out. Twice today they'd been subjected to unnecessary sarcasm and frankly, she was getting sick of it. Why couldn't Home Land Security just handle this?

Professor Karl gave Marco a critical look over his glasses. "What are you? Arm candy?"

Marco's mouth opened, but he didn't respond.

Peyton felt her jaw clench. "No, he's here to shoot people who get too mouthy. Look, Professor, you called us."

"I called the precinct and asked for some real detectives, not two cub scouts with merit badges."

Peyton rose to her feet.

Marco closed his eyes and shook his head grimly.

"Let's get something straight here, Professor. Yesterday, we saw a woman who bled out in an alley from a screwdriver that had punctured her jugular vein. The tip of her nose was burnt away in the blast and she died alone, searching for something to eat in a freakin' dumpster."

He leaned away from her, his hands gripping the arms of his chair.

"So why don't you help out *two cub scouts with merit badges* and tell us where to find this little prick before someone else dies?"

A knock sounded at the door behind them.

Marco reached over and patted the professor's knee. "Don't strain yourself, Professor. Let the arm candy get it for you."

* * *

"According to Housing, he lives in this dorm," said Sergeant Nelson, pointing to a cluster of white buildings on the campus map.

"Isn't that off-campus?" asked Peyton.

Everyone looked over at the campus police representative, Patrol Officer Comphel. "Yeah, in the hills, right behind Frat Row."

A trip to the administration building and Student Affairs had led them here. According to Housing, Will Taber's roommate had requested a dorm change because of "strange smells, weird contraptions, and general creepiness." He now had a double room all to himself.

Once they got that report, Marco had called for a search warrant and Peyton had called Sergeant Nelson. Thankfully, he'd arrived in the hour with his bomb squad. Both campus and city police had immediately agreed to let San Francisco run point on this case.

"When he asked about detonators, what did you tell him, Professor?" asked Sergeant Nelson.

Professor Karl seemed happy to deal with the middle aged sergeant. His attitude had changed dramatically on the walk over to the Housing office. "I didn't tell him anything, but it's not like he can't figure it out on his own. A few internet searches and voila." He held out his hands.

Peyton removed her pad and scribbled a note to confiscate Taber's computer, so they could review his search history. The D.A. would need all the evidence he could get, since the bomb itself provided nothing.

"Ted Kaczynski used match heads and a nail. Others have used alarm clocks, trip wires, you name it. When you go in there, I'd be very careful about opening anything unless you know what's inside," instructed the professor.

"We've got this." Nelson turned to Peyton and Marco. "I'll send my squad in first to evacuate the building. Do we know where Taber is supposed to be right now?"

"He has a class until 4:00PM on the other side of campus," replied Comphel.

"Let's get someone out to detain him immediately."

Comphel reached for his radio and turned away so he could give the order.

Nelson focused on Peyton and Marco. "The two of you wait outside the building until we give the all clear. Then you can come in and do your investigation."

"Understood."

"Wear your flak jackets. We don't know what we're facing."

Marco nodded.

"Comphel?" said Nelson.

"Yes, sir."

"Lead us up to this dorm. Radio ahead and have your people begin clearing the building, but don't go inside."

"Got it."

"Set up a perimeter and keep everyone out. We need Taber's room number."

Comphel passed him a slip of paper.

"What do you want me to do?" asked the professor.

"Stay here," answered Peyton, following behind Nelson as he moved toward the exit.

They rode in Comphel's university-issue sedan to the Charger. As Marco started the car and pulled in behind Comphel, Peyton leaned over the seat and hooked their flak jackets. Once they got on city streets, Comphel turned on his light and they rushed up the hills toward the collection of white buildings on the other side of campus.

Comphel drove them down a narrow, single lane road, winding through redwood trees and eucalyptus. They parked in a narrow parking lot outside the dorm and climbed out. The smell of eucalyptus enveloped them, mixed with the faintest touch of sea air.

Peyton took off her shoulder harness and tugged on the flak jacket, surveying the scene. White buildings, two and three stories tall, spread around them, topped with red tiles in a Spanish mission style. Fountains and planter beds interspersed the buildings, softening the harsh stucco walls.

A moment later, students began streaming out of the buildings, looking at the cops with bewildered expressions, talking on cell phones, or huddling together, muttering anxiously. They were ushered toward the streets by campus police.

Nelson approached Marco and Peyton. He nodded at the building closest to them. "This is where he lives. Once they finish evacuating, my men and I will go in. You wait out here."

Peyton nodded, adjusting the straps on her jacket, then reached into the car and pulled her gun out of its holster. "Be careful, Sergeant."

"Always am."

A moment later he got the all clear and started down the hill toward Taber's building. A number of students came out of the building behind them and wandered toward Comphel, asking him what was going on. Comphel stepped across the parking lot to meet them, leaving Peyton and Marco alone.

Peyton shifted weight. "I hate this."

"The threat?"

"No, the waiting."

"You don't think he'd be stupid enough to have bombs in there, do you?" Marco indicated the building with his chin.

"Who the hell knows? He's had a room all to himself for how long?"

"Who wakes up one day and says, hey, I think I'll make a bomb and see how many people I can kill?"

"You could ask that about any killer, couldn't you? If we had that answer, we'd be super heroes."

"I guess so."

Peyton paced across the parking lot. How long would it take them to search his room, secure whatever they might find there?

Shifting around, she studied the building. A homeless man appeared around the bend in the road, aimlessly moving toward the dorm. Peyton hurried across the parking lot and caught up with him, turning him back the way he'd come. "You have to go that way," she said, giving him a gentle push with one hand, while holding her gun out of his line of sight with the other.

He accepted her guidance and wandered a few feet away, then he stalled, bending over to inspect some plants. Peyton released an annoyed breath and moved toward him, but motion in the corner of her eye caught her attention. She turned and looked behind the dorm. Someone was running up the incline behind the buildings, heading toward the densely wooded hills.

"Marco!" she called, and began moving to cut the person off. It had to be Taber.

They jogged down to a loading dock at the side entrance to the building. A retaining wall blocked the incline and Peyton searched for a way to climb it. Behind them was a wooden fence, enclosing two dumpsters.

Placing her hands on the top of the wall, Peyton looked up at the person climbing toward the hills. "Stop!" she shouted.

He hesitated and looked over his shoulder. Shaggy brown hair flopped down over his eyes and he held something to the side of his face.

"Give me a boost!" she called back to Marco.

He started toward her, but a cell phone suddenly rang behind them. They both turned around, bewildered. The sound was muffled as if it were blocked by something. Marco moved a few steps back toward the dumpster with Peyton a stride behind him. The ringing was coming from inside.

"What—" Peyton began.

Marco whirled. "Get down!"

The next instant everything exploded. The top flew off the dumpster, Marco leaped for her and knocked her onto her back, the air slamming out of her lungs. She felt his body cover hers, his arms folding over her head as debris rained down on them.

Peyton fought to catch her breath, but her lungs seemed incapable of expanding. The weight of Marco's body pressed her into the unforgiving asphalt and her head rang.

Finally, she felt her body heave upward and blessed oxygen rushed into her laboring lungs.

"Fornicators!" came a voice above them.

Peyton blinked open her eyes and stared into the shaggy bearded face of the homeless man.

"Fornicators!" he shouted, wagging a finger at them.

Marco lifted his head, blinking his eyes, then he began searching over Peyton. "Are you hurt? Peyton, are you hurt?"

She caught his hands. "I'm okay. Knocked...the air out of me." She still struggled to get enough oxygen. "Help me up, please."

He shifted off her and pulled her to her feet, his hands roving over her shoulders and sides. "Are you sure you're not hurt?"

She opened her mouth wide to clear her ears. "I'm all right. Are you hurt?"

"Fornicators!"

Marco placed a hand in the middle of the homeless man's chest and pushed him back a pace. Suddenly Comphel was next to them.

"I called for an ambulance. Nelson's on the way out here."

Marco walked Peyton backward to the red painted curb and urged her to sit. Her knees were shaking so badly, she complied.

"Are either of you hurt?" came Comphel's worried voice.

"We're all right," said Marco, but his eyes searched Peyton's face. He reached up and pulled a long, white string out of her hair.

Peyton watched it. "Is that cheese?"

He nodded and tossed it away.

She shuddered involuntarily.

He gave a grim laugh. "It could be worse." Pointing to the side, he motioned at a bit of half-burnt rubber. "That's a condom."

Peyton shivered again, gagging.

"Here." Comphel handed Peyton her gun. She didn't remember dropping it.

"Do the Berkeley police have K9 units?" she asked, checking to see if the gun was damaged in the fall.

"Yeah."

"Can you get one out here? I think our suspect just took to the hills."

"On it."

Comphel stepped away to make the call.

Nelson suddenly appeared, racing around the corner. In the distance, Peyton could hear the sounds of sirens.

"Where are you hurt?"

"We're all right," said Marco.

The other bomb squad officers fanned out around them.

"Get that ambulance over here," Nelson ordered.

"We don't need it."

"The hell you don't." He hunkered in front of Peyton and tilted her head back, peering into her eyes. "You could have head injuries and don't even know it. A day from now, someone finds you dead."

Marco and Peyton exchanged anxious looks.

"And there wasn't even any fornicating," she said sadly.

Marco burst into laughter.

*   *   *

Peyton walked gingerly down the hall of the hospital and peered into Marco's room. He had his back to her as he struggled to pull on his shirt. A massive black and blue bruise covered his entire right side.

"Good God, D'Angelo, who's been beating on you?"

He turned and sucked in an agonized breath at the motion. "Thanks a lot, Brooks."

"Did they x-ray that?" she said, pointing at the bruise.

259

"Yeah, couple of bruised ribs." He gave her a narrow eyed look. "What about you?"

"Just sore. Nothing broken. Thanks to you." She crossed the room and stopped before him.

He had the shirt up to his forearms, but lifting it over his head seemed to be problematic.

"Should have worn a button-up."

"Yeah, I never dress appropriately for a bombing."

She smiled. "They caught Taber."

"Good."

"His room was full of evidence. Apparently it was quite a sight."

"I'll bet." He lifted the shirt, wincing, and got his head inside, but he struggled to pull it down.

She reached up and helped him. "I thought we had a rule about this."

His eyes glittered with pain. "About what?"

"You running around naked in front of me." She smoothed it over the taut lines of his belly.

"Yeah, well, you seem pretty damn intent on breaking all the rules, Brooks, so I wouldn't talk if I were you."

She reached out and caught his hand. "Thank you for saving my life."

He gave her a skeptical look. "Nelson said it wasn't strong enough to kill us. Maim us, yeah, but it probably wouldn't have done much worse."

"Well if that's all." Moving forward, she lifted on tiptoes and kissed his cheek.

He blinked at her in surprise.

"Thank you," she said, giving his hand a squeeze.

"Forget it. That's what partners do."

She smiled and released him, taking a step away. "You're right. That's what partners do."

* * *

260

"Holy shit," breathed Ferguson. "The two of you have been through hell together."

Peyton lifted her eyes to him. "Is that a clinical assessment, Dr. Ferguson?"

He blinked at her. "What?"

"Holy shit?"

He gave a short laugh. "No, it was an honest reaction."

Peyton glanced at the clock over his head. Bracing her hands on the table, she rose to her feet. "Let my partner come back to work, Dr. Ferguson," she said. Then without another word, she left the room.

CHAPTER 16

Peyton parked her Corolla next to the Charger and sat staring up at Marco's apartment building. Glancing down, she noticed her hands were shaking on the steering wheel. She tightened them into fists. She had to confront this thing or there was no way she and Marco would ever get back to a working relationship. Alcatraz loomed large in her mind, dominating her every thought.

Throwing open the door, she climbed out and began walking toward the building. Just as she neared it, the door opened and Marco's mother appeared. She stopped and looked Peyton over, then she continued on, forcing a smile.

"Peyton, how are you, sweetheart?" she said, opening her arms for a hug.

Peyton stepped into her embrace and smiled as Mona kissed her cheek. "I'm all right. How are you, Mona?"

Marco's mother stepped back, but she slid her hands down and grasped Peyton's fingers. "I'm fine." Her eyes seemed liquid in the fading light of the day. "Actually, I've been better."

"What's going on?"

She glanced over her shoulder at the closed door. "He worries me. I come over here, bring him food and try to clean up, but I find the food half eaten in the refrigerator and the dishes sitting in the sink."

"Well, he's a bachelor, Mona."

Mona leaned close to Peyton. "And I think he's picking up strange women."

Peyton reared back, but Mona wouldn't let her go. "Strange women?" She didn't want to get into a discussion about this with Marco's mother.

Mona nodded. "Vinnie says he has a new girl, but when I ask him, he says he doesn't. All this time and he doesn't get married." She dropped her voice. "He's thirty now."

Peyton squeezed her hands in comfort. "He doesn't believe cops should marry, Mona. You know that."

"I know, and it's not really that."

"What is it?"

Mona met Peyton's gaze. "He needs to go to confession. I ask him every day and he gets angry at me, but he has to go. He won't be at peace until he does. He has to ask God for forgiveness." She pressed Peyton's hands to her heart. "Ask him for me. Tell him to go with me this Saturday."

Peyton pulled back a bit. "I can't do that, Mona."

"Please...please. He'll do it for you. He'll do it if you ask him to."

"Why do you think that?"

"He thinks the world of you. He'll do it if you ask him. Please, Peyton, please help me save my son's soul."

Peyton released her held breath. Oh, lord, Marco was going to get pissed at her if she brought this up. Why the hell did his family think she had so much influence with him? Still, she couldn't deny the pain and worry in Mona's eyes. "I'll talk to him. I can't promise anything, but I'll talk to him."

Mona kissed Peyton's hands and released her. "You are a good girl. Your mama must be so proud of you."

Well, that was a can of mess she wasn't about to open right now. Instead she gave Mona a smile.

"Thank you," Mona said, moving past Peyton. "Thank you, sweetheart." Then she bustled off to her car.

Peyton watched her pull out of the parking lot, then she went to the door and climbed the stairs to Marco's apartment. Knocking, she thought about what Mona said. Marco needed to go to confession to save his soul. Maybe this visit of hers was her version of confession.

He opened the door abruptly, then seemed surprised to see her. "Hey, partner."

"Hey yourself. Can I come in?"

"Of course."

Peyton stepped into his living room. She had to admit, she'd never seen it so clean before. The coffee table was free of dust streaks and there weren't empty beer cans lying around. The couch cushions were actually on the couch, instead of strung across the floor.

Marco walked around the coffee table and muted the sound on the television. He wore a white t-shirt and a pair of athletic shorts. She couldn't help but admire the defined muscles in his calves.

"Have a seat." He motioned to the couch. A light breeze blew in from the kitchen, rustling the curtains. "Can I get you a beer?"

"Thanks."

He walked to the refrigerator and pulled it open, grabbing two beers in one hand. He twisted off the caps, tossing them into the sink, and carried them back into the living room, handing one to her. She took a sip to steady her nerves.

"I saw your mom in the parking lot."

He hesitated, then he sank into his arm chair, bracing his forearms on his thighs. He studied the label on the bottle for a moment. "What did she say?"

By his tone, she knew he guessed the direction of their conversation. She wasn't about to lie to him. "She wants you to go to confession with her on Saturday."

He didn't respond.

Peyton shifted on the couch, tucking one leg under her. "That's not what I want to talk about though."

He looked up through his thick lashes. "Okay?"

Peyton rubbed the back of her neck. It prickled with anxiety. "I need to talk to you about Alcatraz."

"There's nothing to talk about."

"There is for me."

"Okay. I'm listening."

Peyton rubbed at her temple, closing her eyes briefly. "I keep replaying it over and over in my mind, and I keep coming to the same conclusion." She opened her eyes and forced herself to look at him. "I should have been the one to take the shot."

"Peyton…" At her inhalation, he hesitated. "Brooks," he amended. "Stop torturing yourself. The shot was mine, I took it, the priest died. It's that simple."

"He was shooting at me."

"Which is why I had the better shot."

Peyton shook her head. "I can't believe that."

"Why? Why can't you believe what everyone else believes…knows?"

Peyton leaned forward and placed the beer on the coffee table. "Okay, here it is. When Peña held a gun to your head, I didn't take the shot. Rosa did."

"If you had taken the shot, I would have had a bullet in my brain."

"And then on Alcatraz, I froze. I didn't do anything."

"You were lying on your back, Brooks. He was shooting at you."

Peyton swallowed hard and forced herself to look him in the eye. "You've got to be asking yourself whether I'm capable of taking the shot when it counts. You've got to be wondering if I'm a liability to you. You must have asked yourself if you wouldn't be better off with another partner." There, she'd finally said it.

He didn't respond for a moment, simply stared at her. Then he leaned forward and placed his beer on the coffee table. Rising, he came to the couch and took a seat beside her.

Reaching out, he covered both of her hands with one of his own. "Listen to me, Peyton, and listen well. Not once in the last eight years have I wanted another partner. There is no doubt in my mind, no time when I have ever once questioned you. I trust you with my life." He reached up and fingered a curl that had slipped out of her ponytail. "I know that if I ever need you, if I ever need you to take the shot, you will." He tucked the curl behind her ear. "Please stop doubting yourself."

She turned her hand over and clasped his. "You know I love you, right, D'Angelo."

She wasn't sure, but she thought he might have winced. Still his fingers tightened against hers. "I know."

"About your mother."

He wearily tilted back his head and exhaled heavily.

"Maybe you should go to confession."

His eyes snapped to her and narrowed.

"Not for you, but…for her. Give her peace of mind."

He blessed her with a gentle smile. "You have a point."

She leaned forward and kissed his cheek.

As she drew away, he released her hand and patted her knee. "You gotta get out of here now."

"What?"

He pushed himself to his feet and loomed over her. "Yeah, I gotta get ready. I've got a date tonight."

"A date?" Peyton rose with him. "Not some blond bimbo, D'Angelo."

"That's none of your business. Now go."

She rolled her eyes, but she moved toward the door. "I swear, you'd think after all these years, I'd have taught you to have better taste in women."

"You'd think," he said, pulling open the door and leaning on it.

Peyton walked through and paused on the other side. "Talk to you tomorrow?"

"Of course."

She offered him a smile, then walked away, pushing open the door for the stairwell and jogging down toward the parking lot. She couldn't help but feel disappointed. She was really hoping that they could watch a baseball game together, reestablishing their equilibrium with each other, but just as she reached the Corolla, her cell phone rang.

* * *

Marco shut the door behind Peyton, then turned and leaned against it. He surveyed his apartment. Utilitarian furnishings, big screen TV, no books, no magazines, no frills. The only thing feminine he had were the curtains on the kitchen window, but his mother had picked those out.

He walked to the refrigerator and pulled it open, bending to peer inside. She had left him a number of little plastic boxes filled with something. He grabbed the first one and pulled off the top, studying the contents. Minestrone. He carried it to the microwave and shoved it inside, punching buttons to heat it.

Then he wandered back to his armchair and flung himself into it, grabbing the remote off the coffee table and pressing the sound button. Reaching for his beer, he filled his mouth with it and swallowed.

The announcer was calling the starting line-up. Marco wished he'd asked Peyton to stay. There was plenty of food and he liked watching the game with her. She didn't feel the need to question everything the way Abe would.

The buzzer on the microwave dinged, but he didn't move, staring at the brilliant green of the in-field. Leaning forward, he grabbed his cell phone off the table and thumbed it on. He pulled up his contacts and studied the familiar numbers to Peyton's phone.

He knew she'd come back if he called her. He knew she would do anything to make this distance go away between them. And he wanted nothing more himself. He hated the way she watched him, wary and afraid he was going to blame her, curse her for not taking the shot. That damn shot had changed everything between them.

Not that their partnership had ever been equal, but she had always been the one he deferred to and he liked it that way. Let her run point. Let her do the interrogations. She was the better cop. He always saw his role with such simplicity. Keep her alive, so she could figure things out.

Now, though, in her eyes, their roles were somehow reversed, up-ended, even though he didn't agree. He felt like he had fulfilled his role in her life, why couldn't she accept it?

Closing his eyes, he tightened his grip on the phone, then he leaned forward and placed it on the coffee table without making the call. Now was not the time to fix things between them. Especially not now when both of their emotions were running way too close to the surface.

If he wasn't careful, he was bound to say something that would ruin everything between them forever, and he couldn't risk it. He just couldn't take that chance. Not now, and probably not ever.

* * *

Peyton climbed behind the wheel, but didn't start the car. She pressed the screen on her phone and lifted it to her ear.

"Brooks?" Cho's voice.

"Hey, what's up? Stan get a hit?"

"No, but we got a body."

Peyton felt her heart sink. "Are you sure it's one of ours?"

"Yeah, it's ours. Just ran the name. The vic was arrested for lewd conduct with a minor two weeks ago."

"Where?"

"Presidio. How quick can you get over here?"

"I'll be there in twenty." She started the car and put it in reverse. As she passed the Charger, she wanted to cuss. It felt completely wrong to be going on a call without Marco. "Have you called Jake?"

"Yeah, he's here right now. We're probably going to send him to Abe with the murder weapon though. You want the details?"

"Not yet. I'm driving. Tell me everything when I get there."

"Okey dokey." He hung up.

As she raced to the scene, she couldn't believe how defeated she felt. Everything they did to stay in front of this bastard wasn't working. How were they ever going to get him?

By the time she arrived, the press had converged on the scene. The Presidio was a sprawling tract of land once operated as a military base, but now it was overseen by the park's department. For over 200 years, it had been a fortified location, occupied at different points by three separate countries. An act of Congress had saved it from being auctioned off, preserving the historic buildings under the Presidio Trust Act. Despite its size, Peyton had no trouble finding the crime scene with all of the cars and people standing behind yellow police tape.

She parked the Corolla and climbed out, taking her badge from her belt. She showed it to the uniform and he lifted the tape for her to duck beneath.

"Inspector Brooks?" came a voice behind her.

Peyton turned and surveyed the crowd. The reporter, Genevieve Lake, pushed between the people and stopped on the other side of the tape.

"Inspector Brooks, is this another attack by the Janitor?"

Peyton felt her jaw clench. She reached out and caught the uniform's sleeve, pointing at Genevieve. "Have someone escort that woman off the premises."

"Yes, Inspector," he said, reaching for his radio.

Peyton walked to Cho where he stood over a blanket-covered body. "You said you have a name?"

"Bruce Weller, computer programmer," said Cho. He hunkered over the body and reached for the blanket, pulling it back.

The man's eyes bulged and his throat was black and blue. Capillaries had burst on his cheekbones and the whites of his eyes were red. Peyton fought down her grimace of distaste.

"Strangulation?" she said, hunkering down across from Cho.

"With a dog leash."

Peyton's eyes lifted to Cho's face. "Dog leash?" She glanced around. "Where's the dog?"

"Didn't find one." He pointed across a grassy area where Simons stood talking to a woman. "She jogged past him earlier, down by the bay, and she said she didn't see a dog then either."

"Where's the leash?"

"Jake took it to Abe. The killer had to exert a lot of force to strangle someone this big. We estimate the vic at about 200 to 220lbs. He fought back. He's got split nails and fibers imbedded in the quick. We were hoping the killer might have left some DNA on the leash. We wanted to get it to Abe before it has a chance to degrade."

Peyton nodded. "How'd he get the drop on someone so big?"

Cho pointed to a bench a few feet away. "We think he came up behind him when the vic was tying his shoes." He pulled back the blanket from his feet. One shoe was missing. "The struggle brought them over here."

"No one saw it?"

"No one that we've met."

"Who called it in?"

"Another jogger. Holmes is talking to him." He pointed over his shoulder.

Peyton studied the bruising around Weller's neck. "It's getting more personal."

"Yeah."

She met Cho's gaze. "Escalating."

"Looks that way."

"Did he have the *Clean-up Crew* card on him?"

"Yeah. It was just sitting on his chest. Jake took that as well, hoping maybe the killer is getting sick of it and wants to be caught. He's not even trying to hide it anymore."

"Do we have any idea how the killer found this guy?"

"Not Megan's List. We found out about his record from the police database. The arrest was too recent to be on Megan's List."

Peyton frowned. "Could the killer be a cop?" It was the only way she could think he'd have access to their database.

"Anything's possible."

"We need to get this guy's computer. See if there's anything on it."

"When we found his wallet and ID, I sent Smith over to get it. He's bringing it to Stan."

"Good thinking. Was the vic married?"

"Not even once."

"It really worries me that the killer might have access to our data bases, Nathan."

"Let's get the computer and see what's on it."

Peyton reached out and covered Bruce Weller's face. "To strangle someone, you gotta really want them dead."

"I know."

She bowed her head. God, she was so sick of this case. There was simply no way to shift the advantage in their favor. If they didn't discover how he found Weller, there would be another body before the weekend. They just couldn't lose ground anymore. They just couldn't lose. She might not know the rules of this game, but the stakes were mounting.

* * *

Jake juggled Abe's box of whatnots and reached into his pocket for the key.

"Just knock."

"I don't want to disturb her if she's sleeping."

"It's only 8:00."

"But the lights are off." He dug the key out, bracing the box against the doorjamb. Struggling to put the key into the lock, he turned it and pushed the door open.

Abe brushed by him and found his way in the dark to the kitchen, carrying his own bags of crap, while Jake used the edge of the box to flip on the living room lights. Looking over his shoulder, he saw Peyton sitting on the couch, in the dark, holding Pickles. Jake wondered why the little dog hadn't barked his head off when they came home.

Walking around the end of the couch, he looked down at her. "Sitting in the dark? Way to go all Goth on me."

"Emo."

"Emo? You sure?"

"No." She shook her head. "It's probably some other annoying abbreviation by now."

He gave her a once-over. "You aren't wearing black. Did you get some tattoos?"

"Not yet."

"Do you want to bring my supplies in here, Jake, or do you want to keep on with this cute repartee?" Abe leaned over the counter. "Heya, sweetie, come in here. I got something to fix up the mopes."

Jake backed to the kitchen, then settled the box on the counter. Abe grabbed it and then shooed him from the room. Peyton set Pickles down and walked over to the bar stools, climbing up on the one closest to the couch.

"What's up?" asked Jake, leaning on the end of the counter.

Peyton watched Abe unpack his box. "Nothing much."

Abe pulled out a blender, a bottle of crème de menthe, one of cream de cacao, and vanilla ice cream. Next he removed four martini glasses. "Call my Angel and tell him to get his gorgeous hiney over here."

"He has a date with a blond bimbo."

Jake gave her a critical look. "Is that why you're sitting in the dark?"

She stared at him as if he were an imbecile. "No."
Then she hesitated and sighed. "Well, not entirely. Did you get anything off the dog leash, Abe?"

"Trace DNA," he said, grabbing his shopping bag and pulling out ice and some chocolate ice cream topping.

"Is that the ice cream stuff that hardens when it gets cold?" she asked.

"Sure is." He tilted the martini glass and poured a looping pattern of chocolate around the bottom and edges. He did the same for two others.

"Will you be able to identify it?"

"The DNA?" Abe shrugged. "Only if we get a match in the system. That would mean our serial killer has been caught before." He reached for the blender and began pouring the contents of the bottles into it. "Most likely, we'll get DNA only from the victim. The last tests were clean. He was probably wearing gloves."

Peyton braced her head on her hand.

Jake reached over and squeezed her other hand where it lay on the counter. "We'll get him. Maybe this last guy's computer will let us know how the serial killer found him."

Abe began spooning ice cream into the blender. "He's bound to screw up one of these times."

"Yeah, how many more people die before he does? And did you see the media out there, Jake? You watch. Tomorrow there's gonna be another *Janitor* article."

Abe threw in a cup of ice cubes, then gave Peyton a glance. "You eat anything tonight?"

"I grabbed a burrito."

He punched the button on the blender and the whir of it filled the room. Pickles scampered over to Jake and pawed his leg to be picked up. Jake scooped him into his arms and covered his ears. Abe reached over and scratched him, then turned off the machine.

Removing the lid, he poured the concoction into the three glasses over the spirals of ice cream topping. Then he dropped a wooden stick with a crepe paper ball into the glass, added a straw, and slid it across the counter to them.

Peyton picked it up and gave it a skeptical look. "What is it?"

"Well, technically it's a Grasshopper, but once you add the pretty beach ball and the swirls of chocolate, it becomes something more. I call it *Sex in the Tall Grass*."

Jake took an experimental sip. It was actually quite smooth and refreshing. "Why not call it *Sex with a Grasshopper*?"

Peyton almost spit out her drink. "I like it. *Sex with a Grasshopper*."

"*Sex with a Grasshopper*," Jake repeated, smiling at her.

"I think you got something there."

"I think so too. Just imagine. Pretty soon all the latest movie stars will be asking for it."

"Then it'll show up on sitcoms."

"And before you know it, even politicians will be having *Sex with a Grasshopper*."

Peyton shrugged, twirling her straw. "They probably already are."

"You're probably right."

Abe's face grew dark and he glared at the two of them. "Well, enjoy it," he said, lifting his own drink. "Because after tonight, it goes into retirement."

*   *   *

Marco entered the precinct a little before his 10:00AM appointment. He really wanted to see Peyton before he had to let Dr. Ferguson psychoanalyze him. He was getting sick of these morning meetings and wasn't sure how much more he could take.

"Hi there, handsome," said Maria, beaming a smile at him. "You're early?"

"Hey, Maria. Is Brooks in yet?"

Maria looked disappointed. "She's in a meeting with Defino, Cho and Simons. They're in the break-room."

"Did she have her session with Dr. Ferguson?"

"Yeah, but he cut it short. She was out by 9:00."

"Hm, I wonder if that's a good sign."

"It's Brooks. He probably got tired of looking at that rat's nest she calls hair."

Marco chuckled, but he didn't take the bait. He pushed open the half-door and moved toward the break-room. "I think I'll just go poke my head inside."

"You're liable to get it bit off by Defino."

"Oh well," he said with a smile. "I'll just have to take my chances."

He walked toward the break-room and found the door open. Glancing inside, he was surprised to see everyone huddled around Stan Neumann and a laptop. Peyton looked up at him and her face lit with happiness, then she dropped her eyes again.

Marco hid the confusion her dismissal caused and stepped inside. Cho was the first to break away and he offered Marco his hand. Then Simons gave him a bear hug and set him away, clapping huge hands on his shoulders. Jake gave a nod, but Captain Defino looked like she was about to explode.

"Hey, Marco," said Stan.

"Hey, Stan."

Captain Defino fixed her hands on her hips. "'You better have a good reason for being here."

"My session with Dr. Ferguson?"

She gave him a suspicious look.

He decided to change the subject. "I had reporters outside my apartment this morning."

"Did you talk to them?" she demanded.

"Not a bit, ma'am."

"Good. Don't."

He gave her a salute.

Peyton met his eye again and offered him a slight smile. "Did you find anything on the vic's computer, Stan?"

"He played *Warriors of Terrabelthenia*."

"Terrawhatenia?" said Peyton, frowning at him.

"An RPG."

"A what?"

"Role Playing Game."

"You like RPGs, Peyton?" asked Jake mischievously.

"What?"

"You like RPGs, you know, the way you love comic books and Star Wars?"

She punched his shoulder behind Stan's back. Defino glared at Jake.

Marco couldn't help but smile. Lord, how he missed this.

"What does that mean, Stan? He plays this terra-thingy?"

"Terrabelthenia. It's not very popular. Most people don't bother with it. The storyline is hackneyed and the graphics are…" He made a rude noise.

Peyton gave the captain a helpless look.

"The point, Stan?" Defino said.

"I didn't set up a profile on this game like I did the others. I'm trying to get into the system now, so I can review his chat logs, but I've got to figure out his password."

"Can you?"

"Of course. He's an amateur. He has a password keeper program."

Marco moved into the room and sat down at a table close to them. They didn't seem to notice.

Stan's fingers flew over the keyboard. "There we go. Gotcha!"

Peyton moved so she could look over his shoulder. Stan tilted his head, so his cheek just brushed against the wisps of curls that escaped her ponytail. Marco resisted the impulse to refocus him with a slap upside the head.

Peyton's dark eyes shifted across the screen. "Is this what I think it is, Stan?"

Stan blinked, then focused on the text. Marco and Cho exchanged an annoyed look.

"What?" demanded the captain.

"It looks like he was arranging a meeting with someone on-line."

"Can you get into that other profile?"

"Of course I can."

"Where were they meeting?"

Peyton looked up. "The Presidio."

"Was he meeting a boy or girl?"

"Boy," said Stan. "Sixteen."

"Give the information on the boy to ICAC, Stan, so they can follow up and find out if the meeting took place."

Stan nodded.

Peyton rose to her full height and rubbed her lower back. "Now what?"

"Stan needs to set up a profile on that game and see if we get another bite," said Jake.

Defino considered that. "It fits the pattern. He changes his search after every two deaths."

"No. When he used the church event board, he killed three people that time," said Simons.

"Right, except he said the ranger was collateral damage. So really, he changes after he kills two pedophiles," corrected Peyton.

Marco covered his mouth with his hand, thinking. This was their one chance to catch the serial killer before someone else died. If so, they couldn't wait for someone to take the bait. They had to lay out the bait and take it themselves.

"Stan, can you set up a profile as a teenager, but also create a second one as a perp?"

"As easily as I breathe." He looked adoringly up at Peyton.

She patted his shoulder.

"What are you thinking?" asked Defino.

"We meet ourselves on-line and arrange a meeting."

"Like a snake eating its own tail," said Jake, earning a round of glares.

"Then we can set up the meeting and control the situation," finished Peyton.

Marco gave her a wink. The smile she returned made something ease in his chest. He hadn't realized how much he'd been wanting that.

Defino considered it for a moment. "If we arrange a meeting, someone will have to go as decoy. It could be dangerous."

"We've done it before, Captain," said Marco. "And if we select the meeting site, we can have officers stationed there ahead of time."

"It would have to be somewhere remote to protect the public," said Simons. "But he might not come if the location is too remote."

"He's getting increasingly bold and reckless," reasoned Peyton. "He might."

Marco pointed at Jake. "We could have Ryder stationed some place inconspicuous and have him snap pictures. Maybe we can get him on film, even if he doesn't approach our decoy."

Defino nodded. "I like it. It's certainly better than anything else we've got. Set up the profiles, Stan, and start the conversations. The rest of you figure out a location to have our meeting. Once you've got that, go out there and get the lay of the land." She gave Marco a nod. "Nice work, D'Angelo."

"Thanks, Captain. Can I have my gun back?"

She shook her head with an amused smile and glanced at her watch. "No, but you can go have your session with Dr. Ferguson right now."

Marco sighed as she walked past him and out the door.

Cho and Simons were on her heels.

As he climbed to his feet, Peyton stopped in front of him. "You done good, D'Angelo."

"Yeah, well, with all the free time I've got, I think my brain is desperately trying not to go to mush."

She smiled and pushed him in the chest. "Go meet with Ferguson."

He gave an aggravated moan. "I hate meeting with him."

"So do I, but I went."

"Maria said you finished your session early. What happened?"

"That little gossip. Who the hell does she think she is?"

"Brooks."

Peyton shook her head. "I'm sick of the sessions too, so I took a page out of Marco D'Angelo's book and refused to talk."

Marco laughed and allowed her to propel him out of the break-room. "Someone's gonna get her gun pulled."

She gave him a sarcastic nod and tried to turn him around. "Go on, D'Angelo. No more stalling." She pressed her hand in the middle of his back and tried to move him forward. "I got work to do."

He watched her head to her desk and then started for the conference room. She had a point. Today was going to be his last session, no matter what decision Ferguson made. He needed to get back to work too.

CHAPTER 17

Marco entered the conference room.

Dr. Ferguson was busy writing on his yellow legal pad and didn't immediately look up.

"Take a seat, Inspector D'Angelo." He motioned to Marco's usual spot.

Marco shut the door behind him and pulled out the chair, sinking into it.

After a few minutes, Ferguson leaned back. "Let me make something clear before we begin, Inspector. I'm not going to sit here listening to silence for another hour."

"Got it." Marco laid his hands flat on the table. "Let me make something clear."

Ferguson's brows climbed.

"I'm not going to meet with you after today. This is our last session."

"I don't think that's within your sphere to decide."

"I think it is. Either you restore my badge or you don't, but this has gone on long enough. If you haven't come to a conclusion yet, you're just milking the department for money."

Ferguson clasped his hands on his legal pad. "I get paid a salary whether I meet with anyone or not, Inspector, so that assessment is erroneous. And you are aware that many people spend years in therapy before they make any progress."

"Is that what we're doing? Therapy?"

"No, I'm evaluating you."

"Well, you've done enough evaluating. So get whatever else you need today, then let's move on."

"I want to talk about your partner."

"That's all we've talked about."

"She wouldn't speak to me today. I finally had to let her go. If I wanted to pull her badge right now, I would be within my rights to do so."

"But you won't because Defino needs her and you really don't have any solid reason to do so."

"I think I do."

"What? What did she say?" Marco frowned. What the hell could Peyton have said that would have caused him to doubt her mental stability? And didn't talking about another patient break some code or something?

"I asked her about her father, his death. I asked her if that was why she clung to you, felt her very self-worth was tied to your partnership." Ferguson held up a hand. "I got nothing."

Marco shifted uneasily. Peyton's self-worth wasn't tied to him and she didn't cling to him. In fact, their friendship really was one sided. She didn't need him. She had a circle of people as loyal to her as he was.

"Isn't this an ethical violation for you?"

"How so?"

"You're telling me about your session with her. I thought that was private."

"As you so aptly put it, this isn't therapy, Inspector, this is evaluation and to evaluate the two of you, I have to talk about you to each other. I'm not telling you any secrets she told me, I'm telling you what she didn't tell me. I can't violate her trust by divulging silence."

"She has operated just fine for years after her father's death. You don't have to question that."

"Why won't she talk about it?"

Marco gave him a disbelieving look. "Because it was the single most painful moment of her life. Why do you want her to keep dredging it back up?"

"I don't, but I don't think burying things helps either."

"I get the feeling we aren't talking about Peyton anymore."

"That's right. Everything in your life is a lie. You bury your true feelings about everything – your family, your religion, your guilt, your partner. You put up a wall between you and everyone else. Have you had an honest conversation with a single person?"

"What does that mean? Of course I have."

"When was the last time you told your parents you loved them?"

"What?"

"Do you tell your brothers?"

"Men don't go around doing that." What the hell!

"Do you know when you had your last honest conversation?"

"I'm certain you're going to tell me."

"In here, when you tell me the stories about you and Peyton. You let your guard down and you show what's important to you, but the minute that clock reaches noon, you shut down again. Until you have an honest conversation with yourself, you won't move past the priest's killing, just like Peyton won't move past her father's death."

Marco slumped back in his chair. "That's all this is for you, isn't it? You want us to pick the scabs off our wounds for your entertainment. You want me to keep reliving the moment I took that shot because it somehow validates you, who you are. As long as you keep me picking at that, keep me raw, you feel like you're doing something, accomplishing something. That's why you want Peyton to talk about her father. You want her to relive the most devastating moment of her life, so you can feel alive."

Dr. Ferguson didn't answer.

"She is the strongest person I know. Strength doesn't come from being able to look at dead bodies or reacting in an instant and firing a gun. Strength is in getting someone to confess to the most heinous crime imaginable, strength is seeing a perp as something more than an animal, strength is seeing that a whore or a drug addict is a person. I rely on that strength. I expect it, but that day, the day her father was shot, I saw her crumble. I saw her..." He looked down at the table. "I saw her come apart. Why the hell would you want her to relive that moment over and over again?"

Marco passed her a paper coffee cup. The fog had come into the City, folding around it and shutting out the rest of the world. A gust of wind sent food wrappers and paper cups skittering across the sidewalk.

"What's this?" She held it to her nose and sniffed. "Hot chocolate?"

"Yep, I got it with whipped cream."

She gave a little shiver of happiness and took a careful sip. "And marshmallows?"

"You got it."

She pointed to the draped body, lying on the floor of the garage. Chuck Wilson, their crime scene processor, was studying the lay of the body and beside him was a man Marco didn't recognize, snapping off pictures.

"You wanna take a look while I enjoy my cocoa?" said Peyton.

He smiled. The cocoa had nothing to do with it. Carrying his own paper cup of coffee, he walked into the garage. "Hey, Chuck, what we got here?"

Chuck came over to him, but they didn't shake hands because of his rubber gloves. "If it isn't the young hotshots. Where's my coffee?"

"Sorry. I wasn't sure if you liked it all sugared up like my partner."

He gave a low laugh.

"Who's that?" Marco pointed at the photographer with his chin.

Chuck rolled his eyes. He was in his mid-fifties with grey hair. A pair of dark sunglasses dangled from the pocket of his uniform and he wore ass-kicking Dock Martins. He was the toughest bastard at the precinct and a lot of the younger cops avoided him. The last of a dying breed, he was a cop turned CSI. "Greenhorn they want me to train. He's a little boy with a camera."

Marco smiled. "He have a name?"

"Bob Anderson."

"Is he going to another precinct?"

"Shit no. You're getting stuck with his prissy-ass when I retire in two months."

Bob Anderson was using the camera as a barrier, taking pictures as far back as he could from the body. He hadn't even lifted the drape.

Marco turned to face Chuck. "You sure about retiring?"

Chuck shrugged. "My wife hasn't been feeling well lately. They're running a bunch of tests."

"I'm sorry about that."

"Thought I'd retire now, so we can do some traveling like we always wanted." He gave him a tense smile. "You young ones don't get it, but there's a time when you just can't put yourself in the line of fire anymore for crazy-ass strangers who just wanna kill each other."

Marco thought of the bombing they'd just survived. Chuck had a point.

"I hope it isn't anything serious with your wife."

He nudged Marco with his shoulder. "I think it's all made up to get me to quit."

They both laughed.

"You might tell little Bobby over there to actually lift the drape on the body, while I go take a look around the house."

Marco nodded his assent and then walked over to the vic, hunkering down next to him. Lifting the drape, he scanned him for cause of death.

The vic lay on his back, blond hair swept away from a strong forehead. No obvious injuries were visible on his upper body and head. His eyes and mouth were open, the mouth contorted in an expression of surprise. Marco lifted the drape further and sucked in a breath.

The man's crotch was covered in red and a pool of it had formed beneath him. "Did you get pictures of this?" he said to Bob.

"Oh, yeah," said Bob with a shudder. "Good thing the poor bastard died, I'm thinking."

Marco gave a nod of agreement. Tilting his head, he looked at the man's hands where they lay, flung out beside him. A gold wedding band wrapped around his left ring finger.

"He was married."

"Yeah."

"You sure you got pictures of it?"

"Yeah, but I can take some more if you think I should." His hands shook on the camera.

Marco forced himself to be patient. At least he wasn't vomiting like someone he knew. "That might be a good idea."

Bob sidled over and squatted, aiming the camera at the man's crotch or well…what was left.

"I'm Marco D'Angelo. My partner's Peyton Brooks."

"Bob Anderson."

"How you like CSI?"

"It's…great."

Marco smiled and shifted toward the street. "Brooks? You wanna come in here now?"

"Not really."

Bob looked up at him.

Marco shrugged.

Peyton came into the garage with her cup of hot chocolate. She moved to his side and bent over, taking a quick look, then she hesitated and leaned closer, putting her hand on his shoulder to steady herself.

"Shot him in the…" She glanced up at the photographer. "Hi, I'm Peyton."

"Bob."

Peyton gave a nod. "Where's Chuck?"

"In the house," said Marco. "This is his replacement for when he retires."

"Oh, that's nice. We should get him a cake or something."

"We should. And maybe we can all pitch in and buy him a present."

"I like that idea."

Bob cleared his throat. They looked at him. "We have a dead body here. Could you show a little respect?"

Peyton nodded. "You're right. So, someone shot him in the willy and he obviously bled out here on the floor."

"Probably a wife," offered Marco, pointing his coffee cup at the ring.

"Or the mistress," reasoned Peyton.

"We should probably talk to the neighbors and see if they heard anything."

"Good idea." She looked at Bob. "Why don't you go into the house and see if you can find a name for the wife?"

"And just leave the body here?"

Marco pointed out to the driveway. "There's a uniform out there protecting the scene."

"And clearly, the vic's not walking away," said Peyton.

"True," finished Marco.

Bob Anderson climbed to his feet. "What's going on here?"

Peyton and Marco exchanged a look.

"We're working a case," said Peyton slowly, rising to her full height. "When someone gets shot in the willy, we have to find out who hated him enough to do it, so we ask questions, we look around his house, we search his possessions, then we arrest the person who did it."

"That's a dead body." He pointed at the vic.

"Right. That's step number one in homicide."

Bob shook his head at her, then turned around and walked rapidly into the house.

"He's not going to last long."

"I give him a few months."

"Months? I give him a few more minutes," she said.

* * *

Peyton jogged down the steps and met Marco and Chuck Wilson on the street. "Those folks made the call to dispatch. They heard arguing in the garage and then the shot."

"I found information on the wife. She works for an insurance company on Market," said Chuck.

"I called and she showed up today. She was more than an hour late," said Marco.

"Well, let's go have a little chat." She glanced at her phone. "It's almost lunchtime. See ya later, Chuck."

Chuck lifted a hand in goodbye, then moved back toward the garage.

As they reached the Charger, Peyton's cell phone rang. Marco unlocked the doors and climbed behind the wheel as she pulled the phone out of her pocket. Pressing it on, she lifted it to her ear. "Brooks here," she said, sliding into the seat next to him.

Marco could hear a muffled voice on the other side.

"Hey, Captain. Marco and I have a lead on the wife. We're headed over to her place of employment to have a chat with her."

More muffled words.

Peyton covered the mouth piece with her hand. "You have the name of the insurance company and an address?" she asked him.

He reached into his pocket and pulled it out, passing it to her.

Peyton read the location into the phone. Marco frowned at her. Defino hadn't interfered in an investigation before. What was going on?

Peyton shrugged.

"Wait. What? We're on our way there right now, Captain. We can get there faster than Cho and Simons…" Her voice trailed away and her grip on the phone tightened. "What?"

He saw her eyes go wide and her breathing picked up.

"Brooks?"

She motioned at the ignition frantically.

He reached over and started the Charger.

"How?" Her voice came out breathless and strange. "San Francisco General? On Potrero?"

Marco slammed the car into gear and pulled away from the curb.

"What? No, I don't understand. Wait. What about my mother?"

Marco could feel his heart begin to pound. He gripped the steering wheel harder as he flipped a U-turn.

"Okay, okay." Her breath hitched as she exhaled. "We're on our way right now. Uh, I don't know. I don't know how far."

She looked over at Marco and her eyes swam with tears.

"About fifteen minutes," he told her.

"Fifteen. Yes, yes, I understand. Okay, Captain." She lowered the phone to her lap and sat staring out the window.

Marco swallowed hard, but he didn't know what to say. Something was terribly wrong. He reached over and covered her hand where it gripped the phone. She gave a little start, then released her breath.

"Uh, my father…" Her voice failed and she closed her eyes for composure. "My father's been shot, Marco."

* * *

They arrived at San Francisco General. Patrol cars fanned out across the entrance and choked the parking lot. Peyton sat staring at them as Marco parked the Charger. He unhooked his seatbelt and climbed out, then went around the car and pulled open her door.

She looked up at him.

He held out his hand and she took it, letting him pull her out of the car. As they walked across the parking lot to the emergency room doors, she stared at her feet as if she needed to consciously think about walking.

When the automatic doors swished open, she stumbled to a halt. A line of police officers stood in the waiting room, their hats in their hands. As soon as they saw her, they bowed their heads.

Marco felt his heart kick against his ribs. There was no way this could be good news.

Peyton trembled next to him, but she lifted her chin and started moving. Marco hesitated behind her. He'd seen few things as brave as her walk down the gauntlet of police officers, her back straight, her chin raised.

A middle aged woman with brown hair detached herself from one of the officers and ran at Peyton, throwing her arms around her. Tears streamed down her face.

"He's gone. He's gone!" she sobbed, then her knees buckled, dragging Peyton forward.

Marco caught Peyton's elbows and slowed their descent to the floor. There they huddled, Peyton's mother sobbing violently, Peyton holding on to her, her eyes wide. Around them the police officers stood, bowing their heads in respect for a fallen comrade.

*   *   *

After the funeral, Peyton's mother, Alice, held a reception at her house. It wasn't an exceptionally large house and with all of the cops, it quickly became crowded. The funeral had been a ceremonious, solemn affair with a long procession of both police and fire to the cemetery. Marco had stayed back with Captain Defino and the rest of the officers from the precinct, while Peyton sat with her mother.

He hadn't been able to stop looking at her. She'd never once shed a tear, never once broken down. Alice had sobbed throughout the whole thing, but not Peyton. She maintained a stoic façade that hid what he knew she had to be feeling inside. He didn't want to see his partner come apart, but her lack of emotion scared him a bit.

Now he couldn't find her. He'd ridden over to the reception with Smith, but he'd been here about ten minutes and he still hadn't seen her. Pressing through the bodies, he searched the living room chairs. Alice was sitting in a recliner before the fireplace, a circle of women around her, urging her to eat and drink. She held the folded American flag they'd given her and wouldn't part with it. He could see her resemblance to Peyton, especially about the eyes, but she didn't have Peyton's wild curls or her exotic looks.

Marco knew he had to offer his condolences. He tugged at the uncomfortable uniform and made his way over to her.

"Mrs. Brooks," he began, holding out his hand.

She took it and stared up at him.

"I'm Marco D'Angelo, Peyton's partner."

Recognition dawned and she rose to her feet, setting the flag on the chair. "Marco, yes. Peyton's told me about you. Thank you for coming."

He gave a brief nod. "I'm so sorry for your loss, ma'am."

"Thank you." She patted his hand. "I think I'm still in shock."

"If there's anything I can do..."

"Thank you."

"I was looking for your daughter. Do you know where she is?"

"She was just here a moment ago. She might be in the kitchen, helping with the food."

"I'll look for her."

He released Alice Brooks and wandered toward the kitchen. He found Abe manning a make-shift bar, mixing drinks for people who wanted something stiffer than beer. Abe looked up and gave him a subdued smile.

"Hey there, sexy. Look at you in your uniform." He wore a black silk shirt with black trousers and wing-tipped shoes.

Marco pulled at the tight collar. No matter what size he got, the police issue uniforms, including the dress blues, always strained across his shoulders. "This is the very reason I took the detective test."

"The uniform?"

"Yeah."

"Well, you wear it well. Can I make you a drink, Angel'Delicious?"

"No. Have you seen Peyton?"

Abe shook his head, his dread locks swinging. "I was going in search of her when I got roped into doing this. Maybe she's with her mother?"

"I already checked."

Someone came in. Marco didn't recognize him, but he gave Marco a nod and moved up to Abe's counter.

"What'll it be?" Abe asked.

Marco moved back to the living room. To the right branched a hallway, so he ducked inside. He had to sidestep a woman leaving the bathroom. She gave him a kind smile as she headed back to the main part of the house.

Marco moved past the bathroom and surveyed the other three doors. He didn't want to go snooping around, but he was worried about Peyton. Knocking at the first door, he got no response, so he moved to the other side and knocked at the next door.

"Come in," came a muffled voice.

Marco turned the knob and poked his head inside. Peyton was sitting on a twin bed in the dark. She had a police officer's hat in her hands. He pushed open the door and approached her. Glancing around, he saw there was nowhere else to sit.

The twin bed took up the middle of the room. At its foot, against the wall, was a dresser and on either side of the bed were nightstands. This had to be her bedroom from when she was a child. Unlike most girls, Peyton didn't have pink, frilly things. Her comforter was neutral colors and above the dresser was a bulletin board with scraps of paper, concert tickets, and playbills arranged in a pattern.

At the head of the bed was an enormous poster of the rock star, Joshua Ravensong, his head thrown back, microphone in hand, his black hair cascading over his shoulders. Marco gave it a wry look, then decided the only place to sit was beside her on the bed.

A little brown stuffed dog blocked him, so he picked it up and set it on her pillow. "Hey, partner, I've been looking for you." He sank down on the mattress beside her.

She turned the hat around in her hands. "When I was a little girl, I would sneak my father's hat out of his room and pretend I was solving cases in here. He never scolded me for having it when he was trying to get ready in the morning."

"I'm thinking there wasn't much you could do that would make him mad."

She lifted the hat and hooked it on the post of the footboard, running her fingers over it. "I just don't understand how everything can change so quickly. One minute you're fine. The next…"

"No one understands that, Brooks."

"You think you understand the dangers, you know? Police get shot, but the reality…the reality is so different."

He didn't know how to answer, so he said nothing.

"I keep trying to remember the last thing I said to him." She clasped her hands tightly. "I keep hoping it'll come to me. What if it was unimportant? Silly? What if his last thought was that he wished I'd told him something more?"

"Peyton." He put his arm around her. She was trembling. "It doesn't matter what we say to people, especially family. They know our feelings without us having to say it over and over again. And I have no doubt he knew how much you loved him. I saw it when you were with him."

She closed her eyes and the trembling grew worse. "I need to know that what I said meant something, Marco. I need to know that he understood. In that final moment, I need to know that he was sure he was loved."

Marco tightened his hold. "He knew, sweetheart. He knew."

She began to sob, deep, wrenching sobs, folding over on herself. He kept his arm around her as she slumped into his lap, burying her face in her hands. Reaching up, he stroked the curls that tumbled around her, blocking her face.

He lost track of time as he sat in the dark room with her, letting her sob out her devastating loss, and in that moment, he knew what his duty was – he didn't want anything like this to ever happen to her again.

* * *

Marco stopped talking, staring at the table in front of him. If he thought about it, he could bring up the feeling in that room again. Some memories are so powerful they stayed with you forever. That was one of them.

Dr. Ferguson didn't speak. Marco was fine with that. There really wasn't any more to say. If he didn't understand why Marco wasn't guilty for the priest's death, he never would. Defino would simply have to go to bat for him with Internal Affairs.

"You're right," he finally said. "This is our last session."

Marco blinked and looked up at him. He wanted to feel elated, but something in Ferguson's demeanor seemed off. "Good."

The doctor tilted the legal pad and let the papers slip back into place. "I will be giving Captain Defino my final report by the end of the week."

Marco resisted the impulse to ask him what it would say.

"I do, however, wish you the best, Inspector D'Angelo. I wish you'd consider seeking real therapy. I'm happy to recommend someone if you'd like."

"I'm good, Dr. Ferguson."

"As you wish. You have my number if you change your mind."

"I do." Marco rose to his feet. "You do know that nothing I've told you makes me incapable of carrying a gun, right?"

Ferguson gave him a slow smile. "I'll have my report to Captain Defino by the end of the week, Inspector D'Angelo. You will know then."

Marco let his fist fall against his thigh. So be it. He would just have to wait for the report before he decided his next course of action. "Good bye, Dr. Ferguson."

"Good bye, Inspector D'Angelo. May you find peace."

Marco hesitated, then he decided it wasn't worth it and went to the outer door, pulling it open.

CHAPTER 18

Peyton locked the door on her Corolla, then paused as she heard the rumble of a large engine pulling off the street. The Charger came around the side of the building and stopped next to her. Marco climbed out.

His dark hair was pulled back in his usual ponytail and he wore a ribbed t-shirt that showed off his muscular forearms. Coupled with loose fitting jeans and his boots, he looked healthy and hearty, a man in his prime.

"Hey, partner."

"Hey, yourself. What are you doing here?"

He stopped in front of her. "It's been three days since my last session with Dr. Ferguson. He promised a report by the end of the week."

"I see. So do you plan to sit here all day, waiting for it?"

"I plan to demand my job back whether Ferguson gives his report or not."

Peyton gave him a once-over. "Ooh, you going all bad ass on me here, D'Angelo?"

He smiled.

Her phone vibrated in her pocket and she reached for it. A text message from Defino blinked across the display. She pressed it. *Meeting. Conference Room. Now.* She showed it to Marco. "You think she'd learn to speak in complete sentences, wouldn't you?"

"I don't know. I think she's a very effective communicator, especially with you." He put his arm around her shoulders and directed her toward the precinct. She leaned into him a little, it felt so right for them to be headed the same way together again.

As they entered the building, Maria looked up. "Brooks, Defino wants…"

"…me in the conference room." She pushed open the half-door and turned directly into the conference room. She was surprised when Marco walked in after her.

Stan Neumann was there with Cho and Simons.

Defino looked up when Marco entered. "D'Angelo, out!"

"With all due respect, Captain, I'm reporting for duty this morning. Unless Dr. Ferguson has given you a good reason to bench me, I need to do my job."

"He hasn't given me a good reason to bring you back either."

"But I can give you a reason. You need all hands on deck for this case and it makes no sense to keep me sitting at home."

"Bench you, all hands on deck?" said Peyton, giving him a wry look. "You've been watching too much TV."

Marco sighed. "You have no idea. Do you know they have a slicer for your banana? It cuts it into little bite size pieces."

"I have one of those," said Cho. "It's great for cereal. Every slice is uniform that way."

"Where'd you get it?" asked Simons.

Defino threw up her hands. "We have a serial killer running around and this is what you want to talk about."

"In their defense, Captain, they were talking *cereal*," said Peyton.

Defino's eyes swung to her and narrowed.

Peyton held up her hands. "Just saying."

She pointed at Marco. "You are not reinstated yet, but you can park yourself over there. Clearly you need the mental stimulation."

Marco shared a smile with Peyton and obediently went to the chair she indicated.

"Brooks, where's Ryder?"

"He should be here soon."

"You sit there." She pointed to the spot next to her, diagonal to Stan.

As Peyton took her seat, Stan smiled and gave her a little wave. She started to wave back, but Defino glared at her.

296

"Gentlemen," she said, encompassing Cho and Simons.

They moved to the table and took a seat.

Just as she opened her mouth to begin, Jake threw open the door and bustled in, carrying his camera case.

"Sorry, the Daisy didn't want to start today."

"Maybe you need new spark plugs?" offered Cho.

"Or a starter. Starter would be a bitch, though," said Simons.

Defino rolled her eyes toward the ceiling. "Maybe you need a banana slicer," she growled.

Jake gave Peyton a bewildered look. Peyton knew better than to comment.

He glanced around, spotting Marco. "Hey, Adonis, you back?"

Marco gave him a nod with his chin.

Defino tossed her pen onto the table. "Mr. Ryder, do you mind? We're trying to hold a very important meeting right now."

"Of course." He slid into the nearest chair and braced the camera case on his lap.

"Stan?" said Defino, then took her seat.

"We got a hit on our profile."

"The teenager one?" asked Cho.

"No, the other one. Someone contacted me last night, said he was fifteen and we talked for about an hour, mostly about graphic novels. On a hunch, I mentioned a really rare one that I have and he got excited about it, said he'd like to see it. I told him I'd be willing to trade it for one of his. Before he signed off, he asked me to meet up with him."

"What did you say? About the meeting?" asked Peyton.

"I tried to pick one of the locations we talked about, but he wouldn't go for it. He said we had to meet in public, his parents had warned him about meeting strangers, but he really wanted to see that novel."

"It's probably just a dumb kid," grumbled Simons.

"I thought so too, so I tried to trace back his profile to the source. It's encrypted."

"Are you saying a kid wouldn't be able to do that?" asked Defino.

Stan shrugged. "I suppose, but it was pretty sophisticated. Plus, when I checked his history, he just started playing *Warriors of Terrabelthenia* about a week ago, and it doesn't look like he's done many quests. Mostly he just chats with people."

"A week ago? About the time Bruce Weller died," said Peyton.

"That's what I thought."

"Where does he want to meet, Stan?" asked Marco.

Stan scratched at his chin. "That's the problem. He wants to meet at Pier 39 tomorrow at noon. He has a specific bench picked out and he wants our decoy to wear a green baseball cap."

"I'm not sure that's our killer then," said Defino.

"Well, hold on a minute, Captain," said Peyton. "His third assault was on Alcatraz with people all around. He then killed Lewis Booker at the campground with people around. Bruce Weller was in the Presidio. He's gradually evolved into doing public killings. Pier 39 makes sense."

"Plus I think you're missing something," Marco said. "You damn near got him with Lewis Booker. You figured out his two-pedophile pattern. After Bruce Weller, he's got to be thinking that you might figure him out again. Maybe he wants a public place so he can see if cops are around before he acts."

"Why not change the two-pedophile pattern, then?" asked Jake.

"Serial killers evolve, but they don't change major patterns, even if it means they might be stopped," answered Peyton.

Defino turned to Cho and Simons. "Do you two agree?"

They both nodded.

Defino looked down at the table. "I don't like this going down in a public place. If he starts shooting…"

Peyton shifted to face her. "We'll have the place surrounded prior to the meeting."

"I think we need to do more than that," said Marco. "We need to have a physical decoy out there in a green cap."

"That's dangerous, D'Angelo. Even for a cop."

"It can't be a cop, Captain. He knows Brooks and me from Alcatraz and he might have been watching Simons and Cho work the earlier murders. I'm not even sure Jake can be a decoy. He's taken pictures at each of the crime scenes."

"Gosh darn it," said Jake. "I've worked really hard on my *decoy* acting lately."

Peyton smiled, but dropped her eyes when Defino focused on her.

"We'll probably need a cop from another department."

"I'll do it," said Stan.

Every eye turned to him.

Peyton was impressed by his bravery. "No, Stan, it's too dangerous."

"I can wear a flak jacket right. It gets breezy out at the piers, so I can wear a windbreaker over it. And you'll all be there with guns, right?"

"But we won't be right next to you, Stan. He strangled his last victim with a dog leash."

Marco leaned forward on the table. "Give me back my gun, Captain. I can guard Stan, while everyone else mans the rest of the location. I can stay out of sight, but be close enough to react if someone approaches him."

"What if he goes back to shooting his victims?"

Defino seemed particularly worried about that.

Peyton understood. A gun going off in Pier 39 would create panic and chaos unlike anything they could imagine.

"I don't think he will, Captain," she said. "He's evolved into more personal killings. He has to look them in the eye or be in close proximity to do it now."

"I hope you're right, Brooks."

"What choice do we have, Captain? We have to stop this guy."

"I know. I just don't like it, but we're out of options. Every day I see some news report about the *Janitor* and it just makes me feel as if we're losing control of this narrative. What if he makes our people before he approaches Stan?"

"That's why Jake has to be there. We'll position him away from Stan and he can snap regular images. We might get lucky and stumble on something later."

"Wait. I thought you said he might recognize me," Jake said, looking worried.

"Don't worry, Preacher," said Cho with a mischievous smile. "We can give you a clerical collar."

"Oh, that'd be great. He's real fond of priests."

"Then what about a fake nose and mustache," offered Simons.

Defino shook her head and pushed herself to her feet. "Why not a banana slicer? Look, I want everyone to diagram this whole thing out, then I'll be back to review it." She pointed at Marco. "You, come with me to call Internal Affairs, so we can get you temporarily reinstated. But I promise you I'll pull your badge again if Ferguson's report comes back with anything hinky."

Marco nodded and rose to his feet. When she turned her back, he gave everyone in the room a wink and followed her to the door.

"What the hell is this banana slicer?" asked Jake when they left.

Cho leaned back in his chair and folded his hands on his stomach. "A slicer that slices bananas," he offered and gave Jake a smirk.

* * *

Jake took a seat on the benches surrounding the planter bed at the entrance of Pier 39. He resisted the impulse to glance around because he didn't want to give anything away. He had a clear view of the bench where the meeting was going to take place, so he settled his camera bag at his feet and removed the camera, trying to look like any number of tourists crowding around them with their own cameras. Saturday in the Wharf was busy.

Pier 39 was a collection of tourist shops on a wooden boardwalk. Directly behind him was the giant crab sculpture and to his right was the blue canopied entrance to the Aquarium of the Bay. The bench the serial killer had indicated was just within the entrance, tucked back into a corner beneath the wooden mezzanine, a perfect place to attack someone without it being immediately seen.

He knew Peyton was behind him to his left, close to the Embarcadero. She was trying to blend in with the tourists, but if anyone looked closely enough, they'd notice the gun strapped to her side and the curving white wire of the headset in her ear. Cho and Simons were deeper in the Pier and a number of uniforms patrolled up and down the Embarcadero, trying to appear natural.

He fought the shaking of his hands. He didn't know why he was so nervous. He felt fairly sure this was all a mistake, that the contact on-line had been exactly what it seemed, a boy wanting to see a comic book, but if it wasn't, if the serial killer really showed up...

Jake removed the lens cap and shoved it in his pocket, glancing quickly around at the tourists crowding the area. Street performers lined the sidewalk behind him. Men who were living statues, or jugglers, or magicians all plied their trade within feet of him, drawing small crowds. He felt a moment of anxiety when he realized he couldn't spot Peyton any more, then he schooled his features. He couldn't give this away. Besides that, she would never leave him unprotected.

Stan Neumann came into view in his borrowed green baseball cap, carrying the graphic novel in his hands. He went straight for the bench and took a seat. His movements were a little too scripted, but Jake hoped the serial killer would mistake it for anxiousness to meet the "boy" he'd met on-line.

Jake sat at the farthest edge of the bench at the back of the planter bed. The benches were arranged in an octagon around the crab statue, so the one next to him was to his left and behind his shoulder. An older Asian man sat down in that spot, tugging a toddler with him. The little boy jerked his hand out of the man's and tried to walk away, but the man caught him by the tail of his jacket and hauled him back.

Jake glanced over his shoulder at them. So many people, so many vulnerable, innocent people who had no idea a sting was going down. He watched the toddler stagger over to a garbage can that was bolted into the cement before the older man's bench. The little boy hooked his fingers in the diamond shaped metal sides and tried to pull himself up on it. The older man went after him and returned him to the bench.

Jake glanced back at Stan. He was pretending to read the graphic novel, but he kept looking up over the top of it to survey the area. Jake lifted the camera and looked through the viewfinder. A tall, broad shouldered man moved into his line of sight, standing a half dozen yards to the right of Stan. *Adonis.* Jake forced himself to take a deep breath and release it, steadying his hands on the camera.

The toddler went toward the garbage can again. This time when the man went after him, he collapsed into a heap and began crying. The man reached down and picked him up, then walked toward the Pier, struggling to hold the kicking, screaming child.

Jake lifted the camera again and scanned the crowd. There, on the upper mezzanine, was Cho, his sunglasses obscuring his face as he looked out over the Embarcadero.

Bringing the camera down to Stan, he swung it over to Marco.

"Don't turn around, and don't move," came a voice.

Jake went still, his heart slamming against his ribs. He sensed someone had taken the bench the older man had vacated. Shifting the tiniest amount, he heard the man behind him hiss.

"I have the little detective in my sights, so I'd do exactly what I say, unless you want me to shoot her."

Peyton. Jake released a shivery breath.

"Nice sting. Damn near fell for it. Who thought it up? Her?"

"No," Jake choked out.

"So it was Handsome, huh? Surprising, and here I thought he was a big, dumb bag of muscle."

Jake lowered the camera. Involuntarily he looked toward Marco, but Marco was faced away, staring down the Embarcadero.

"I said don't move. You don't really want me to shoot her, do you?"

"No. And I don't want you to shoot me either."

"Relax, I don't shoot innocents."

"She's an innocent too."

He made a scoffing sound. Jake could just get a sense of him, large, husky. "She stopped being innocent the moment she strapped on a gun."

"You need to turn yourself in. You can't keep killing people."

"Now here's where we disagree. I think I'm doing a service to this country. And more than that, I'm engaged in a great social study."

"Social study?"

"Of course. You see, I've observed something during all of this. People cling to life. No matter how wretched, how pathetic our existence, we go out fighting. Take the priest for instance. When I put the gun in his hand, I thought he'd go out there, hold it up and beg not to be shot. He'd never held a gun before. I had it all planned. The police would see him and before they could understand what he was saying, they'd gun him down."

Jake shifted just his eyes toward Marco. Marco turned at that moment, scanning the entrance, his gaze coming to rest on Jake. Their eyes met, then Marco's focus went beyond him. Jake saw him tilt his head and speak into his shoulder, then he reached for his gun.

"Tell him to stay where he is," came the warning.

Jake frantically shook his head.

Marco staggered to a stop and spoke into his shoulder again.

"Good job. Now where was I?"

Jake shook so badly, he could feel the bench moving. "The priest…"

"Right. The priest. I thought he'd wave the gun in the air and surrender. What does he do? He starts shooting. Shooting. Surprised the hell out of me. He damn near killed the little detective."

"So you shot him."

"Didn't really have to. Handsome there had already put a couple of bullets in him. Mine was more of a precaution."

"Then you don't really want to kill her. You tried to protect her."

"Don't go placing noble motives on me. I will kill her. In fact, you should see her right now, staring at me with such hatred. She is all fired up to come over here, but she's afraid I'll shoot you. She doesn't even realize she's the one I'll go after."

"Why are you doing this?"

"Someone has to."

"The cops. Let them handle it."

He made another scoffing noise. "They're outnumbered and outgunned. Besides that, every time they lock one of these bastards away, some parole board lets them out again. You stamp and you stamp and there's always more cockroaches. You'll never get them all."

Jake locked eyes with Marco. He had to do something. He couldn't let this bastard get away from them. "You're talking about people, not cockroaches."

"Same difference. No matter what you do, you can never get them all. It's like holding back the tide with a bucket."

Jake went still. Something in the voice sounded familiar. He shifted the slightest amount toward his left.

"I told you not to move!"

A deafening sound went off near his head. Screams rose all around him and he hit the deck, covering his head with his arm.

"Down! Down!" came Marco's voice and someone dropped next to Jake, huddling on the concrete, breathing heavily.

He closed his eyes as people ran past, someone kicked him in the side, and he could see feet careening around him.

"Get back! Get back!"

Suddenly Marco was there, grabbing Jake's arm and hauling him into a sitting position. "Are you hit?"

Jake shook his head, unable to find his voice.

Marco's eyes scanned him. "Jake!"

"I'm all right. What about Peyton?"

"I'm here, Jake." She knelt in front of him, placing a hand on his shoulder, the other wrapped around her gun.

"He said he was going to shoot you."

"He shot the garbage can."

Jake closed his eyes and tried to calm his frantic breathing. Marco was talking rapidly into the radio on his shoulder, standing over them, his feet braced.

"He's headed down the Embarcadero. You have to head him off."

"We need a description," came the voice over the radio.

"Did you see him?" Jake asked Peyton.

"He was wearing dark glasses and a Panama hat with a wide brim. I wouldn't be able to pick him out of a crowd. Did you get a look at him?"

"No, but his voice sounded familiar."

"Panama hat, brown, dark sunglasses. I think he was wearing a black wind-breaker," shouted Marco.

People continued to run around them, frantically trying to find cover.

"We need to block off the pier," shouted Marco.

"We're trying to get in position," came the response.

"What did he say, Jake?" asked Peyton.

Jake shook his head. "I'm not sure. He talked about the priest and that he's doing a social experiment. I don't know. I was so freakin' scared the whole time. I should have listened better."

"It's okay."

"We need to get patrol cars here, block the entrance," came a voice over the radio.

"How are you going to block the whole entrance? Better to block the Embarcadero. Shut it down!" shouted Marco.

Sirens blazed around them, panicking the people more. Suddenly uniforms were swarming the entrance to the pier, trying to subdue the crowd, but there weren't enough of them yet.

"Holmes!" shouted Marco into the radio. "Holmes, do we have a visual?"

The radio crackled.

"Holmes!"

More crackle, then silence. Finally, Holmes' voice came through. "We lost him."

"How?"

"I don't know. We just lost him. He disappeared into the crowd."

"Disappeared?"

"Yeah, he just freakin' disappeared."

EPILOGUE

Jake sat on the couch with Pickles on his lap, stroking the little dog. Peyton took a seat on the coffee table in front of him and reached over to rub the dog's ears.

"You okay?"

He nodded, staring at Pickles rather than her.

Abe leaned over the back of the couch and handed him a shot glass. Jake automatically took it. "What crazy name does this drink have?" he asked, looking up at the medical examiner.

"Bourbon."

Jake gave a nod. "Good name." He tossed it back and grimaced, curling his fingers around the glass.

Marco sat on the barstools behind him. "You should eat something before you start pounding shots. What about Chinese?"

The concern was actually touching. Jake realized Adonis might not consider them friends, but he himself appreciated his cool head and caution today. He'd chosen to protect Jake over catching the serial killer. If he'd moved in, Jake had no doubt either he or Peyton would have been shot.

"Chinese is good," he said, passing the shot glass back to Abe. "So is another Bourbon."

The murmur of Marco's voice in the background coupled with Abe's humming in the kitchen created an insulated bubble around Jake. It was hard to comprehend that he'd been conversing with a serial killer just hours before.

He wished he could remember everything the man had said to him. He'd tried to recreate as much of it as he could for Captain Defino at the precinct, but he'd been so terrified at the time that he just wasn't sure of anything.

"Jake, I was wrong to bring you into this. You don't belong in this line of work."

"Why do you say that?"

"I can't lie to you. It could have gone horribly wrong today. And now he knows you, he's marked you."

307

"He did that already when he sent me the card after the priest died."

Peyton reached over and covered his hand where it rested on Pickles. "Jake, I think you should go home to Nebraska."

Jake gave a sad laugh. "This is home now, Peyton. Look, it scared the shit out of me today and I don't ever want to go through that again, but I'm not running away from this. I spent my life being careful. Careful degree, careful career, and look what happened. I lost my wife. No one writes us a check on our life, no one promises us anything."

"Yeah, but most people don't face down a serial killer, Jake. It isn't being careful to stay away from that madness."

Abe passed him another shot over his shoulder. Jake accepted it, staring at the amber colored liquid with the pink umbrella dangling over the side.

A laugh escaped him and he met Peyton's eyes. "This is home now, Peyton, this crazy, screwed up City with its crazy, screwed up people. Shit, after this, everything else would just be vanilla."

*   *   *

Captain Defino heard the knock on her office door. She looked up from her laptop. "Come in."

The door opened and Dr. Ferguson poked his head inside. "Do you have a moment?"

"Of course." She motioned to the melamine chairs across from her desk.

He came in and took a seat, trying to smooth out his hopelessly rumpled jacket. "I wanted to give you my report on your two detectives."

Defino leaned back in her chair. The knot in her stomach tightened. If she wasn't careful, she was going to get an ulcer. "Great," she forced herself to say. She hadn't yet told him that she'd reinstated Marco.

"Let's start with Inspector Brooks."

Oh, boy. She plastered a smile on her face. "Certainly."

"Inspector Brooks is undisciplined and impetuous. She tends to get personally involved in her cases, viewing the suspects as more than suspects."

Defino bit her inner lip. He certainly wasn't easing into this.

"She doesn't outright disobey orders, but she doesn't outright obey them either. She creates attachments with people that she uses to fulfill the unsatisfactory relationship she has with her mother."

Defino squirmed in her seat.

"She has yet to overcome the death of her father, which makes it difficult for her to make a personal attachment to a monogamous relationship with a man because she has a fear of abandonment. She has a sharp tongue and a lack of respect for authority."

Defino blew out her air. "And?"

"She's an exceptional police officer."

A smile teased at Defino's mouth. "Really?"

"Do you doubt it?"

"No, it's just…well, she's Peyton."

"Yes, and we'd do well to have a dozen more cops like her with her dedication."

"Excellent. I appreciate your analysis."

"Now, let's talk about Inspector D'Angelo."

Defino felt the knot tighten. She didn't know how she'd pull Marco's badge now. "Go on."

"Inspector D'Angelo is the consummate professional. He has a strict code he lives by, is disciplined, and has a strong personal network to support him. He is respectful of authority and does not feel the need to buck the rules."

Defino blinked away the tension, forcing her shoulders to lower. "Thank you, Doctor…"

"I'm not finished."

He was interrupted by the sound of shouting in the squad room. Both of them looked toward the door, but the commotion quickly subsided.

Defino turned back to him. "Go on, please. By the sounds of your report, I thought…"

"Captain Defino, Marco D'Angelo is a fine cop; however, he has an Achilles heel."

"A what?"

"A weakness, a fatal flaw."

Voices rose outside the door again. Defino found her attention divided between the doctor and whatever was happening in her squad room. Holding up a hand to the doctor, she started to rise to her feet, but Simons' booming bass suddenly filtered through. Bill Simons could handle whatever was going on out there.

"I'm sorry, Doctor. Please continue."

"I was mentioning that Inspector D'Angelo has a fatal flaw."

"Right."

"And I fear that if you don't take action and I mean soon, you may lose him."

"Lose him?" Defino sank back into her chair. "*Lose* him?"

"As in get him killed."

"What? How?"

"Captain …"

The cacophony rose once more. Defino tore her eyes from the doctor and looked at the door. What the hell! She didn't have time for this right now.

Suddenly the handle turned and Cho poked his head inside. "Captain, we got a problem. The squad room's filled with reporters, led by that Lake chick, and they want answers about the serial killer."

Defino's gaze shifted between the two men. Damn it all, could nothing get done without her? "I'll be right back,

Doctor," she said, climbing to her feet and moving toward the door. "Whatever you do, don't go anywhere."

*   *   *

Marco pulled into the parking lot of St. Matthews' Church. Father Michael, his grey head bent, was working on the roses in the front courtyard. Marco climbed out and crossed the parking lot to the priest.

"Father Michael?"

The old man looked up from where he knelt in the planter bed. "Yes, my son."

"I'm Marco D'Angelo. I work for the San Francisco Police Department."

"Yes, yes." He held out an arthritic hand. "Help me up, young man."

Marco braced him as the old priest climbed to his feet. "You spoke with my partner, Peyton Brooks, a few weeks ago."

"Oh, yes, the young woman with the wild curls."

"That's her."

"What can I do for you? Is it something to do with Father Reynolds?"

"No, I'm not here on work. Actually, I need some advice, but I haven't been attending church regularly. Lately, that is. I was at St. Mary's when you met with Peyton and I thought…" He sighed and looked away. "I thought you might be someone I could talk to."

"I understand." He motioned toward the church. "Do you want to use the confessional?"

"No, I'm not here for confession. Like I said, I just want some advice." He looked around at the courtyard. The warmth of the summer sun baked the terra cotta tiles and the roses gave off a pleasant odor. "Do you mind if we talk out here?'

"Not at all. Wherever you feel most comfortable." Using Marco's arm to brace himself, they walked to a bench

311

at the other end of the courtyard, out of the direct sunlight, and sat down. A few pigeons fluttered into the soil beneath the bushes.

For a moment, Marco just enjoyed the quiet, the peace, the serenity.

"Whenever you're ready."

Marco faced the priest. "I feel I should tell you who I am first."

Father Michael gave him a nod. "Go on."

"I…" He rubbed a hand over his chin. "I was on Alcatraz with Inspector Brooks."

Father Michael's eyes widened. "You are the police officer who shot Father Reynolds?"

"Yes."

"I'm glad you came to me, my son. In order to be forgiven, you must…"

"That's not why I'm here."

"I don't understand."

"I did what I had to do. I took a shot and killed him before he had a chance to kill my partner."

"The purpose of your action doesn't matter in the eyes of God. You must confess your sin to be absolved, my son."

"I don't want to be absolved for that. I did it and I would do it again if the situation came up."

Father Michael looked uncomfortable. "I feel this is a grave miscarriage of our sacrament, young man. You took a life, you broke one of the commandments."

"And I saved a life. I protected my partner. I won't ask for forgiveness where that's concerned."

"Then why did you come to me?"

"I came for something else, something that I'm not sure how to handle."

Father Michael's watery blue eyes searched his face, then his expression softened. "How can I help you, my son?" he said.

*   *   *

Abe settled the picnic basket on the grass at Crissy Field, then he shook out the blanket and laid it down. Other families were arranged around them, also setting out their supper. Jake sank onto it and stretched out his legs.

July in San Francisco could be foggy and cold, but not this one. Although a breeze teased in off the bay, it was warm as the sun set beyond the City. Peyton sat down across from him and Marco took the rear of the blanket, leaning his weight against a backrest.

Abe pulled the picnic basket onto the blanket and knelt in front of it, fussing with the buckles.

"So what'd you bring?" asked Jake, nodding at it. "Hot dogs and apple pie?"

Abe looked up. The beads on the end of his dreads were in alternating patterns of red, white and blue. "Hot dogs? Good God, no. Do you know what's in those?"

"I don't care. They're American and that's what we should be eating on the 4ᵗʰ of July."

Abe waggled a long finger at Jake. "Do you know that hot dog inspectors actually allow so many rat hairs and droppings in the…" He gave a frown and looked at Peyton. "What is it called when you make a hot dog? Not batter? Not mix?"

"Ooze?"

Abe held up a hand. "Precisely."

"Okay, so if we're not going American, what are we doing?"

Abe unhooked the buckles and lifted the lid. Then he pulled out a plastic tin and held it out. "Finger sandwiches."

"Finger sandwiches?"

"I have egg and chicken salad both, and for my Angel, cucumber and cream cheese." He winked at Marco.

Marco gave a short nod.

"Finger sandwiches?"

313

"I also made a pasta salad." He tapped Peyton's knee as he settled the sandwich container on the blanket. "I used those multi-colored pastas and a delightful Italian vinaigrette dressing."

"Tell me you at least brought good old fashioned domestic beer to drink," complained Jake.

Abe rolled his eyes. "Of course not." He reached into the basket and pulled out a plastic jug, filled with a burgundy red liquid. Pieces of orange swam in the mix. "Sangria."

Jake looked over his shoulder at Marco, but Marco simply shrugged.

"And for my soul sista..." He reached out and touched Peyton on the tip of her nose. "I brought a beautiful chocolate cake." He lifted out a cake tray and twisted off the lid, displaying a perfectly frosted confection that was sure to make them all diabetic.

As he set it beside the rest of the fare, Peyton grabbed him around the neck and began spreading kisses on his face.

Abe nearly toppled over under her enthusiastic assault.

"Peyton, stop! You're getting girl cooties on me!" he complained, struggling to escape her grasp, but she just continued to kiss him.

Jake laughed, glancing over at Marco, but Marco was definitely not looking at him.

"Peyton, stop!" shrieked Abe as a golden shower of glittering light spread over the City.

* * *

The San Francisco Examiner lay spread open across the rustic picnic table. The front page article had a picture of Pier 39, shot from the Embarcadero, showing the blue awning above the Aquarium of the Bay and in the far corner the crab sculpture.

The headline streaked across the page, bold and brass, proclaiming SERIAL KILLER FIRES SHOT AT THE WHARF. He spread the paper with both hands and chuckled. The by-line read Genevieve Lake, Contributing Reporter. What the hell was a *contributing* reporter? Didn't all reporters contribute something? Humans and their stupid labels.

Like this one – the Janitor. The Janitor? That stupid Lake woman had slapped that label on him herself.

Actually, when he thought about it, he didn't mind the moniker. After all, his *Clean-up Crew* cards led her down that path. She wouldn't have come up with it on her own. He had to do everything for these people. Clean up their city, protect its children, and then think up clever names for *contributing* reporters.

He focused on the picture beneath her by-line – pretty, young woman smiling like a cat in the cream. So damn proud to get a front page story and never once thinking that it might not be a good idea to put her picture on an article about a serial killer. Oh, the sheep, the poor, pathetic sheep, making it so easy to prey on them.

His eyes zeroed in on one paragraph in particular. *The San Francisco Police Department nearly captured the killer in an elaborate sting. Captain Katherine Defino stated, "We have a good lead on the suspect and the next time, we'll get him. There is no place in this city that he can hide. Rest assured, we will find him."*

He smiled at that and crossed his arms on the picnic table, lifting his head and looking up at the towering redwoods all around him. Blue jays cawed in the branches and a chipmunk scurried across the open ground from one burrow to the next, disappearing into a hole. He'd always liked Big Basin, especially in the summer. 'Bout time he got out of the City for some R and R. Folding the paper in half, he climbed out of the picnic table and made his way back to the RV, whistling as he went.

THE END

315

Now that you've finished, visit **ML Hamilton** at her website: authormlhamilton.com for more information on the **Peyton Brooks'** mysteries and her other contemporary fiction novel, *Ravensong*.

If you missed the first three novels in the **Peyton Brooks'** mystery series, *Murder on Potrero Hill, Murder in the Tenderloin* and *Murder on Russian Hill,* buy them now!

Then check out her fantasy series, *The World of Samar,* at worldofsamar.com.

All **ML Hamilton** titles available at Amazon in Kindle and paperback formats.

The Complete *Peyton Brooks' Mysteries* Collection:

Murder on Potrero Hill Volume 1

Murder in the Tenderloin Volume 2

Murder on Russian Hill Volume 3

Murder on Alcatraz Volume 4

The Complete *World of Samar* Collection:

Emerald Volume 1

The Heirs of Eldon Volume 2

The Star of Eldon Volume 3

The Spirit of Eldon Volume 4

Made in the USA
Middletown, DE
30 June 2015